TRASHED

By Jasinda Wilder

TRASHED

ISBN: 978-1-941098-20-2

Cover art by Sarah Hansen of Okay Creations. Cover art © 2014 by Sarah Hansen.
Interior book design by Indie Author Services.

CHAPTER ONE

"...And if you'll look over to the right, you'll see the old fort. It's the highlight of the island, really, situated on the bluff the way it is. Built in 1780 by the British, it was intended to replace the older wooden structure of Fort Michilimackinac, which was built by the French around 1715."

The driver of the horse-drawn carriage pauses to cluck at the two huge Percherons, encouraging them up the hill, and then he continues, "The British commander thought Michilimackinac would be too difficult to defend, so he began construction of a new fort here on the island, using the plentiful natural limestone as the primary material. The fort was used to control the Straits during the Revolutionary War and, despite the terms of the treaty, the British didn't relinquish control of the fort until 1796."

My co-star, Rose Garret, lounges on the bench beside me, a half-empty bottle of water in one hand, and her phone in the other. She's as bored as I am. The driver tugs on the reins; the carriage swings around a corner and we're approaching the main thoroughfare. It's a hot day, and even the shade of the carriage roof isn't enough to cool us off.

The director, Gareth Thomas, as well as the two executive producers and some of the supporting cast, are sitting ahead of us. We're all hot and bored, and ready to go back to the hotel, but the carriage ride will last over an hour and a half, taking us all the way around the island. I've heard the tour is supposed to be a lot of fun, but so far—less than ten minutes in—I'm bored, hungry, irritable, and restless. It's nearing dinner time, and I can be a dick when I'm hungry.

I tap my fingers on my knees, my gaze roving from one side of the carriage to the other, tuning out the constant drone of the tour guide and driver. No one is paying attention; we'd all rather be back at the Grand Hotel. I know I would. That place is the shit. A little fancier than I usually like, but there aren't many hotels like it, even among the five-star places I've stayed at on location shoots.

We're on Mackinac Island for the weekend, doing a huge fundraiser gala for charity. It's a publicity event, the kind of over-the-top Hollywood affair I hate attending, but don't have any way out of. I'm *really* not looking forward to the dinner. It's a swanky black tie deal, the kind of thing where you need a date and a jacket with tails, where you have to use the right cutlery and your inside voice. It's going to be stiff and formal and awkward, and I hate wearing suits, tuxedos even more so.

Worst of all, the only appropriate date I could get to go with me is my ex-girlfriend, Emma Hayes. I'd rather stab myself in the fucking face than see that bitch again after what she did to me, but I don't have much choice. You can't bring just anyone to these things. The paps will be there, cameras flashing, which is just all the more reason to not be seen with Em, because then the tabloids will start howling that I took the cheating skank back.

I'm lost in thought, trying to figure out how the hell I'm going to get through an entire gala with Em and remain civil. I'm not paying attention to anything, ignoring both the sweat trickling down my nose and Rose as she yammers into her cell. I'm doing my best to ignore everything while praying for this sightseeing tour to be over.

And then I see her.

All I see is her hair. Fuck, her hair. Must be damn near waist-length, a river of black locks. She's facing away and has her head tipped backward, her hair loose and cascading down her back in a glimmering, glinting black waterfall. Her hair is like a raven's wing, so black it's almost blue, catching the sun as she shakes it out. She pulls a hair tie from off her wrist, and then pulls her hair back into a ponytail, which then gets twisted up into a loose bun at the nape of her neck. My sister Lizzy would call it a chignon. I don't know how I know that, but that's the word that pops into my head when I see it.

And god, her neck. When she tilts her head back, her neck is a delicate curve, baring her throat to the sun. It's the kind of throat a man could spend hours kissing.

She lifts her bun with one hand, wipes her palm across the back of her neck and rolls her shoulders. She pivots and she is turned toward me.

I'm mesmerized. Caught. Trapped. I can't blink, can't look away.

Her skin is tan, not olive, just naturally tan and made darker by hours in the sun, and her eyes, they're huge, wide and dark brown like pools of chocolate. I'm less than ten feet away from her as the carriage passes her by, and she looks right at me, pausing with one hand on the back of her neck, her eyes finding mine and widening when she realizes who I am.

I'm not even aware of moving, but the next thing I know I'm hopping off the carriage and jogging back to meet the girl. Rose just rolls her eyes at me and Gareth is leaning out the side of the carriage shouting, "ADAM! What the hell are you doing? Adam?"

The girl grabs something she had propped against her legs, and then turns swiftly away from me, starting to walk as if afraid, or embarrassed. Or both; I've been told chicks get intimidated around me sometimes.

I catch up and slow to walk beside her. "Hey," I say.

She ducks her head and keeps walking, not looking at me. "Hi." Her voice is pitched low; as if she's not sure she should even be talking to me. Which is stupid, since I approached her.

I take a long step to get in front of her, then turn to walk backward, ducking my head to try and get those big brown eyes to look at me. "I'm Adam."

"No shit."

Not the response I was expecting. I laugh. "All right then, I guess you know my name." I wait, walking backward in front of her. "Gonna tell me yours?"

She shakes her head and brushes past me, swerves to one side, and uses a little broom to sweep an empty, crumpled water bottle into a handheld dustpan, and then she moves on, not looking back at me. For the first time, I realize what she's wearing: a one-piece jumpsuit, light gray with green trim running down the sleeves and down the sides of the legs. She's wearing scuffed black combat boots, and the front of the jumpsuit is unzipped to just above her navel, revealing a white wife beater-style tank top.

Shit, is that a hot look.

And that's when I realize how *tall* this chick is. I'm six-three, and she's not much shorter than me—three and half inches, four at the most. And she's fucking *stacked*. I mean, even with the fairly shapeless jumpsuit disguising her frame, it's clear the girl has curves for days.

"What are you doing?" I ask. Not my most intelligent question ever, I'll admit.

She pauses in the act of sweeping a stray napkin into the dustpan, gives me a look that says *"what are you, stupid?"* And then, deliberately, each motion screaming sarcasm, she finishes sweeping up the napkin.

"Working."

"You work on the island, then?" I'm not usually this slow, but I'm scrambling for some way to get this girl to interact with me.

She rolls her eyes at me. "Well, this is an island, I'm pretty sure, and...yep! I'm working. So it would seem that, yes, I do in fact work on the island."

She keeps walking until she reaches a rolling trashcan, then dumps her dustpan into it. She pushes the trashcan with one hand, holding the broom and dustpan in the other. I stand and watch her walk away, realizing how stupid I sounded. Shaking my head at myself, I glance across the street. There's a fudge shop, and I can make out the shape of a glass-door beverage refrigerator. An idea strikes me, and I head across the street and into the fudge shop. Or shoppe, as they seem to all be called here. I buy a pound of fudge in three different flavors and two bottles of water, trying my damnedest to act casual, keeping my head down and hoping no one notices me.

The clerk girl behind the counter, however, gasps when I set a fifty-dollar bill on the counter. "Holy shit! You're—you…you're…" She's stammering, clearly distraught.

I smile at her, my brightest, fakest, photo-op smile. "Adam," I say, holding out my hand.

She takes my hand in hers, a goofy, shit-eating, delirious grin spreading across her features. She's pretty enough, for a seventeen-year old schoolgirl. "Adam Trenton." She has my hand now and won't let go, until I literally tug my fingers free from hers. "Holy shit. Holy shit. You're Adam Trenton."

I nod. "Yep. That's me." I slide my bill closer to her. "Gonna let me pay for my fudge, sweetheart?"

She stares blankly, and then starts. "Yeah. Yeah! Sorry, sorry, Adam. Mr. Trenton, I mean. Um. Yeah. Change."

There's a crowd behind me now, some quiet conversation, cell phone cameras clicking. Had to stop for fucking fudge, didn't I? Dumbass. I get my change, offer the girl another million-dollar smile, and turn away.

"Would you—I'm sorry, I'm not supposed to do this, but—I've never met anyone—I mean, um..." she stammers.

I turn back, take the napkin she's holding toward me, and sign my name with the Sharpie I always carry in my pocket.

"Here ya go, hon." I hand the signed napkin to her. "I really do have to go now. Nice to meet you."

I try to slip past the crowd, but someone else is calling my name, and someone else is shouting "Marek! Marek!" Which is the name of the character that made me famous, the hero from a popular graphic novel series. I stifle my sigh of irritation, shuffle my bag and the bottles of water so they're all clutched in one hand. I sign two backpacks, three hats, six notebooks, three receipts, and pose for ten pictures before I can slip out and away from the fudge shop. Shoppe? What the hell is a 'shoppe' anyway?

By now the girl is gone. I scan the streets as I keep moving, ignoring the long stares I get every now again from the crowds on the sidewalks. I'm nearly run down by a pair of massive black horses pulling a long carriage and have to dance backward out of the way. Then I cross the street, heading back the way I came. I hear casters rolling across the cobblestones far ahead of me, and I set off in a space-eating jog.

I catch her as she's rounding a corner, heading into a courtyard. "Hey! Hold on!"

She stops, turns, and rolls her eyes when she sees it's me. "Still working, dude."

Although, judging by the surroundings, she's about to be finished for the day. There are other people in similar jumpsuits coming and going, and there's a sign reading 'Sanitation Personnel Only' on one wall.

"You're clocking out now, right?"

She wipes a strand of hair out of her eyes. "Yeah. Why?"

I hold up the bag of fudge and the water bottles. "Have dinner with me?"

She actually laughs at this, and her smile lights up her face, makes her eyes shine like there's sunlight behind the brown orbs. "Fudge? For dinner?"

I shrug. "Sure. Why not?"

She gives me a skeptical look. "What do you want?"

"Just your name. And for you to have some fudge with me." I crack my water bottle and take a long swig.

It doesn't escape my notice that, even though she's trying to act unaffected, her eyes follow my throat when I swallow, flick down to my chest and arms when she thinks I'm not looking.

She hesitates. "Why?"

I shrug. "I'm bored, and you're gorgeous."

She frowns. "Nice line, asshole."

I laugh. "It's not a line! That tour was hot and boring as hell and I'm hungry. And you really are beautiful."

Her cheeks color, but she gives nothing else away. "Uh-huh. Sweaty, stinking, and dressed in a jumpsuit. It's a sexy look, I'm sure." She turns away from me. "Not sure what you're after, Adam, but I'm probably not the kind of girl you think I am." With that parting shot, she pushes through a set of double doors, shoving her trashcan ahead of her.

Shot down. Jesus. That hasn't happened in a while.

I grin. I've always enjoyed a challenge.

What the hell is Adam goddamn Trenton doing on Mackinac Island? And more importantly, why is he talking to *me?* That was Rose Garret in the carriage with him. I'm positive. *Rose Garret*. As in starred in *Gone With the Wind* with Dawson Kellor. She's got three Oscars and two Emmys, and she's one of the hottest actresses in Hollywood, as well as being one of the most desirable women in the world.

I shake my head, pushing the mystery out of my mind. A freak occurrence, obviously. Probably figured I'd fawn all over him, maybe beg him to let me blow him behind the shop.

Right.

But his eyes won't leave my mind as I dump my bag of garbage into the dumpster and put away my can, broom, and dustpan. Those eyes, such a strange shade of green, so pale they were almost pastel in color. And so, so vivid, so piercing. He looked at me like he was actually seeing *me,* like he could read my secrets by looking in my eyes.

I clock out, wave goodbye to Phil, the supervisor, and then unzip my jumpsuit the rest of the way, tying the arms around my waist. It's a hot, humid, sticky day. I stink. I'm dripping sweat, and all I want is to get back to my little room and take a shower. Cold first to cool off, and then hot to get clean. Maybe meet Jimmy and Ruth for some drinks later.

I'm out of the shop and through the courtyard at a quick walk, lifting the neck of my wife-beater to wipe the sweat off my face. With the shirt in front of my face, I'm momentarily blinded as I walk, and so I don't see him. I feel him, though. Or rather, I feel the icy plastic of a water bottle against the back of my neck.

Instinct takes over; I'm not the type of chick you want to startle, given the kinds of neighborhoods I grew up in. I pivot and shove, and my hands meet a solid, heavy, hot mass of man, sending him stumbling backward a couple steps.

"Fuck, man, I was just trying to cool you off." He's laughing, though, not angry.

I'm a tall girl. Strong. And I've had to defend myself more than once, so I know I can push pretty damn hard. But this guy? He barely moved. Like, two steps, if that. After a shove that hard, most men would have gone flying.

And yet, despite my reaction, he's laughing, shuffling toward me as if approaching a dangerous dog, the water bottle extended. "Here. Take it. I won't hurt you, I swear," he says, using a low, soothing voice. "Take it. It's all right. Take it."

I shake my head and huff out a laugh, wanting to be irritated, but he's too fucking gorgeous, and also funny. He's massive. Only a few inches taller than me, making him maybe six-three or -four, but his body is...solid, sheer muscle. Which makes sense, since Adam Trenton is the biggest action star since The Rock—big in terms of muscle mass and stature as well as fame and popularity.

I take the water bottle, twist the top off, and take a long swig. So cold, so good. I can feel him watching me as I drink, and I pause to glare at him. "What?"

He just shrugs and shakes his head. "Nothing."

I finish the water in two more long swallows. "Thanks," I say lifting the bottle in gesture.

"No problem." Awkward silence. "So. Dinner?" He pulls out the box of Ryba's fudge. "I've got dark chocolate, chocolate peanut butter, and chocolate with nuts of some kind."

"Walnuts," I tell him.

"Walnuts?" He seems puzzled. Is he not good at keeping up with conversation?

I point at the fudge. "The nuts in the fudge. They're walnuts." I draw out and emphasize the word so it drips in sarcasm.

"Oh. Right. Yeah, I knew that." He peers at me as if assessing something about me. "You look like a dark chocolate girl."

God, if only he knew. I steal another glance at him as he breaks the dark chocolate fudge into huge slices. He has dark skin, as if his heritage is from the South Pacific or somewhere like that, naturally dark, and tanned even darker by the sun. His eyes, though, the pale, pale green, throw me off. I'm not sure what his heritage is, but I'll take his brand of dark chocolate any day.

Not that anything of the sort will be happening. Not with him and certainly not with me. He's A-list Hollywood. He probably has Natalie Portman's phone number in his cell or something. And I'm nobody. Less than nobody. A garbage collector.

A distraction for him, if that.

My thoughts have soured the moment.

But then he hands me a hunk of fudge, and obviously I can't turn that down.

"You still haven't told me your name." His voice is close.

Too close. I look up, and he's leaning against a lamppost, mere inches from me. His voice is like the purr of a lion. He has a piece of fudge stuck to his lip, right at the corner, and he doesn't notice. He takes three more bites, and still doesn't notice, and then wipes his hands and his mouth, and somehow misses the bit of chocolate. I want to reach out with my thumb and wipe it way, maybe even lick it off my thumb.

What the hell am I thinking?

But my hand clearly doesn't have any common sense or restraint, because I'm touching his mouth, his actual real mouth and I'm wiping the dark spot away. He's frozen, tensed, and both of us are watching my hand and wondering what I'm doing.

It only gets crazier.

I feel something huge and rough wrap around my wrist, look down, and realize that he has my hand pinioned in his, and even though I don't exactly have dainty little hands, his are paws, actual paws. The spread of his hand from pinky to thumb could easily engulf both of my hands together, and his palms are callused, his fingers gentle on my wrist but implacably powerful.

"I'm sorry, I—I'm not sure why I did that," I admit, realizing he has to be pissed that I would touch him like that. "You just had something—" I'm not sure where I'm going with that, so I stop talking abruptly.

He doesn't respond, his leaf-hued eyes boring into mine, bright and intense and inscrutable. I can't fathom what he's thinking. Can't even begin to wonder.

And then, absurdly, he brings my hand toward his face. My hand is splayed out, fingers spread apart. He twists my hand so my thumb is pointing toward his mouth.

No.

No way he's going to—

Yep. He is.

My heart actually literally and totally stops beating, just freezes solid in my chest, and my lungs seize, and his mouth is hot and wet and warm around my thumb, his tongue sliding over the pad of my thumb, licking the chocolate away. His eyes never leave mine, and now I have to breathe, have to suck in a gasping breath, and his eyes flick down to my tits, which, admittedly, are fairly prominent at the moment, even in my sports bra and tank top. But his gaze doesn't linger, just notices and appreciates and returns to my eyes, and my thumb is *still* in his mouth. He's pulling it out, his lips wrapping around my knuckle and then my thumb is free.

And he still has my wrist in his hand, not letting go, just holding, gently but firmly.

I swallow hard, blink, and then jerk my hand free. I step away from him before I combust, or do something utterly idiotic, like agree to whatever he's about to ask me.

"Have real dinner with me."

"No."

"Yes."

I stare at him. "Um. Not sure you're getting how this yes and no thing works."

He just grins at me. No, it's not a grin. It's…a *smolder*.

I remember sitting in the living room of my last foster home in Southfield, visiting with my favorite foster-sister. She insisted that I watch *Tangled* with her, so I did, and the main character, Flynn Ryder, has this moment where he goes, "I didn't want to have to do this, but you leave me no choice." Then he looks at Rapunzel with this meaningful look in his eyes and says, "Here comes... *the smolder.*" And he does this cute little grin that's obviously meant to be knock-em-dead sexy.

This is that kind of smile.

But, unlike Flynn, this one works for him. Like, *really* works. The way his lips just slightly curl at the corners, the way his eyes narrow to intense, piercing slits, the press of his lips against each other, those lips, just begging to be kissed...it works. God, does it work. I can't look away. I'm trying, but I can't.

He's just so fucking *hot.*

And it works, because I want to say yes. I want to have real dinner with him. I want to pretend that this ripped, famous, gorgeous hunk of a man could actually like me, and want to spend time with *me.*

He starts walking, pulling me with him, and again he's gentle but totally and irresistibly powerful. I'm pulled into motion behind him, and somehow my hand is in his, clasped palm to palm. Our fingers aren't tangled together in that intimate way of holding hands, he's just holding my hand and pulling me behind him, and I can't help but follow, watching his long, tree-trunk thick legs move in his khaki board shorts, his sculpted calves rippling. Even his calves are muscular. It's totally ridiculous. I didn't think guys this built actually existed in real life.

Yet here he is, pulling me, walking ahead of me, larger than life and holding *my* hand.

What the actual fuck is going on? What's happening?

"Where are we going?" I manage to get intelligible English words out, arranged into a grammatically correct sentence.

"Dinner." He's leading me, and I'm wondering if he knows where we're going, since he's got us headed in a direction away from the restaurants.

"But I said no."

He glances back at me. "Yeah, so?"

"Which means I don't want to have dinner with you," I say, sounding reasonably firm.

That's a damned dirty lie, but he doesn't need to know that, and I'm not going to admit it to him. Or to myself. Because going to dinner with Adam Trenton is a bad idea.

He's going to expect something from me that I won't be willing to give.

He stops, and then somehow he has *both* of my hands in his, and his eyes are sliding down to mine and searching me and reading the lie in my heart. "Do too."

I may be many things, but I'm not a liar. "I'm in my work uniform. And I've been outside all day, sweating."

He leans toward me. "Sweaty is sexy." He says this in that leonine purr of his, and manages to make it sound promising and dirty all at once.

It's hard to swallow or even breathe, because he's so close to me you couldn't fit a piece of paper between my chest and his, and his presence is overwhelming, dominating, blocking out the island and the *clip-clop* of a horse-and-carriage trotting past us and the caw of a seagull overhead.

"Nice line, asshole." That was good. That sounded like I'm unaffected.

He ignores that. "It's just dinner. I'm only here for the weekend, okay? What can it hurt?"

"Just dinner?"

He nods. "Just dinner. Promise."

"Okay. But let me shower and change first."

He grins, and follows me as I lead the way to the co-op dorms I stay in for the summer.

Did I just agree to have dinner with Adam Trenton?

This is a bad idea.

I know it is, but for reasons I can't fathom, I'm ignoring my gut.

CHAPTER TWO

I SIT ON THE FRONT STEP OF HER BUILDING, WASTING time on my phone while she gets ready.

I still don't know her name. That's kinda fucked up, actually. I've licked fudge off her thumb. I've been so close to her that I could almost feel her heart beating, I could see her pulse drumming in the strong curve of her throat. I've gotten her to agree to go to dinner with me, yet I don't know her name.

I expect to be sitting here for a while because, in my experience, chicks invariably take hours to get ready. Yet, barely twenty minutes later she's coming out the door wearing a pair of tight, faded blue jeans with rips in the thigh. They don't look like the type of expensive designer jeans that come pre-ripped; rather, they seem to be actually that old and worn and faded that the rips are from age and wear. I hear her before I see her, so the first thing I see is her feet, in a pair of Chucks. The white stripe of rubber around the base of the shoes on both feet have been colored with a black marker into a checkered design. These, as well, are the kind of shoes you just know she's had for a long time. My eyes travel up her legs, encased in those tight, faded jeans, and *Jesus*, the girl's legs are absolutely fucking killer. She's got mile-long legs, but not the skinny tall-girl legs. These are curvy with muscle and flesh.

God, I look up at those legs and in that moment I want nothing more than to feel her wrap those legs around me and hold on tight. It's a hot, hard, intense thought, and I can't shake it.

I'm staring.

And then my gaze travels farther, up to the plain black V-neck T-shirt she's wearing. My mouth goes dry, and I've got to stand up and turn away and adjust myself discreetly, because the image of those powerful legs wrapped around my waist is only the beginning.

Tits. Jesus, just…Jesus. I can't look away. The shirt is molded to her body, the V-neck baring an expanse of deep, tanned cleavage that hints at a glorious pair of breasts. And then I force myself to make actual eye contact, because I've been ogling her far too openly for far too long.

And I'm stunned into a breathless, speechless stupor.

Let's be clear about one thing: I've been on set with some *hot* women. I've been to parties with some of the most beautiful and famous women on earth. I dated Emma Hayes for nearly two years, which is an eternity by Hollywood standards. And Emma is… stunning. I can't take that away from her, no matter how big a bitch she is.

But this girl, in old ripped jeans, inked-up Chucks, and a cheap black V-neck…she's drop-dead gorgeous. I don't think she knows it, either. She can't have any clue how intensely, heart-stoppingly beautiful she is. She wouldn't be sweeping up fucking trash on Mackinac Island if she did.

She's put on makeup sparingly, just a hint of eye shadow and mascara to highlight those big brown eyes, some color on her cheeks and lips.

Mmm, those lips. Plump and red and begging to be kissed.

Even her ears are beautiful. She's got detached earlobes, a single small diamond stud in the lobe, with three hoops climbing up the shell on both ears.

And her hair….my god. So thick, so black, so long. My hands twitch, itching to bury my fingers in those ebony locks, feel them slip like silk between my fingers and pull her against my chest and kiss the ever-loving shit out of her.

"Take a picture, dude. It'll last longer." She's got a wry smile on her lips, somewhere between amused, baffled, and flattered.

I hold up my phone and swipe up on the lock screen, opening the camera app, and snap a picture of her. She's got one hand tucked into the back pocket of her jeans, the other hanging casually at her side. Her hair is loose, a mass of black framing her face, a few strands fluttering in a breeze. She's got that wry smile, and a sharp, piercing gaze.

As soon as I snap the photo she lunges for me, grabbing at my phone. "I didn't mean *actually* take a picture, you dumbass! I wasn't ready!"

She reaches for my phone, which I hold out of reach. Most girls, if I hold something above my head, it may as well be on Mars. This girl, this nameless beauty, she's so tall that she's able to hop and get my hand in both of hers, and holy shit is she strong. She's pried my phone out of my hands before I know what's going on.

"Hey!" I snatch it back before she can delete the picture. "It was a good photo, no reason to freak. You wanna see it?" She lunges for me again, and I dart out of reach, laughing as I bring up the picture and hold the phone so she can see it. "Look."

She frowns. "It's *horrible!* The angle is all wrong. You can't take a picture of a girl with the camera pointing up like that. Don't you know anything?"

"So quit trying to steal my phone and I'll retake it," I say.

Surprisingly, she complies. She puts her weight on one leg, the other knee bent, her torso twisted and her hands buried in her hair, her head tilted back slightly. It's the perfect pose for her, accentuating her hair and her height. I snap several, put a filter on it, and then show it to her.

"Is that better?" I ask.

She shrugs. "Sure. It's okay."

"*Okay?*" I shake my head. "You're nuts. It's an awesome picture. You're insanely photogenic. I know some photographers who would love to get you in front of their cameras."

She tosses her hair and rolls her eyes. "Yeah… okay, sure," she says, sarcasm thick in her tone. "Tell me another one."

I shove my phone in my pocket and move so I'm in front of her and walking backward, then stop so she bumps into me. "You really don't know how gorgeous you are, do you?"

She shoves me away hard enough that I trip and have to catch my footing. "I've already agreed to have dinner with you, so you can lay off the flattery, all right?"

I don't think she realizes who she's pushing around. I move fast, darting toward her and putting my shoulder in her stomach, lifting her off the ground and running three long steps, and then I set her down and press her back to the wall of a building. She doesn't even have time to protest or wiggle, and I have her up against the wall. I grab her hands, both of them, and press her knuckles to the siding, my fingers tangling with hers. I pin her hips in place with mine, and I'm drowning in the clean scent of her skin and hair, in the crush of her tits against my chest, her breath coming in short, sharp gasps of surprise.

"It's not nice to push," I murmur, my face inches from hers. Her eyes are wide and I can feel her trembling. "Listen to me. You think I'm going to waste my time on flattery? I don't fucking think so."

"I just—"

I don't let her finish whatever bullshit she was going to say. "Now. Before either of us takes another step, I need one thing from you."

She's shaking all over, her eyes wide as saucers, brown and deep and dark and rife with thoughts and emotions I can't decipher. "What's that?" she asks, her voice shaky and small.

"Your name."

"Des." Her voice is a whisper. "My name is Des."

"Des what?"

"Ross. Des Ross."

"Des." I draw the syllable out, accentuating the 'z' sound at the end, tasting her name, rolling it on my tongue. "Is that short for something."

"Just Des."

I can't resist any longer. I just can't. I release one of her hands and slide my palm past her ear, into the thick mass of black hair. It's cool and silky and still damp. Her mouth falls open slightly, and I'm a breath away from claiming those red lips of hers, but I don't, I save that, save the kiss. I look at her, try to read her, but she's just breathing, her lips parted, her eyes searching mine. She's not moving into me, not trying to take the kiss I'm holding back, but she's also not pushing me away or trying to escape. She's shaking though. The fingers I've still got twined in mine are trembling as if she's barely holding back some powerful emotion. Is it nerves? Desire? Or fear?

The wind has picked up, blowing strong through the alley, carrying a heaviness with it. It's not a cold wind, not this time of year, but it's a wet one, a thick, damp wind.

I force myself to let her go, to back away from her, and when there's space between our bodies, she seems to go limp, deflating, letting out a long, harsh breath. She straightens after a moment, visibly composing herself, and glances at the sky. "It's going to rain, I think."

I follow her gaze skyward, and see that low, angry gray clouds have rolled in suddenly, covering the blue sky and the sun. It's dark now, and cooling off quickly. My skin prickles, and a deafening clap of thunder splits the air, accompanied by a blinding flash of lightning streaking across the sky, stabbing and then gone. There's a drip, a drop, two and three and four, and then before either of us can even move, the clouds have opened up, releasing rain in torrential buckets.

"Holy shit!" I grab her hand and pull her into a run. "Where the hell did this come from?"

She's running with me and laughing as the rain pounds on our heads, soaking us to the bone within seconds. I have no idea where I'm going, I'm just running, and she's following me.

"Where are we going, Adam?"

"I don't know!"

We're at an intersection and she jerks me to the left, pulls ahead and leads down a short street that dead-ends at Main Street. She's opening a door and leading me into an old bar, low ceilings and aged wood floors and thick beams, sports channels on TVs, a dartboard on one wall, a small bar with eight or ten stools. There are two or three rooms to the bar, several tables and booths in each, with the bar itself in the corner as the centerpiece. It's a warm, dark, and comfortable place, the kind of bar I can imagine the handful of year-round locals drinking at when the tourists have all gone home.

"Jesus, that was fast," Des says, wringing her hair out. "That came out of nowhere."

I rub my hand over my short, spiked black hair. "No kidding. Sunny one minute, pouring down the next."

How the hell can I be expected to have dinner with this girl now? She's soaking wet, her shirt plastered to her skin, outlining the cups of her bra and the flat of her stomach and the curves of her back. I can see the erect nubs of her nipples poking through the fabric of her shirt and bra.

I'm wet too, though, and my shirt is a plain white undershirt. And now that it's wet, the thin cotton is basically see-through. And yeah, being an athlete and an action-movie star, I'm expected to be in top shape, especially during filming. And I am. I spend hours at the gym every day to retain the bulky physique the producers expect for my role, which is a renegade roughneck superhero. Kind of like Wolverine meets Batman. He's dark and brooding. He wants nothing to do with his superpowers, though, and avoids using them, until events conspire to force him into action. In the graphic novel on which the movie is based, my character is drawn to be impossibly proportioned, even more so than most superheroes, and when the film people started casting, they knew they had to find someone who was capable of achieving the level of bulk needed to fill the role. The Rock could have played it, but he's older than they were looking for, and too well known. They wanted a relative unknown, someone who'd done enough acting to pull off the lead role, but not famous enough to be immediately recognizable on a household level.

That's where I came in. Marek in *Fulcrum* was my breakout role, but I'd had supporting actor roles here and there, enough to establish my chops. And I'm naturally big enough that with the right regimen and training, I could bulk up enough to fill the massive profile the character demanded. Which meant that, at the moment, I'm bulked out to the max. Even in my one season with the San Diego Chargers I wasn't this shredded, and with my T-shirt soaked through I might as well be shirtless.

Des is eyeing me pretty openly as she wipes the moisture from her face with a stack of bar napkins. "Good thing I just took a shower," she says.

"Good thing for you you're not wearing *this* shirt," I joke, plucking at the sopping, translucent fabric.

"You probably wish I was, though," Des says, and slides onto a barstool.

"Damn right I do." I slip onto a stool beside her and try to keep my eyes north of her shoulders.

A slightly awkward silence then, as she probably wonders what I'm expecting from her, and I'm wondering what the hell it is I think I'm doing. The last thing I need right now is a distraction, or media attention. Gareth, the director, and Parker, the head executive producer, have both been adamant that everyone attached to the project keep media exposure to a minimum. We're shooting the long-awaited and highly anticipated sequel to *Fulcrum,* which means I'm reprising my role as Marek. Everyone from the big magazines to minor blogs is speculating about who's in the movie, where the plot is going to go, all the usual chatter. But because it's been more than three years since the original, and since Gareth, Parker, and I were all vocal about the impossibility of a sequel, the rumor mill is running on all eight cylinders. Which means media attention of any kind has an effect on the shoot, and could lead to possible leaks.

And apart from the need to keep myself out of the media professionally, I'm in no position to get into anything. After what happened with Em and the shit-storm that engendered, the last thing I need is to be photographed with some other girl. Especially, both of us soaking wet, on what's supposed to be a fundraiser weekend.

I don't know what I'm doing. I don't know why I jumped off that carriage, why I'm here with her, why I'm so intrigued by her, why her tough-girl persona has me twisted and heated and hungry.

I just don't know.

And I have no idea what's going to happen or what I expect from her.

"So tell me about yourself, Des," I say, to distract myself from the internal self-questioning.

She shrugs. "I'm a college student, here for the summer on a co-op program. This is my fifth year here on the island."

"Major?" I ask her, and then turn to the bartender, who has stopped in front of us to get our orders. "I'll have a Sam Adams and whatever she wants."

"Usual, Des?" the bartender asks. Des nods, and the bartender slides me my Sam Adams, and then pours a vodka tonic, setting it in front of Des.

"You have a usual here?" I ask.

Des nods and shrugs. "Sure. I'm here after work a lot. Probably more than I should be, but there's not much else to do in the evening, you know?" She sips at her drink and then sets it down. "I'm majoring in social work, with a focus on foster care."

"Foster care, huh?"

"Yep." She keeps her gaze on the TV screen in the corner and sips at her drink, her posture closed and tensed. Clearly, that subject is off the table.

"So you've been coming here for five years?"

She opens a little at that. "Yeah. I came here the summer I graduated high school. I'd already been accepted to Wayne State at that point, and my counselor at the high school suggested I do the summer co-op program. She knew the program liaison at

Wayne, so she got me in before I'd technically started college. Been coming back every year."

"Just for the summer work, or what? What keeps you coming back?"

She answers right away. "I don't know. A lot of things. It's a good way to save up money for the school year. It's good work experience, looks good on a résumé. It gets me away from Metro Detroit for a few months every summer. Plus, I just like it here. The horses, the atmosphere, the tourists. It's just so fun and different. My best friend Ruth comes here with me every year, and it's just kind of what we do." She glances at me. "What about you? What brings you to little old Mackinac Island?"

"There's a fundraiser dinner at the Grand Hotel tomorrow night. It's a big deal. Couple grand per plate, silent auction, red carpet, and photographers and the works." My head aches just talking about it.

Des must hear something in my voice. "You don't sound all that excited."

I shake my head. "I'm not."

She stares at me in disbelief. "Why the hell not? That sounds like fun!"

I laugh. "You've clearly never been to one, then. They're boring. Stuffy. You just sit there all dressed up and have quiet little conversations about the weather or whatever. The whole thing is just a pain in my ass. I *hate* wearing suits, for one thing. Tuxedos are the worst. I'm an actor and an athlete, not a wine-and-dine and be all haughty and hoity-toity kinda guy, you know? I like beer and football, not champagne and golf, and that's all these sorts of events are about. Everyone is drinking expensive fucking champagne, which is gross if you ask me, and talking about golf and the latest gala in Beverly Hills, and gossiping about who cheated on whom, and who got funding for their latest script. It's boring and stupid."

"So you're just an average guy that gets dragged to fancy events against his will, huh?"

I laugh. "Yeah, pretty much. I swear, you act in one blockbuster movie, and everyone goes fucking nuts." I deliver the line casually, but I'm trying to feel Des out, see how she feels about my status as a relatively famous movie star.

"Price of fame, or something like that, right?"

I nod. "Pretty much. You do a movie, and then you have to do the junkets and the press release events, and these fundraisers and whatever. I just want to shoot the film and be done, but no, that's not how it works. Gotta play the game their way, I guess."

"What are you shooting?" She's pivoted slightly toward me, now. Finally her posture and body language is relaxing and opening up a little.

"I can't really talk about it, actually. The whole project is on the down low. The script is super-secret. I have to check my script in and out every time I take one. You can't just walk around with it, can't risk someone getting a look at it. The whole thing is crazy secretive."

"Really? Why?"

I hesitate, unsure how to answer that with really giving anything away. "Well, it's one of those things where the director and producers don't want any spoilers or leaks, just because of the nature of the project."

She grins at me. "Nice non-answer."

I duck my head and laugh. "Well, I *told* you I can't talk about it. I've gotten good at not really answering interview questions by now, I suppose."

"Well, I wouldn't want you to feel like I'm interviewing you or anything," she says, and then slides a food menu toward me. "We eating, or just drinking our dinner?"

I scan the options as I answer. "Oh, we're eating. I'm fucking starved, and this is a cheat weekend for me."

"Cheat weekend?"

"My trainer has me on a wicked strict diet. Like, when I started training for the shoot he gave me a one-page list of things I could eat, and when, and how much."

She seems to find this hard to believe. "That's nuts! Why?"

I curl my arm up, flex my bicep, and slap it. "Gotta look a certain way for the role, babe. You don't get guns like these by accident."

"Oh my god," she snorts. "You did *not* just say 'guns', did you?"

"I believe I did."

"That's just...I can't even. I just can't even."

"Can't even what?" I ask, glancing at her.

She laughs into her vodka tonic. "It's a meme... white girls who just can't even...'"

I shake my head. "Not familiar with that one."

She sits up straight, and her face twists into a prim and proper expression. She flips her hair. "Like, ohmy*god,* did you *see* her shoes? I just can't *even*."

I choke on my beer as I laugh, picturing the exact stereotype she's mimicking, the kind of girl who populates L.A. so thickly you could hit six of them every time you throw a stick. "That's a good one. I know exactly what you're talking about now."

"But seriously. You don't *really* call them guns, do you?"

I frown at her. "I hope to *fuck* I'm not coming across as that type of guy."

She shakes her head. "No! No, I'm just—I barely know you. I just met you. You never know, you know?"

"Fair enough." The bartender swings by and we both order burgers and fries, and when the bartender leaves to put in the order, I turn on the stool to face her. "So anyway. Be assured I am *not* that guy. You will never, *ever,* hear me in any seriousness refer to my arms as guns or pythons or anything fucking stupid and vain like that. They're just arms."

"But they are very *nice* arms," she points out. "Just saying."

I grin at her. "Thanks."

Another awkward silence descends, because I'm not sure what I can ask her about. From the way she froze up over me asking about her focus on foster care, I'm guessing questions about family are going to be off limits at this point. And that's usually what I lead with, to get conversations going.

"How'd you get into acting?" Des asks, eventually.

I lift my beer in a signal for another. "Well, it wasn't something I ever thought I'd do. It just wasn't on my radar, you know? I was an athlete. Football. I played football from the time I was ten all the way through college. Played in school. Stanford. That was really what I thought about. But then, my senior year at Stanford, a friend of mine who is a filmmaker asked me to be in his movie. 'You don't have a lot of lines,' he promised. Only, the other guy he had as a lead quit halfway through, and Rick conned me into taking the lead role. It was just this tiny little thing, you know? A film school project, that's it. But it was fun. A lot of fun. Rick was raving about how good I was, but whatever, I just had fun doing it."

Our food arrives, and I pause to take a few bites, relishing each morsel. Burgers and fries aren't exactly on the approved list. "Anyway. I got drafted after I graduated, and played a season in San Diego. But then Rick got hired to direct a bigger project, and he wanted me in it. So during the off-season, I worked on his movie. And this one got the attention of a director who was looking for a male support who looked a certain way, which I just happened to fit. And that role? It was a big deal. *Big*. The kind of thing that could start a real career, you know? And I knew at that point that I had the chops to maybe really act, so it was a dilemma. Training season was about to start, and I had a role on the table. I had to choose, you know? Football, or acting?"

"When you say you played a season in San Diego..." she trails off expectantly.

"The Chargers."

"You mean the NFL?"

I nod. "Yeah."

"You played pro football?"

I shrug. "For one season, yeah."

"What position?"

"Fullback."

"I don't know anything about football, so I don't know what that means."

"A fullback can be either a blocker or a running back, depending on the team's playing style. I was more of a blocker." I wave my hand. "It's not important. Not anymore."

"Do you miss football?"

I shake my head. "Not really," I say immediately, but then have to backtrack and try again. "Well, that's not entirely true, actually. There are some things I do miss, I suppose. Practice with the guys. Working out with ten or fifteen guys is a lot more fun than spending four to six hours every day in the gym with just one hard ass trainer. I miss the rush of competition, too. That most of all. The all-out exertion, pushing yourself past your max. Making the block, being out there on the field with these massive guys coming at you, and just being as fucking dominant as humanly possible, stopping them and making the block to get the ball down the field. It's a rush, you know? I miss that part."

"What don't you miss?"

"The pressure to perform at your peak every single game, every single practice. You can't slip, not once. There are so many guys itching to come up, all these huge, talented guys that are just hungry to take your place on the starting line-up. And I also don't miss getting hit. Even with the pads, when a guy that stands six foot six and weighs three hundred and twenty pounds of solid muscle drills into you, it fucking hurts. I don't really miss that at all." I notice she's turned the conversation back to me again. "Enough about me. Tell me something about yourself."

She shuts down immediately. Until I asked the question, she was facing me, knees apart, one foot propped on my stool, sipping her drink and nodding and watching me intently. As soon as the question leaves my mouth, she turns away, returns her foot to the rail of the bar, ducks her head, stares down into her drink.

"Not much to tell." She lifts a shoulder in a small, dismissive gesture. "Grew up in the suburbs outside Detroit. Went to Southfield-Lathrup High School. Just graduated from Wayne State University with my bachelor's in social work, starting on my master's in the fall. I'm a janitor at U of D Jesuit, and I live in downtown Detroit."

I sigh. "Des. That's like…the abbreviated Cliff's Notes version. There's got to be more to tell than that."

She shrugs, shakes her head, and drains her drink. "Not really." She glances out the window. "Looks like the rain has slowed down a bit. Guess I'll head home. Thanks for dinner. And, you know…stalking me."

Before I can register her words, she's slapping a ten-dollar bill onto the bar and is out the front door, jogging back up the hill. I growl in frustration. She's the most closed-off person I've ever met. It's ridiculous. Clearly, she has something to hide, or something she just *really* doesn't like talking about.

I leave a one hundred-dollar bill on the bar and slide her ten into my wallet, and then jog out into the rain after her.

She's not getting off the hook that easily.

CHAPTER THREE

I RUN OUT OF THE BAR AND INTO THE WET STREETS. I have to escape him. I have to get away from his piercing, knowing eyes, from the heat of his body that seems to just suck me in, draw me closer. Something about Adam is just…magnetic. Hypnotic. He makes me want to talk to him. Trust him.

But…I don't trust. Not anyone. Not ever. Not even Ruth knows much about me, or about my past. We both went through the foster care system, so she understands that part. She doesn't ask, and I don't tell. We're friends because we get the need to let the past stay in the past, to forget and move on and pretend none of it ever happened.

I can't trust Adam. It'd be beyond idiotic. He's a famous movie star here for the weekend. I'll never see him again, no matter what happens. Or would have happened, now that I've made my escape. He had expectations. When someone like him shows interest in a random girl when he's on a weekend trip, he's only interested in one thing. I am most definitely not the type of girl to go back to some movie star's hotel room for a night of debauchery. Nope, nope, nope. Not me. For a lot of reasons, that's just not me. And he doesn't need to know any of the reasons.

I'm soaked. I was already wet, but within half a block, I'm even more thoroughly drenched. Every inch of me is dripping with rain. My shoes squish with each step, my hair is a heavy, sopping wet mass of tangles on my back, and my jeans are pasted to my legs. I slow to a walk and keep trying to convince myself that I made the right choice in leaving Adam at The 'Stang.

I did make the right choice, though. The more he asked me about myself, the more I felt myself just shrinking in, closing off. Not fair to him, I suppose, since he was asking normal questions, but I just can't start answering those questions. How do you explain to someone you just met what it's like growing up in the foster system? Being bounced from house to house, family to family? How do you explain that not all the families were stable, or…safe? Or that you never bothered making friends or getting close to anyone because you knew it wouldn't last? You don't.

I learned that the hard way. People don't want to know. People don't care.

I'm rounding the corner and approaching my dorm when I hear footsteps on the pavement behind me. I turn, and there he is. Huge, bulky with muscles upon muscles, yet quick and quiet on his feet. He's lit by the street lamps, passing through the circle of dull yellow light, and his T-shirt is clinging to his torso, pretty much sheer now. I can see every ripple and ridge of his abs, the deep grooves at his sides, the heavy slabs of his pecs…his shoulders are so broad he could be Atlas, carrying the weight of the world on his back. His arms are nearly as thick around as my waist, toned to perfection and solid as granite. He's jogging after me in a lithe, easy stride that belies his enormous size, his body shifting and rippling. He looks like a predator, like a lion stalking through the shadows, all muscle and grace and power.

I stop and wait for him, heedless of the rain now. I'm so wet at this point it doesn't even matter.

Lightning stabs the blackness, a quick flicker of brilliance, followed by a roar of thunder so loud my eardrums hurt and my bones rattle.

I force myself to remain motionless as he approaches me at an easy jog, even though he's so huge it's scary. He exudes power and threat and confidence and I shiver all over in his presence, he steals my breath and my capacity to make sense. I'm *not* that girl; I'm always totally unaffected by guys.

But Adam? He's all man, all masculinity and raw sexuality and aggressive beauty. And I just don't know what do.

I want to back away from him, creep deeper into the shadows and hold still and hope he doesn't see me, as if I were a mouse and he was a tomcat hunting me and toying with me. But I'm not that girl either. I don't back down for anyone. I don't let anyone control me or push me around. I am my own person, and I will not be cowed by *anyone*.

Especially not movie stars who happen to be far too gorgeous for their own good. No matter how interested in me he seems to be.

So I stand my ground as he stops in front of me just within arm's reach, and I lift my chin to meet his eyes, and I resist the urge to fit my fingers in the grooves of his abdominal muscles. My breath sticks in my throat as he erases the inches between us until his chiseled, rugged features are all I can see, until his scent is in my nostrils and his heat is billowing against my skin. His hands cup my upper arms momentarily, and his palms are rough and his hands are the size of dinner plates and callused, and though his hands feel strong enough to crush stones into powder, his touch is gentle, so gentle. And then one of his palms slides up my arm, missing the wet cotton of my shirt and he cradles the side of my neck, a thumb tracing over my ear. Surely he can feel the hammering of my pulse in my throat? His other hand moves to the back of my head and eases me forward, and I cannot for the life of me remember why I ran away from him, because I know all too well what he's about to do, and I want it and have absolutely zero chance of stopping it.

The rain is a cascade, harder rain than I've ever experienced in my life, and the wind is a brutal, raging force, knocking us sideways, blowing rain in sideways curtains, and thunder is banging and crashing in explosive tympani, lightning crackling and spearing and sparking.

Adam twists so his back is to the wind, taking the brunt of the storm's force upon himself, and I fit inside the cavern of his arms just perfectly.

A kiss is the meeting of lips, an expression of tenderness and affection, a physical demonstration of emotion. A kiss is a mutual act, two people giving and taking in equal measure.

What comes next—it's not a kiss. It's a statement of possession. A claiming. His mouth demands mine, his tongue seeks out mine, and his hands clutch at me, refusing to let me escape, and his arms encircle me, imprisoning me.

I should beat him away, push at him, curse at him. Flee. Call him names: Brute; Oaf; Cave man; Troll.

But I don't do any of that. I only press closer, melt into him, burrow deeper into his warmth and his protective shelter, and I kiss him back.

I let myself be claimed, possessed in that single kiss.

I've known him for two hours, max.

He pulls away enough to move his lips, and I feel his words more than hear them. "I won't ask you any more questions, Des. I promise."

Not what I was expecting him to say. "Okay," is all I can manage.

"Come on." He pulls me into a walk, away from my dorm, in the direction of the Grand Hotel.

"Where are we going?"

"My room."

"That's a fifteen-minute walk."

"So?" He tilts his face to the sky, baring his teeth. "We're already as wet as we can get."

I don't bother arguing. I just let him pull me back to Main Street until it turns into Lake Shore, and then I nudge him onto Market Street and then left on Cadotte Avenue. He doesn't speak and neither do I, although I have a million questions and a billion doubts and I know what he's going to expect from me and I can't let that happen, because I'll get attached and he'll go back to shooting a movie and it won't mean a goddamned thing.

But I can't take my hand from his, because his fingers are laced into mine, and he's absolutely sure I'll follow him, rightly so because I *am* following him, and anyway something tells me he'd just pick me up and carry me with him if I tried to escape. And I don't *want* to escape, that's the part that has me shaking with fear. I want to follow him, I want to see his room, want to let things happen even though I know I can't go through with what he wants from me.

A bolt of lightning shears the air mere feet in front of us, thunder shaking the ground beneath our feet. Just ahead is The Little Stone Church and I pull him across the street, jerk open the doors and we're in the foyer, dripping on the carpet. The air in the church is musty and old, and it's darker in here than outside, no lights lit, and only a couple stained glass windows for ambient light. I can't see him, can't see a thing. Wind and rain batter the windows and rattle on the door, and he's a warm solid presence in behind me.

"What is this place?" His voice rumbles in my ear.

"The Little Stone Church."

"Smells weird."

"It's old," I say.

He spins me around, his mouth is suddenly and fiercely moving on mine, his hands firm and unrelenting on my back, spanning my spine and sliding down to the small of my back. I'm being pulled against him, body flush to body. It's inexorable, like the tides. My breasts touch his chest, and then they're crushed between us, and my heart is pounding against my ribs so hard the bones become drums, and I know he can feel it.

Where are my hands? I've lost all sense, lost track of what's happening, of what I'm doing, what he's doing. All I know is his mouth, his lips scouring mine, his teeth nipping at my lower lip and then the upper, and I can feel his hands too, inching downward and downward, into dangerous territory, to the upper swell of my ass and I don't know how I'm tolerating this, how I'm doing it, how he's erasing my doubt and my fear and my lack of trust in anyone—especially men—and somehow igniting inside me this…heat. This need. This ravenous hunger, this desperation the likes of which I've never felt, never knew I *could* feel, especially after—

No. *No.* I will not allow that monster control over me, not anymore. Not again. Not ever.

Adam has a double handful of my bottom, clutching me against him possessively, as if he has a right to me, a right to touch me, hold me, grope me, caress me, squeeze me. I don't know which word is right, because he's doing all of them at once, and I'm *letting* him.

Oh, this kiss. It has no end. It's an ocean and I'm drowning in it.

And my hands? They're gripping the soaked fabric of his shirtfront as if I'm holding on for dear life, as if he's all that's keeping me tethered to the earth.

I shiver, and he releases me abruptly and gasps for breath, almost as if he's as blown away by the power of this thing between us as I am.

But that's impossible.

"Come on. You're shivering. Gotta get you warm." He pulls me out of the dry warmth of the church foyer and out into the bucketing, howling, raging storm.

The sky flashes with lightning and shakes with thunder, and it's not so much raining as upending the contents of a sea from out of the clouds. We run, now, hand in hand, barreling up the hill toward the looming white colonnades of the Grand Hotel's world-famous porch.

We enter through Sadie's, the nearest door, where all is white walls and black, white, and red checkered benches, and the scent of vanilla and baking pastries and coffee, and then we're in the florist shop and it's all geraniums and roses. I've never been past Sadie's. You have to pay a ten-dollar fee to go past the front door, unless you're a guest, and I've never had the time or inclination to spend the money merely to indulge my curiosity. Dripping with each step, shoes squishing, we go down a long marble-floored hallway, windows showing the road on one side, and shops on the other. The road is dark and glistening wet, flashing white with lightning now and then; a carriage passes, lit lamps on the back, and the horses clop-clop-clop along, tails swishing. There is a jeweler, a clothing boutique, a coffee shop, and then the front desk.

"Hello, Mr. Trenton," the small Asian woman behind the desk says.

"Hey," Adam responds, with a smile and wave.

There are whispers and mutters from the crowd standing around the front desk, people twisting and craning to get a glimpse of *the* Adam Trenton. A few people lift their cell phones and snap pictures, and a blonde girl of maybe fifteen or sixteen shuffles forward, offering a silver cell phone to him.

"Can I have your autograph, Mr. Trenton? Please?" She's timid, and tiny.

I notice an immediate shift in Adam. He's gone from lithe and loose to stiff and tense in the space of a breath. But I only notice that because I'm clinging to his arm. Outwardly, he's smiling and taking the cell phone, digging a Sharpie out of his pocket and scrawling his name across the back. As if the one signature was a dam breaking, half a dozen people surge forward, shoving receipts and hats and tourist maps at him.

And he signs them all.

He smiles at each person as he hands them their autographed item, not once betraying any irritation or haste. A crowd has formed at this point, and I can see that Adam's smile is becoming strained, even though he's still signing and shaking hands and posing for pictures. I move to stand over to one side and try to be inconspicuous, melting back into the crowd.

"No more, no more," a doorman says, cutting between the crowd and Adam and I. "No more, now, please. Let Mr. Trenton go on his way, please."

Adam grabs my hand and pulls me with him as the doorman escorts us away from the crowd; another red-suited doorman keeps the people at bay. Adam hands the doorman a fifty-dollar bill as he calls the elevator.

"Thanks," Adam says.

"Of course," the doorman says, with a wide white grin splitting his black skin.

Adam pushes the button for the fourth floor and the elevator doors close in front of us. As soon as the doors are closed and the elevator is moving, Adam lets out a relieved sigh and leans back against the wall.

"Does that happen a lot?" I ask.

I knew he was famous, obviously, but I've never seen anything like that before, at least not in person.

He nods. "All the time. Happened once already today, when I was getting the fudge."

"It looks exhausting." I stare down at our joined hands, wondering why he's still holding my hand.

He laughs, a harsh, sarcastic sound. "You have no idea. It was cool the first few times I got recognized out on the street, you know, but it's just so tiring. It's part of the gig, though, so I can't bitch about it too much."

"I was impressed, to be honest," I admit. "You gave everyone your full attention."

He shrugs, but his smile is bright and genuine, and a little shy, actually. "Well, they're the reason I'm where I am, you know? They like my movies, they like me. So as much as I don't enjoy it in some ways, because I can't really go anywhere without getting recognized like that, I do love it, too. It's a validation that I'm doing something right, I guess."

"That makes sense," I say.

The door slides open and Adam leads me off the elevator, turning right. Everything is green. The carpet is a deep forest green, and the walls are a pale mint, and there are framed photographs of woodcut artwork from hundreds of years ago lining the walls.

"This hotel is weird," I say as we pass a replica of a Greek sculpture in a corner. "It feels like it's…I don't know how to put it. Like we've stepped back in time or something."

Adams digs a key out of his pocket. It's an actual physical key, not a swipe card like you see in pretty much every other hotel in the world.

"That's the point," he says. "That's part of the appeal, why they can charge so much for the rooms and whatever. It's an experience. You have to be dressed in formal clothes to even go down to the parlor level after six o'clock."

"I've heard about that. I've never actually been in the hotel itself, though."

"It's kind of fun," he says as he unlocks a door. It's a double door, in the corner where the hall turns to the right. A sign above the lintel announces that this is The Musser Suite. "It's kind of like being in a movie. We got here late yesterday afternoon, so we all had dinner down in the main dining room. I wore a suit and tie and everything, and it was very, very fancy."

"Sounds like fun," I say.

It does, too. I own one nice dress, and I never have an opportunity to wear it. I don't even dare think about what it would be like to be dressed up and go down to the dining room on Adam's arm. That's not going to happen. He wants one thing from me, and once he gets it, he'll send me on my way. That's how this works, and I know it. Panic shoots through me as Adam leads me into the room, dragging me by the hand through the doorway and closing the door behind us.

My panic is momentarily subsumed by shock. The Musser Suite is unlike anything I've ever seen before. It's...overwhelming.

As you walk in, there's a large foyer that also functions as a kitchen, with a sink, a wine refrigerator, and a stainless steel microwave drawer and a dishwasher, beside which is a rack containing half a dozen bottles of wine. The foyer floor is a dark parquet wood, with a round green, white, and black rug with an elaborate 'M' in the middle. Three steps up lead to the sitting area. The floor here is plaid carpeting, a white background with blue and red stripes in a squared-off pattern. The ceiling is painted a pale mint green with white beams meeting in a starburst pattern, from the center of which hangs an ornate gold chandelier. There is a violently purple satin couch against one wall, and the opposite wall, above the white mantel fireplace, is covered in the same intensely purple satin. There's a flat-screen TV mounted to the purple wall, which seems poignantly out of place in the otherwise archaically decorated room. The curtains framing the window are a sheer turquoise, and centered beneath the window is glass tabletop mounted on a white spindle. The matching chairs have crimson satin cushions. There's another table and two chairs set in front of the fireplace, but these are large overstuffed armchairs done in a busy floral pattern. Behind the couch is a matching set of four oil paintings, but I don't know enough about art to say what style they're in.

I take two steps into the sitting area, staring at the room.

"Something else, right?" Adam says.

"I don't even know what to say." I take a few steps in, leaving puddles on the floor, keeping my hands tucked against my stomach. "It feels like I'm not supposed to touch anything. Like it's a museum or something."

He grins. "Well, it's not how I'd personally decorate anything, but I'm a typical macho dude, so what do I know?"

I roll my eyes at him. "You're anything but a typical macho dude, Adam," I say.

Somehow he's behind me, and I can hear his breath in my ear, feel his chest expanding at my back. His hands come to rest on my hips. "Oh yeah? So what am I, then?"

I swallow hard and fight the urge to lean back into him. "I—um. You're Adam Trenton."

"Cop-out," he murmurs.

Teeth nip at my earlobe, and I can't breathe, and my eyes are sliding closed against my will, and somehow I'm losing strength, my spine melting inside me, leaving me no choice but to fall back against him.

His hands trace the waist of my jeans, pausing on my stomach, his hands covering mine.

I shiver again, both from being cold and from his proximity, from his lips on my neck, on the curve where throat meets shoulder, clavicle, and breastbone. His hair tickles my ear, and his lips are touching, kissing, moving.

"You need a hot shower," he murmurs.

I'm compliant, his lips having stolen my will with each delicate touch. He pulls me back down into the foyer, and back up into a bedroom. There's a bed with a flower-print comforter and an elaborate purple headboard surrounded by drapes that match the bedspread. That's all I see, and then I'm being pushed into the bathroom. He halts, spins me, pressing my back against the frame of the door, so we're half in the bathroom, half out, our bodies crushed together. His lips touch my throat, and then my neck, and I'm tilting my head to the side with a sigh as he kisses beneath my ear.

I don't know what's happening. What I'm doing. I should stop this. Stop him. Have him get me one of the horse-drawn carriage cabs back to my dorm. If I stay here, I won't stop him. I'll let this happen.

He squeezes past me, into the bathroom, opens the glass door of the shower and turns on the water. In moments, steam is billowing from the spray and filling the small room. And now he's here again, in front of me, curling a finger into a belt loop of my jeans. His hand frames one side of my face, fingers curling into my wet hair, pulling me toward him. His lips devour mine more slowly now, and his other hand deftly unbuttons my jeans, lowers my zipper.

Now my heart is crashing and hammering and I'm kissing him but I'm so, so scared, because I'm *letting* him do this, allowing him to undress me, even though I'm scared and know I shouldn't be and know this can only end badly for him and for me… mostly for me.

God, what the actual fuck am I doing? I'm helping him, that's what. I'm pulling my arms through the sleeves of my shirt and shrugging out of it, tugging it over my head and letting it plop to the floor at my feet, and the air is cold against my skin, even though steam is enveloping us, wreathing around us. I'm in my bra and jeans, and his hands are on my flesh, sliding up my back, smoothing beneath my bra strap and up over it, to my shoulders. My feet are toeing off my shoes and socks, and now, oh no. No. No.

Yes.

He lets me peel his shirt off.

Jesus, the man is perfect. I have to wrench my eyes open and gaze at him. His body is not just bulky and built, but is also incredibly, perfectly toned. Each muscle is so clearly defined they may as well be chiseled into place. His khaki shorts are heavy from being wet, and they hang low around his hips. The waistband of Polo underwear peeks out, and a wickedly deep V-cut disappears under the elastic.

My hands itch and twitch. I want to touch him so fucking bad it hurts. He's a fantasy. *This* is a fantasy. It's not real. I'm asleep at home in Detroit, in my bed, dreaming. There's no way this is really happening. It feels real, but I know it's not. It can't be. It's all happening so fast, meeting him in the hot sunshine of late evening, and then the storm hitting out of nowhere, and the leisurely hour of dinner, and now suddenly I'm in this extravagant hotel room being kissed and stripped by an actual god.

Hot, rough-skinned, massive hands slide up my sides and in, around, to my ribs. I glance at him, and see that his eyes are open and roving over me, staring at me as if he can't get enough of me. As if I'm something he likes. Which is just crazy. I'm not stupid or self-conscious. I know I'm pretty enough. I'm in shape. But I'm not dainty or skinny. I'm just shy of six feet tall, and I'm curvy. I don't look like Hollywood actresses, or models. I'm me, and I'm confident in myself, content with the way I look.

But I'm just not what a man like Adam Trenton goes for.

And now, with his leaf-green eyes taking in my skin and my tits and my hips, I wonder what he's thinking. If I'm being naïve. Maybe he's not picky and I'm just a conquest for the night.

"You are so fucking sexy, Des," Adam growls, his voice a low rumble in my ear. His lips trace along the shell of my ear. "You know that? Do you know how fucking incredible you look right now?"

I can only shake my head, because that's just the honest truth. I don't know. I don't feel sexy. I'm wet and cold and my hair is a tangled mess and my makeup, what little bit I put on earlier, is either smeared by the rain or washed away entirely.

"I'll have to show you, then."

He pivots, and my back is to the towel rack, and I can see over his shoulder to our reflection in the mirror. His back is as ripped as the rest of him, of course, and god, a man's muscular back is a thing of beauty. His muscles shift and ripple as he leans down and his teeth nip at the delicate skin at the side of my neck. And then he pivots again, and I'm facing the mirror and he's standing behind me. He doesn't tower over me, but he still dwarfs me. His hands wrap around my waist, just above my jeans, and now I can see myself.

Black bra. It's an old one and doesn't fit, so my breasts spill out over the top of it, the edge of my areola peeking up from the top of one cup. My stomach isn't entirely flat, a fact which doesn't usually bother me, but now with his scrutiny on me like a laser, all I can see is the slightly rounded pooch of my belly. My jeans are undone, showing my green cotton underwear in the 'V' of my open zipper.

I am in no way prepared for this. I'm not even wearing a matching bra and underwear set. As a broke, orphaned college girl barely making rent and tuition, the last thing I need or have the money for is sexy lingerie. But now I'm wishing I'd bothered, because I'm in a hotel bathroom with *Adam Trenton,* in my jeans and my bra, and my bra is easily ten years old, the silk of the cups fraying at the edges, and it doesn't fit because I've filled out since I bought this bra, but it's one of three I own and the other two are in the wash. And my underwear? Well, thank god they're not granny panties; I don't wear those, even on period days. These are basic cotton, which isn't really sexy, but at least they're boy-shorts, which, considering how big my ass is, look pretty good on me.

But am I sure I want him to see my underwear? Meaning, am I sure I'm willing to let him take my jeans off and see me in just my underwear?

No.

Hell no.

But his fingers slide down my sides and over my hips, slipping between the denim of my jeans and the cotton of my underwear. And then, somehow, I'm stepping on the cuff of one leg of my jeans and pulling my leg free, and then again, and now I'm shaking all over and his eyes are raking over my curves in the mirror, and I can feel him behind me. He's a huge mountain behind me, his chest at my shoulders, and I can feel something hard and thick between us, and I know what it is, but can't think about that.

"Des." He says my name in a rumbling whisper.

"Adam."

"You're shaking."

"I'm cold." That's true, but that's not really why I'm shaking. The truth slips out of my mouth. "And scared."

"Why are you scared, Des?"

"Because…I mean, isn't it obvious?" The real truth behind my fear isn't something I'd ever admit to, not even under torture.

"No." He cups my hips, and then his hands are palming my butt, lifting the heavy weight of one cheek and then the other, playing with me, enjoying it, kneading and caressing.

I couldn't stop him if I wanted to, and I don't. I don't want to stop him. I *like* the way his hands feel on my ass. I like being touched like this. I didn't know it would feel so good to have a man's hands on my bottom. But it does, it's incredible, it's heady and I'm shaking from how good it feels and from the ever-present fear and doubt and nerves.

I have to regain some kind of control over myself, and over the situation. "Well, let me spell it out, then. You're a famous Hollywood movie star. You got mobbed in the hotel lobby. I'm no one. I'm a trash collector." I have to pause to breathe, because his hands are finding the elastic waistband of my underwear and digging under to cup bare flesh and muscle, and my underwear are perilously close to coming off now, baring my core. "I'm a fucking garbage girl. A janitor. And like you said, you're only here for the weekend, and Adam? I'm *not* this type of girl."

"What type?" he demands, meeting my eyes in the mirror. "What do you think is happening?"

I glare at his reflection. "You're seducing me. And I'm letting you, but I have no fucking clue why. And I don't know why you'd want this with me. Why you'd bring me up here, when I'm nobody, when I look the way I do and you're you and—"

"The way you look? What's that mean?" He sounds almost angry.

"It just means I'm not a size two, okay?"

"And what? You think I somehow missed that fact?"

I'm stunned for a moment. "Wow. Okay." I rip myself out of his arms. "Fuck you." I push past him.

I don't make two steps before he's wrapping an arm around me and stopping me, spinning me in place and pulling me hard against him, so my bra is pressed against his chest and my breasts are actually and completely spilling out. And I can feel his cock between us, big, thick, and hard.

"Stop, Des."

"Let me go." I hate being restrained. It triggers a fight-or-flight reflex in me. Violently, if I feel threatened enough.

"Des, just listen—" His hold on me is inexorable and unbreakable, triggering rage and panic in me.

"Let me fucking go, *now,*" I growl, pushing against him with all my strength

He releases me immediately, and I'm having trouble breathing, memories flashing through me. "Des? It's okay. It's okay. Breathe. Breathe." He's got a hand on my back, and I want to both knock it away and beg him to put both hands on my back, to hold me, touch me.

I force my breathing to slow, and straighten. Fixing my eyes on his, I stab his bare chest with a finger. "Do not *ever* restrain me like that again."

He holds his hands up, palms out. "I won't. I swear, I promise. I just—"

"Damn right you won't," I say, and snatch my shirt off the floor. "Because I'm leaving."

"Hold on a goddamned second," he says, moving in front of me. "You misunderstood me. Deliberately, something tells me. You're not a size two, and I know that. I see that. I saw that the first time I laid eyes on you. You're here, Des. I brought you here, on purpose. Because I like you. Because you turn me on."

He's inching closer to me, hands outstretched, daring to reach for me after what just happened. He takes my shirt from me, and he is now standing chest to chest with me, and his eyes are palest green and knowing and kind and fierce and sharp and intelligent.

"Des. Hear me. I'm a man who speaks the truth, no matter the consequences. So here's some truth for you." His palm fits against my cheek, and his fingers tilt my face up so I'm looking at him, our lips kissing distance apart. "I'm intrigued by you. You're fascinating. I can't figure you out, and I like that. You're not impressed by who I am, and I like that even more. You're so drop-dead fucking gorgeous that I can't stand it. You're so sexy it's not even right."

I can't move, can't breathe. No one has ever called me beautiful before, much less gorgeous or sexy. More frighteningly, he seems to mean it. I want to pull away and run before I give in, but I'm not moving and I'm already giving in.

He's not done, though. "And yeah, I'm only here for the weekend. And you're not no one. You're you. And I like you—what I've seen so far. I promised you I wouldn't ask you any questions, and I won't. But I hope you'll trust me enough to tell me a few things about you on your own. Whatever *this* is, whatever it is that's happening between us, I want it. Whether it's just for tonight or tomorrow too, or something beyond that, I want it. So I'm going to go with it." His other hand moves possessively and with intimate familiarity to the small of my back, holding me in place. "You're scared. I can see that. I don't know why, and I'm not going to ask because I promised I wouldn't. But you can tell me the truth, whatever it is. If you really want to leave, I'll take you back myself, or I'll get you a carriage back to your dorm. But I don't want you to leave. I hope you'll stay."

"Adam…I just—"

He presses his thumb over my lips to silence me. "So, as much as I'd like to finish stripping you down to skin, I won't. As much as I'd like to have you naked, right here and right now, I'm going to back away. I'm going to let you get in the shower, and I'm going to give you time to think. Decide what you want, and I'll go with it. I'm not going to pressure you into anything. You know what I want. I've made it clear, I hope."

He takes three backward steps and then stops, leans in and kisses me, hard and fast, and then turns goes into the sitting room, out of sight.

I stand trembling, confused, and half-naked in the doorway of the bathroom, steam billowing around me.

What do I want?

Fuck if I know.

Well, that's not true. I want Adam to kiss me. I want this dream to be real. I'm still not convinced I'm not going to wake up in my dorm room and have it all be a fever dream. I pinch the inside of my arm, and it hurts, and I'm still in The Musser Suite of the Grand Hotel, with Adam Trenton one room away, waiting for me.

Wanting me.

How is that possible?

But it seems to be true, and I have to decide what I'm going to do about it.

I peel my clothes off and step into the shower.

CHAPTER FOUR

It takes every ounce of self-control I possess to remain sitting on the couch, waiting for her. I want to go into the bathroom and watch her. I want to peel my shorts off and step in the shower with her.

I want to push her up against the tiled shower wall and take her there.

Instead, I wait until I hear the bathroom door shut, and then I grab her wet clothes off the floor and bring them to the foyer. I use the hotel phone to have the front desk send someone up to take her clothes to be dried. Once the maid has taken the clothes, with an assurance that she'll have them back in less than half an hour, I have a bottle of Pinot Grigio sent up, along with an order of chips and salsa.

I change into a pair of gym shorts, not bothering with underwear.

I'm hopeful, what can I say?

Minutes pass in taffy-slow increments, and eventually I hear the shower shut off.

"Hey! Where are my clothes?" Des's voice rings out.

I grab a robe from the closet and stand outside the bathroom with it. Des has the door open just enough to poke her head out, and I can see a towel across her chest.

I hold up the robe. "Housekeeping is drying them for you."

"So I'm your hostage until they're dry, is that it?" A gleam of humor in her eyes tells me she's not mad.

"Exactly. Half an hour, they said. Until then, wear this." I hold the robe toward her.

She pulls the towel more tightly around her torso, and then opens the door. My eyes soak up her beauty. Her hair has been towel dried, but it's still wet and hangs down over one bare shoulder. God, I want so badly to tug the towel away, but I don't. Instead, I hold the robe open for her, and she turns away from me, slides one arm through the sleeve, and then the other. My throat closes as she unfastens the towel from beneath her armpits and lets it drop to the floor. And just for a moment, she's naked and in the same room as me, but then she wraps the robe closed and ties it off and the moment is lost.

"Feel better?" I ask.

She nods, and sighs. "Yeah. A hot shower does a world of good. You're next?"

I shrug. "Nah. I'm fine." I grip her shoulders gently and turn her to face me. "So."

Her big brown eyes meet mine briefly, but then flicker down over my chest and down to my shorts, and I wonder if she can tell I'm not wearing any underwear.

"So," she repeats.

A knock on the door interrupts this eloquent and fascinating exchange, and I leave her standing in the bedroom to answer it. It's the wine and chips, and then coming up behind the young man delivering the food is the maid with the clothes, folded and dried and placed discreetly in a white linen bag. I take the tray and set it on the counter, sign the charges to my room with a hefty tip, and then take the clothes.

When I turn back, Des is leaning a shoulder against the doorway to the steps to the sitting room, pulling a hotel-provided brush through her hair. I hold up the bag with her clothes in one hand, and the bottle of wine in the other.

"Choose," I say.

Her eyes narrow, and she tosses the brush across the room and onto the bed. "Choose?"

I move up onto the bottom step, looking up at her. "The bag has your clothes in it. Take the bag, put on the clothes, and I'll get you home. Go your way, I'll go mine. Or, I open the wine and we see where things go."

"That's a tough choice," she says, and somehow there's no irony or sarcasm in it.

It really is a hard choice for her, for reasons I can't fathom. She stands on the top step, looking down at me, and I can't read her eyes. She reaches out with one hand and touches the linen, and then the chilled glass of the bottle.

"If I stay, what will happen?" She moves her gaze to mine, and waits.

She expects the truth, so I give it to her. "If you tell me you want to stay, I'm going to take that robe off of you and I'm going to lay you down on the bed over there, and I'm going to kiss and touch every beautiful inch of your body. I'm going to make you come over and over and over, until you can't stand it anymore. And then, when you can't possibly come again, I'm going to put my cock inside you and make you come again." Her eyes go wide, her mouth falls open, and she stops breathing. I ascend the steps until I'm face to face with her, and she's backing away and I'm following her. Her palms go flat on my bare chest, as if to push me away, but she doesn't. "That's where I'll start. We'll drink some wine, eat some chips and salsa, and then I'll ravage you over and over and over until you beg me to stop."

"Holy shit." It was a breath, a curse, a prayer. I'm not sure which.

"Is that what you want, Des?" I set the bag on the floor, and then put the bottle on a little table just inside the doorway. She watches my every move, her hands toying with the knotted belt of the robe.

"I…I don't know," she says.

I move toward her, taking a deep breath to swell my chest, my arms swinging, my eyes fixed on her brown, inscrutable gaze. "You don't know?"

"You talk like that, and yeah, I want that, but—"

"Do you want me to take you home?"

"No." Her voice is small, and she's looking up at me from beneath thick black lashes. "Yes. I don't know."

"Des." I take the knot in my fingers, work it loose, but don't untie the belt. "Do you want to stay?"

Her breath catches, and I can see her pulse beating in her throat. Her fingers touch the backs of my hands, but she's not stopping me as I slowly untie the belt. Her arms go across her torso then, keeping the robe closed.

"I don't know." Her voice is barely above a whisper, and she's not looking at me.

"You don't want to leave, but you're not sure you want to stay?" I ask.

She nods. "Right."

"You're really testing my resolve to not ask you any questions about yourself right now, you know that?" I take the edges of the robe and hold them closed, and close in so my lips brush hers. "I'll be gentle, Des. I'll go slow. You want to stop, at any moment, and I'll stop."

"Am I a conquest?" she blurts.

I'm taken aback. "What? Are you a *conquest?*"

"Are you doing this to prove you can? Is this just because I'm here, and you're horny? Is this what you do? Seduce random girls? What is this, Adam? Tell me the truth." She grips my hands in hers, keeping her robe closed, holding tightly to my hands as if I'm all that's keeping her upright.

"No, Des. That's not what this is." I pause to gather my thoughts. "I haven't been with anyone in months, and before that I was in a relationship for almost two years." I hope she doesn't push that line of questions, because it's not something I want to rehash. Not now, not ever.

I can see the curiosity in her eyes, but she doesn't ask the question. Instead, she frowns and asks, "So why me?"

I shake my head and shrug. "Because you're beautiful. You're secretive and mysterious and sexy."

I gather her thick damp black hair in my hand. "Because the moment I saw this hair of yours, I wanted to bury my hands in it. Because the first time I saw your big brown eyes and those lush lips, I wanted to know you. Kiss you. Find out who you are, get to know you."

"Lush lips?" she breathes, as if disbelieving.

I brush my lips across hers, lightly, teasingly. "The lushest." I kiss her cheekbone, and she turns her face to the side, giving me access to her neck, so I kiss her there too. "I'm intrigued by you. I don't know what this is any more than you do, Des. The last thing I have time for right now is to get involved in anything, but I can't seem to stop myself."

Her fingers release mine, release her robe, and she grasps at me, clutches at my chest. I move closer, press our bodies together, and she sighs, a desperate exhale. Her fingers scrape over my chest, curl and dig into my pectoral muscles, and now she turns her face and tilts it to look up at me, and all I can see is her eyes, wide and the color of liquid chocolate and so deep, fathomless, so expressive and yet giving away nothing of what she's thinking.

"I'm not mysterious."

I laugh. "Yes you are."

She shakes her head without breaking our locked gazes. "There's just…a lot I don't like to talk about."

"Fair enough."

My hands are on her back, resting lightly. I leave them there, and I shift forward, slant my mouth across hers. I taste her breath; feel the shaking in her body. But she's pressing closer, her magnificent tits crushed between us, and I'm losing the fight to keep her clothed. I can't hold back anymore.

"I have to see you." I whisper it, my lips moving against hers.

Her lips move on mine, and she lifts up on her toes, deepening the kiss. I groan at the taste of her lips, the feel of her body against mine, and then her tongue slips between my teeth to slide against my tongue, and I'm lost. I'm gone.

I reach up and curl my fingers into the thick collar of the robe, just beneath her chin. She's on her tiptoes, so tall I don't have to bend at all to match our mouths. The last of my will is shredded by the way she grinds her tongue against mine, and I slowly pull my hands apart as I slide them down the center of her torso. The robe opens, revealing tan skin and inner side boob. She gasps into my mouth and her fingers claw into my shoulders. I'm this close to having the robe off of her, to having all of her gorgeous body bare to me.

"No." She grasps the edges of the robe and pulls them back together, jerks backward, out of my reach. "Adam, I—I can't. I can't." She's gasping, her eyes wide and wavering back and forth.

I hold up my hands in surrender. "Des, it's okay, I'm sorry, I—"

When my hands go up, she stumbles away from me, as if scared of me, of my hands, and her eyes are wet with tears. "Don't! Don't touch me, don't—please—"

"Des? What's wrong? What did I do?" I'm totally baffled. I barely touched her, and as soon as she said the word "no" I had my hands off. This is an extreme reaction to a simple situation, and I don't know how to handle it, what to do, or what caused it.

She hits the end of the bed with her knees, sits down, and then scrambles away from me, and she's sobbing, and I'm totally helpless.

This is a panic attack.

I've only had one before this, and that was the last time I let a man touch me. It was a guy from a two hundred-level psychology class, someone I'd been in several classes with. He was a nice, attractive guy, easy to talk to, easy to look at. We had coffee after class one evening and then a few drinks and then we were in his car and we were kissing. Then his hands were under my shirt, and I wasn't sure I liked it but I let him grope my boobs anyway, just to see how it would feel.

But then he got greedy and tried to undo my pants and I freaked. He stopped right away and apologized, and I could tell he didn't know why I was freaking, but I couldn't stop. I couldn't breathe and couldn't see, dizzy and lungs aching. Eventually I managed to get it under control and the guy took me home, confused and frustrated and still nice as ever.

That was a year ago.

This panic attack is wracking and unending, terrifying in its intensity. I'm crying, and the more I cry the more I can't breathe, and the more I can't breathe the worse my terror gets, which in turn only worsens my weeping. It's a cycle I don't know how to break.

I hear Adam saying my name, but that's somewhere outside myself, and all I can grasp are the tears and the need to breathe and the terror. And somehow the tears come harder and faster and I can't breathe. I'm choking and rolling away from him and crawling up the bed to curl into a ball near the pillows, sobs wracking me.

The bed dips with a heavy weight, and I feel something warm drape over me. A blanket. He's covering me. He wraps the blanket over me, and then slips his hands under me and lifts me like I'm a child, weightless. He settles on the bed with me, my head against his chest, and I can hear his heart beating steadily, a little fast, his breathing even and easy, and his arms are around me and his lips are at my ear, and he's murmuring something rhythmic and soothing.

I focus on his heartbeat, focus on his breathing, and try to match my breathing to his, try to will my heart to beat in time with his. Slowly my terror recedes and the hyperventilating lessens to ragged gasps. His hands rest on my shoulder and my hip; I'm curled on his lap like a child. I hear his voice now, and realized he's singing some pop song, the kind of song you hear on the radio a dozen times every day but never really know the title or artist, just the hook and chorus. His voice is low, quiet, and melodic.

I'm still crying, but quietly now.

I have to stop this. I have to calm myself. I move off him into a sitting position. Breathing deeply and slowly, I slow my heartbeat back to normal, and I wipe at my eyes with the heels of my palms.

I can't even look at Adam now.

He slides off the bed and goes to the kitchen. I hear water running, and then the gurgling of a kettle. I need to get up, need to get dressed, need to get out of here, but I can't seem to move. I'm not thinking of the panic attack now, I'm thinking about what preceded it.

I've never been so embarrassed in my life: I let a man I've known for a matter of hours almost get me naked, let him touch me, let him kiss me. And he's not just some random *guy,* he's a rich and famous movie star.

What the *fuck* was I thinking?

And then I go and have a panic attack.

God, I'm a freak, and a mess.

He comes up the stairs and into the bedroom with a mug in his hand, the string and tab of a tea bag dangling over the side of the mug. He's wearing nothing but a pair of black gym shorts, and even after everything that just happened I catch myself staring at his crotch, watching the bounce and sway of his dick in his shorts as he walks toward me. I can see the tip in the folds of the shorts, a thick round thing. I force my eyes away and blink hard, keeping my eyes down on the floral-print comforter and accept the mug of tea from him.

He sits on the edge of the bed and watches me sip the tea. Waits. "Des, I—" he stops, sighs, and tries again. "Are you okay?"

I shrug. "I'm fine. Thanks."

"I want to ask what happened, what I did to make you have a panic attack, but I—"

I interrupt him. "It wasn't you. I just…have issues."

"I should have backed off. I'm sorry, Des. I saw—I knew you were nervous or something, but I didn't realize—"

I finally meet his eyes, and see that he's genuinely upset. "Just…forget it, okay? It wasn't you."

"Don't feed me the 'it's not you, it's me' bullshit, Des. You don't just have panic attacks that bad out of nowhere." He says this gently, reaching out to trace my cheekbone with his thumb. "Drink your tea, babe. I'll get dressed and take you home."

Babe. He called me *babe*.

Why do I like that so much? And why do I feel this crazy urge to explain everything to him?

Instead, I follow him across the room with my eyes as he snags a pair of jeans and a black T-shirt out of a suitcase in the corner of the bedroom area. He goes into the bathroom and comes out dressed a few seconds later. I notice he didn't put on any underwear, and that does things I can't quite figure out to my insides.

I take a long sip of the tea, which is some kind of minty lemony herbal tea, and it's exactly what I needed even though I didn't know it until now. I listen as he calls down to the front desk and requests a private carriage.

"What kind of tea is this?" I ask when he comes back.

He goes down to the kitchenette and grabs the wrapper off the counter. "Harney and Sons. Mint Verbena."

"It's really good." I try to smile at him. "Thank you."

"You're welcome." He smiles back at me, but the questions that keep piling up in his eyes are all I can see.

"I'm sorry for freaking out on you, Adam. It really wasn't your fault."

He shrugs. "Don't be sorry. "

I want to tell him how good what he did made me feel, but I don't know how. "And thank you for..." I wave my hand vaguely, hating the way I'm flushing. "This."

His gaze narrows and heats. "This what?"

I try a different tack. "I had a really...*really* good time. Until I wigged out, that is. But dinner, and everything. Just...thank you."

A smile brightens his face, his eyes gleaming. "I really enjoyed everything, too, Des. So thank *you*."

I finish my tea in two long swallows, burning my mouth a little and not caring. I have to get home. He's too much. This is too much. I'm embarrassed by my freak-out, shaken by how intensely attracted to Adam I am, not just physically but to him, to the man, and I just don't know what to think or feel or do.

I still can't believe I almost let him get me naked. That can't happen. He'd see things no one has ever seen except Ruthie, and I don't know how he'd react.

I take the linen bag containing my clothes into the bathroom and dress quickly, and when I emerge Adam has a pair of cross trainers on and his room key in his hands. We walk to the elevator in silence. We ride down to the parlor level together in silence, and he walks me out to the covered driveway, not holding my hand and not speaking.

A closed carriage waits, two tall black horses stomping and swishing their tails and shaking their heads. The driver is hunched over, wearing a slicker and gloves and looking miserable. A doorman opens the carriage door, and Adam hands me up.

"Goodnight, Des," he says.

"Goodnight, Adam."

A million things lie between us, all unspoken.

Rain still falls in wild, windblown curtains, and thunder still crashes and lightning still splits the sky. I'd forgotten, for a while, that it was storming.

Adam hands a folded bill to the driver, tells him my destination, and then closes the door, shoving his hands in his pockets and watching as the carriage jerks into motion. I watch him until he's out of sight.

When I finally get home, Ruth is on her bed reading.

She frowns at me over the top of her book. "I thought you were meeting Jimmy and me for drinks?"

"I was going to," I start, and then realize I have no clue how to explain what just happened, to myself, let alone to my friend. "Something came up."

Ruth knows me well enough to know when I'm evading, when I don't want to talk about something.

"Okay," she shrugs, and then looks at me more closely. "Are you okay? You look like you were crying."

I owe her something, at least. "I don't even know where to start, Ruthie. I just don't. I'm okay, though. I just…I need some sleep."

She stares at me, one pierced eyebrow arched in suspicion. And then she goes back to reading. "Fine. But if you ever want to talk, you know you can tell me anything."

"I know." I lean over and hug her, but quickly, so she doesn't smell Adam on me. "Thanks, Ruthie."

Sleep is a long time coming. I can't stop thinking of Adam, of what he made me feel. I realize he knew exactly how to handle my panic attack, and somehow I'm not surprised. He just took care of me, and he didn't ask any questions.

And when I finally fall asleep, I dream of his hands and his mouth and his eyes, and his words. I dream of his big warm hard body beneath mine, just holding me, and I dream of listening to his heartbeat.

CHAPTER FIVE

It's late afternoon, the day of the fundraiser dinner. I've managed to spend the day in my room, answering emails and working on my script and studiously not thinking about Des. Eventually, I'm compelled by my restless nature to head downstairs for lunch. After eating, I find Gareth on one of the couches in the parlor, sipping tea and staring at his cell phone, a sour look on his face.

"Bad news, Adam," Gareth says to me.

I sit down beside him, and he sets his phone on his knee. "Bad news, huh?" I glance at him. "What's up?"

"I just got a call from Emma." He doesn't look at me as he says her name. "The storm is still out of control. They ran the ferries all day yesterday despite the storm, but today they're saying the waves are well over fifteen feet in places. They're shutting down the ferries for a while, until the waves go down a bit."

I frown. "I didn't think they ever shut the ferries down."

He shrugs. "I didn't either. First time in like, twenty years or something. One of the ferries almost capsized this morning, apparently." He taps at the screen of his phone. "Anyway, point is, Emma can't make it for the dinner."

"Well, damn," I say, my tone dry and droll. "I'm so upset."

Gareth rolls his eyes and grins. "I'm sure you're heartbroken. But you still need a date for the dinner."

"I might be stuck going on my own. It's not the end of the world."

"Fine, whatever." Gareth pokes me in the shoulder. "But you *will* show up, Adam. Alone or with a date, you have to at least make an appearance."

"I will, I will."

He sets his tea down with a clatter, and picks up a tiny triangular sandwich with something pink on top of the bread. It's a formal English type of tea setup that they do every afternoon, apparently, complete with weird sandwiches and bizarre pastries.

"Well, I'd better go make some calls," I say, slapping my knee.

Although, by the time I get up to my room, I already know what I'm going to do. It's reckless, and sure to get me in trouble, and probably make a huge scene for everyone, but I don't care. I shower and dress in my tux, fighting with the bow tie for nearly twenty minutes before getting it to look right. Fucking bow ties.

I ask for a private carriage and bring an umbrella, not that it'll do much good, as it's still raining really hard. I hop into the waiting carriage, tell the driver where I want to go, and then sit back to think about what I'm going to say. And try not to think too closely about what I'm doing, and how bad an idea it is.

It's only a few minutes before the carriage is stopping outside her dorm. I jump out and jog to the entrance, which is luckily unlocked. A girl with blue-streaked blonde hair and an eyebrow piercing is exiting one of the apartment doors and locking it behind herself.

"Excuse me," I say, fixing my public-appearance smile on my face. "I'm looking for Des Ross."

The girl starts and presses a hand to her chest, having not seen me as I approached. "Holy shit, you scared me, dude." And then she actually sees me and her eyes go wide. "Holy shit. Holy motherfucking shit."

I ignore her unblinking stare of disbelief. "Do you know where I can find Des?"

She tilts her head to one side. "Why?"

"I met her yesterday, and I wanted to…talk to her." I take a step closer and let a silence hang. "Do you know where I can find her?"

The girl has a calculating expression on her face. "She came home last night looking like she'd been crying."

"Home?" I glance at the door behind the girl. "She's your roommate?"

"Ruth Nicholson." She extends her hand, and I shake it, squeezing gently.

"Adam Trenton."

"Nice to meet you, Adam." She withdraws her hand and fixes me with an impressively hard look. "So why did she come back looking shaken up?"

I hesitate, not knowing what to say. Finally, I decide on neutrality. "I think if she didn't explain, neither should I. But how about you just tell her I'm here, and let her decide if she wants to see me."

Ruth nods. "Good enough." Her eyes rake up and down. "Nice tux, by the way."

"Thanks."

She goes back inside, and then returns after only a moment. "You can go in." She closes the distance between us and looks up at me, a fierce expression on her face. "You better be nice to my friend, dude. I don't care *who* you are. Don't hurt her."

"She's in good hands," I tell her.

She nods, a rueful expression crossing her features. "Yeah, that's what I'm afraid of."

And then the small but fiery girl with blue-streaked hair is out in the rain, ducking and running across the street and into a coffee shop. The door to her and Des's apartment is cracked open, so I knock on it and push in. It's a dorm room, exactly like you'd find in any college in the country. Small, a bunk bed on one wall, a bookshelf and two small bureaus on another, a bathroom behind a partially open door. There's an actual closet too, shallow and narrow, but more than most dorms have. There are girl clothes everywhere, a bra hanging off the hook of the bathroom door, inside-out jeans on the floor, a hairbrush on the desk under the window, a tiny scrap of thong underwear on the floor just inside the bathroom. Having sisters, I'm unfazed.

Des is sitting at the desk, her hair in a ponytail and hanging over her shoulder. She's wearing yoga pants and a hoodie, and she manages to be a knockout even in that.

Her eyes find mine. "Hi."

I move to the desk and perch one hip on the edge. "Hey."

She eyes me warily, but doesn't move away from me, even though I'm suddenly in her personal space. "What's up? Why are you here, and why are you wearing a tux?"

"Do you have a nice dress here with you?"

She just blinks at me. "A dress?"

I nod. "Yeah. Like, a nice one. An evening gown type of thing."

I can see the wheels turning in her head. "I do, actually, yeah." Her gaze flits over me. "God you look hot in that tux." She closes her eyes slowly and presses her lips together, as if she hadn't meant to say that.

I laugh. "Thanks. So. How long will it take you to get ready?"

She frowns. "Ready? For what?"

"The ferries are shut down, so the person I was bringing to the dinner tonight can't get here. I want you to come with me."

"The dinner? The fancy fundraiser dinner?"

"Yep."

She shakes her head. "No. No fucking way."

I lean closer to her, brush my palm against her cheek and inhale her scent. "Please?"

She nuzzles her face into my palm, closes her eyes and lets out a shuddering breath. "Adam, that's crazy. I don't belong at a dinner like that."

She really doesn't. Neither do I, if you ask me. But no one's asking me.

I just grin at her. "But I want you there. I really don't want to go, but if I have to, it'd be better if you were there." I don't know what I'm saying, but it feels true. "Please? I need you to go with me."

She hesitates. And then she stabs her finger into my chest. "You can't leave me alone. Not for one second."

I'm leaning into her finger, closing the inches between us, inhaling her scent. I take a strand of her thick silky black hair between my fingers and spin it so the end twirls.

"I won't." She smells so good and looks so good and I want to kiss her, so I do. Slowly, carefully, briefly. "I'll stay by your side the whole time."

She seems shaken by the kiss, as if she wasn't expecting it, and doesn't know how to deal with it. "Promise?" she asks in a whisper.

"I swear."

"Give me forty-five minutes."

"No problem."

She stands up and I move out of the way. She slides past me, her eyes finding mine. A smile crosses her face, but then she ducks her head and goes into the bathroom. I catch a glimpse of her as she tugs the band out of her hair and shakes it out, and then shrugs out of her hoodie. I catch a glimpse of a bare shoulder and a hint of tattoo ink just before she closes the door.

Ten minutes later, she's out of the shower and emerging from the bathroom wreathed in steam, a towel turbaned around her hair and another wrapped around her torso. I get another glimpse of the ink, but it's hidden by the towel and I can just see the edges of it. It looks like words, text of some kind, but that's all I can make out. Des just out of the shower, dripping wet and flushed from the heat, is a version of her I'm starting to really like. She offers me another small smile, rifles through the clothes on one side of the closet, and withdraws a red dress. Then she goes to a dresser where she withdraws a bra and a pair of underwear, but I can't make out what either looks like. She vanishes into the bathroom once more, and this time she's in there for a full half an hour. I hear a hair dryer going for a while, and then further silence.

The intimacy of waiting for a woman to get ready is not lost on me. Even in the year and a half that I was with Emma, we didn't share these kinds of intimate moments. I never saw her just out of the shower. Never waited for her to get ready. We always met somewhere, or I picked her up at her house, waiting in the foyer for her to come down.

At long last, the bathroom door opens and I catch a glimpse of red, and then my heart stops beating, my lungs seize, and my dick goes rock hard.

"Jesus, Des." I stand up, move closer. "You're… there just aren't words for how incredible you look."

She smiles brightly, shrugging one shoulder. "It's just a dress I've had for awhile. Never even worn it."

It's not an elaborate or expensive dress, but it's molded to her goddess body like it was made especially for her. It's strapless, the cups pushing her incredible tits into mouth-watering prominence, and the hem hangs to brush the tops of her toes on one side while not quite hitting her knee on the other. It's unbearably sexy without being slutty.

Her hair…god, her hair. She's brushed it to shining perfection, leaving it loose to scintillate in waves around her shoulders and down her back, and she's put on just enough makeup to accentuate how lovely she is, highlighting the bright brown molten brilliance of her eyes and the tanned clarity of her skin.

I wrap my hand around the small of her back and pull her closer to me. "Des…I'm speechless."

She's wearing a pair of simple black heels, so the difference in our height is almost eliminated. "Really?" She sounds skeptical.

I shake my head. She really doesn't understand what she does to me. "You're so gorgeous it's sinful. I don't know how I'm going to make it through the evening without attacking you." I tug her body flush against mine. "You're so fucking sexy it actually hurts to breathe looking at you. Now come on, the carriage is waiting."

I don't think she's ever been complimented this way, judging by her unsure reaction. Eventually she shrugs and then looks me over again. "You look pretty damn sexy yourself," she says.

I just smile at her and offer her my hand. She takes it, and we go to the entrance, brace ourselves, and run for the carriage.

I bought this dress on a whim, a year ago. At full price it'd have been so far out of my reach I wouldn't have even bothered trying it on, but it was on clearance, so I gave it a try. I'm not an insecure girl most days, and I'm also not vain. But when I put on that dress, I knew it looked good on me. *Damn* good. So I bought it, even though I never went anywhere that such a dress would be appropriate. And more baffling still, I stuffed it and a pair of heels into my bags when I packed for the summer on Mackinac. Why, I wasn't sure, even then. I collected trash and drank with the other co-ops and locals. Why the hell would I have brought an evening gown and heels? But, for reasons unknown, I did, and now I'm glad I did.

I'm also glad my hair is long enough to cover the upper edge of the tattoos on my back that peek up over the dress, because I'm pretty sure an event like this isn't the kind of place to go around showing ink. I wonder if Adam saw the ink? I wonder what he would think if he saw it all, if he likes tattoos or if he's against them.

And then I wonder why I care.

The ride from my dorm to the hotel is quick, which doesn't leave me a lot of time to mentally prepare. We're pulling up under the covered portico, and there are two lines of uniformed hotel employees forming an umbrella tunnel from the carriage up to the famous covered porch.

My heart is suddenly hammering. Above, where I know the porch to be, cameras flash like nonstop lightning. The carriage door opens, and the wind buffets against me, carrying the sound of a thousand voices all raised at once. A white-gloved hand appears in front of my face, and I take it, stepping out onto the red carpet leading up the stairs to the porch and then into the hotel parlor. The line of umbrellas protects me from the rain, and I take a step away from the carriage to make room for Adam. He descends, tugs his tux jacket straight, and then his eyes fix on me.

He offers me a smile, and I see nerves in his eyes. If *he's* nervous, I should be terrified.

And I am.

"Ready?" he asks, extending his elbow to me.

I wrap my fingers around his arm. "No?"

He laughs. "Yeah, me neither. I hate these things." He glances past me, up the stairs to where the flashes pop endlessly, and then back down to me. "Listen. This might be…crazy. They're not expecting you, so they'll have a million questions. Don't answer, okay? Just smile, give them a few poses, and don't let them see your fear. They're like sharks, you know, they can smell it."

"They?"

He frowns. "The paparazzi? Photographers, journalists."

My knees quiver. "Paparazzi?" I'd either forgotten or hadn't realized there would be media at this thing. What the hell did I get myself into?

He rolls his shoulders, lets out a quick breath, and smiles at me. "You know what? Don't worry about it. All you need to do is be you. You'll be the most beautiful woman in the room, guaranteed. Just be confident, okay?"

Confident. I can do that. He asked me to go with him. He wouldn't have done that if he didn't want me here. He thinks I'm the most beautiful woman in the room.

I stiffen my spine, straighten my shoulders, lift my chin, and smile back at him. "Let's go."

His grin widens, and his eyes roam my face, and then down my body. He leans in, touches his lips to my ear. "That's my girl."

His girl? I should be so lucky.

He moves forward and I go with him, watching the steps. I'm not used to high heels, so the steps present a challenge, requiring focus. I hear cameras clicking and flashes popping, voices clamoring louder and louder, and then the stairs level off and I'm surrounded by a wall of humanity behind red velvet ropes, and all of them are shouting at me, at Adam.

"Adam! Adam! Where's Emma Hayes?"

"Who's your date, Adam?"

"Who is she?"

"What's your name? Tell us your name!"

"How tall are you?"

"Over here, Adam!"

"Give us a smile, beautiful!"

My heart isn't beating. It's not even in my chest anymore, it's somehow simultaneously in my stomach and my throat. I force my lips to form a smile. Adam's hand descends to my opposite hip, resting on my waist, his thick arm a supportive bar at my back. He takes three steps through the barricaded crowd, then stops, guides me into a pivot so we're facing one bank of the journalists.

His arm remains around me, and he is actually holding me upright for a few moments. There are so many of them. The flashes blind me, illuminate me.

And suddenly, it hits me: *What the FUCK am I doing here?* I did my own makeup, my own hair. This dress came from the fucking bargain rack at Kohl's.

I feel a panic attack coming on; I force the smile to remain on my face, force myself to breathe slowly.

Adam pulls me closer, so I'm molded to his side, so I don't fall over. He leans down, whispers in my ear. "You're doing great. Smile. Stop thinking. It's fine."

The questions are a nonstop barrage, coming as hard and fast as the flashes, but I've stopped hearing them. I'm not sure I could answer anyway. I'm not sure I have a voice right now. I'm not sure of anything, except that I've gotten myself into something huge, and I'm in no way prepared.

Adam turns with me, presents us to the opposite rank of photographers. He seems totally oblivious, at ease, as if this is totally normal, an every day occurrence. He's a natural. Loose, smiling, shifting his gaze from one camera to another. I try to mimic him, try to focus on making my smile seem more natural and less deer-in-the-headlights. I stand taller, turn into Adam slightly, shake my hair and turn my head. The cameras go nuts when I do that, and the shouted questions become a repeated refrain:

"Who is she?"

"What's her name?"

"How long have you been dating?"

"Where is Emma Hayes?"

Emma Hayes? Adam's ex-girlfriend. Oscar-nominated for *Margo and Me.* Golden Globe winner. Three-time Emmy nominee for *Garden of Evil.*

Jesus. I'm so out of my league, out of my element. I'm a fish out of water; I'm drowning, unable to breathe.

I toss my hair again and focus on a single camera, stare into the black lens; focus on the lens rather than the face above it. Another lens, to the left. Another, and another.

And then we're moving and I have to focus on each step, because I can't feel my feet. The sheer terror and overwhelmed panic has made me numb, I think.

Now we're stopped again, this time in front of one of those checkered backdrops plastered with logos of companies I've never heard of. Adam steps away from me, gesturing to me as if silently saying to the cameras, *here she is.* The questions still come in shouted rolling waves, and the flashes have me seeing stars, but I dig deep, dig down into my reservoir of strength, that place I go when I've got nothing left but can't give up. It's where I went when LeShawn would get drunk and angry and I'd be the only target, when Frank would come into my room late at night —

I viciously shove those thoughts down. I smile. I pose. I don't know what I'm doing, why I'm here, why Adam dragged me into this, but I'm here and there's no escape, so I have to keep going. I turn, smile, toss my hair and look in another direction, and then Adam has my hand in his and he's pulling me through the doors and into the parlor of the Grand Hotel. The flashes and the questions are left behind, but now I'm faced with an all-new crisis.

Rose Garret is standing directly in front of me. Gareth Thomas, one of the most well-known directors and producers in the world, with over a dozen films to his name, all of them blockbusters, is standing next to her. Lawrence Bradford is there, an older supporting-role actor, one of those guys you've seen in dozens of roles but never in the lead. Amy Jones, as stunningly resplendent now as when she was a fresh-faced actress in the late sixties and early seventies. I see other faces I recognize, even more I don't.

And they're all staring at me.

Conversation stops. Drinks pause in mid-air.

Rose Garret is the first to step forward. She smiles at me, but it doesn't quite reach her curious hazel eyes. "Hi. I'm Rose."

I take her hand and shake it briefly. "It's an honor to meet you, Rose. I'm Des."

"Des." She says this as if judging me by my name alone. She eyes me, examines me, and then shifts her eyes to Adam. "I thought you were bringing Em."

"I was. But she couldn't make it. They shut down the ferries."

Rose grins. "I bet you're devastated."

Adam nods. "Completely. I cried."

I'm missing something, obviously. I know Adam and Emma broke up a while ago, which I suppose could be awkward if they were supposed to attend a gala as a couple.

"So, Des. You're a model, I take it?" Rose asks.

A server drifts up to us, a silver tray balanced on his palm, and offers us each a glass of champagne. Adam takes two, hands one to me, and I sip it delicately, slowly. The last thing I can afford in this situation is to let alcohol cloud my judgment or loosen my tongue.

"I—" I have no clue how to answer that. She thinks I'm a model?

"Des is a college student. An intern." Adam answers for me.

Which is true enough, but probably not in the way Rose is assuming. Maybe that's Adam's intent, though. I don't know.

Gareth Thomas moves into the circle beside Rose, and Adam introduces us. "Des, hmm? A unique name for a uniquely beautiful young woman." He shakes my hand vigorously, and his eyes cut speculatively to Adam. "You've been holding out on me, Adam."

"Man's gotta have a few secrets, Gareth," Adam says, nudging the director with his elbow. It's a joke, but it's not. I'm a secret? Not so much anymore, obviously.

Lawrence and Amy join the circle next, and now I'm suddenly surrounded by Hollywood royalty, and it's hard to breathe. I try not to stare at each of the people surrounding me, people I've seen in movies and on the covers of *People* and *OK!* and *Time* and *US Weekly*, and on *Entertainment Tonight* or *TMZ*.

Again, the thought hits me like a ten-pound sledge: *What am I* DOING *here?*

Adam deflects all the questions directed at me, introducing me without explaining who I am in relation to him, or what I do. I'm an impostor, surely? I don't belong here: I'm a trash collector.

I smile and nod and take tiny sips of champagne, and do my best to keep my emotions buried and off my features. Rose drifts away from the circle, but I see her eyes go to me more than once as she joins a different conversation. Eventually Adam pulls me away from Lawrence, Amy, and Gareth, and moves me through the crowd, waving to one person or another, pausing to chat with this person or that, and he always introduces me politely but neutrally, and leaves no room for probing questions. But I can sense, in every new person we meet, every conversation Adam steers us away from, that everyone is curious. Everyone wants to know who I am, where I came from, and why I'm here so unexpectedly at Adam's side.

I ask myself the same questions, and find about as many answers as the journalists are getting…i.e., none.

I keep smiling until my face hurts, and I shake dozens of hands. Either Adam's arm is around my waist or he's holding my hand. I meet so many people I'm dizzy and have no hope of remembering anyone's name except those whom I already recognized. I manage to make a single glass of champagne last over an hour, and even then I feel disconnected in my head, but that may be as much from the surreal experience as the alcohol.

At last, people begin to filter into the dining room, each couple greeted by the maître d' and passed off to a server who leads them to a table. The Grand Hotel dining room is almost as famous as the porch, so I've seen pictures of it, but I've never been here for a meal. I know, though, that it's been transformed for this event. Usually, there are small, rectangular two-top tables in three rows on either side of the main aisle, with big round tables for larger parties interspersed throughout the room. Now, however, the usual setup has been replaced by twenty or so of the large round tables, all centered around a raised dais placed against the wall of windows overlooking the famous porch. There's a podium and a microphone, and a long rectangular table on either side of the podium, each one set with six places.

Adam and I are directed to the dais, sitting in the middle two places at the table to the left of the dais. Rose sits beside me, and a ridiculously hot guy sits in turn beside her, closest to the stage. I recognize the guy with Rose, but it takes me a few minutes of thinking to place him. He's tall and lean with messy brown hair and sharp features. Dylan Vale, that's his name. He's a newer actor, from an edgy new cable show about a feud between two rival clans of shape-shifters. I haven't seen the show, but Ruthie likes it, and she's always raving about how hot Dylan Vale is. Now that I see him in real life, I can see that Ruthie has, if anything, understated how absurdly beautiful Dylan is.

He's not Adam, though, and he's clearly enamored with Rose, leaning in and nuzzling her neck, saying something that has her laughing and blushing.

On the other side of Adam are Gareth and a striking, middle-aged woman who must be his wife, judging by the easy, comfortable way they interact with each other. The table on the other side has Lawrence and his wife, Amy and her husband, and a man with salt-and-pepper hair and vivid blue eyes, who I assume is a producer or something, and his date.

The rest of the tables are seated quickly, and servers appear bearing bowls of soup and trays of water and silver pitchers and bottles of wine. A dozen young men and women in white coats with a towel over one arm move from table to table, listening and taking orders, and then return with a bottle of wine, which he or she then opens with elaborate formality, pouring a tiny amount into a glass and waiting for approval.

As we wait, Adam leans into me, and I hear his voice buzz in my ear. "You're amazing. You're a natural at this, Des, for real. Everyone is absolutely nuts over you."

I turn to look at him. "What the hell were you thinking, bringing me here? I'm so out of place it'd be funny if I weren't terrified." I say this in a tiny, tight whisper, pitched so low he has to put his ear to my mouth to hear me.

He laughs as if I've said something funny. "I know you feel out of place, Des. I get it. I feel the same way, every time. Just keep faking it. No one will ever be the wiser."

"That I'm a fucking janitor, you mean?"

He frowns at me. "Does that really matter?"

I give him an incredulous expression. "Um... yeah? If these people find out you brought a garbage collector as your date to a Hollywood A-list fundraiser gala...I don't even know what would happen, but nothing good. For me, or you."

He shakes his head. "Des, you're overthinking this. It's going to be fine. Just be you. You're beautiful.

None of the guys can take their eyes off of you." His hand, resting on the table, lifts and a finger inscribes a small arc to indicate the dining room. "Look around you."

I sip at the glass of wine that appeared in front of me at some point, and try to unobtrusively scrutinize the room. When I do, my heart rate skyrockets. Adam is right. Everyone is looking at me. *Everyone.* Not just the men, but women, too. The men are more obvious about it, glancing at me, and then away, around the room, and then back to me. But the women are watching me too, and that's almost more frightening. They're more judgmental. I can feel their scrutiny. I can feel them examining my hair, my makeup, my dress, the cheap silver bangle around my wrist, and the cheap cubic zirconium earrings in my ears. At least I'm sitting down, so my height and shape are mostly hidden by the table.

"Thanks," I tell Adam, darting a quick glance at him. "I'm even more self-conscious now that I'm aware that everyone in the room is wondering who I am and why the hell I'm here."

"They're wondering how I managed to get someone as sexy as you to come with me on such short notice."

"Bullshit," I say, but it lacks venom.

The fact that Adam seems to honestly think I'm sexy does something to me, makes my brain and my stomach and my heart all quiver with a weird, restless energy.

The eyes in the room eventually stop staring at me as the dinner progresses, and I find a measure of comfort. I'm still hyper-aware that I'm out of place, that I'm a nobody in a room full of famous people, but Adam engages me in conversation.

By the time the main course is done, I'm stuffed full and my bladder is screaming. "Adam? Where's the restroom?"

Rose overhears my question and stands up. "I have to go, too. I'll show you."

I'm hesitant, but I can't very well get out of it now. I glance at Adam, who is half-standing, watching me, concerned. I can't look scared just to go to the bathroom, and everyone is watching, so I let out a small breath and shake my head at him subtly, then I follow Rose out of the dining room and down a short, wide set of stairs to a narrow hallway. There's a gift shop opposite, closed and dark now, and then an opening leading to the front desk. A velvet rope blocks the stairway, guarded additionally by a pair of hotel doormen and another pair of huge, black-suited bodyguard types. They nod respectfully at Rose, and the rope is pulled aside to let us through. The bodyguard steps in front of us, opens the door to the women's bathroom, and calls out to see if it's occupied. A woman's voice calls back, and she comes out a moment later, staring at the hulking bodyguard and then at Rose, and then at me. Her eyes go wide, and she opens her mouth, but a hotel employee is adroitly escorting her away, and Rose pulls me into the bathroom after her. The door closes slowly, and I see the bodyguard take up position in front of the doorway, massive arms crossed over a broad chest.

Rose and I take care of business, and then wash our hands, and then Rose plucks at a strand of platinum blond hair, tucking it back into position, adjusts her breasts in the bodice of her Valentino gown, wiggles a foot in her Jimmy Choo heels. And then she fixes her hazel eyes on me.

"So. Des." She turns to face me and props one slim, perfect hip against the counter. "What do you think about your first event?"

I swallow hard and try to smile. "Is it that obvious?"

Rose laughs, but it doesn't feel mocking. "Yeah, it kind of is. You haven't said two words to anyone but Adam, for one thing."

I shrug. "I don't know anyone but Adam."

"Clearly." She waves a hand. "The men probably aren't as aware as I am, though. They're all too hypnotized by that cleavage of yours."

I laugh with her, but I'm not entirely sure she's kidding. "Is it too much?"

Rose makes an incredulous face. "Des, honey, if I had your tits, I'd have them on display too. But no, it's not too much." She trails a finger through my hair. "Who did your hair and makeup? It's simple and understated. It really works for you."

My cheeks heat and I want to look away from her in embarrassment. "I did," I say.

She nods. "Well, you did an amazing job. I'm not sure I'd have the balls to do my own hair and makeup for an event like this."

"It was kind of last minute," I say, which is true enough, but doesn't really address the fact that there was no one to do it for me, as she's obviously used to.

"Adam *did* explain what he was bringing you to, didn't he?"

"Sort of?"

Rose's eyes go wide and concerned. "Look, sweetie, you're really beautiful, and I can see why Adam's attracted to you. But, just between you and me, it's pretty obvious you're not...in the industry, so to speak. And now you're telling me he brought you to this event without preparing you for what you'd face?"

"Like I said, it was last minute." I take a deep breath. "I should probably get back."

Rose sighs. "I can't believe him. You can't just spring a thing like this on a girl. I hope you're ready, babe."

"Ready?" I swallow hard. "For what?"

"The attention. You've just been put under an international spotlight, Des. There may not be television media here, which is fortunate for you, but it's still one of the most widely covered events of the year. The photographs from this are going to be in every magazine in the developed world. *Especially* since Adam came with you instead of Em." She shakes her head. "I honestly don't know what he was thinking. Nothing against you, it's just—"

My heart sinks, and my stomach flips. "What?"

"Well, it's just that the rumor mill surrounding Adam is kind of rabid." She smooths her dress over her hips and glances at me. "Any time he goes anywhere, all the rags make up these speculative stories about what he's doing and where he's going and who he's with. When he and Em broke up, it was the talk of the whole community. It was ugly. Really, really ugly. And every appearance since then has been the subject of a million rumors. Bringing you, to *this?* Last minute, no explanation? It's going to start the mill all over again, and anyone connected to the media is going to be looking for you."

"Looking for me?"

Rose nodded. "And they'll find you, too. They're relentless."

I feel faint. "Awesome." I steady myself with both hands on the counter. My breath is coming in short gasps. The panic attack I've been fending off all night is pounding in my throat and at my temples and in my lungs. "Good thing I'm not a super private person or anything. Jesus."

A small, cool hand touches my back. "Breathe, sweetie. It'll be fine. They'll print whatever they want to print, and eventually they'll lose interest. Just don't do any interviews, 'kay?"

"Why would I do an interview? About what?"

Rose laughs, and this one does sound condescending, but not cruelly so. "Oh, honey. You really have no idea, do you? They'll want to know every detail about you and Adam. And they'll offer you money, and book deals, and all sorts of things like that. If you want to remain a private person, don't answer. Just tell everyone 'no comment' and live your life. Eventually someone will come along who actually wants their attention."

A deep voice beyond the door rumbles loudly. "Sorry, Mr. Trenton. Can't let you in."

I hear Adam's voice. "You gonna try and stop me, Zach?" Silence, and then the door opens, revealing Adam, with the bodyguard behind him. "Didn't think so." Adam crosses to me, I feel him beside me, feel his hand on my lower back.

"Hi, Adam." Rose's voice is neutral, careful. "The little boys room is next door, I think."

"What did you say to her, Rose?"

"Just the truth." She passes me and stops in front of Adam. "I'm not sure you did yourself or her any favors, bringing her here, Adam."

"Goddamn it, Rose—"

"She's really stunning, though. Even in an off-the-rack dress."

"Don't be a bitch, Rose," Adam growls, his voice low and threatening.

"I'm not!"

I stand up, push between them, hating how they're talking about me as if I'm not here. "Adam, stop. It's fine. She wasn't being a bitch." I let out a wavery breath. "Thanks for the advice, Rose. Adam, let's just go, okay?"

I sweep past Adam and Rose and out the door, past Zach the burly bodyguard...right into a gaggle of photographers waiting for me on the other side of the rope.

They're less than four feet away from me now, ten of them, and their cameras come up and start clicking, flashing.

"What's your name, honey? Can you tell us your name?" The questions come in a sudden burst, variations on a theme. They all want to know my name, and I'm frozen, staring at them, eyes wide, panicking.

And then Adam is behind me, a hand on my waist, propelling me up the stairs, away from the cameras and the questions without so much as a word to any of them. The event is still going on, but now Gareth is at the podium talking about "a noble cause" or something. Adam guides me away from the dining room and into what seems like a small library, a few tables and plush couches and elegant chairs, bookshelves lining all four walls, and a small bar behind which is a pretty, middle-aged black woman with thin dreadlocks, dressed in hotel livery.

"Two Labatts," Adam growls, tossing a twenty-dollar bill on the bar.

He drags me into a corner of the room, guides me to a seat on a couch, then sits beside me and tucks me against his side. He's huge and solid and real, and his arm is curled around me, and now everything is crashing down around me, in me, on me. Everything Rose told me, how out of place I felt, how out of place I am.

A cold bottle is pressed into my hand, and I take a long gulp, breathe, and then take another. Finally, I look at Adam. "Why am I here, Adam? What were you thinking? I don't belong here. Everyone can tell what a fish out of water I am."

"Fucking Rose. She doesn't mean to be mean, she just doesn't have a filter. She says whatever she's thinking, regardless of whether it's a good idea or not."

"She was right though. I look as out of place as I feel: cheap. Cheap dress, cheap shoes, cheap makeup.

I'm…" I swallow hard and start over. "And she said reporters would come looking for me. What am I supposed to do, Adam? God. And the whole thing with you and Emma Hayes?"

"We're not talking about her." He says this with a cold note of finality, and then sighs wearily. "The media's going to speculate regardless. They always have and always will. I don't care what they say. Just don't answer them. Don't look at them. Pretend they don't exist."

"Easy for you to say. You're used to it."

"You never get used to it," he says. "Maybe I didn't think through what this might mean for you, I guess. I'm sorry."

"Can I go home, now?" I say, only half-joking.

"I'll take you back if you want, but…I'm hoping maybe you'll stay for at least one dance."

"Dance?" I glance at him over the mouth of my beer, which is somehow almost gone already.

"Yeah. After dessert, which I think they're serving after Gareth quits running his mouth."

"Maybe one dance. Can't get all dressed up and not dance, right?"

He grins at me, and drains his bottle in two long pulls. "Right."

I finish mine as well, and he leads me back into the dining room. I feel the eyes on me, and I try to keep my back straight and my head high. There's a plate of delicate-looking chocolate mousse waiting for me, and thank god for that. I force myself to take small, demure, lady-like nibbles of it, even though I want to gulp it down greedily.

Couples and groups are filtering out of the dining room, and Adam leads me with them, his huge warm hand engulfing mine. We make our way to a ballroom, a small, intimate room with a parquet dance floor and a stage surrounded by round tables.

There's a string quartet on the stage, all middle-aged men in tuxedos. They're already playing, and a few couples are dancing. Adam pulls me onto the dance floor, wraps one large hand across the small of my back and tangles the fingers of his other hand through mine, and we're slow dancing. His body is huge and his pale green eyes are hot and intense and focused entirely on me. Everything falls away, then, except Adam and the music.

We spin slowly, our bodies pressed close together. I can feel his chest swelling with each breath, the faint tum-tum—tum-tum of his heart beating, and his shoulder is a broad slab under my left hand. I don't really know how to dance, but this is slow dancing, just easy circles, step, step, step. Around us, a few people are doing more elaborate waltz steps, dips and twirls and things, but Adam seems content to just step-pivot-step with me. Which is fine. It gives me a chance to catch my breath, to push away the swirling doubts and fears.

And then I feel Adam stiffen.

"Can I cut in?" The voice is smooth, boyish.

A pair of amused, roguish blue eyes meet mine. Dylan Vale wants to dance with me? Gah. Ruthie is going to lose her shit when I tell her this.

"Piss off, Dylan," Adam growls.

Dylan just laughs. "Aw, c'mon Trenton. You can't keep a gorgeous girl like this to yourself all night, you know."

Adams looks down at me. "Go dance with Rose."

"I have been." He winks, making it a lewd insinuation. "It's just one dance, dude. I'll give her right back."

Once again, I'm trapped by circumstance, forced to brave when I don't feel very courageous. "It's okay, Adam. It would be my pleasure to dance with Dylan."

Adam's eyes narrow. "Just one."

Dylan slaps Adam on the back companionably. "Loosen up, man."

And then Dylan's hand is in mine, another on my waist. He's maybe an inch taller than me, although with my heels on I have a slight edge on him. His blue eyes are speculative, intelligent. He moves gracefully, leading me in faster circles than Adam did. There are a few inches between us, and nothing about his posture or demeanor makes me think this is anything other than a friendly gesture.

"So. Your name is Des, right?"

I nod. "Yep." I'm not sure where to go with that, conversationally. "And you're Dylan."

He grins. "That's me. Seen the show?"

I shake my head. "No. It's not really my thing. My roommate raves about it though." I let a small smile touch my lips. "Well, more about you than the show, if I'm being honest."

"Not really your thing, huh?" He doesn't seem insulted, and doesn't acknowledge my compliment.

I shrug. "Vampires or whatever, zombies, that kind of thing, no."

He claps a hand to his chest dramatically. "I'm wounded. It's not *vampires* or whatever, Des. It's *shapeshifters*. Big difference."

I laugh. "Okay, fine. Shapeshifters, then. Still not my thing. Mythical creatures do not interest me. No offense."

"Well, I can't take too much offense, I suppose. I mean, I'm just a co-creator and lead writer. No big deal."

"I didn't know that. I thought you just acted in it."

He shakes his head. "Nope. I was a writer before I was an actor."

I can't help but feel amused. He's so unlike Adam it's shocking. Adam seems reticent to talk about work, eager to downplay his success and fame. Dylan, on the other hand, spends the entire dance talking about the show, about how he and Ed Monighan wrote it together and pitched it, and how the studio demanded to see him audition for the lead, over his protests that he wasn't an actor, of course. It's not exactly arrogance exuding from Dylan, just…eagerness. Excitement. And it's a little nerdy. Cute, endearing, and slightly annoying.

He's beautiful, yes, and his eyes are vibrantly blue and he's lean and toned and breezily confident in the way of a guy who's always been popular and who's always had everything come easily to him.

I find myself much preferring Adam's enormous, masculine, animalistic intensity, his brawny bulk, and his quiet self-assurance.

The song ends, and Adam swiftly reclaims his place, and this time his body is hard against mine, almost inappropriately close, and his hand is dangerously low on my back, resting barely an inch above the swell of my buttocks.

"Fuckin' pretty boy," Adam growls. "He's an ass."

I laugh. "Not really. He's nice. Cute, and eager."

"Cute and eager, huh?" A smile quirks the corner of his mouth.

"Did you know he's the co-creator and lead writer for *Shifters?*" I try to mimic Dylan's excited tone.

Adam laughs out loud. "Yeah. That's him." His eyes are suddenly leaf-green spears of heat. "You ready to get out of here?"

I nod. "Absolutely."

Something thrills through me at the way Adam ushers me out of the small ballroom, waving good-bye to Rose and Gareth and a few others. He's eager to be gone, his hand on my back keeps me moving, his big body shielding me from the paparazzi as we board an elevator.

CHAPTER SIX

I just can't handle it anymore. I can't handle the scrutiny, the whispers. Everyone is talking about her. I shouldn't have brought her here. She's too beautiful, too dominating and mysterious a presence, too captivating. The fact that she's totally oblivious to her hypnotic charm only serves to make her that much more appealing. Gareth was mesmerized. Rose was puzzled and a little jealous, I think. And the reporters? Ravenous. They couldn't get enough of her.

So I take her up to the Cupola Bar, find a table in the darkest, most intimate corner of the upper section. There's a window on our left, looking out over the island. When it's clear, you can see the bridge in all its splendor from the Cupola Bar, but it's still bucketing rain, so all we can see is darkness and the occasional flash of lightning.

Once we have drinks and solitude, I touch her chin with my thumb, turn her face to mine. "You okay, Des?"

She doesn't answer right away. When she does, her voice is hesitant. "I guess. It was just…a lot. Sudden, and surprising. I didn't know what I was getting into. I'm not a public kind of girl, Adam. I'm just not. I wasn't ready for that."

I sigh. "I'm sorry. I brought you on impulse, and didn't really think about how it might affect you."

"It's okay. I survived." She pulls her hair over one shoulder, dragging her fingers through it.

"You more than survived, Des. You killed it."

"Killed it?" She sounds skeptical.

"Everyone was talking about you."

"It's not every day you see a six-foot-tall giant of a girl like me. Especially wearing these heels." She shrugs a shoulder.

I lift her chin again. "No, Des, that's not it. You're tall, yes, but you're beautiful. You dominated the room."

She tries to shake her head and look away. "Whatever, Adam."

"Don't '*whatever*' me," I tell her, leaning down.

Her lips, red and plump, beckon me. She stops breathing, and so do I. I go slow. I give her time to stop me, time to pull away, time to realize what I'm about to do. An exhale of sweet breath past those red lips, and then my mouth is on hers, and I'm tasting her lips, touching my palm to her neck, beneath the coal-black sheaf of her hair, my thumb just beneath her earlobe.

"Adam…" she breathes, withdraws her lips from mine, but doesn't pull away entirely.

I sigh. "Too much?"

She shakes her head, brushing the tip of her nose against mine. "No. Yes. I mean…" She lets out a breath that's part sigh and part self-deprecating laugh. "*You're* too much, Adam. This. Everything. It's just too much."

I pull back, take a sip of my drink, and tangle one of my hands in hers. "Explain."

She takes a drink, and then a moment of silence to think. Eventually she lifts a shoulder in a shrug. "I just don't get you. Or what you want from me. Why I'm here. Why you're wasting your time with me. I mean, you're a famous movie star. I'm a trash collector. We have literally zero things in common."

"I'm just a guy, Des. Sure, my job is making movies, and some of them have done all right. Which is awesome. I have fun. I enjoy what I do, and plan to do it for a long time. But…it's not who I am. I'm not a movie star. I'm just Adam." I touch a fingertip to her chin, and she looks at me. "You're wrong about you and I not having anything in common, though."

She frowns. "Oh yeah? So name one thing."

"I'm attracted to you, and you're attracted to me."

She doesn't disagree. She just looks at me for a long moment. "Is that enough?"

"Enough for what?"

"For...whatever it is you want from me."

I trace a finger behind her ear, down her neck, across the ridge of her shoulder. "And what is it you think I want from you?"

She shivers under my touch. "I don't know. That's what I'm asking."

"I told you yesterday what I want. I thought I made myself pretty damn clear." I lean in and touch my lips to the crook of her neck, her shoulder, her throat, and then to the shell of her ear, and I whisper softly. "I want *you,* Des. *All* of you. I want you to let me show you how good I can make you feel. I want your skin. I want your mouth. I want your body. I want *you*."

She closes her eyes and I watch her hands curl into fists in the material of her dress at her thighs. "Yeah, but for how long?"

"Honest answer? I don't know."

"An honest answer for an honest answer then," she says, turning her head so my lips brush across her cheekbone. "I don't know if I can give you what you want."

"Why not?"

She shakes her head, as if she doesn't know how to answer that, or won't. "Because...I just can't. I just can't. I don't know how."

"I can show you."

"How?"

"Like this." I put my palm to her cheek, tilting her face to mine.

And once again, I lean in as slowly as I can. My eyes are open, hers are, too. Her eyes are wide and brown and scared, and I wish I knew what this girl has been through to put such fear in her eyes, what she's endured that has such high, thick walls between herself and the rest of the world. I want to know what's behind those walls, but I'm not sure how to get past them without spooking her.

So I kiss her. Gently, slowly. Just lips, at first.

And this time, she melts. Not all at once, like butter in a microwave, but like a chunk of ice in a cool, shadowy pond: slowly, gradually. She leans into me, a shoulder touching mine, her breasts squishing against my chest, and then her hand is on my shoulder and stealing up to my chin, then to my neck and she cups my skin beneath the hairline and she's not breathing and neither am I. I circle my arm behind her back and hold her close, and she twists in the booth so she can press closer, and our mouths move, seek, claim. Her tongue slips out first this time, touches my lip, my teeth, and then I'm tasting her tongue and she's sighing into my mouth.

I remove my lips from hers and maybe it's my imagination, but it sounded like she made a little moan at the loss of the kiss.

"Des…" I breathe her name, a single syllable whispering between our mouths. "Come to my room with me."

I stand up, toss back the last of my drink, and then hold my hand out to her. She stares up at me, and I can see thoughts whirling in her eyes, see desire warring with doubt. Or fear. Or whatever it is that is holding her back. After a long moment, she stands up, taking my hand. We start forward, and then she stops, turns back, and downs her drink. She sets the empty beer bottle down a little hard, with a sigh as she swallows the beer.

"Kiss me again," she says, leaning into me.

I don't need to be asked twice. I pull her to my chest, press my palm to her lower back and cradle her cheek with my other hand. She delves into my mouth with that sweet, strong tongue of hers, and her hands curl at my chest, fingertips digging into the material of my jacket.

I'm hungry for her, my hands desperate to slip lower, to drag that sexy fucking dress off and reveal her curves and her skin, needing her mouth on my skin, her flesh under my lips, her essence on my tongue. I can't stay here with her either. I need her alone. I'm hard, aching, throbbing.

I break the kiss with a low, almost inaudible growl and lead her by the hand down the steps to the green-on-green hallway to my room. I'm so consumed by the need to resume the kiss that I fumble with the key. I finally get the door open, and I don't even notice the gaudy purple explosion in the sitting room, or the bizarrely archaic headboard and canopy of the bed.

All I see is Des, her bright expressive eyes, and her hands, and the fall of black hair around her shoulders. She stops, her back to the door, hands flat against the surface at her hips, arms slightly bent, just her ass, hands, and shoulder blades touching the door. It's a stance of readiness, preparation for flight, for battle. Her eyes shine, fixed on me. Her lips are slightly parted, her chin tilted slightly upward.

I stand three feet away, and she's just staring at me, me at her. And then I move. I take a step toward her, and I tug at my bow tie, tossing it aside. I shrug out of my jacket. Unbutton the cuffs of my shirt. I finish unbuttoning my shirt and shrug out of it, my torso clad in a skin-tight white T-shirt. The slim shiny black dress belt is next, tossed aside. Shoes, kicked off. Socks, toed off.

Her nostrils flare, her eyes go wider, if that's even possible, and her chest heaves as she sucks in a deep breath.

"Des," I say. "It's okay."

She doesn't answer, doesn't do anything, and just holds her about-to-bolt pose, her eyes following my every motion. She hasn't moved, and is barely breathing.

I close the space between us, stopping just shy of pressing our bodies together. I just look at her, for a moment, assessing the turmoil in her eyes. She wants me, her eyes roaming my arms and chest and face tell me that. The swell of her chest with each breath tells me that; it also tells me she's nervous, or scared, or something.

Why, I don't know, and I'm not going to ask. I just have to be attentive to her mood, to how she responds to me.

I descend to my knees slowly, and her eyes follow me, but her head doesn't tip down. Her mouth falls open a bit wider, and then a breath leaves her in a whoosh as I palm her knee just beneath where the hem of her dress ends on one side. I curl my fingers around the back of her knee; slide my hand down the plump musculature of her calf. Her breath hitches. I wrap my hand around her ankle, lift her foot, and slide the shoe off. She goes down flat-footed, and I slip my fingers between her legs, under the slinky fabric of her dress, to the back of her other leg. I caress her kneecap, around to the back, feather my fingers across the crease, down over the curve of her calf, and lift her foot, remove her other shoe.

I stand up, dragging both hands up the backs of her legs, lifting the hem of her dress as I rise. When I'm at my full height, her dress is bunched at mid-thigh and she's breathing deep and fast. I lean in, press my nose to the side of her throat and inhale, slipping my palms around her thighs.

"Adam..." she breathes.

I move one hand into her hair, bury my fingers in the thick shimmery cool weight, and bring my mouth to hers, my other hand moving of its own volition up and up and up to the firm globe of her butt. She breathes into my mouth, and then her teeth click against mine as she closes in suddenly and ravenously for the kiss. Her hands lift, press flat against my chest, and her tongue seeks mine, and I pull her flush against me. She feels my erection, I know she does; there's no way she can miss it. It's a hot iron rod between us, straining against my boxer-briefs and the fly of my tuxedo slacks.

She breaks free from the kiss, and her head thunks against the wood of the door.

"Des? Do you want to go?" I let her dress go, move my hand from the bare smooth hot flesh of her ass out to rest on her hip over the fabric. "I don't want you to be scared. Or do anything you don't want to do."

"I don't want to leave," she whispers.

"But you seem like you're about to freak out."

"I'm nervous. I've never done anything like this before."

"Like what?" I tug her hair gently so she has to look at me.

"This. You and me. I barely know you. I just met you. This is *crazy*." Her hands rest on my chest, her eyes seek mine. "This isn't what I do."

"Me neither," I say.

Her head tilts to one side. "It's not?"

I laugh softly. "No. Not even close." I bring my hand to her face, and she presses her cheek into my palm. "Just because I'm an actor doesn't mean I'm a player or a man-whore."

"You're just being…aggressive about this."

I kiss her cheek, the corner of her mouth. "When I see something I want, I make it mine."

"And you want me?"

"Hell yeah I do."

She bites her lower lip between her teeth and then releases it. "So…you're making me yours?"

"Yes." I tighten my grip on her hip. "Do you want that, Des?"

She blinks at me, and I can tell she's deciding. Determination solidifies in her eyes, and she pushes at my chest. I take a step back, give her some space.

"Yes. I do." She lets out a long, slow breath. "Just...I need one thing from you first."

"What's that?" I ask.

"Don't make promises you can't or won't keep."

I smile at her. "That's a basic life principle, for me," I say. "I never make promises or commitments unless I'm one hundred percent sure I can hold my end up. And this, with you and me? All I know is I like it. I like you. I'm attracted to you in an insanely intense kind of way, and all I know is I want to explore it. I don't know where it's gonna go. I just want to try and find out. That's all."

She smiles, but it's a little shaky still. "I can deal with that."

And then, instead of reaching for me, or kissing me, or touching me, she turns her back to me, pulls her hair over one shoulder, baring her shoulders and upper back, and the zipper of her dress. She twists her head to look at me over her shoulder, and her gaze on mine is expectant. Offering.

Instead of ripping at the zipper like I want to, I sidle across the inches separating us, capture her biceps in my hands, and kiss the ridge of her shoulder. The round spot where her arm becomes her shoulder. Across the base of her neck. I tease the edge of her dress at her back; slide my finger between fabric and skin, following the path of my finger with kisses across her warm smooth flesh. She inhales sharply, and I pinch the cold metal pull of the zipper between finger and thumb. I drag my lips across skin, up her neck to behind her ear. She's not breathing, and I'm not either; we are both breathless with anticipation.

The opening of the zipper is a loud sound in the silence. Her dress opens to the small of her back, baring an expanse of spine and the black band of a strapless bra, and the tattoo running across her back from shoulder blade to shoulder blade.

The tattoo is simple, handwritten script, elegant and feminine. It says: *The ache for home lives in all of us…*

I run my hands over her ink, wondering what it means to her and not daring to ask. I feel her tense as I touch the tattoo, and I know she's bracing for the question. So I slip my palms up her back and over her shoulders, down toward her cleavage. Another sharp inhalation, but I'm teasing her, playing games with her. I'm not ready to touch her yet, oh no, not yet, I have to see her first, have get her bare so I can soak up her beauty. I merely brush the cups of the dress away, run my palms between skin and dress to push the material down. It falls, pools around her feet. She steps out, and stands facing away from me clad in a strapless black bra and a matching black thong.

I'm breathless. "You…are incredible," I tell her.

"No, I'm not—"

I don't give her a chance to finish. I spin her, crash my mouth against hers to silence her protest. "Yes. You are." I pull back to look into her eyes. "'I'm beautiful.' Say it."

She turns to face me. "Adam, I—"

"Say it." She blinks hard, bites her lower lip, and I can't handle that, not at all. I take that plump lower lip between my teeth, stretch it out, let it go, and claim her mouth. "Des. Say it."

"I'm beautiful." She can't help smiling as she says it. "Is that better?"

"A little." I grin back at her.

I reach for her, but she dances backward. "You can't get me naked without letting me have some of you bare, too."

I hold my arms out. "Go for it, babe."

She takes the corner of her lower lip between her teeth again, steps forward, slips her fingers under the stretched cotton of my undershirt. Instead of lifting it off me like I was expecting, though, Des does the unexpected: she unhooks the fly of my slacks, tugs the zipper down, and her eyes go to mine. Her hands slide under the loosened waistband of the slacks and then they are around my ankles and I'm stepping out. Her eyes drift down to my tented underwear.

She blushes.

I reach for her again, but she shakes her head. "I'm in nothing but my underwear, so I get to have you the same way."

I laugh and let her peel my shirt off, and she tosses the white undershirt onto the pile of our clothes, hers and mine mixed together on the floor of the foyer. My eyes roam her body. Tan, taut skin, curves for days, legs long and strong, and her eyes, bright and liquid brown and feverish.

I take her hand, walk backward, leading her up into the bedroom. She hops up the last step, and her breasts bounce heavily. I don't let her get two steps into the bedroom before I'm jerking her towards me so she stumbles into me. I slide my lips over hers, and she responds immediately, lifting up on her toes to deepen the kiss, and my blood pounds like thunder in my ears and my heart hammers in my chest. Her hands are moving in slow circles on my back, from shoulders to waist, shoulders to waist, each time dipping lower, as if working up the courage to grab my ass.

I find the hook-and-eye fastener of her bra, pull the edges together and loosen one eyelet, the second, and then the third and last. She's pressed against my chest, so the bra is caught between us; I lean back without breaking the kiss, and the undergarment falls to the floor between us. Des's mouth goes still against mine, her body tensing.

"Let me see you," I say, stepping back and taking both of her hands in mine so she can't cover herself.

I stare at her. Take in her beauty. God, I knew she had curves galore, but…damn. The girl is a goddess. Big, heavy tits, high and firm, round and peaked with dark areolae, thick nipples puckered into hard beads. Thighs I want to bury my face in, and her ass…goddamn. I've had my hands on it, but now that she's bare, I have to touch it again. I step closer, slide my hands over her hips and clutch her full, round ass, which is delightfully bare except for the string of the thong.

I'll go ahead and say it: I like a big ass. So with Des, I'm in heaven.

I spin her around and let go of her hands, run my palms down her arms and get a good long look at her ass, and then I have to touch it again, have to hold it. Have to press up against it, and I know she feels my desire. I can't help but nestle my painfully rock-hard cock between those lush, round globes and imagine burying myself deep inside her, just like this.

Not yet, though. She's shaking, trembling, and she's barely breathing. Need to go slow, prime her. Get her ready.

It's time to make good on my promise from yesterday.

"I need to hear you moan." I guide her gently toward the bed, and she trips, rights herself and turns, covering her chest with her arms. I pull her hands away. "Never cover yourself, Des. Those tits of yours are too fucking perfect to ever be hidden."

"Adam, Jesus. You act like you've never seen tits before." She shrugs, and pulls her hands free, but doesn't bar her arms over herself again.

"Not like yours I haven't." I step up to her, run my hand up her side, and then, finally, at long last, I have her breast in my hand.

God, so big, so heavy and soft. I run my palm over the swaying mound of her left boob, then thumb her nipple. She gasps and flinches.

I look into her eyes and flick her nipple with my thumbnail, and she flinches again, hard, her mouth falling open. "You're sensitive as hell, aren't you?" I ask.

"I guess so," Des murmurs, her eyes wide and fearful and searching mine.

"Then you'll really love this," I say.

I lift her breast to my mouth and run my tongue over her nipple in a slow, wet lick.

"Jesus...Adam—"

"Same thing," I say, grinning at her, and then close my lips around the erect nub and suckle.

"*Fuck!*" she curses, and her hands go wild, passing over my shoulders, clutching at me, and one of her hands scrapes over my scalp and she grips my short black hair in her fist.

"You like that?" I ask.

"Adam..."

I lick again, and then suck, flick her nipple with my tongue back and forth a dozen times until she's gasping. "You like it?"

"Yes..." She cups the back of my head, holding my face against her breast. "I like it. A *lot*."

I push her so the bed meets the back of her legs, and she sits, involuntarily. I go to my knees between her thighs, pressing kisses to the tender flesh of the inside of her breast, moving across her sternum to the other side, and I take her right nipple in my mouth and make her moan again.

I skim my hands over her thighs, grip the crease where hip meets leg and press my thumbs into the flesh and muscle, drive them closer and closer to her core. Her head falls back on her neck and she's breathing so hard she's nearly hyperventilating, but her hands are clutching my forearms for dear life, but she isn't pulling me away or stopping me. I fall back to sit on my heels and just look at her.

Looking up at her, watching her, I hook my fingers in the string of the thong circling her waist. She's watching me back, brown eyes wide, a little nervous, anticipatory. I tug down, and the triangular scrap of fabric covering her core rolls down and away. Her chest swells with a breath, and catches. Her eyes narrow and her mouth falls open. I pull some more, and the thong catches on her butt.

"Lift up, babe," I say.

She hesitates, and then lifts her backside up off the bed, and I strip the underwear off, toss it aside. And now she's totally naked for me, bared, vulnerable, and beautiful.

"God, Des. So fucking sexy." I run my palms up her thighs, and back down.

I feel her body tense, but she doesn't move otherwise. This time, my hands drift up between her legs, pressing her thighs open, and she complies with delicacy and demure hesitancy, her eyes sliding closed.

Even her pussy is gorgeous. She's trimmed but not shaved, and her lips down there are as plump and kissable as the ones on her face. She opens her eyes and sees me staring at her core.

"Oh my god." She blushes, her tan skin flushing, and she tries to close her legs, but I'm between her knees. "Stop, Adam. Don't look at me like that."

"Like what?"

She shrugs uncomfortably and tries to cover her pussy with her hands. "Like I'm—"

"Beautiful? Delicious? Someone I want to spend hours pleasuring?"

She closes her eyes and squeezes them tight, as if fighting with herself, warring about something internally. "You're nuts."

"How about this?" I say, and let her cover herself with both hands. She's shy, suddenly. I trail my fingers down the tops of her thighs to her knees, and then drag my fingertips back up along the insides of her thighs. "How about I let you cover up, and I'll just see if I can get you to move your hands on your own. I want to see you, Des. All of you. I want to touch you. I want to kiss you."

"Kiss me where?"

I let a hungry smile play across my lips. "*Everywhere,* Des." I slide my fingers around the circumference of her thighs, as close to her core as I can get. She shivers and I can feel her fingers trembling. Her fingers splay, and I slip one long middle finger between the gaps of her fingers, touching slick skin. "Here. I want to see and touch and taste you *here*."

She makes a sound in the back of her throat, and then opens her eyes, fixes them on me. "Jesus."

"That's not my name."

"Adam."

"Better." I put my hands over hers. "Now. Look into my eyes and tell me you want me to stop."

"I can't."

"I know you can't." I brush my thumbs across her nipples, lift her breasts and let them fall with a bounce. "Because you know you want this. You want to let me touch you."

She keeps her eyes on mine, and I see the internal war raging and I want to know what she's afraid of, what has her so conflicted. But I don't ask. Instead, I skate my palms over her thighs, over her hips, up her ribs to her tits and back down. I see her eyes waver with indecision, and then she lifts her chin, determination filling her gaze, and moves her hands away, resting them on my shoulders.

I grin and trace her opening with my index finger.

She moans, and her eyelids flutter.

I've touched myself. I've given myself orgasms. But that is totally unlike the sensation of Adam's finger sliding up my opening.

I can't stop this. I want to, and yet I don't. I want to feel his fingers inside me, and I want to feel his mouth on me. I know he's planning on going down on me, and I want that. I do. Fuck, I do, so badly.

But I'm scared. I'm terrified.

I should tell him I'm a virgin.

But I'm not going to. He'll stop, and he'll make a big deal over it.

And all he's doing right now is touching me.

He'd want an explanation as to how I can be a twenty-two-year-old virgin. He'll want the story, and I can't give him that. I can't. I won't. It's not something I tell anyone, ever. It happened a long time ago, and I should be over it, but I'm not. And that's part of why I'm doing this, why I'm still here, why I'm fighting my fears and the turmoil in my soul, why I'm shaking like a leaf, my heart hammering and my breath coming in fast, deep gasps. I don't want to let my past dictate my present or future anymore. I want this, really truly deeply *want* Adam, want to do this with him, but I'm afraid. Which is why I have to push myself past my fear, why I have to let this happen: so I can move on. So I can find some semblance of normality. And as long as I let my fear rule me, that'll never happen.

It's not normal to be terrified of letting men get close to me. It's not normal to freeze up when male hands reach for me.

For some reason, Adam scares me the least of anyone I've ever met, even as he simultaneously terrifies me more than I ever thought possible. I feel safe with him. I feel like I can trust him, like he'd stop in an instant if I said the word. Like he'd be furious for me if he knew the root cause of my fear. And I want him. I want him so bad. I want to touch his skin, his muscles. I want to see all of him. I want to pull his underwear off and see and feel that massive, iron-hard thing they so completely fail to disguise.

I'm not some innocent, lily-white fainting daisy. I grew up hard, and fast. I'm not innocent or ignorant. I've had a few…experiences. I've just never been capable of letting anyone get close enough to me to give them my virginity. I've just never been able to withstand touch, however gentle.

I've seen cocks before, and I know he's packing something rarely and uniquely amazing. Just like the rest of him.

I *want* him. I want *him*.

But I'm scared of letting myself go there. I'm scared of what will happen. Not to my body, but my heart. And I'm scared I'll freak out at the last second, and mess everything up.

Oh god, he's touching me everywhere. Hips, breasts, nipples, ribs, thighs. And he's telling me he wants to touch me—and *kiss* me—everywhere, all over, and I know I want it and can't keep a curse of embattled need and fear from escaping.

"Jesus," I hear myself say.

"I keep telling you that's not my name," Adam jokes again, a grin on his lovely, talented mouth.

"Adam…" I breathe.

"Better," he says, covering my shaking hands with his.

I'm covering myself. No one has ever seen me like this, naked, bared, open, vulnerable. And the way he's looking at me, like I'm something yummy he wants to eat, is both dizzyingly wonderful and scarily intoxicating.

"Now look into my eyes and tell me you want me to stop."

He knows that's impossible. I've let this go too far, and there's no turning back now. "I can't," I admit.

"I know you can't," he says, an arrogant smirk ghosting across his lips. "You know you want this. You know you want to let me touch you."

How the fuck can he read me so well? How does he know what I want so unerringly? It's unnerving.

I can't look away from him. There's not the slightest desire in me to look away from his pale, green eyes. His gaze heats me from within, makes something quiver inside me. More even than his arrogant words and confident touch, the knowing, patient, hungry look in his eyes has me acquiescing to my own desires.

I want to let him see me, touch me, and so…I do. I force my hands away, and cling to his broad shoulders. I can feel his muscles shifting under his skin as he keeps his eyes on mine, that cocky grin curling on his lips, as he traces the seam of my pussy with one thick forefinger.

I feel a sliver of heat knife through me, beginning deep within my core, deep down just below my belly. The heat is damp, thick, and pervading. And then his finger drags from the apex of my vagina back down, pauses, and slides back up. The upward journey parts my labia ever so slightly, and a moan escapes my lips. My eyes want to close, but I refuse to let them. I make myself watch. I force my eyes open and watch his finger skate up and down my opening slowly, slowly, again and again, slipping in a little further with every upward and downward motion. And then he's *in* me; his finger is inside my pussy to the second knuckle. His palm faces up, his finger curling in. His eyes go to mine, watching my every reaction. My eyes are heavy, fluttering with the aching fullness of one of his fingers, my core hot and wet now, made all the more damp by his touch. Wetness moves through me, until I'm sure I must be dripping, and I'm embarrassed, but he doesn't seem to notice.

Or maybe he does. He pulls his finger out of me, and I feel so empty, suddenly. And then, making sure I'm watching, he puts his index finger in his mouth—the finger that was just inside me. I gape at him in disbelief, but can't summon any words. It was mortifying and erotic in equal measure, and I don't know which reaction to show, so I don't show either, I just stare at him. His finger, glistening with his saliva and my essence, slips back into me now, piercing me slowly, and I squirm at the invasion, breathe out a moan.

I ache. There's a pressure within me, building and building, mounting with every appreciative, desire-hot sweep of his eyes over my body, with every gentle, skillful touch of his hands and mouth on my skin.

I ache, and I know somehow that only Adam could ever release the pressure, could ever provide the relief I need.

He slides his finger upward and finds the nexus of the aching pressure: my clitoris. The heat and the wetness and the pressure and the need, it's all centered there, and he knows it, and he finds it, and his finger presses the diamond-hard nub of nerves and I have to bite my lip to keep from moaning too loud.

"You like that, Des?" His voice is a low rumble, coming from deep in his chest.

"Y-yeah. I do."

"Then let me hear you say it."

"I like it," I say.

He circles my clit again, not touching me directly, but the indirect pressure is somehow worse, or better, I'm not sure which. All I know is the circling and swiping of his finger has me wiggling, has my hips wanting to move, has the heat and pressure coiling higher and hotter and moving closer to the surface.

And then he flicks my clit with a fingertip, and I have to muffle another groan.

"Don't hold back," he growls. "Let me hear you."

He wants me to be noisy? Why?

Thoughts are erased as he moves his finger in circles again, and my hips are moving now, out of my control. I can't stop them. I should. I know I should.

I'm being crazy and embarrassing. But I can't control myself anymore.

He controls me with his touch.

I'm too late to bite back a loud moan when he flicks my clit again at the same time that he leans forward and takes my hardened nipple in his mouth. The moan is loud and embarrassingly breathy, but this only seems to make him touch me faster, mouth my breast all the more hungrily.

And then he nudges me backward, and I fall to the mattress. My legs hang over the edge of the bed, and I know I'm bared to him, my thighs spread open for him. I feel his gaze, and I feel his finger moving inside me, descending from my clit to my channel, slipping in and then moving out. My eyes close involuntarily, and I feel so full from just his finger, and then somehow I'm even more full, spread open inside until it almost aches, and I force my eyes open and sit up on my elbows to see that he has two fingers inside me. He's not moving his fingers all the way in, and I wonder if he can feel the barrier of my innocence, if he can feel my virginity with his fingers. If he does, he doesn't say anything. He just curls his fingers into me and moves them. It feels so good I have to fall back to the bed, have to close my eyes and let my hips lift in the rhythm of his moving fingers.

My eyes are closed, so I don't see him do it. I'm aware of nothing but his fingers and the ever-mounting sun-hot balloon of pressure aching inside me, and so I'm shocked into a breathless scream when I feel something wet and firm and slippery and hot at my opening. I feel my clit being sucked on, and then his tongue is moving against my clit and I'm moaning, moaning, and I can't even remember my name or his, but I know nothing, nothing has ever felt this way.

I open my eyes and peer down the length of my body to see his face buried between my thighs, moving from side to side as he flicks his tongue against my clit faster and faster. Shit, shit, shit...that's a vision I'll never forget, Adam's broad shoulders and the massive curve of his back and his short spiky black hair and the feel of his tongue in my most sensitive, most private, most delicate place, and the heat is exploding and I'm groaning past clenching molars. I'm grinding against his mouth, and I'm gasping with wantonly erotic need, and his tongue is flicking my clit with hungry vigorous speed, and I'm lifted off the bed, his hands cupping my ass and physically lifting me as if I weighed nothing, and he's pulling me against him and Jesus, holy shit, he tosses one of my legs and then the other over his shoulder, and his face moves crazily and his tongue circles madly, and my hips gyrate, driven by an engine of relentless heat.

This is surreal.

This isn't happening.

It can't be.

But it is.

And then I'm making a wild sound, a teeth-clenched scream and the world is imploding and my body is wracked and my core is shaken and exploding and I'm writhing, and Adam is growling into my pussy and his fingers are driving in and out and rubbing somewhere high inside me that has the explosion going hotter and the heat spearing even more sharply.

My thighs clench around his neck, and my heels scrabble at his back, and my hips move on their own. I'm screaming. I don't recognize the sounds coming from me, but then I don't recognize anything in this dizzied chaotic world where all is spears of ecstasy rifling through my veins and muscles and pores, where all is hotter than the sun and Adam's hands clutching my ass and his mouth sucking my clit and his fingers sliding in and out of my pussy. He's playing my body like an instrument, like he's a virtuoso and I'm his art, taking each sound and shiver and making it into music.

I can't breathe, can't do anything but shake and whimper and moan, and eventually his mouth pulls away from my pussy and I'm being bodily moved up to the top of the bed, and he's beside me, looking down at me.

"Ho—holy shit," I gasp. "Holy shit."

I look up at him. His mouth is shiny with wetness, and I'm mortified to realize that it's my essence on his face, smeared on his skin. As I watch, he wipes his palm across his lips, and then his forearm, and I blush. He smirks knowingly, his palm skating across my stomach, up to my breasts. He brushes his index finger over my nipple, and I flinch, so sensitive even that slight, gentle touch is almost too much.

I rake my gaze over his broad shoulders, his thick pectoral muscles, his tree trunk-huge arms, the heavy sculpted slab of his abdomen, and then I see the thick ridge of his cock bulging the stretchy gray fabric of his CK boxer-briefs.

He's watching me watch him.

I turn toward him, reach a hand out, rest it on his side. He doesn't move, doesn't even blink. I run my fingertips over his firm skin until I come to the elastic band of his underwear. Can I do this?

My emotions are a jumble. I'm not a virgin because I don't feel desire, or because I'm a prude, or because of religion; I'm a virgin because I experienced things that caused deep wounds inside me, left thick scars and impenetrable walls between me and the world. I'm a virgin because I don't trust anyone to not hurt me. But I feel desire. I feel need. I ache. I'm lonely. I'm a twenty-two-year-old girl with the same hormones and drives and appetites as any other, but so far my fear and distrust has won out.

Now, somehow, for reasons I don't understand, desire is winning. Attraction and desperation is winning. Adam is all man. He's huge and strong and sexy and beautiful, but he's also kind and funny and reassuring and down-to-earth despite his fame and wealth.

And I want him.

I want to touch him. I want to see what he looks like totally naked. I want to see his cock. I want to touch him. I want him to kiss me and get lost, and I want to get lost in him. I want to drown myself in this with him, future and consequences be damned.

I want to conquer my fear.

So I caress my palm over Adam's chest and stomach and shoulder, and then push him down to his back, and I sit up. Hooking my fingers in the elastic, I let out a long breath, lick my lips, and pull his underwear down. I have to stretch the waistband away from his body to free his erection, and then he's lifting his hips for me and drawing his foot out of one side, and then kicking it away.

I'm naked with Adam Trenton.

He's still, watching me, and only his eyes move, flicking from side to side, then down to my breasts and between my thighs, and back up.

My gaze is locked on his cock. Holy hell is he big. Tall, thick, and straight, standing erect, pointing away from his body ever so slightly. My pulse is crashing thunder in my ears, my hands trembling ever so slightly. Or maybe a lot. Adam seems totally at ease, one hand tucked behind his head, the other resting with proprietary familiarity on my thigh.

The fingertips of my right hand trail down the slight dusting of dark hair on his chest and stomach, but I chicken out and skirt his crotch, dragging my fingers down his thigh. His posture is loose and relaxed and confident but, jerking my gaze from his impressive erection to his eyes, I notice that his expression is as shuttered as mine is, as if he's feeling a weltering wealth of emotion and has as many walls up as I do. Maybe I'm reading too much into his blank expression, but I don't think I am. I summon my courage and draw on my desire, bring my hand back up his opposite thigh, to his stomach. He tenses, sucks in his stomach as my hand nears his erection. His eyes narrow, his nostrils flare. The hand tucked under his head clenches into a fist, and the hand on my thigh squeezes, and then relaxes.

Hovering over him briefly, I finally let my palm descend, and the thick, veined, dark organ is in my hand. I close my fingers around him, and he inhales a long, deep breath. I've got him in my fist, now, and his flesh is hot and smooth. It's exactly as hard in my hand as it looked, yet also softer, silkier. Like satin cushioned around a core of steel. I slide my fist down, and the bulbous head emerges from the top of my hand, straining. I touch my thumb to the very top, and find it springy, squishy. A bead of wetness oozes from the tiny hole at the tip, and my thumb smears over it. Adam's jaw is clenched, his breathing coming in deep, even inhalations. I move my hand up, and then back down, and Adam's hips lift slightly. He likes this. I mean, duh, I knew—intellectually—that he would like it, but knowing it mentally is not the same as seeing as his reactions, feeling his stomach tense and his thighs contract, and feeling his hips lift into my touch, seeing his eyes go hooded and hot.

I twist my fist around his thickness as I bring my hand down, and then twist again as I bring it slowly back up. The clear fluid beading at his tip is all over my hand now, and smeared all over the thick, soft, broad bulb the head of his cock.

"You'd better stop," Adam says. "Or this is gonna end real fast."

He was that close to coming? I didn't realize it would be that easy. Part of me wants to keep going, wants to make him come. I want to watch that happen, and know that I did it. Maybe I'll get that chance another time. For now, I let go, and then he's lifting up, his torso leaving the bed, his mouth finding mine, his tongue thrusting into my mouth, and heat fills me. Energy sluices through me, desire floods me. My hands find his chest, his shoulders, his arms, caressing the great muscles, tracing the contours and indentations.

I'm on my back, somehow, and I don't mind it. I like his bulk above me, like his mouth on mine, like the warmth billowing from his skin. I like the press of his body on mine. I feel his knee slide across my thigh, press down on the mattress between my legs, and then his other knee does the same, and we're devouring each other's mouths, his tongue wrestling against mine, seeking and scouring and I'm giving as good as I'm getting, lost to the kiss. Pressure coils low in my belly, and my hands come alive, scraping over his back and now finally I find the courage to grab his ass, and I find it hard and taut and I like it, like the way it feels in my hands, so I spend time caressing him there, exploring, kneading, down to his thighs and back up to his spine, and then return to palming both cheeks in my hands.

His knees nudge my thighs apart, and my heart crashes in my chest.

It's happening. It's going to happen.

And I want it to. I'm going to let it.

Not just let it, but welcome it. I'm going to go into this eyes wide open, knowing that I may never see this man again, but I'll have this with him. There's still fear boiling deep down, but it's buried and subsumed and weakened. Adam's gentleness and patience and his obvious attraction to me, his compliments, his reassurance, his understanding of my reticence to answer questions, all of this has weakened the hold of fear, has undercut the hold of the past on me.

Now, I'm alive, and I'm ravenous for Adam, I'm buzzing with energy, my skin tingling with the feel of his against mine.

I feel his cock against my inner thigh, and his mouth leaves mine. This is it.

I look up at him. And instead of pushing into me, he moves back. "Touch yourself, Des."

"Wh-what?"

"I'll be right back," he says, slipping backward off the bed. "Now let me see you touch yourself."

"Why? Where are you going?" I'm losing my heat, the pressure, the need. Fear is bubbling back up. Where is he going, why is he leaving, why does he—?

He's back on the bed and his hands are on mine, and he's pushing my fingers between my thighs, and I feel a zing of electricity as our joined hands find my core, and then our fingers circle my clit and I gasp, and his fingers move into my opening, and I moan, and I push my fingers inside me beside his, heat billowing and pressure clenching and clamping and spreading, and I close my eyes and my head falls back to the pillow. I barely notice him leave the bed, focused on the building crescendo, and then I hear a crinkling of plastic. My eyes flick open to see him ripping open a condom, rolling it over himself.

My eyes go wide with apprehension now, as I see once again exactly how fucking massive his cock is, and I wonder if this is going to hurt. I've always heard it does the first time. I'm not afraid of a little pain, but I'm worried I'll give away the fact of my virginity.

I have absolutely no intention of telling him I'm a virgin. None. He doesn't need to know. He only has this one weekend here, and then he's going back to Hollywood to make his movies and I'll just be a memory. That's fine. I know what I'm getting myself into. I don't want this to be a big deal. It's long past due, and he doesn't need to know, and there's no way I can explain it all to him.

He's watching me, and I wonder momentarily if he can read my mind, if he can see my thoughts somehow, because he's watching me and his eyes are so sharp, so intelligent, so perceptive, seeing so deeply into me that surely he can perceive the source of my nerves. He's kneeling between my thighs. I'm no longer touching myself, lost in my thoughts, in my inner discourse.

And then his fingers find me, and I gasp as he rubs a fingertip against my clit. He circles twice, three times, and then delves his fingers into my opening, and I'm sucking in a harsh breath as lightning rips through me. My hips lift, and he circles, and lightning strikes again, and I'm moaning, then he delves in and finds a spot deep inside me that has me gasping a whimpering groan and lifting my hips clear off the bed.

And then I'm coming again just that easily, that quickly, grinding against his fingers and moaning and I feel him over me, rip my eyes open and fix my gaze on his pastel green eyes, and I know now is the moment, *now*—

I'm spread open, his cock is a hot and hard pressure at my entrance, and he's watching me intently. I whimper as he inches forward just a little, whimper from the aching burn of accommodating him. Oh, it hurts. It *hurts*. I'm breathless from the pain, but I'm still coming, his fingers are at my clit and circling to milk the waves of orgasm from me but it can't bury the burn.

I'm filled. I can't take it, can't take it…he's on me and over me and *in* me, and I'm full to bursting, crazed by the sensation of being entered, penetrated, pierced.

But it's not frightening. His eyes are gentle and sure, watching me, and I think he has to know this is my first time, but if he does he hasn't said anything and I don't think he will.

He's not even fully inside me yet, but he stops, his face showing the strain of holding back. Now that he's stilled, my muscles have a chance to learn him, to stretch, and the burn fades, or morphs into something else, something hotter and deeper.

"Okay?" he rumbles.

I nod. "Yeah. Yeah. God, yeah." I palm his butt, pull at him. "More."

And I'm not saying that for any other reason than I want *more*. The ache and the burn and the looseness of post-orgasm is turning into *something* powerful inside me, and the intensity of his presence above me, his eyes, his hand fisted in the pillow beside my face, his other hand now finding my boob and rolling my nipple to make me gasp, it's all conspiring to make me desperate for something, for *more,* for him.

For this.

Sex.

I'm having sex.

With Adam Trenton.

He leans on an elbow, supporting his weight on one arm, the other still toying with my nipple. His mouth finds mine, and his hips move toward mine, and he's pushing deeper.

He pulls back with his hips, and then surges forward and I feel a brief, sharp, pinching spasm of pain, like something tearing, but it's so quick that by the time I gasp, he's all the way inside me and the pain is gone, not even a memory and he's sliding back out and his eyes are on mine, a curiosity in them.

I kiss him, lifting up and wrapping my hand around the back of his neck, pulling myself toward him to push my tongue into his mouth and he's moving now, slowly, and it's so good, *so* good, a burn and a stretch and a fullness and a sense of utter completion, being filled with Adam as he moves, draws out, pushes in, and the burn is pleasure now, such pleasure.

He's going slowly, and each withdrawal makes me whimper from the loss of him, and each surge to fill me makes me groan with relief to have him back inside me.

"Oh god, Adam." I can't help saying it. I want him to know I like this. He has to know, from the sounds I'm making, but I want to say it. "So good. You feel so good."

He buries his face in my neck and pushes deep, and I gasp a shriek at the depth of his thrust, at the surge of ecstasy of having him so deep. "You're so fucking tight, Des. God, you feel perfect."

He withdraws, and I move without thinking. I wrap my heels around the backs of his thighs and pull him back toward me. "No, I need—oh god…"

"What? Tell me what you need."

"You. Deeper. More. I need more of you, Adam." I blush furiously to hear myself talk that way, to say that, but he growls and leans back to sit on his heels.

His cock is stretched away from his body, and I wonder how comfortable that can be, and what he's doing, and then…oh—oh Jesus. He rises up onto his knees, takes my thighs in his hands and slides his hands under my ass, lifts me, drags me toward himself. And oh god, I'm absolutely *stuffed* with him, he's all the way in me, surely he can't go deeper—

But then he grips my hips and holds me aloft, somehow, I don't know how he manages it, but he does, and he drags his hips back, pulling out, and I knot my fingers in the sheets beside me, my mouth falling open, eyes widening, and then he thrusts into me.

"FUCK!" I scream, my entire body jolting, my hips driving on their own into him, and Adam's chest rumbles, his fingers dig into the flesh at my hips and he pulls me into him.

"Fuck me, Des, you feel so good. I wanna make this last, but you feel too good." He pulls back again, slowly, and then glides in, quickly and smoothly.

I know what I want now; when he pulls back again, I wait until he's about to start his inward thrust, and I roll my hips toward him, meet his thrust, and when our bodies clash together, I gasp breathlessly from the dizzying, heady ecstasy that thrills through me. He's so deep, now, pushing into me until I can't physically take any more. He thrusts, and my clit smashes against his body and I'm shaking, and then he pulls out and I groan at the emptiness, and he's growling now with each thrust.

His whole body is tensed, as if he's exerting all his significant power to hold back. Each thrust in is measured and careful and slow, and I realize this is because he *is* holding back, being gentle and careful.

I don't want gentle or careful, not totally. I don't think I'm ready for Adam to totally unleash, but I want him to loosen just a little, at least. I move with him, grind against him, and he starts to move faster, so I move faster with him, and I can almost predict his motions now, and I'm greedy for him, needing him more fully, needing all of him, needing his heat and his weight.

I feel the upwelling of pressure, the coiling heat, and I know full well what that means: I've got an orgasm coming, and I want it. But I want even more to feel Adam come, to feel him explode, to feel him take his own pleasure.

So I rock against him, wordlessly urging him faster, and he mirrors my increased tempo, and even begins to increase it on his own. His eyes close and his hands grip my hips more tightly, almost painfully, but I like it, I like the little signs that he's losing control. And now he's growling nonstop, grunting, really, and I like the sounds of his exertion too, like the low throaty rumble of his voice as he begins to grind against me now, not thrusting and pulling back but rolling, pushing deeper and deeper.

He releases my hips and falls forward with both hands beside my face and his hips begin to circle faster and faster. I run my hands down his back, greedy to touch him, to feel the sinuous ripple of his massive muscles, and then I take his ass in my hands and pull, pull, urge him onward.

God, this is amazing. He's close, I think. And the closer he gets, the better it feels for me. Each rolling thrust drives the heat hotter, pulling moans from me, and ratchets the pressure tighter within me. His face is buried in my breast and his spine arches and straightens, glistening with sweat, and I cup his head and hold him, and I say his name…

"Adam, yes, god…don't stop, don't stop…YES Adam, yes!" I don't even care how I sound, if it's cliché, because I now realize why those clichés exist, that you can't even help what comes out of your mouth when he's in you and losing control and taking your control and you're exploding and he's on the verge of detonation inside you.

"Oh fuck, Des, I'm right there, babe, I'm so close…"

"Me too, Adam, oh god…fuck me harder!" Holy shit, I don't even know where *that* came from, but it makes him wild.

He growls loudly and scoots closer to me, deeper between my thighs, and I wrap my ankles around his ass and clutch him to me and rock my hips against his and he's groaning, his face showing strain now.

I don't dare close my eyes, even though I feel an orgasm ripping through me, even though I'm gasping and shrieking as fire sweeps through me and the pressure implodes inside me and has me writhing beneath him and clinging to him and rocking with him. I watch him, and I see the moment he lets go. His eyes flick open and his pale green gaze is like fire, razor sharp and intense and unwavering, and his lids go hooded, his thrusts become mad and wild, and then he pounds deep, once, hard, and then again, and our gazes are locked, something intangible but potent exchanging between us in that moment. I can't hear, can barely see, can only register the shredding pulsation of my climax and the way his cock throbs inside me and heat fills me and his sweat coats my skin and his mouth crashes against mine, because it's impossible to not kiss in this moment.

It's not just a kiss.

I absorb this truth with the saliva on his tongue and with the power of his lips and the dig of his fingers in my hip and the nova-hot rupture of our mutual orgasm. It's something else, something deeper.

Spent, his lips move on mine, wet and desperate, and I kiss him back with all that I have, knowing something momentous just occurred between us.

He falls to his side, bringing me with him, falling out of me, and a breath whooshes from him. "Holy shit, Des. Holy motherfucking shit."

I can't even form words yet. "Y-yeah."

His eyes cut sideways to mine. "That was… incredible," he says, and then slips off the bed and goes into the bathroom.

I watch as he uses a long strip of toilet paper to peel off the condom, wrapping it up and then discarding it. Surreptitiously, I lift up to check the sheet where I was lying, but the sheet is clean and white. If I bled, it wasn't enough to stain the bed, apparently, and thank god for that.

He returns to the bed, slides in beside me, and reaches for me. I settle in with him, my hand resting on his shoulder, my breast draped across his side, my thigh on his.

I've never been more content in my life. Drowsy, I let myself drift.

CHAPTER SEVEN

THIS...IS NOT WHAT I EXPECTED. *SHE* ISN'T WHAT I expected. Sweet, responsive, eager. She's a tough girl, independent, closed off. But once she gave in to wanting this with me, she transformed. Just utterly....changed. Morphed into a voracious, insatiable, erotic woman.

I want more of her; it's dangerous.

Questions boil inside me, and I know if I ask even one, she'll freak out and bolt.

So I hold her and keep my questions to myself. My hand skims in circles on her back, and her breathing goes even, her body nestled against mine goes limp. Her hand is on my chest, the fingers curled slightly. I examine her hand. It's a delicate, feminine hand, but her nails are cut short and filed into perfect curves. Well kept, but not long, and not painted.

My fingertips stutter across her back, between her shoulder blades where I know the tattoo to be. There are bumps where I know the ink is, long raised welts. Scar tissue. I crane my neck and peer at her back. Trace the letters of the text inked onto her skin, and find the scars beneath. The tattoo covers something. The text is large, each letter at least half an inch tall. The scars are significant. I can't quite figure out what kind of scars they are, though.

And then I notice another tattoo. On her ribs, high on her left side. Even wearing a tank top or strapless dress, the tattoo would go largely unnoticed unless you were looking for it:

...The safe place...

My fingertips skim the inked letters running on a slight diagonal from just beneath her armpit toward her back. And yes, beneath this tattoo as well is more scar tissue. The same as on her back, raised welts, rough, ridged lines of an old scar of some kind.

Jesus. What has this girl endured?

She makes a sound low in her throat, a sleepy murmur, and rolls away from me. And as she does so, I see two more tattoos done in the same neat but simple script. One is on the opposite side of her body as the one under her armpit, on her right side low by her hip, again running on a diagonal from just above the hip upward and toward her back:

...Where we can go as we are...

And yes, beneath that as well is more scar tissue.

My throat seizes, my heart clenches. I need to know.

The last tattoo is on her left leg, on the outer side of her thigh, high up, almost tucked under the swell of her buttock. The scar tissue here is thicker, harder. The text yet again runs on an angle, from the outside of her thigh to the inside, slanted high to low:

...And not be questioned.

Des rolls again, and I see a fifth tattoo on her right leg, on the front of her upper thigh where it'd be hidden by all but the shortest skirt or shorts. It's the smallest, and it wraps from the front of her thigh around to the side, and this one is straight, not angled like the others:

~ Maya Angelou

I snag my phone off the side table and bring up a Google search bar, type in the beginning of the quote, and it auto-fills the rest. I click the first link and read the quote in its entirety: *"The ache for home lives in all of us, the safe place where we can go as we are and not be questioned."* —Maya Angelou.

The ache for home.

The scars are all on her back and legs, angled in such a way as to suggest that whatever was striking her to create the scars was coming from above, and she was turtled to protect herself from it.

I can't help tracing the text on her thigh, the ridged tissue beneath the ink, and she stirs, blinks, sees where my fingers touch, and I feel her tense.

Her eyes go wide, the rest of her expression carefully blank. "Adam, I—the tattoos are—"

I touch her lips with a finger, stopping her. "Des, I told you I wouldn't ask. I'm not asking. All I'm going to say is, I would be honored to know more about you. If you feel like sharing, I will listen and I promise you I won't judge."

She blinks hard. "Fuck. Adam, it's not that simple. I can't just…share. It's nothing like that. It's too much to…even know where to start." She sits up, holds the sheet against her chest, and I feel her withdrawing emotionally. "And besides, you're leaving…what, tomorrow? Monday?"

I sigh. "Tomorrow."

She glances at the clock, which reads 12:15 a.m. "And guess what? It's tomorrow. So there's no point in getting into it."

I nod, although something in me rebels against the idea of just letting this go so easily. "I get it."

"And it's not like you've told me much about yourself either. That's not what this was, Adam. It's not what it's ever going to be. I know that. I'm fine with that." She scoots toward the edge of the bed. "I should go."

I grab her wrist, stop her. "Don't leave. Just stay here for tonight."

She neither pulls away nor returns. "Why?"

I release her wrist and slide my palm up her forearm, crawling across the bed toward her, and then bring my hand from her bicep to her shoulder to the back of her neck. "Because I'm not done with you."

She leans toward me, by accident maybe, automatically. "You're not?"

I kiss the base of her neck, bury my fingers in her thick black hair and tug her head back to bare her throat, kissing her there. "Nope. I haven't had my fill of you yet."

What I don't say is that I'm not sure I'll ever be able to get my fill. I trail a line of small feathery kisses up her throat until I reach her chin, and then her mouth, and then I've got her tongue between my teeth and my palm on her inner thigh, reaching in and around. She gasps into my mouth as I find her wetness and heat with my fingers. Another gasp, and then her hand skates across my stomach and finds my cock.

Her eyes flick open, and I see her gaze flit around the room, seeing the extra condom I tossed onto the bedside table. She pushes me down to the mattress, slides astride me and reaches for the square packet. She rips it open with her fingers, pulls free the circle, tosses the empty packet aside. Sitting on my thighs, she toys with the condom, rolling it one way and then the other until she determines which way it opens. Taking my cock in one hand, she fits the circle around the tip and rolls it down one-handed, then uses her other hand to push it down the rest of the way.

I rest my hands on her hips, deciding to let her do what she wants, for now. She leans forward, and her tits slide across my chest, soft and warm against my skin, and her weight presses me down against the mattress. Her lips touch my shoulder, my chin, my jaw, the corner of my mouth, and then we're kissing and my breath is gone. Her kiss is sweet, slow and deep. One hand supports her weight, a palm in the mattress beside my ribs, another smoothing over my chest as we kiss. She inches forward a bit more, and her free hand sneaks between our bodies. She doesn't break the kiss as she guides my cock to her entrance, no, she deepens it, opening her mouth to mine and demanding my tongue. I feel her labia part and accept the head of my cock, and then she pauses. Breaks the kiss, sighing quietly, and then her forehead touches my chest and she's watching our bodies join as she flexes her hips downward, taking me deeper oh so slowly, centimeter by centimeter, and with each increment she takes short shallow breaths in and out, and she's watching, watching my cock enter her.

"I don't know how you fit, but you do," she whispers.

"Does it hurt?" I ask.

She shakes her head. "No. Well, yeah, a little, but it's good. Oh god, yeah, it's good." She's fully impaled on me now, her ass nestled against my hips.

Both of her hands go to my chest, supporting her weight on me, and I use my own hands to caress her lush tan skin everywhere I can reach, hips, thighs, ass, back, and then I cup her heavy tits as they sway above me, and she gasps when my fingers find her nipples and pinch and roll and twist. She rolls her hips, keeping me deep. Slow, driving, grinding sweeps of her hips, her mouth hanging open and her eyes wide and fraught on mine, her hair a thick black curtain over one shoulder.

Her head hangs, then, and she finally lifts up off me, and her teeth catch at the corner of her lower lip. God, I love that, the way she bites that one corner of her lip, like she wants to say something but is too overwhelmed to form words. Oh fuck, fuck, fuck, her pussy is tight, so tight, so incredibly tight, squeezing me like a vise, so hot and slick and perfect that I can't take it, can only growl and groan as she plunges her hips down now and I'm pushed deep inside her and we both cry out loud.

"Shit, Adam. Jesus, it feels so good."

"Des. Don't stop. Let me feel you come, just like this."

She's finding a rhythm now, rising and sinking, and I'm tensed and tautened, holding it back. I'm not close yet, but I can feel it rising and she's just now finding her rhythm, gasping with each plunge downward. And now she's moving a little faster, and I'm gritting my teeth and moving with her, thrusting up as she sinks down on me, and I can't look away from her. Her tits are bouncing and swaying, her nipples hard and thick, and her hips are soft and generously padded with sweet silky flesh, and her ass is slapping against me and her lips are stuttering across mine, sloppy kisses exchanged as she begins to lose control.

I hold back, because I want to watch her come apart, want to see every expression, read every emotion, glean whatever I can from the way she comes for me.

"Adam, oh my god, Adam, I'm coming!" She frantic now, her face pressed into the crook of my shoulder, her fingers clawed into my pectoral muscle, and her hips are driving relentlessly, hard and fast and wild. "Oh god! Oh fuck, oh…"

"Look at me when you come, Des," I order, taking one hand from her hip to tilt her chin up. She resists, burying her face deeper in my neck, so I grab a handful of hair near her scalp and tug gently but insistently as she shrieks wordlessly. "*Look* at me, babe, let me see those big brown eyes while you come."

She brings her head up, and she can barely keep her eyes open, but she fixes them on me and her mouth is wide and her fingers dig almost painfully into my chest, and she's grinding on me, her pussy sliding wet and slick up and down on my cock, which throbs with the need to come, but I hold it. I hold it.

And she comes. Lifts up, almost losing my cock in the process, and then slams down. Gasps. Lifts up, hesitates, and slams down again, and this time she actually screams, a loud, rasping sound of release.

I use that moment to flip her off me, levering her onto her back, and then guiding her onto her stomach. I settle behind her, lift her up by the hips, and she moves with me, bringing that big fine round ass of hers to face me, baring it for me, presenting it to me. I palm it, taking a second to appreciate it, and then I move to my knees, reach between her thighs to find her opening and guide my cock in. I'm throbbing painfully, aching, thick and fighting the urge to come right then. She rests on her shins and elbows, and sucks in a sharp breath as I slide fully into her in one smooth thrust.

She lets the breath out slowly and shakily as I pull back slowly and push in even more gradually. I want to take my time with this. Make it last. Savor it. I hold her ass in both hands, caressing each cheek with my palms. I can't hold back any longer, then. It feels too good. She pushes back against me as I thrust slowly, rhythmically. Again, and again. And now I feel the come boiling in my balls, feeling desperation welling up inside me, and I'm moving faster.

Des is moaning too, now, and the sound of her voice, the vocal evidence of her enjoyment of this has me driving harder, deeper, and that only makes her louder, and I'm close to losing it. She stretches out her hands in front of herself, grips the sheet in both fists, and then snakes one hand between her legs.

"Yes, Des, touch yourself. Touch your clit while I fuck you."

"Are you gonna come soon?"

"Yeah, babe, I'm close…I'm right there."

I take the crook of her hips in my hands and pull her back into my thrusts, and now the room is filled with my grunts of exertion and the sound of my thighs slapping against hers, my hips and stomach smacking against her ass as my cock fills her. I feel her fingers moving, and now she's whimpering in time with me, her hips meeting mine thrust after thrust.

"Now, Adam, come *now*. I'm coming again too. Oh god, oh my fucking god…" Her voice goes hoarse and she presses her torso to the mattress, and I slide even deeper.

"Oh fuck, Des. So good. I'm coming so hard." I grunt the words, bite them out, and then I can't form words because I'm exploding and she's pushing back hard and fast into me.

My entire body seizes and it feels like fire pours through my veins and coalesces in my gut, shooting out of me, emptying me. Her orgasm has her shaking and growling and grinding her ass against me, and I feel the walls of her pussy clamp down around my cock, and I'm still coming, unable to control or temper the driving slam of my hips. She takes it, takes every hard crash of my body into hers, and moans in pleasure for more.

God, she's heaven, she's shaped perfectly to take all I've got and she loves it, needs it, wants it. That's what I feel coming from her, in that moment, and I wonder if I'll think differently when the moment is gone, when our heat is spent.

She falls forward and I let her, pull out and take a moment to rest before stripping the condom off and cleaning myself. When I get back to the bed, she's lying on her back and watching me, her eyes going to the bounce and sway of my softening dick, then to my eyes.

Neither of us speaks as I cradle her against me. She settles in easily, naturally, fitting into the sheltering nook of my arms and we are like two pieces of a puzzle fitting together.

She falls asleep quickly, and I'm not far behind.

I'm panicking. God, am I panicking. Adam is up and about already, even though we were up till after one this morning and it's barely eight. He's ordered breakfast and he doesn't know I'm awake.

I don't want to go home. I don't want him to go back to L.A. I'm watching him through slitted eyes, and my heart squeezes. Last night he was so attentive, so gentle, so sweet. Until the end, when he started to lose it, and then he was powerful and primal, and that was honestly the hottest thing I've ever experienced, the way he flipped me over and positioned me the way he wanted, and just…took me.

I wouldn't mind letting him have his way with me more often. I would play games with him, play hard to get and make him take me. I'd push him around and take him for myself, when I wanted.

But that won't happen.

He's leaving, and in a week I'll be headed back to Detroit for morning classes and late-night classroom cleaning. And we'll never meet again. This is all I'll have with him, so I'm trying to absorb it all. Soak up the hard lines and angles of his body, the heavy planes of muscles, the slabs of masculine strength.

The intelligent pastel green of his eyes, the gentle power of his hands.

The way he kisses me, like he's trying to devour me, and drown in me, and subsume me in his essence all at once.

The way he moves into me, slow and careful until he can't hold back and loses control and turns into a huge hard and hungry beast, a beast that is sexy and dominant and exotic and headily addictive.

I'm so fucking sore. Or…sore from fucking. My thighs ache, the muscles burning from exertion. My sex is what hurts the worst, though. It's a sensation I can't really describe, even to myself. It's a soreness, a stretched-out feeling, a post-fullness burn…and I love it. It's an incredible sensation.

I'm not a virgin any longer.

I want to squeal and kick my feet, especially when my eyes land on the extreme hotness that is Adam Trenton, shirtless, wearing nothing but a pair of basketball shorts low on his hips. There's the V of abdominal muscles leading down to his cock, and god, I want that again. See it. Feel it.

Maybe even taste it.

My heart flips and flops and my stomach goes weightless and my mind whirls. I can't believe the past two days have been real. That I'm really here, naked, in Adam Trenton's bed. That we just had mind-blowing sex…

Mind-blowing for me, at least.

Which makes me wonder what he thinks about all this. If this is par for the course for him, or if this was as expectation-shattering for him as it was for me. I mean, I know *I'll* never be the same again.

My heart squeezes, and I force myself to keep calm, to breathe slowly and push the glut of emotions away. It was just sex. For him, and for me.

Just sex. Don't get attached. You know nothing about him, or he about you. He owes you nothing. You owe him nothing.

My entire being rebels against that line of thought, though. I *want* it to be more. I want him to want it to be more.

A knock at the door has me shutting my eyes and feigning sleep. Adam answers the door, speaking in low tones. The door shuts again, and I hear his weight on the steps leading up to the bedroom.

"You can get up now, Des." His voice comes from beside the bed.

I sit up slowly, bringing the sheet with me, clutching it to my chest. His eyes are all over me, taking in my hair—which must be a rumpled rat's nest—and my eyes and my shoulders. "Hey," I say.

He has a mug of coffee in each hand, one black, one creamed to a medium khaki color. "How do you like your coffee?"

I grab the one with cream. "This have any sugar in it?"

He shakes his head. "No, you want some?"

I take it and sip. "No, thanks. This is perfect."

He sits, drinks his coffee, and watches me drink and watch him. It's a very meta moment. "Wasn't sure what you like for breakfast, so I got a little of everything. Bagel, an omelet, French toast, scrambled eggs and bacon, some rye toast."

I grin at him. "French toast and bacon."

He sets his mug down on the bedside table, goes down to the foyer and picks through the metal lid-covered plates, transfers bacon from one plate to another, the toast and the omelet to a second, and carries both plates up to the bed. He arranges them on the foot of the bed, and then returns for silverware, butter, syrup, and the carafe of coffee. He settles on the bed next to me, reaches for the plate with French toast and bacon on it and hands it to me, along with a fork and knife, and then he takes his plate.

"Dig in, babe," he says.

I sit cross-legged, and try to figure out a way to eat while keeping the sheet tucked under my arms. Adam watches me for a few seconds, fighting a grin.

"What?" I ask, giving him a sideways glare.

He shrugs, the smile ghosts across his lips, gone again immediately. "Nothing. You're just so fucking cute it's ridiculous."

"And that means...?" I prompt.

He shovels a bite of eggs into his mouth and speaks after he's chewed a few times. "You're being so modest all of a sudden. It's just cute."

I sigh. "I didn't care when we were in the moment, but now, it's different. I'm not...I don't even get changed in front of Ruthie, and I've known her for years, and we share that shoe box of a room every summer."

"Why?" he asks, as he snags his T-shirt off the floor and hands it to me.

I put it on with a grateful smile at him.

"Why what?" I cut my French toast into tiny squares and take a bite. I can't help a moan of bliss from escaping as the rich flavors explode in my mouth. This is no IHOP French toast. It's fancy gourmet food, bursting with spices and ingredients I can't identify, but I know I've never had them in French toast before.

"Good, huh?" Adam says. "Why are you so uncomfortable being naked?"

I shrug and keep my eyes on my breakfast rather than him. "I just am. For lots of reasons."

He sighs and takes several bites. I can feel him thinking, processing. "You really won't tell me one single thing about yourself, will you?" he says eventually.

"It's not like that, Adam. I just...don't see the point." I swipe a chunk of French toast through syrup, wash it down with coffee.

Again he doesn't respond immediately. "There's no point in getting to know each other?"

"Not really." I finally look up at him. He's troubled, judging by the expression on his face. "I mean, it's not like you've told me much either."

Adam scrapes the last of the eggs into a pile. "What do you want to know?" He laughs, but there's no humor in it. "That you can't find with a quick Google search, I mean."

I groan in frustration and set my plate aside, empty except for the bacon, which I saved for last. "Adam, god. It's not about information. I'm sure you would tell me whatever I wanted to know. I'm not doubting that. And I'm not *hiding* anything."

"Then tell me anything. One fucking thing."

"Why?" I nibble at a slice of bacon. "What's the point? Let's not make this something it isn't, Adam."

He growls in irritation. "You keep saying that. 'What this is, what this isn't.' I thought we'd already gone over this."

"Adam. You don't have sex with someone you've known barely forty-eight hours and think it's gonna be a match made in heaven. Especially not when you're leaving. That's all I mean." I have to push away the disappointment I feel when he doesn't disagree.

"I've had a great time, Adam. You're amazing. This has been incredible. Honestly, the best two days of my life, and that's the truth. So thank you."

"So you're going to tell me you didn't feel…I'm not sure how to put it…a—a connection? Last night, you didn't feel that?" His eyes bore into mine, and I'm trying desperately to deny what I see there.

I have to protect myself. I can't go there with him. I can't let him know that I did feel it, that I *still* feel it. I can't get attached. Can't let my emotions out of their cage. So I lie, sort of. "I mean, maybe? I don't know. It was incredible sex, I felt *that*." Which is true, and I hope that came out casual. It's not as if I have anything to compare it to.

Adam stares at me for a long moment, his eyes piercing, demanding, and open. I see his emotions. I see that he felt something, just like I did. But it still means nothing. He's leaving, and I'll never see him again, so what's the point? I keep my eyes neutral. It takes every ounce of strength I possess to do so. I've got a lifetime of experience in burying my emotions to draw from, a lifetime of denying the pain of loneliness, the pain of a foster-father's fists or belt, the pain of never fitting, never belonging, of never having a real home. I know how to block everything out, how to pretend I'm unaffected. I know this like I know how to breathe, because it's what I do, what I've always done, what I'll always do. So I do it. I imagine a brick wall going up, brick by brick, around my heart, around my soul, around my emotions, and I build it high, build it strong.

After an eternity, Adam tosses back his coffee and sets the mug down on the side table with excessive gentleness, as if to combat the urge to smash it. And then he stands up, squares his shoulders, lets out a breath, and walks with stiff precision to the balcony, closing the door behind himself.

I stay where I am, still and silent and cold.

But I can't leave him like this. I can't walk out and let him think this meant nothing to me. I can't walk away yet, not when I can see the hurt in the slump of his shoulders as he leans his forearms on the railing of the balcony. It's a sunny, beautiful morning, no clouds in the sky today. A gull wings past the window, cawing. Adam is utterly still, his broad back a frozen sculpture of muscle and skin. I want to go out there, run my hands over his spine, over his shoulders. I want to kiss each vertebra of his spine. I want to feel his skin, slip my hands under the elastic of his shorts. I want one more moment with him.

My feet are carrying me out there. I'm unable to stop them, even though I know that whatever happens next, I'll still shut down, close him out. But I can't fight the momentum of my feet, can't stop my hands from pulling open the sliding door. Can't stop my palms from touching his sides.

"Change your mind?" He doesn't turn when he speaks.

My lips are pressed to the wide arc of his back, between his shoulder blades. *Yes,* I want to answer. But I can't lie to him. I haven't changed my mind, and if I speak, he'll know the truth. If he looks at me, he'll know. So I just touch him. Explore the bulk of his chest, palms moving in slow circles. He hangs his head, as if he knows I'm avoiding his question. Perhaps he doesn't. Of course he does. He's so smart, so perceptive. He can read me, somehow. He takes a deep, deep breath, his chest swelling.

The sound of a door opening alerts us that we're not alone. The balcony we're on is part of a shared structure. The floor extends across at least three or four rooms, each room's balcony made into a separate area by a pair of white, wooden, seven-foot-tall partitions that is part wall and part bench. If you stand at the rail, like we are now, you can see the other room's balcony. I hear voices, an elderly man and woman. They talk about how beautiful it is out here, how lovely the view is. The wood beneath our feet creaks as they move toward the railing.

Adam spins, pushes me backward, takes me by the shoulders and moves me toward the partition bench-wall. He turns me to face the wall, takes my wrists in his huge hands and presses my palms to the wood. His foot slips between mine and nudges my feet apart. His body is a mountain behind me, blocking out everything— the sun, the rippling blue of the Straits, the balcony. My heartbeat increases, begins to hammer in my ears. His hands slide up under the shirt. Touch my waist. His front presses against my back, and I can feel his heart thudding against my spine, feel his breath coming deep and fast, feel his cock thickening and rising against my ass.

His lips touch my ear. "Don't make a sound," he whispers. "Don't even breathe loud."

I nod, and feel dampness coat the inner walls of my vagina, feel heat curl in my belly. His palms slide over my stomach, up, up, and cup my boobs, lifting and caressing, thumbs scraping across my nipples. The heat and pressure tighten inside me. And then one hand dips down between my thighs, the other remaining at my tits, toying with one nipple and then the other. I have to bite my lip hard to keep from gasping, from moaning as he slides not one, but two fingers into my channel.

Those fingers, god…they drive in, smear my juices over my clit and circle and circle and circle, and I'm grinding my pussy against his touch, silently begging him to make me come. He knows, oh he *knows* exactly what I need, what I want, and he gives it to me. He doesn't draw it out, doesn't play games. He brings me to orgasm within seconds, and I taste the tangy salt of blood as I split my own lip in the effort to keep silent.

"Oh, my. Why didn't we come here sooner, Bob?" a shaky, elderly female voice says, mere inches away, just on the other side of the thin wooden wall. "It's just so lovely and pleasant."

"I don't know," the man says, his voice coming from the balcony's edge. "But we'll come again next year."

Adam's voice is a hot breath in my ear, barely audible. "Don't move."

And then he's gone from behind me, and I tilt my head to watch him carefully, silently slide the door open, step through and snag the square packet of a condom from the bedside table. I hold my position and watch him, pulse pounding, climax still tremoring inside me, keeping me breathless and shaking. He leaves the door open, standing just inside. His eyes find mine, and now he's making sure I'm watching. When he knows he has my full attention, he drops his shorts, baring his erect cock. It strains, juts high and proud. He rolls the condom down his length and takes cat-silent steps out onto the balcony, completely naked and fearless. When he's behind me, he drags his fingers up the backs of my thighs, over my ass, lifting the T-shirt as he goes. My ass is bared, then my breasts, and then he's guiding one of my arms out, then the other, and now I'm naked too. I shiver, not from the cold but from being nude in broad day-light, and I'm about to be fucked.

Adam leans into me, and his hands run over my shoulders, along my arms, to my hands. His fingers tangle in mine, my palms pressed against the wood, his palms against my knuckles. His chest is hot against my spine, and his cock is a thick, rubber-coated rod nestled between the globes of my ass. His breath heats my right shoulder, and then his lips touch the back of my neck.

"Ready?" The word is a warm thread tickling my earlobe.

I nod. It's all I can manage. I'm not breathing. I couldn't move a single muscle but for that incremental inclination of my head. I feel Adam dip, bending at the knees. He pushes his hips against my ass, and I feel the broad tip of his cock nudge against my clit. He rolls his hips, and I have to stifle a gasp. Another nudge, I have to hang my head and suck in as silent a breath as I can. And then he draws his hips back ever so slightly and pushes, and the head of his dick is spreading the lips of my pussy apart, and I'm angling myself to let him in, sinking down and pushing back.

My mouth falls open in a silent scream. He exhales in my ear as he slides his cock into me, inch by inch, until he's fully seated within me.

"Not a sound, Des," he whispers in my ear. I shake my head, and his teeth nip at my earlobe.

He pulls back and thrusts in, and I'm shaking all over, filled, spread apart, aching and burning and needing and replete. And then he drags my hands down the wall to bend me at the waist, and his fingers curl around my wrists and slide up my forearms, up my biceps, and then he's cupping my hanging, swaying tits as he pushes into me. There's no warning, just his cock driving into me with a sudden and punishing rhythm. He's careful, though, and every thrust is silent, not even the wet sound of joining giving us away.

Inches away, Bob and Martha quietly discuss their grandchildren, upcoming birthdays, their son and daughter-in-law's marital difficulties.

Tension in my core become unbearable, thick and hot and taut, and every drive of his dick into me makes it worse, or better, or something. Increases the fire's potency, tautens the wire coiled inside me, swells the balloon of pressure expanding in my sex. He holds my tits in place, uses them for leverage as he fucks into me hard but slow.

Then, abruptly, he buries himself deep and releases my tits, grabs my hips and pulls me backward. I'm forced to bend even further, so I have to press back into him and push against the wall with my hands to keep my balance. And now he's thrusting in even more slowly, gently, and his palms caress my ass, my back, the crease of my hips.

I have to suck in a breath, realizing I'd stopped breathing entirely for a few moments. I'm bent double, and he's driving into me. I'm motionless, taking what he's giving me and soaking up the ecstasy. I don't need to move, don't want to. I just want to let Adam do this to me, to take me.

But then the volcano within me rumbles and begins to detonate, and everything I thought I knew or wanted or needed is erased. All I want and need is to come, is to have him deeper, is to get him to keep going, keep fucking me. I want to say that to him, but I can't speak. I don't remember why not, but I know I can't. I'm breathing hard, and I hear a barely-audible whimper escape my lips.

Adam's hand goes across my mouth, muffling me. His other hand is at my hip, pulling at me, urging me. I move back into his thrusts, push, push, and I spread my legs farther apart. Adam's hand slides down my thigh, grips me at the knee, and lifts. I put my foot on the bench, straighten, and I feel Adam lift up on his toes behind me, thrusting hard. And in this position, he reaches so deep it's impossible to not whimper, but his hand is there quieting the sound. His foot goes up on the bench too, on the opposite side, and now he's thrusting and thrusting and his breath is raspy in my ear. One hand is on my tits, cupping one and then the other, massaging and kneading and tweaking nipples. His other slides over the inner thigh of my propped-up leg, touching the delicate, sensitive crease between thigh and labia, and then his fingers are rubbing at my clit and I'm gritting my teeth to keep silent, the climax spreading through me from the tips of my toes and tingling fingers to the sun-hot fires burning in my core, and I'm dipping at the knee, needing him harder and deeper.

I feel him rumble deep in his chest, and his breath catches, and his cock spasms inside me, his rhythm faltering, and he's coming with me, coming hard, his face burying in my neck, my hair a black mass between us and around his head and face, and he's still rubbing at my clit to make me come harder, or again, or still, or something, all I know is that I'm going supernova, being torn apart by the orgasm and he's fucking deep and hard and fast and his voice is murmuring quietly in my ear:

"You feel it, don't you? I know you do...*fuck,* Des, you have to feel this." He bites my shoulder; a sharp nip that I know is going to leave a mark. "Deny it if you want, but I know—I *know* you feel this connection."

I want to whimper, as much from the unerring truth of his words. I feel them like an arrow striking my secret heart.

"Don't make a sound, Des. Don't say a word." He's thrusting to the rhythm of his words, milking our orgasm even as he sends arrow after arrow of truth into me. "You don't need to. I feel you. I know you. Fuck, *fuck,* you're so incredible. I know you feel us. You do, don't you? Yeah, you feel it, you fucking feel us, Des."

We're both exhausted, shaking, tremoring from the orgasm, but he's still thrusting, and I'm so sensitive, so sore, aching from having taken him so hard, so many times, yet I can't get enough even though I'm so post-climax sensitive that it's unbearable.

And then he pulls out, sweeps me off my feet and into his arms, carries me into the room and lays me on the bed. I watch him strip the condom off and wrap it, discard it, close the sliding door, and then he's back on the bed, hovering over me. His mouth descends so slowly, so gently, and that almost breaks me, almost jerks the truth from me.

I feel us, Adam, I want to say. But I don't.

Because I'm afraid. Because I can't trust anyone.

Because anyone I've ever trusted has hurt me. Those I don't trust have hurt me, too. Everyone hurts me. It's inevitable. Home after home, foster parent after foster parent. I wanted to trust them, to love them, to belong, and they always turned on me, hurt me, betrayed me.

So I don't say a word. I just kiss him back and hope he can feel the regret and the buried emotions.

But the kiss doesn't end. He breaks it, his lips parting from mine, his breath on my mouth, and then he kisses my throat and my chest and my breasts, and I want him *again,* even though I know I've had all I can physically withstand.

His cock nuzzles my thigh. I can't help touching it, grasping it, and can't help caressing its marvelous length. I feel wonder course through me as it responds, and I watch between our bodies as it comes to life in my hand.

He kisses my nipples, and then gasps and looks at me. "What are you doing, Des?"

"I don't know."

"Again?" It's a suggestion.

I shake my head. "I can't…I want to, but I…can't. It's been…a long time and I'm…sore."

"Then what are you doing?"

I can only shrug. "I don't know."

He doesn't stop me, though. He remains on his hands and knees above me, and we both watch as I stroke him to life. He watches, and I watch, and my hand slips and slides, back and forth along his length. I rub my thumb over the head, and he flinches. I do it again, and again, stroke and rub the tip. He lifts his head, and his eyes meet mine.

I don't know why I'm doing this. I'd rather have him inside me, and I know he'd rather the same thing, but neither of us suggest this. He doesn't move, and I keep stroking.

"Des…" His voice is shaky, low and rumbling.

I keep my eyes on him, and I know that everything I'm feeling is shining out of my eyes. The conflict, the wish that I could say what he wants me to say, that I feel us, that I don't want him to go, that I want this to last forever, that I wish I could stop time and have this with him for days or weeks or months, that I want this to just *last,* and *last.* And I know the fear is there, the fear that I'm already attached and that I know he's going, and so am I.

I feel us. The thought bubbles at my lips.

He's arching his back and pushing into my touch ever so subtly. He's close. I want to watch this happen. I want to see it. His face is strained, his eyes hooded and dark.

He thrusts into my hand, and I feel him thicken and pulse in my palm. I slow my strokes and squeeze. He grunts in the back of his throat, and I feel him tense. I put both hands around his thickness and pump one hand near his base and the other at the head, and his eyes lock on mine and refuse to waver, not even blinking, and his mouth is open and he's gasping, moving only his hips now.

"Des…"

He's about to say something I can't lie to or not respond to, so I lift up and kiss him, but then he breaks it and we both watch as he comes. A stripe of white spurts from him and hits my stomach. He thrusts again, and another jet gushes out of him and this one lands hot and wet between my breasts. I keep stroking him, and more seed spurts out of him, dripping onto my skin.

So…much…come.

I like the way it looks against my skin, the wetness of it on me, the fact that I brought it out of him.

He's shaking, sucking in deep breaths, and I caress his length a few more times with one hand, and feel a few more drips on my belly, and then he flops onto the bed, gasping.

"Jesus, Des."

"Same thing," I say, using his own joke on him.

I glance down at my chest and belly, considering the white pool of Adam's come glistening and cooling on my skin. God, I wish I could stay. I wish he could stay. I want more of him. I don't want to be closed off and untrusting. I want to tell him things about myself.

I felt him touching my tattoos, and I feel an explanation in my mouth…

But he's *leaving*. He's going back to his Hollywood life, and if I open up now, it'll only hurt that much more.

So I get up and move into the bathroom. I feel his seed dripping down my body, and I wonder if I should feel ashamed for what I just did, the whole night, and just now. But I don't. I turn the water on and step in while it's still scalding.

I rinse him off me.

When I get out of the shower, he's dressed in dark blue jeans and a black T-shirt. He hands me a clean, folded pair of gym shorts and a T-shirt. "Figure maybe you'd rather wear these home, instead of the dress."

Saving me the walk of shame, basically. So fucking considerate. Damn him. I take them, and put on my bra and underwear, then the shorts and T-shirt. He even lets me wear his sports sandals instead of my heels. My dress and shoes go in a bag, and he walks me in silence to the elevator, and we ride down to the lobby. Eyes go to me, and then away. If it's obvious that I spent the night with him, the gazes don't give it away. I don't feel shame. I only feel regret that this had to feel like so much more, when it couldn't ever be more than just one night.

A carriage taxi waits, and Adam hands me up, and sits beside me. He hands a hundred-dollar bill to the driver. "Another one for you if you take just the two of us."

"Sounds good," he says, and snaps the reins. "Where to?"

Adam gives him my address, and the horses start to move forward.

The ride is long, and tense. Neither of us is willing to speak freely, especially not in front of the cab driver. We stop at my building, and Adam gets out, hands me down, walks me to my door.

"I'm leaving in a couple hours," Adam says. "Probably as soon as I can pack."

"I know."

Silence.

"Des....listen," he starts, then lets out a breath. His fingers touch my chin. "You know, there are so many things I want to say right now, but I'm not sure where to even start."

"This is what it was always going to be, Adam." I lean in to kiss him, and feel my heart contract, feel it close and go cold. "You're amazing. Last night was... and this morning...god. I don't even have words."

He seems to be fighting his own emotions, hunting for something to say. He touches his lips to mine, but this is a cold and passionless goodbye. "What's your number?" he asks.

Such a lie. It's not cold, or passionless. I'm just refusing to feel anything.

I can't quite look at him. "I don't have a number. I don't own a cell phone."

He seems puzzled by this. "You don't have a phone?"

I shake my head. "Nope. No point. No one to call. I see Ruthie every day, and she's...pretty much it. Plus, cell phones are expensive."

"So how am I supposed to find you?"

I sigh. "God, Adam…"

He lets out a breath and steps back, accepting that I'm pushing him away. Accepting, but angry. "Okay, Des. Fine. I get it." He steps backward again, hesitating, as if waiting for me to change my mind. I don't, and he wipes at his face with a hand. "Goodbye, then." He says this far too casually.

"'Bye, Adam."

My heart completes the process of calcification as he turns and climbs into the carriage without a backward glance.

CHAPTER EIGHT

Adam is gone, long gone. It's for the best. But god, does it hurt—it never stops hurting. I've still got a few days left on Mackinac Island and I can't wait to leave. I just want to get back to Detroit and to school and to the shit life I'm used to.

I don't cry, because I don't do that. And except for that stupid panic attack, I haven't cried in a long, long time. But that doesn't mean I'm not all sorts of fucked up. I sit on my bed and try not to think, not to remember, not to dwell. I completely fail at this. I'm still on my bed half an hour later, when I remember that it's Monday, and I have work in…an hour ago.

Shit.

I scramble into my uniform and run pell-mell across town to the office.

When I stumble, sweating, into Phil's office, he's surprised to see me. "Des? Ruth stopped by earlier this morning to say you were sick. What are you doing here?"

God bless Ruthie, covering my ass. I wipe at my face. "I—I'm feeling better."

Phil stares at me for a long moment, clearly sussing out the fact that something is wonky. Eventually he just shrugs. "Whatever. You're here. Might as well get to work." He gives me my assignment, and I set out.

I work hard, and when the shift is over, I work an extra hour to cover my tardiness this morning. And then I head to the stables and find Mack, the stable master.

Mack is a short, heavy, late middle-aged guy with a thick beard and gentle brown eyes. He's hard on stable hands and easy on the horses, but he loves me because I love the animals. "Hey there, Des," he mumbles, and hands me a manure rake. "Glad you're here. Far end could use some help."

"Sounds good." I exchange the combat boots I work in for a spare pair of muck boots Mack keeps around for me.

I muck out the empty stalls with a will, stopping by the stalls that have horses in them to pet their noses and murmur nonsense to them. I'm delaying. I don't want to go back to the dorm. I don't want to talk to Ruthie. I don't want to have to think about things.

So I work. I scoop horseshit and toss it in the wheelbarrow until it's full, and then dump it, and start over again. I muck until my hands are blistered and my muscles ache.

More than they already did, that is.

Mack shows up and stands by a stall a few feet away, watching me work. Muriel, a black and white seventeen-hand Clydesdale, sticks her head out into the hall and bumps Mack with her nose. When I finish the stall, Mack takes the wheelbarrow from me. "Get outta here, Des. Gotta leave something for the other hands to do, you know." He's gruff and taciturn, but he understands my need to stay busy, and he never questions me.

It's past sunset when I leave the stable and head back to the dorm. My hands throb, my back aches, and everything else is on fire. Ruthie is on her bed, reading on her Kindle. She sets her Kindle down when I come in, and stares at me expectantly. I ignore her, changing out of my jumpsuit and into a pair of shorts.

Which, belatedly, I realize, are the pair Adam left me. I sniffle, and Ruthie continues to stare at me.

"Des. Out with it already."

I continue to ignore her as I make a mug of tea. Finally, I sit at the foot of her bed and lean back against the wall. "I don't want to talk about it."

She snorts. "No shit. You don't ever want to talk about anything. But…you gotta give me *some*thing. I mean, Jesus. I turn around and Adam fucking Trenton is standing there, asking for you. Add that to how shell-shocked you looked the night before…something happened to you, and he has something to do with it, and then you don't come home last night, and now you're here at…nine o'clock the next night, and you look like hell. So I say again, out with it, bitch."

I pluck at the soft, slinky fabric of Adam's shorts and hate how much I love that they smell like him. The shirt even more so. "I met Dylan Vale last night."

Her eyes narrow. "Do not try to distract me. You'll tell me EVERYTHING about that once you've told me why Adam Trenton was here, and why you're wearing his clothes, and where you were last night."

The only person on earth who knows I am—or *was*—a virgin, is Ruthie, and not even she knows the full reason why, although I think she suspects the truth. I shrug. "I was with Adam last night." I trace my finger up and down my thigh and refuse to look at Ruthie.

"With Adam." I feel her processing all the possible meanings, and then she sits up, scoots toward me, and takes my face in her hands, forcing me to finally look at her. "And when you say 'with Adam' you don't mean *with Adam,* do you?"

I just stare at her for a moment, and then pull my face out of her hands. "Maybe," I mumble.

"You lost your virginity to Adam Trenton?" she all but shrieks, and then claps her hand over her mouth. "Des! What the fuck? Have you lost your mind? What were you thinking? Holy shit. Holy shit. What were you thinking?"

"Ruthie, Jesus Christ woman, calm down."

She bounces on the bed. "Calm down? Calm down? How the hell do you expect me to calm down? How did this happen? *Why* did this happen? What was it like? Speak, woman, speak!"

I clear my throat. "If you'll shut the fuck up for five seconds, I'll tell you what I can." I take a deep breath and let it out. "I met him the other day. Friday. He was on a carriage tour, and he saw me, and for reasons I can't pretend to understand, decided to jump off and come talk to me..." I tell her about the fudge and the ensuing visit to the bar, and the storm, and the church, and making out with him, and the panic attack. When I get to him showing up and taking me to the gala, Ruth freaks out again.

"Wait. Waitwaitwait. He took you to THE PARTY? Like the huge Hollywood event everyone at the hotel has been talking about ALL FUCKING

SUMMER? Adam Trenton. *The* Adam Trenton. Took YOU…to the gala?"

I shrug miserably. "Maybe? Yes. Okay? Yes, he did. I didn't know it was going to be like that. Jesus, I thought it was going to be…I don't even know. I don't *KNOW* what I was thinking." I thunk my head back against the wall hard enough that it hurts. "Ow."

"Holy fucking shit, Des."

"Yeah."

"Did they take your picture?"

I laugh sarcastically. "Only about a million times." I grin at her. "Now do you want to hear about Dylan Vale?"

"You really met Dylan Vale? Like in actual real life? You spoke to him?"

My grin turns evil. "Spoke to him? I slow danced with him."

Ruth stops breathing and waves her hands at her face. Why, I'm not sure. Eventually she gasps out a question. "Slow…slow danced? With *my* Dylan?"

I shrug. "Well, from what I could see, he belongs more to Rose Garret. But yeah, that Dylan. It wasn't a big deal. I mean, he *was* every bit as hot as you keep telling me, plus maybe even a little hotter. But he was total nerd. He spent the entire dance telling me about the show, how it was HIS idea and how the producers had to beg him to read for the lead role, blah, blah, blah. You would have loved it, but it bored me to tears. I couldn't care less about that show. But he was pretty fucking cute." I twist a lock of hair in my fingers and look away. "Nowhere near as hot as Adam, but…still."

Ruthie can't quite breathe yet. "Jesus, Des. I'm so jealous I don't think I can be friends with you for a few minutes."

She gets up and rummages in our little freezer, pulls out a fifth of Absolut. She sits down on the bed with it, unscrews the cap, and takes a long chug directly from the bottle. She swallows, hisses, and hands it to me. I regard the bottle for a moment. I'm not a hard drinker most of the time, but this is a situation that calls for vodka straight from the bottle. I take a swig and chase it with my tea.

Ruthie takes my mug from me and steals a drink, then hands it back. "Dylan Vale aside—and you know I'm serious now, because Dylan is literally EVERYTHING—what *happened,* Des?"

I'm dizzy now. "We fucked."

"Unpack that a little, sweets."

"I wasn't going to. I had a panic attack, for god's sake. But…he's just incredible, Ruth. I couldn't not. I *tried*. But he kissed me, and I lost all sense. He's sweet, and yet he doesn't take no for an answer, and that's just incredible. I mean, when I freaked out, he held me and didn't ask what happened. He made me tea and held me, and then took me home. No questions asked. And then after the party, I just…I *wanted* him, Ruthie. I wanted him so bad. And I didn't want to be a virgin anymore. I didn't want to be afraid anymore, you know?"

Ruth takes a long time to answer. "Yeah. I do. I really, really do." She takes another smaller sip and hands me the bottle. "Does he know?"

I shake my head. "I didn't tell him anything. I mean, how do you explain that? Am I just supposed to stop him in the middle of the most amazing foreplay that's ever happened and just be like 'hey, by the way, I'm a virgin?'"

"Yes, Des, you are, if necessary. That's not something you can just not tell a guy. That's a big deal."

I groan and take a drink, and let the warmth spread through me. "Exactly. And I didn't want it to be a big deal. I just wanted him to want me, and to go with it. I would have chickened out if I'd told him. And he probably wouldn't have kept going if I'd told him."

She shrugs and nods at the same time. "I guess I get that. I still think it's shady as fuck, and I'd be pissed if I was him, but I get it. So are you going to tell him?"

I shake my head. "Nope. He's long gone."

She's sitting beside me, sideways on the bed, our heads against the wall and our feet hanging off the edge of the mattress. She rotates her head to stare at me. "He's gone? Where'd he go?"

"He was only here for the weekend. He's back to wherever they're filming his movie. Some studio in L.A., I'd imagine."

"So, let me get this straight: you gave your virginity to *the* Adam Trenton in a one-night stand, and he doesn't know it?"

I nod. "That's about right."

"Are you going to see him again?"

I shake my head. "How? He'll never come back to Michigan, and even if he did, how would he find me, or me him? And why? It was just a…one-time thing. I know it, he knows it. The end."

Ruthie, even though she's clearly starting to feel the vodka, looks at me far too perceptively. "You're a shitty liar, Des Ross. You *like* him. You're upset. You wouldn't be drinking all my fucking vodka if you weren't all kinds of messed up over this."

I'm suddenly too drunk to argue. Thank god for that. At least now I can stop missing Adam for a few minutes.

I take the bottle of vodka and drink even more, until Ruthie snatches it from me and stumbles to the freezer and puts it away. "You're a lightweight, babe. Gonna be sick if you keep that up."

Babe. Adam called me babe. That was his thing. 'Babe' this and 'babe' that. I liked it.

No more babe.

"Don' call me babe," I slur.

"He call you that?"

I nod, and I can't quite figure out why I'm horizontal, or why my pillow smells like Ruthie's shampoo. Ruthie pats me on the head, and I realize I'm lying across her lap. She holds me, strokes my hair, and now I'm wondering why her lap is wet. "It's gonna be okay, Des. You'll be fine. Hush, sweetie. It's okay."

Oh.

I'm crying.

Damn it.

The ferry ride back to the mainland is the longest boat trip of my life. And it's followed by the quietest, longest, and most awkward car ride of my life. I'm in the back of a massive black Navigator with Gareth and Ruth, and we're on our way back downstate. Back to filming. Back to life.

Eventually, after approximately three hours of tense silence, Rose groans in frustration. "Jesus, Adam. What the hell happened to you? You're acting like somebody shit in your Wheaties."

I can't help but laugh. "Wow, Rose. Quite a turn of phrase there."

"Well, it's true."

Gareth has dozed off in the front seat, and Oliver, the driver, is talking to someone via a Bluetooth headset.

I stare out the window for a long moment before answering. "Just...things didn't go the way I expected."

"With that girl? What was her name? Des?"

I nod. "Yeah. Des."

She pats my arm. "Well, it's not like you have time for that kind of thing right now anyway. But I'm not sure you did that poor girl any favors by putting her in the spotlight like that. She's gonna get attention, and I'm not sure she's ready for it."

"Not much I can do now, is there?"

"No. I guess not." She leaves it there for a moment, and then snorts. "I mean, if that's how it is for you, then that's how it is."

I turn to stare at her. "What the hell's that mean?"

She shrugs. "Nothing."

I roll my eyes. "I'm not in the mood for fucking games, Rose."

"There's always something you can do, you big dumbass. You want her, you do something about it."

"It's not always that simple."

She shrugs. "Of course not. When was the last time anything was simple?"

"She made herself pretty clear: One night, and that was it."

"But?"

I turn back to staring out the window. "But...it feels like she's the one that got away."

"If that's what she wants, then you gotta respect it." Rose sweeps a hand through her loose blond hair. "But then, sometimes, we women tell ourselves and act like we want one thing, when really, deep down, we want something different and we're just… unwilling for whatever reason to let ourselves have it. Usually because we're afraid of one thing or another."

"Well that clarifies things. Thanks, Rose."

She slaps my knee. "No problem."

CHAPTER NINE

"Um. Des?" This is Ruthie, speaking from her spot curled up in the corner of the couch in our Detroit apartment. We just got back to Detroit last night and I never thought I would say this, but I'm glad to be here. I had one more week on Mackinac Island after Adam left—and it was one of the longest weeks ever.

I don't look up from my book. "What?"

"You need to see this." When I don't answer, she gets up and slams her three-year-old ASUS down onto my lap. "Des. You *need* to see this, right *now*."

It takes a moment to register what I'm seeing. It's an article in some celebrity gossip magazine.

There are photographs…

Of me.

With Adam.

I look hot.

Adam's hot new flame? the headline reads. And by headline, I mean huge, bold letters across the top of the website, like size one hundred font. Accompanied by photograph after photograph. A close-up of Adam and me holding hands. His lips at my ear, whispering something to me. His arm around my waist. Us slow dancing...me with a look of utter rapture on my face.

"You're in *Entertainment Now,* Des." She's stepping into flip-flops and snagging her purse off the counter. "I gotta go and get a hard copy of this."

I sit in shock as she vanishes out the door. I skim the text, but it's the usual conjecture:

Action movie heartthrob Adam Trenton was recently photographed at a charity dinner with a mysterious new love interest. The pair refused to comment to our on-scene reporters, but sources say they were spotted together more than once over the weekend. Adam, who rumors say is filming a sequel to last-year's box-office smash Fulcrum, *hasn't been spotted with anyone since he and* Garden of Evil *star Emma Hayes split early this year amid a swirl of volatile rumors. His new love interest isn't anyone we recognize, but if these photographs do her any justice, something tells us we'll be seeing more of her—and soon.*

And, at the bottom of the article, a long-distance photograph of me climbing into the carriage outside the Grand Hotel. Wearing what are clearly Adam's clothes.

Shit. Shit.

Shit.

Ruthie sweeps back into the apartment, a glossy magazine in her hand. She's staring at the article even as she sits down on the couch beside me. "Holy shit, Des!" She shoves the magazine into my hands. "This is incredible! Perez Hilton is blogging about you, girl! This is huge. HUGE."

"Hugely *bad,* Ruthie."

She stares at me in bafflement. "Des. You spent the weekend with one of the most eligible and sought-after bachelors *ever.* When he and Emma were official, the female population of the world went nuts. And when he and Emma broke up, they went even crazier. And now that he's been seen with a new girl, things are going to go even crazier yet, especially since you're a mystery to everyone. No one knows who you are or where you came from, and believe me, sweetie, they're gonna find out."

She grabs my hands in both of hers and squeezes hard. "What the *fuck* were you thinking? You are seriously the world's most private individual, and you let yourself get photographed at an über-exclusive A-list charity dinner? And this?" She taps the final image of me in Adam's clothes. "That's like, *obviously* a morning-after shot. You look sexy and gorgeous, in an I-just-spent-the-night-fucking sort of way."

I bury my face in my hands. "What am I going to do?"

She shrugs. "Baby doll, I don't even know."

"I didn't know any of this would happen. I—god, I didn't know."

Ruth is in the kitchen mixing a pitcher of margaritas, which she is spectacularly amazing at making. "Good thing is, you don't have a phone number and you're not on the lease for the apartment. So finding you is going to be pretty damn near impossible. I think. I mean, for one thing, you look *nothing* like your normal self in those photographs. Not that you're not beautiful normally, but Des, hon, you've been holding out on me. I had no idea you could clean up that good!"

I accept a margarita in a juice glass, since we don't have actual margarita glasses. "I didn't know either. I mean, I didn't do anything special. I barely put any makeup on! God. If I'd known what he was taking me to, I wouldn't have gone. I mean, it wasn't just Adam and Dylan there. I met Gareth Thomas, Rose Garret, Lawrence Bradford, Amy Jones…I mean, there were some insanely famous people there…and me." I let out a shaky breath. "Rose cornered me in the bathroom at the dinner and she warned me this would happen."

Ruth gives me a sour expression. "Listen to yourself. Talking about *Rose* like she's your buddy. This is Rose fucking Garret, Des. God."

I down the margarita, which is *strong*. "You think I don't realize how surreal all this is? It all feels like a dream. I don't know what else to say, Ruth."

She refills my glass and sits beside me again. "You miss him, don't you?"

"I barely know him. I spent all of…not even two full days with him."

"But…" she pauses to sip and swallow, "you still miss him."

I rest the glass against my forehead. "Yeah. I try not to. Try not to think about him. About that night. But it's impossible not to." I twist my head to meet Ruthie's eyes. "I don't think I'll ever be able to forget that night."

"How could you? That was like…a once in a lifetime thing."

I can't help wishing it was a lifetime thing, and not *once* in a lifetime.

The next day I'm leaving my last class of the day at Wayne State, waiting for the bus that will take me to U of D for my janitor shift. I've got ear buds in and I'm spaced out, tired, not wanting to go to work. I feel a tap on my shoulder, pull out an ear bud and turn to face the person who tapped me. He's a few years older than me, attired in a pair of tight dark blue jeans with the cuffs rolled up to his ankles above a pair of shiny, calf-high, unlaced combat boots. He's wearing a white button-down with a bright purple scarf tied around his neck like a cravat, and a black coat that reminds me of something a Civil War officer might wear, brass buttons and a flaring hem. His hair is blond and slicked to one side, and he's got mascaraed eyelashes, blushed cheekbones, and nails painted the same color as his scarf.

He's gorgeous, in a *fabulous* sort of way.

"Are you Des?" he asks, and if there was any doubt, his voice gives away his sexual alignment.

I keep my expression carefully blank. "Who's asking?"

He hands me a business card:

Thom Rayburn, talent acquisitions

The Sidney Weaver Agency

12345 Fifth Avenue, New York, New York

212-555-6789

My first thought is whether his name is pronounced "Tom" or "Th-om." Second, what does he want with me?

I blink at him, and then hand his card back. "Not interested."

He laughs. "You haven't even heard what I'm offering, Des."

"Still not interested."

"Have you ever heard of The Sidney Weaver Agency?" He moves to stand beside me.

The bus arrives in a squeal of brakes and a cloud of diesel fumes, and Thom boards ahead of me, and pays for two tickets. "What the hell do you want, Thom?" I pronounce it *Tom,* guessing that no one, no matter how gay, would go by *Th-om*. "And why did you pay for my ticket?"

"Sit down, sweetie, and I'll tell you what I want." He waves impatiently at an open pair of seats near the front. I slide in, and he moves in beside me. He smells like expensive cologne and faintly of marijuana. "Since you didn't answer my question, I'm going to assume you aren't familiar with the agency. We are *the* premier modeling agency. We represent all of the most successful and talented models in the world. And Des? We want you. We saw those photos from the gala on Mackinac Island, and honey, you looked *incredible*."

I snort derisively. "I may not know your agency, but I do know models are supposed be size negative two, okay? And I also know I'll never be that skinny. So you're barking up the wrong tree, *sweetie*."

"Negative two. That's funny." He pulls an electronic cigarette from his coat pocket and sucks on it, making the tip glow blue, and then blows out a cloud of odorless smoke. "For real, though. Haven't you ever heard of plus size modeling?"

"So now I'm plus size?" My voice is dangerously even.

He has the decency to blush slightly. "*I'm* not labeling you anything, hon, that's just what the industry calls it. And they need talent." He takes another puff of the e-cig, and then puts it back in his pocket. "You know how many calls we got asking about you after those photos went up? Guess. I want you to guess."

I shake my head. "Four?"

He snorts. "Try two hundred. And that was just the first day. All of them wanted to know if we represented you, and if not, how soon we could get you. Cacique, Torrid, Lane Bryant, Michael Kors, Betsy Johnson…they all want you. Which means *we* want you."

Modeling? Me?

I don't answer right away. "I don't know anything about being a model." I glance at him. "Plus, I've watched TV, okay? I've heard about the modeling industry, and how brutal it is. I've got zero interest in signing some contract that makes me an indentured servant."

Thom looks aghast. "Des. *Des.* We're not that kind of agency. God, I've never been so insulted in my life. Those kinds of contracts come from…god, they're little better than fucking charnel houses, okay? We represent *talent*. Beauty. Class. And we can train you. That's what we do."

"I have tattoos."

He blows a raspberry with his lips. "Um, Photoshop, *duh*. Not to make you look less like you, of course, but that's the kind of thing we use it for. Cover up tattoos and blemishes."

I pinch the extra flesh at my stomach between finger and thumb. "Yeah, blemishes." I look away.

Thom shakes his head and looks sad. "God, you've had a rough time of it, haven't you? You're beautiful, Des. For real. Have you met me? Obviously I know what I'm talking about, right? My job is to find beautiful people and put them in front of a camera. I wouldn't be here on this—" he lowers his voice and whispers in my ear, "very, *very* dirty bus in the middle of Detroit, if you weren't what we represent."

"Thanks, Thom. That's nice of you to say. But all that aside, I've got a career plan. The semester is about to start. I can't just leave."

"A career plan, huh?" He eyes me, long, thick lashes touching his cheeks. "That's good. Great. I'm sure you've worked your ass off to get where you are. But honey, think about this for one second. Really think. This is a once in a lifetime opportunity to get out of Detroit, to do something *different,* something *exciting*. You weren't even posing in those pictures, you were wearing like, *no* makeup and your hair was great, but obviously done by you. And that dress? Honey, think about how amazing you could look in a couture gown, with professional hair and makeup. You have the kind of face, hair, and body that could sell mad copy, okay? I'm serious."

"Thom—"

He takes my hand. "Des, this is coming from one fabulous bitch to another: You've got it going *on,* and you have to capitalize. People want you *now*. School will wait. Your career will wait. This opportunity? It won't wait. You're relevant *now*. I've got work for you *now*. In a month or two or three, they'll have moved on, found someone else. You need to let me get you in front of a camera now. Not tomorrow or next year, but *now,* while they want your look."

"Wow, Thom. You're a *really* good salesman, you know that?"

He grins at me. "Sweetie, I didn't get where I am in my career by sucking." He pauses and puts an index finger to his lips. "Well, on second thought, that may not be *entirely* true…"

I color scarlet. "Oh my god."

He laughs. "I'm only kidding…or am I?" He holds up his hands when I open my mouth. "For real, though. This isn't just a sales pitch, Des. I'm serious." He hands me his card again. "Google us. Think about it. Talk to your friends. And when you come to a decision, call me. But don't wait too long, okay?"

"I'll think about it," I tell him.

"Come to New York, Des. You won't regret it."

The bus squeals to a stop, and Thom gets off. I watch him as he coughs and waves a hand in front of his face to clear the diesel fumes. He gets into a black car that apparently had been following the bus, and then he's gone.

The rest of the way to my stop, I stare at the business card.

All through my shift cleaning classrooms, I think about the card in my purse and what it represents.

All the way home, I think about Thom, and wonder if I could do it.

Ruthie is watching the latest episode of *Orange is the New Black* on her laptop when I come in. I pull Thom's card from my purse and set it on her keyboard.

She pauses her show and examines the card. "What's this?"

"This guy followed me halfway to work today. He claims that a modeling agency wants me to move to New York and be a model."

Ruth gapes at me. "A model?"

I shrug. "That's what he said. A plus size clothing model." I hate even saying that phrase; I am who I am, and fuck labels.

She brings up her browser and types in the name of the agency. I sit down and watch as she scrolls through the results. After a few minutes, she turns to me. "They look legit. I've seen some of these models before."

"But...I mean, me? A model? I don't even know what to think."

She shrugs. "Does it sound interesting to you? You've watched *America's Next Top Model* with me. You know how they portray the business."

"I don't know," I say. "I mean, part of me wonders. Having all those questions shouted at me, that was rough. But actually having my picture taken... that was fine. I mean, not the walk of shame picture, which sucked. But...I don't know. Part of me wants to at least try it, you know?"

"You'd really move to New York? Put your master's degree on hold, leave Detroit, leave me?" She closes her laptop and traces the logo on the top cover. "Look, Des. I want you to be happy. You're my best friend. And if you go, I'll be happy for you, if that's what you want. I just...I mean, I'd miss you. But... this is a big step. And it doesn't seem like...you."

"I've never felt beautiful before, Ruth. I've learned to love myself, to accept the way I'm built and to rock what I've got the best I can. But that's not the same as feeling truly *beautiful*. And I felt that way with Adam, and at the dinner. And Thom, the guy I met today, he made me feel the same way. And I mean, what do I have to lose? My loans and scholarships can be put on hold, right? This is the kind of thing that may never come along again. If I finish my master's and get a job, I'll probably never leave Michigan. That'll be it. This is my chance to…do something. To maybe be something other than what I've always been. Does that make any sense?"

She nods. "Yeah, it does. I get it. I really do." She smiles at me, but it's a sad smile. "Better give him a call, then, huh?" She hands me her cell phone.

I dial the number on the card. It rings once, twice, three times, four, and then there's Thom's voice on the other end. "This is Thom."

"Hi, um, this is Des."

There's a lot of background noise, shouts and laughter and music, and then a door closing and it all is muffled into silence. "Des, hi. You coming to New York with me or what?"

"Yeah. I think I am."

"You're making the right choice, Des. Give me your address and I'll pick you up Wednesday afternoon."

"This Wednesday?" My voice is thin and shaky. Today is Monday; I've been home from my summer job for less than a week.

"I knew you'd say yes, so I called Sidney and she's already scheduled your first shoot for next week. We've got a lot of work to do in the meantime, sweetie. Gotta get you ready for your modeling debut."

"Is there a contract or anything?"

"Oh, sure there is. But I'll explain all that to you when we get to Manhattan. Sidney, Rochelle, and I'll go through the whole thing from start to finish and explain it to you step-by-step, clause-by-clause. You've also got about a thousand appointments with beauticians and stylists and all sorts of things, plus Sidney wants to meet you, and then there are head-shots, and…just a bunch of fun things to do. For now, get packing. I'll see you Wednesday."

And then the line is dead, and my head is spinning.

I'm going to be a model…in New York.

Gareth is pissed as hell at me, but I don't even care. We're supposed to be leaving for London tomorrow, and I'm in Detroit right now. We finished the studio portion of filming, and now we're doing the location shoots. London, Prague, and then Tokyo. I'm supposed to be with the rest of the cast, supposed to be doing the cold read-throughs. But instead, I'm in the registration office of Wayne State University, trying to hunt down a particular black-haired beauty.

I've spent the month since the charity dinner trying to act like I've moved on from Des, but I can't fool even myself. I keep thinking about her, dreaming about her. Even Gareth noticed something has been off with me, and he's typically oblivious to pretty much everything unless it's film-related.

Rose finally dragged me offset and took me out for drinks and told me—in so many words—to quit being a fucking pussy and go find her.

So here I am.

"Can I help you?" The woman behind the counter is older, with graying brown hair and tired eyes. She doesn't seem to recognize me.

"Hi. I'm trying to find a friend of mine who I think is a student here."

"Name?"

"Des. Des Ross."

She taps at the keyboard for a few seconds. "She's not registered. I have her in our system, but it doesn't look like she's registered for classes this semester."

"Do you have an address or phone number you could give me?"

The woman peers at me over the rims of her reading glasses. "I'm sorry, I don't, and even if I did, I couldn't give that information out to you." She squints. "Do I know you?"

Am I above using my fame to find Des? Hell no. "You might," I say, wanting her to recognize me but not wanting to make a scene.

She taps her finger on the desk, and I can see her putting two and two together. "I do. My grandson dragged me to some shoot-em-up movie. Was that you?"

"It may have been. I've done some acting." I lean close, crossing my arms on the desk and whispering conspiratorially. "Look, ma'am. This is important. Des and I...lost touch, and I'm trying desperately to find her. Is there anything you can do to help me?"

The woman clicks her mouse, types something into the keyboard, glancing at me every once in a while. After a moment, I hear a printer whirring, and she stretches to grab the sheet of paper that spits out. She grabs a pen from a cup, and slides the pen and paper toward me; I take it, seeing that she's printed out a promo shot of me from *Fulcrum*.

"What's your grandson's name?"

"Dan."

I scrawl in the white border above the picture: *Dan, you have an awesome grandma. Thanks for watching!* And then I sign my name, large and messy, above my head. I hand her the picture, and she reads the note, and then gives me a look that is equal parts sour, amused, and flattered.

"Well, Mr. Trenton. Do you know Ruth Nicholson?"

"Yeah, I met her once."

"Well, if you wait outside room A-one-thirteen, a class will be letting out in...fifteen minutes. Ruth might be able to help you."

I thank her and leave the registration office. It takes me most of the next fifteen minutes just to find the room, and then I wait at the end of the hallway, my Chargers ball cap pulled low over my face, a pair of wide aviators over my eyes. It's the look that I call "celebrity incognito," meaning that it doesn't actually ever fool anyone if they bother to look right at you, but it makes you feel like you're at least trying to go unnoticed.

I only wait a few minutes, and then a door opens and students file out, most of them chatting in pairs or singly and staring at their cell phones. A few glance at me, and only one kid seems to recognize me. I give him a slight shake of my head, and he grins at me and keeps walking. And then I see Ruth. She's walking beside a young, good-looking Asian guy wearing a Tigers cap, and neither of them notice me.

They're about to pass by when I snag Ruth's sleeve. "Ruth. Got a second?"

She halts and stares at me, and her eyes go wide, but she recovers quickly and turns to her friend. "Hoang, I'll catch up to you, okay?" She inclines her head toward the exit leading outside. I follow her, and she pulls me around the corner into an alcove, lights up a cigarette, and stares at me. "Well, well, well. If it isn't Adam Trenton."

"Hi, Ruth. How are you?"

"Peachy. What do you want?" She's got her arms crossed over her chest, one hand lifting her cigarette every now and then. Her posture is closed and she's either angry or suspicious or both.

"Des."

She frowns at me and blows smoke past my face. "You let her go a month ago."

"Not by choice. She…I don't know how to even put it. She shut me out. Just closed down." I shove a hand in my pocket and scan the area around us, making sure there's no one taking pictures or noticing me. "I really like her. I wanted to…see where things could go, I guess, and she just wasn't having it. I let her go because it's what she seemed to want. But I can't get her out of my head. I need to find her. Where *is* she?"

"Gone."

I wait, but no more information is forthcoming. "Gone where?"

"Did you see the magazines?" She takes a drag and speaks around the smoke. "Reporters hit you guys up, hard. She was in a dozen different magazines."

I shake my head. "I don't read that shit. Never have, not before I got famous, and sure as hell not now. It's all lies and bullshit. Ninety-nine percent of it's as fictional as fucking *Star Wars*."

"Yeah, well, they still had pics of you two. Not just at the dinner, either. After. One where she was wearing your clothes the next morning."

"Shit."

"Yeah."

I let out a frustrated breath. "Did she get harassed or some shit?"

"No." Ruth is definitely guarding her friend's back. Good for her.

I step close to Ruth and uncurl my posture, standing straight and flexing to look bigger, more imposing. "Ruth. You're avoiding my question."

Her eyes widen and she tilts her head back, defiant and bold. "Yeah, I am. I don't know you, and I don't trust you."

"I remember our conversation, before you let me in, you know. I didn't hurt her. I was good to her. I took care of her."

Ruth smirks, and then it's gone, replaced by the same hardness. "Yeah, I'll say."

I roll my eyes. "You know what I mean, goddammit. Where is she?"

She contemplates my question, taking three long drags of her cigarette, and then she tosses the butt to the ground and steps on it. "She moved to New York."

"What? New York? Why?"

"Some modeling agency saw those photos of her and offered her a contract. She took it. She's gone, dude."

"Which agency?" My mind whirls. She's modeling?

"Sam Weaver or something like that. I don't know." Ruth hikes her backpack higher on her shoulders. "I gotta go."

"Hold on a second. What's her new address? I have to find her, Ruth."

She rubs at her lower lip with a thumb. "I don't have her address. She still doesn't have a phone either, to answer your next question. She calls me every couple days and we talk—and no, I don't know that number, it's unlisted. All I know is she's staying with a couple other models somewhere in Manhattan."

I think fast. I dig my Sharpie out of my pocket. "Have a scrap of paper?" Ruth pulls a notebook from her backpack and hands it to me. I write my name, phone number, and email address neatly on the top line and hand it back to her. "Next time she calls, tell her I'm looking for her. Give her that information."

"Okay, I'll let her know."

"And Ruth, I just have to say this: do not share that information with *anyone* except her. If I find out that you've spread my shit around, it will *not* go well for you, okay? I'm not trying to threaten you, but this is serious to me."

She nods. "I got it, dude. I wouldn't do something like that."

I lean in and give her a one-armed hug. "I know. You seem like a really cool chick, Ruth. Thanks."

She goes stiff. "Cool. Now get off me."

I back away. "See ya."

"Yeah, probably not. But I'll pass the message along. No promises, though."

The car I hired is waiting for me, and I slide in and ask him to take me to the Metro Airport. I have a first-class ticket on the next flight to London, which is for early the next morning, so I get a room at the airport hotel and wait.

The night is long, and the flight even longer.

A week of filming in London, two weeks in Prague, and another two weeks in Tokyo and no call, no email, no nothing.

I stop in Manhattan on the way back to L.A. from Tokyo, and spend two days looking for her. I try the modeling agency, which I'd heard of, but they stonewall me. The receptionist won't even tell me whether Des works for them or not. Short of causing a scene and possibly getting arrested, it's a dead end.

Finally, I go home to L.A. and begin the long, painful process of trying to forget her.

Again.

CHAPTER TEN

"Good! Good! Now turn this way. Great. One more. And now try to look aloof—pretend you're too important for this shit. Good, perfect. Now turn away and look at me over your shoulder. No, don't smile, just…look at me. No expression. YES!" The photographer spews a non-stop stream of instructions, encouragement, and sometimes meaningless babble, just signifier words like *stellar* and *fantabulous*.

I'm standing in front of an exposed brick wall in an old warehouse somewhere in the far lower end of Manhattan, wearing a tight pair of jeans and a flowing, low-cut top. There's a huge industrial fan blowing from my left, making me look windblown. There are a dozen people all milling behind the photographer, some of them the photographer's assistants, others for hair and makeup, and others from the clothing line. And there's Rochelle, a glamorously beautiful woman about thirty years old with straight, fine blonde hair hanging just past her shoulders and hard, intelligent brown eyes. She's always perfectly attired, usually in slim slacks of either black, brown, navy blue, or khaki, and tops of varying cut and color. She never wears dresses or skirts, and she never smiles. But she's hideously, frighteningly efficient at her job, which is getting models from one place to another, making sure they're ready for the shoot, and that they look their best. Since most of the models I've met are usually a little on the…flighty side, this can be a challenge.

She also acts, in some cases, as a buffer between the photographer and the model. Some of them are…yucky.

This guy, for instance. I can feel his gaze through the camera, feel his leering stare even though I refuse to look right at him, and refuse to interact with him any more than necessary. He's middle-aged and balding with a shoulder-length ponytail, weak blue eyes, and a potbelly. But, apparently, he's one of the best photographers in the business, and I'm lucky to get him.

He'll make me look incredible…or so Rochelle and Sidney claim, at least.

I turn, pose, smile, don't smile, smolder, and look mysterious. And then I change outfits behind a screen, assisted by two girls no more than eighteen and a flamboyantly gay man with black hair going silver at the temples. And then I pose again, smile, and repeat the whole process over again. Change, repeat. Change, repeat. Hours, and hours, and hours. I've been at it since seven this morning, and I've had three bites of a Caesar salad and half a bottle of water since then, and it's now past six in the evening.

Judging by the rack of clothes, I've still got three or four outfits to go.

I stifle a sigh and change outfits yet again.

I hear Rochelle's phone ring—which happens at least once every ten minutes—and she pokes her head around the screen. "Des, I've got to step outside and take this. You okay here?"

I give her a thumbs-up as Mark tugs a tank top over my head and then drapes a short-sleeved button-down sweater over my shoulders. I stuff my arms through and step out of the jeans. At that moment the photographer, Ludovic, steps around the screen. He acts surprised, like he forgot where he was going, but I see his eyes rake over me, calculating, hungry. Mark shoos him away, and the shoot resumes.

Finally, after two more changes of clothes, I request a break.

Rochelle waves me away. "Ten minutes. Ludovic's time is more valuable than yours, dear."

Yeah, but Ludovic gets to sit down and smoke cigarettes while I change clothes, and while the stylists check my hair and makeup. I get to stand there and be tended to, not sitting, not eating, not drinking, not even given a moment to breathe.

Quickly I head outside, grabbing the clear plastic box that contains my six-hour-old salad and the half-empty bottle of warm water. It's all I've got till I get home, and I'm getting faint with hunger. I perch on an overturned milk crate around the corner and force the salad down my throat.

I feel him before I see him. "Here you are. I wondered where you'd went." Ludovic.

I glance up at him and offer a tight, small smile, hoping he'll go away.

He doesn't.

"You're a lovely girl, you know." He crouches beside me, his back to the wall, and lights a cigarette. His eyes flick sideways and rove up my body and then down. "With the right help, you could go places impossible for you, otherwise."

I ignore him and keep eating the flat, limp, disgusting salad.

"I'm doing a beach shoot next week. Down in Florida. I have spoken to Sidney about this, and she has arranged for you to be in the shoot. Many lovely girls, a big beach. A good time, I think." He eyes me again. "Bikini shoot. You…you will be the sexiest, no?"

I have to stop eating now and respond. "A beach shoot? Sidney didn't tell me about this. I'm not doing a beach shoot."

He smirks, and his eyes latch onto my cleavage. "She has not told you yet." His tongue slides across his lower lip, and he flicks the butt of his cigarette. "If you are nervous, perhaps we could do a…private shoot. Yes?" He grins suggestively.

I fight against the revolt of my stomach. "Let's just finish this shoot." I stand up and move toward the door.

He's in front of me, too close, and he reeks of cigarettes and body odor. His hand grabs mine, forces my hand against his crotch. "Be reasonable, beautiful Des. You help me, I help you." He leans close, his lips touch my neck. "I can make your career, you know. All you have to do is go with me, for drinks, and maybe some *dessert* in my apartment later. Yes?"

I back out of his reach, jerk my hand free, and suppress a shudder. I'm saved from having to respond by the appearance of Rochelle. "It's late and I have a date. Come on, Des. Quit holding me up." I don't argue, god no. I'm grateful she showed up, and something tells me she did so on purpose, judging by the way she floats between me and Ludovic and herds me inside. "Come *on,* Ludo. Let's go."

We finish the shoot and Ludo hovers as his assistants pack his gear. He glances at me, and even winks once when he thinks no one is looking. I change back into my own clothes quickly, and then grab Rochelle and pull her aside.

"Ludovic, he—"

"I know. He does that with all the models. He's a nasty old horn dog, that's all." Rochelle's phone trills and she pulls it from her purse, glances at it.

"Can he make trouble for me for refusing to go along with his offer?"

She shrugs. "Trouble? No, not unless you make a scene or do something stupid like outright insult him. Just avoid him and don't worry about it." She eyes me over the top of her phone. "He *does* have a lot of influence, though. He knows people. He can get you places…if he likes you. Just saying."

"Rochelle! I'm not going to—"

"And I'm not suggesting you do," she interrupts. "I'm merely informing you of the facts. Your job is to be a model. You've done that. What you do on your own time is your business."

I shudder and wipe at my neck where his nasty mouth touched me. "He said something about a beach shoot." I shake myself and grab my purse. "Do you know anything about that?"

"I don't know, let me find out." Rochelle types a text message, her fingers moving so lightning fast it seems impossible. I hear her phone buzz in her hands a few seconds later and she reads the message, then looks at me. "He did indeed book you for a beach shoot next week. A very exclusive group, from what Sid is telling me."

"I don't want to—"

Rochelle's eyes flick to me, hard as stone. "Refuse his advances, avoid his groping hands, whatever. I don't care. But you *don't* deny work. Not when it's Ludovic Perretti." She lowers the phone, indicating how serious she is. "He's a nasty old horny dirtbag and he'll try to fuck you if you'll let him, but he's the best damn photographer in the business."

"Okay, Rochelle. Okay. I get it."

She softens. "Good. Now go home. Tomorrow we find you a bikini."

My stomach twists into a knot and rises into my esophagus. A bikini? Hell to the fuck no.

But I don't have a choice, it seems. Not if I want to stay in New York and continue to get modeling work. Which is what I want, right?

I head home, grabbing a sandwich from a bodega on the way to the subway. It's not enough, but if I'm trying on bikinis tomorrow, I'd better go easy on the calorie intake. None of my roommates are home when I get there, so I take the opportunity to call Ruthie on the landline.

"Des, hey. How are you?"

I groan and flop into the beanbag on the floor beside the phone. "Tired. Hungry. And feeling violated."

"Violated? What happened?"

"The photographer at today's shoot, he propositioned me. Said he could further my career. For a price, obviously, and the price was very explicitly implied." I shudder, feeling his hands and lips all over again. "God, he's so nasty. And worse, he's basically forced me into working a beach shoot with him next week."

"A beach shoot? Won't that be fun, though?"

I snort. "Yeah, when was the last time you saw me in a bikini?"

"Oh."

"Exactly. Oh."

"How can he force you?"

I sigh. "Because he's 'the best photographer in the business'." I lower my voice to make the phrase into mockery. "You don't turn down work. You just don't."

"Will he try something again?"

"Without a doubt."

"So what are you going to do?" Ruth asks, a blender whirring in the background.

"Do the shoot and try not to let everyone see that I'm going to feel like a fucking whale wearing a stupid bikini."

"God, Des. Are you sure you're happy there?"

"No."

"I thought modeling was supposed to be...I don't know, good for your self-esteem?"

"I thought so, too. Only it's not. It's the opposite, if anything. Everyone else I work with is skinnier than me. More tan than me. Higher, tighter boobs than me. Better facial structure than me. Better at posing than me. More willing to suck off the photographers than me. And the unspoken but very real pressure to keep my weight down really does a fucking number on my psyche. No one's outright said in so many words 'Des, you have to lose five pounds.' Not yet, at least. What they do is measure me and weigh me and second-guess my food choices and cluck and tut when I have to wiggle myself into jeans so tight I feel like a stuffed motherfucking sausage. I just want some goddamned cheesecake, Ruthie! I'm in New York City and I haven't had one single piece of cheesecake. It's ridiculous. You know what I've eaten today? Limp, *warm* caesar salad, a small one at that, and a pre-made turkey and swiss sandwich. You know what I had yesterday? A handful of veggie sticks and half a bagel, no cream cheese."

"My god, Des. That's criminal."

"That's modeling."

"Well, fuck modeling."

"I can't quit now, Ruth. I've barely gotten my feet wet."

"You're miserable."

I don't know what to say. I hate it here, most days. It's loud, hectic, high-pressure, intense. And that's just New York. I'm hungry. I've been hungry since the day I landed at LaGuardia. I miss Ruth. I miss Detroit, as crazy as it sounds. I miss Mackinac Island.

I miss Adam.

Ruth is silent, and I know her so well I can tell she's got something to say but isn't sure how to start. "Just say it, Ruth."

I can hear her take a long sip of whatever she made in the blender, a piña colada or something delicious I'm sure. "There's no way to ease into this, so I'll just say it. Adam showed up at school."

"He—what? Adam? At Wayne State?"

"He was looking for you."

My head spins, and if I wasn't already sitting down, I'd have fallen down. "Holy shit. What did he—what did you tell him?"

"The truth. That you're modeling in New York, that I don't have an address or phone number for you." She's quiet again, and I wait for her. "He gave me his contact info to give to you."

"He did?"

"He looked…like he missed you, Des. Like he regretted letting you go."

"He didn't. I let *him* go."

"Why, Des? He seems really cool."

"How is that gonna work, Ruth? I follow him wherever he goes? Sit in some mansion in L.A., waiting for him to get back from filming? I barely know him, and he doesn't know me at all."

"It's called taking *risks,* Des. You should have given him a shot." She sighs, and she sounds frustrated, or disappointed, or just resigned. I can't tell which. "Do you want this info or not?"

"Yeah."

She rattles off Adam's information, and I write it down. We talk for a few more minutes and then hang up. I stay in the bizarrely comfortable yet hideously uncomfortable beanbag chair, staring at the numbers. I find myself writing his name above the phone number, circling it, underlining it.

But I don't call.

My reasoning is vague, even to me. Is it about not admitting that I was wrong? That I should have… what? That I should have handled things differently? Told him more about myself? Told him why I got the tattoos? What difference would any of that made?

So I don't call.

Not that day, or the rest of that week.

I spend a few days trying on bathing suits, and it goes as well as could be expected. Sidney frowns, and Rochelle's plucked and waxed eyebrows lower in consternation. They hand me bikini after bikini, and reject each and every one. Finally, they settle on two. One is a bandeau top and boy short bottoms in basic black, the other a red and orange swirl design in a halter-top and a high-waisted bottom.

And let me just say, even wearing those standing in front of Sidney and Rochelle was hard for me. I squirmed, fidgeted, adjusted the halter-top, played with the bandeau strap, and tried gamely not to pluck at the wedgie the high-waisted bottom gave me.

And then Sidney dropped the bomb. "These are good, Des. As good as they're going to get, at least." Her hazel eyes fixed on me, and she trailed a hand through her expensively-dyed red hair. "You really need to drop a few pounds, though. If you could manage that, the suits would fit just that much better. You have…what…four more days? Even three or four pounds would make all the difference."

My face went red from equal parts of anger and embarrassment. "Sidney, I—"

She held up a hand, palm face-out to me. "I hate having to say that. I really do. You think anyone wants to hear that? You know how many times I heard that, when I was modeling? 'Five more pounds, Sidney.' At least once a week, I heard it. It hurts, I know it does. And I'm sorry. But it's the business." She waved a hand at me, dismissing me. "You can do it. I'm sure you can."

I leave the office with a small bag containing the bikinis, and a heart full of hurt and anger.

I swallow it, and spend the next four days barely eating, walking faster, taking stairs. I try on the bikinis every morning, and every night, and see that, yes, as I shed two pounds, and then three, and then four, they do fit slightly better. My cleavage is accentuated when the rest of me is slightly more…streamlined.

But I'm so hungry.

And the anger percolates in me, deep down.

Florida is hot and humid. We spend a good portion of the first day choosing a location, which means hiking up and down the beach, hunting for exactly the perfect location. Each spot looks the same to me: hotels and restaurants and resorts on one side, sand and the sea on the other, as far the eye can see in both directions. But Ludovic seems to be looking for something specific, so we all follow him here and there like stupid little ducks trailing after their mama.

And then he chooses a stretch of sand exactly like all the others, nods, and announces that this is *it*. His crew scrambles to set up reflectors and all the other gear. Hair and makeup start dabbing and brushing and twisting, and we're peeling off our cover-ups. The other girls all do so easily, confidently. They toss their wraps to the sand and adjust straps and bikini lines, and strut around happily, chattering to each other and kicking at the surf, giggling. A crowd is gathering, watching, and I find myself hesitating. But I can't hesitate. I untie the front of my cover-up and shrug out of it and focus on *not* seeing the crowd of gawking tourists and sunbathers. I fold the cover-up and set it on the sand, kick off my flip-flops and let hair and makeup finish with me. All eyes are fixed on me.

Because I stand out.

The other girls are all rail-thin and lithe with tiny but perfectly shaped tits and bubbly little butts and skin that looks airbrushed even before they grace the magazine pages. I'm the tallest one by at least three inches, and the biggest one by at least thirty pounds.

I'm the only "plus size" model doing this shoot.

I see people staring at me, I feel it. Guys amble by and I feel their gazes on me. Ludovic is taking pictures of the ocean or something, endless pictures, adjusting the settings on his massive Nikon. With the reflector, without, then with some kind of gray lens filter, and without.

Finally, he points at one of the models, a girl from Brazil named Nina. Her bikini is so negligible that it would probably fit in an empty Keurig coffee pod.

She's fucking stunning.

She lays in the gentle surf, rolls around, droplets of water beading just so on her dark skin. Her smile is white and genuine.

Anya is next, a Russian-American girl with platinum hair and massive—but fake—tits. Her waist curves in, and her ass bubbles out, and her thighs are slim but shapely, and she's just absurdly perfect looking. Ludovic pays special attention to her. He shoots hundreds of photos of her, handing his camera to an assistant and kneeling beside her, adjusting her hair and saying charming little things to her that have her giggling. Then he has her roll onto her back so her tits are thrust into the air and her hair is splayed wet and fine on the sand while the waves lap at her knees.

It's an incredible shot. *Sports Illustrated* perfect.

When they're done, he stops her and whispers something in her ear, handing her what looks likes a room key card. She smiles coyly at him. The next model takes Anya's place at the water's edge, and Anya plops down onto the sun-warmed sand beside me.

She uses the key card to scrape a line in the sand between her legs. "God, what a pig."

I play dumb. "Who? Ludovic?"

She nods, not looking at me. "Yes, *Ludovic.* Touching me. Telling me how sexy I am. Of course I'm sexy! I'm a fucking model, yes? Like I'm going to sneak into his room in the middle of the night and let him fuck me. I don't care if he *can* get me on *Sports Illustrated*. Not happening. God, what an asshole."

"Do you want to be on *Sports Illustrated?*" I ask.

She looks up at me and her expression is one of disbelief. "Of course. You think I go on this diet and spend so many hours in the gym to look this way for to get a date or some shit? No. I am a swimsuit model. The swimsuit edition is what every bikini model wants. But to do what *he* wants me to do to get it, I don't think so. I have standards." She glances at me again, curiously this time. "I'm sorry. Did you do something like this to get here? I don't mean to insult you, if you did."

I can't help but laugh. In trying not insult me, she insults me. I shake my head. "No. I'm only here because he's hoping I will."

"And will you?"

I dig my heel into the sand, trying to disguise the anger and disgust. "*Fuck* no." I wiggle my toes. "Not if he was the last man on earth."

"Then we have at least that in common," Anya says, and stands up, brushing sand from her ass.

Another backhanded insult. I try not to let it bother me as I wait for my turn in front of the camera.

Hours later, as the sun is lowering into the sea, and I'm bored out of my mind all the other models have left, except Li Fei. And then she's shoving her feet into sandals and leaving without a word to anyone, and it's just Ludovic, me, and the crew.

I try to leave space between me and Ludovic as I pass him, but he moves toward me, puts his hand on my arm and turns me.

"Just there, yes." He snaps a few shots, checks them, adjusts his settings, and snaps a few more, dropping to one knee.

With no direction, I just stand there, hands at my sides, weight on one leg, unsmiling. My skin tingles where he touched me, and I want to rub at it, slather hand sanitizer on it. He lets his camera hang from his neck and puts his hands on my waist, guiding me toward the sea. I step out of his reach, and I see a flash of irritation cross his features. He closes the space between us and his hands go to my waist again, and he positions me. His hands linger, and his eyes search me.

"Don't play coy, Des," he says to me in a low voice only I can hear. "You know your options are limited."

And with that fury-inciting statement, he backs away and starts snapping, kneeling, bending, standing up, twisting the camera to portrait, changing a setting, shouting pose instructions. The next hour passes slowly, my muscles stiff and sore from changing positions and poses so frequently, holding a particular pose as long as I can every now and then.

He gestures at me at the end of an hour. "Nice, nice. Now change to the other bikini."

There's no screen, and a small crowd is still watching. "Um. Change where?"

He has to stifle a leering grin. "Here, here. They can shield you with your cover-up, if you're so worried."

Two girls on the makeup crew take my cover-up and the light reflector, positioning themselves between me and Ludovic and the crowd, so there's only the ocean to see me as I strip the top off and stuff myself into the halter top. Fortunately, there's no one out paddle boarding or jet skiing at the moment. I feel Ludovic watching me, and I know he can see my feet and calves, and my shoulders. He unashamedly lifts up on his toes to try to watch, winking at me.

When I've changed into the other bikini, we spend another hour going from pose to pose, until the sun is half-buried in the rippling horizon and we're losing the light.

Finally, he waves at the crew. "Good. We're done. You can go." He looks at me, and his expression is dark, hungry. "Des and I are going to finish here alone."

The crew exchange glances, and one of them fixes me with a questioning gaze. She knows his reputation, and what he's trying to do. But they can't do anything about it; assistants and camera crews are even more replaceable than models.

I pull on my cover-up as the crew packs up and drifts back to the hotel. Ludovic is scrolling through the previous shots, nodding now and then.

When he realizes everyone is gone, the crowd of curious tourists included, a smile crosses his face. "Alone at last," he says, his voice low with promise.

I hold my chin high. "I have to go."

He just shakes his head. "No, you don't." He gestures at the restaurant not far away. "We should have dinner, I think."

"I'm not hungry," I lie.

He just grins. "Yes, you are." He steps toward me and I tense, feeling my skin crawl with his proximity. "You've lost weight. It looks good on you. Or off you, more like. Now, if only you would drop, oh, ten more, you'd be truly striking. I could do amazing things with you, Des." He winks, making it a double entendre.

I don't bother to hide my disgust and anger. "I'm leaving." I turn away before I do something rash, like put my fist down his throat.

He jogs after me, leans into me, and his finger hooks in the halter strap of my top, tugging at it. "Come on, Des. You think you can get anywhere in this business on your own? You really don't want to walk away from me."

"Yes, I do." I keep walking, refusing to look at him.

He keeps pace with me, and his mouth is beside my ear. "You wouldn't even have to do much, you know. Not unless you wanted to. Put those plump lips of yours around my cock, Des. You'll like it, I promise. Just that, and I can make you successful. I can get you out of that shoebox apartment you share with all those other girls. I have a big apartment, and a big cock. You can have both." He drifts a hand across my waist, down to my ass. "You know you want to. You know you won't ever get anything better than me."

Everything boils up and out. Rage is hot, and blinding. I spin away from him, take a step back. "*Fuck... you.*" I spit out the words, hissing in blind fury.

And then I do something even more stupid: I take one step toward him, and slap him with my open hand as hard as I can. He blinks at me, a hand to his face, and then starts toward me, anger in his eyes. I shove him away from me. Pussy that he is, he goes flying backward three or four steps, stumbles, and lands on his ass in the sand. His camera thumps against his chest, and he rolls to one side, the Nikon dragging through the sand.

I stalk away, and ignore Ludovic as he shouts.

"You'll regret this, you bitch. I'm calling Sidney right now! You'll never work again. You're finished! FINISHED!"

Trying to make an angry exit across the sand isn't easy. I want to run, but I don't. My tits would smack me in the chin, for one thing, since this stupid bikini top provides absolutely dick for support. And for another, I don't want to give Ludovic the satisfaction of knowing how upset I am.

Rage and shame and hate pulse through me, tears prick at my eyes, making crying inevitable. Not yet, though. Not here.

I feel shame because, just for one single split second, I considered it. For an eye blink, I considered doing what he wanted. But then sanity reasserted itself, and disgust shot through me. Along with a crushing load of self-loathing.

You know you won't ever get anything better than me.

Oh, I could have had something much better. But I ruined that, too.

"Damn it, Des. I warned you." Rochelle meets me in the check-in line at LaGuardia airport.

She has my suitcases balanced on a trolley. Not just the one little carry-on I brought to Florida, but the three big ones that contain everything I own.

"Rochelle?" I stare at my suitcases. "What's… what's going on?"

Her eyes are regretful. "You don't have to fuck him, I told you. Just don't piss him off." She shakes her head. "And you go and assault him? In public, on a beach, in front of dozens of witnesses?"

"You don't know what he said to me, Rochelle."

"And I don't care." She digs in her purse, comes up with a folder. She opens it, hands me two pieces of paper. One is a check for a paltry amount of money. The other is a one-way plane ticket back to Detroit, leaving in thirty-six minutes. "The only reason I'm even paying for your flight back is because I like you. *I* paid for that ticket. Not Sidney, not the agency. Me. This isn't the business for you, Des. It's just not. Go home. Go back to school."

I stare at the ticket. And I find, along with hurt and sadness and embarrassment, a palpable sense of relief. "Thanks, Rochelle."

She offers me a rare smile, and it looks strange on her features. "No, thank *you*. You know how long I've wanted to slap that smug, arrogant pig?"

So I drag my three heavy suitcases through the line as fast as I can, tripping, fighting back confused tears. I barely make the flight, stumbling to the jetway just as they're about to close the door. They let me on, and I find my seat, holding my purse on my lap and staring at the check that represents nearly two months of starvation and stress and insane hours.

Back at Detroit Metro Airport, I realize I'm not sure how I'm going to get home, and wonder if Ruth has found a new roommate. I don't have a credit card or a debit card, and I'm not even twenty-three yet, so I can't rent a car. I don't have a phone or anyone to call. Ruthie doesn't have a car.

I have to call an airport taxi, and the ride costs me the rest of my cash. It's raining when I lug my baggage out of the cab and onto the sidewalk outside Ruthie's apartment building. My key doesn't work in the lock, which I realize is brand new. I press the buzzer, but she doesn't answer.

I have nowhere to go. No money except for the check in my purse, which I can't cash or deposit yet. Everything is closed.

I stack my wet suitcases on the ground and sit on the pavement beside them. The rain batters down on my skull, soaking me to the bone in moments.

I try not to remember the last time I was stuck out in rain like this.

I've lost track of time. Eventually, I doze, despite the rain. Or maybe the term is 'pass out'.

I feel a hand shaking my shoulder. "Des?" It's Ruth. I peer up at her, and realize my teeth are chattering so hard I can't even speak. "Des, honey, what are you doing here? Jesus, how long have you been out here?"

"No—nowhere else to—to go."

"Oh, sweetie. God. Come on, let's get you inside."

A hot shower, a change of clothes, and some Campbell's chicken noodle soup has me feeling slightly more human. I explain everything to Ruth, who is too good of a friend to say "I told you so," but I can see it in her eyes, feel it sitting between us, unspoken. She doesn't ask if I ever called Adam back; she knows better.

She hasn't rented out my old room.

Because she knew I'd be back?

CHAPTER ELEVEN

"TRAIN JUMP, TAKE TWO. AND...*ACTION!*" PRESLEY Miller's voice booms through the megaphone, and I spring into action.

I take off running along the roof of a warehouse, and four feet below me is a freight train moving about ten miles per hour faster than I can run. It's all been carefully calculated and choreographed and tested using a stuntman, so they know it's possible. Hell, I've completed the jump itself once already. It's not the landing that's the problem, it's the moment *after* that's tricky. Presley wants me to make the jump look effortless, so we practice with the train stopped. Full sprint, leap, drop ten feet, land on my feet onto the roof, keep my footing, keep running. I've almost got it. Almost.

I've landed it in practice, and nearly had it the first real take, but I stumbled the first few steps before catching my footing and Presley just won't have the stumble. Won't have it. So I do it again.

"You're a goddamned superhero goddammit!" Presley screams through the microphone. It's his version of a pep talk. "Stick the fucking landing, you big pussy! I'm not backing this fucking train up again, so get it right! Now…Go-go-go! Ready? JUMP!"

I jump. My heart thuds. Air whistles. My feet throb from landing on the metal roof of a train car. My thighs ache from constant sprinting. The train barrels beneath me, and I know I've fucked this up. Or someone has. The train is supposed to get moving five minutes before I start my sprint, and everything is precisely timed so my jump lands me in the middle of a car.

Instead of the reassuring rusted metal of a roof, all I see is a gap between cars. I'm going to miss. I'm going to smash between the cars and get turned into paste.

My heart crashes in my ears. It feels like time is moving in sludge-slow increments, like treacle.

The distance between me and the train congeals, and then my stomach and ribs are slamming into the edge of the train car. Motherfucker, it hurts. I've caught the edge, and I can see the ground whizzing beneath my feet. If I slip, I'm dead. There's no safety backup, no wires. The train is moving too fast. I can sense the difference, feel it. I can't move. Can't breathe. Someone is screaming, yelling, "CUT! CUT!" but Presley is rolling his arm, the signal to keep rolling.

Yeah, don't mind me, asshole, I'm only about to die here.

I strain, claw, scrabble the toes of my combat boots against the side of the car, groaning between gritted teeth. My ribs are screaming, either bruised or cracked. My muscles are on fire.

I get an elbow on the top of the train car, and then the other one. Now I can move myself forward and get my feet under me. The pace car is bouncing along beside the train, and the AD is waving his arm in circles. We're still rolling.

Ahead of me, Israel Price-Vickers runs across the top of the train, oblivious to what's just happened. He's got an AK-47 slung around his back, blanks loaded in the clip. He's the villain, the one I'm supposed to catch. I'm supposed to be running behind him. I have to catch him. The fact that Presley hasn't cut yet tells me he may just go with this take, *if* I can get moving. I suck in a breath and wince at the lance of pain in my chest, put a hand to my ribs, and force myself into a run. Each step hurts, but I've played with worse. I bury the pain, growl through it, push myself into a sprint. Israel glances back at me, and pours on the speed. I leap the space between train cars, and now there's only one car-length between us. Israel doesn't stand a fucking chance. Even with bruised ribs I can still run him down like a dog.

We pass the marker; a telephone pole with a red 'X' spray-painted across the wood, telling us the next phase of the scene is coming. When we see the next X-marked pole, I'm going to tackle Israel and we're going to fly through the air and onto a huge stunt pad.

Except, if the train's moving faster, we're going to miss the landing. In the choreography, Israel spins at the last second and topples backward to absorb the impact of my tackle. That's not going to work now. Israel doesn't know the train is moving faster than it's supposed to, or what that means for the scene.

So I push myself harder. I see the marked pole, and the pad, and it's a lot closer than it's supposed to be.

I dig deep, and force myself to the limits of my physical capability. Israel doesn't see me coming, isn't ready for the tackle.

Six feet.

Four.

And then I'm flying through the air, diving at Israel, slamming into him. The butt of the AK-47 bites into my ribs, but I can't do anything except absorb the pain. Israel is in my arms, twisting, thrashing, and then as we hit the stunt pad the rifle jabs me again, further damaging my ribs.

"What the fuck, Adam?" Israel is rolling away from me, bouncing on the huge, inflated pad and onto the ground. He stumbles, tosses the rifle aside and grabs his side, leaning over and wincing like a pussy. "That's not the fucking choreography, you asshole! What the hell were you doing?"

"Saving your ass, and the scene," I growl, sliding gingerly to the ground.

Presley is here, hopping out of his golf cart and rushing for me. "Holy shit, holy shit! That was epic!"

"You need to fire that fucking train engineer," I bark. "He had that piece of shit train going way faster than it's supposed to be."

"I know, I know," Presley says, waving a hand dismissively. "But he's union, nothing we can do except yell at him. You stuck it, though, and that scene works *so* much better this way! It makes your character seem that much more human and believable! I can't believe it! That was absolutely wonderful! Take five, everyone!"

I lift up my shirt, and see that a massive bruise is already purpling across my torso. "How about I take the day, Pres? Or the week, how about that? I almost died just now, or did you fucking *miss* that little fact?"

Presley winces and looks away. "Don't be so dramatic, Adam. But yes, yes, fine, take till Tuesday. We've got some work to do for Israel's next few scenes anyway, so we don't really need you." He waves at me. "And get that looked at. Need you tip-top for your next scene." He lowers himself heavily into the golf cart, which settles significantly under his bulk. Presley Miller is not a small man.

I watch him go, and then the on-scene medical team is cutting my shirt away and probing my ribs. Bruised tissue and muscle, they say, but no breakage. They also tell me the thick layer of muscle kept me from sustaining any major injuries.

Why couldn't I be a romantic comedy actor? Crack jokes and kiss hot chicks all day. Sounds good to me right about now.

They help me into another golf cart and drive me across the industrial landscape we're using as a set. We're somewhere in the wasteland of the industrial urban blight outside Detroit, filming a big-budget action movie, an all-original storyline and characters for once, which is pretty exciting in this age of remakes, reboots, and adaptations. We wrapped on *Fulcrum 2* three months ago, and I've been working on this movie ever since. We're filming the whole thing in and around Detroit, both for the post-apocalyptic feel of the abandoned warehouse districts and inner-city ghetto areas, and because the newly elected state governor instituted significant tax breaks for the film industry as a tactic to rejuvenate the struggling city.

My driver and bodyguard Oliver is waiting for me beside a sleek black Range Rover, and he drives me downtown to my rented apartment. I shower, change, and toss back some Motrin for the aches and pains, and then have Oliver drop me off at a local bar. I settle into a booth with my script, a pint, and a burger. I spend a couple hours slowly sipping beer and refreshing my lines for the next few scenes, and ignoring the buzzing bar around me.

Patrons come and go, a few recognizing me, but Oliver keeps them at bay.

And then I happen to glance up as I'm reciting a particularly tongue-twisty line under my breath, and happen to see a girl at a table adjacent to mine. She's sipping a martini and flipping through a catalogue of some sort while she chats on the phone. There's a place set across from her, so I'm guessing she's waiting for someone. The girl herself doesn't interest me, though, but the catalogue does. It's for a clothing line, and what catches my eye are the models. Like the girl looking through the catalogue, all the models are curvier. Plus size, I guess the term would be. Although after knowing Des, I've stopped using that term; women are women, and are beautiful regardless of their shape or size or weight.

My heart clenches as I think of Des. She never called. Six months and not a word from her.

The girl flips the page and there she is. Des. In the catalogue. Tall, ink-black hair, beautiful, so beautiful, wearing a long, flowing blue dress and simple white sandals.

Without thinking, I leave my booth and slip into the empty seat across from the girl. She stares at me in irritation, and then she recognizes me. "Beth? I'll—I'll call you back." She ends the call and sets the phone down. "Hi. Um. Hi?"

I point at the magazine. "Sorry to bother you, but could I see your catalogue for a second?" She blinks in confusion. "I know that's a weird thing to ask, I just—I know her, that girl." I tap the image of Des.

The girl slides the magazine toward me and I spin it so it's right-side up.

God, Des.

She really is a model, now. She's a bit slimmer in this image than when I knew her, although that could be Photoshop. She's got a mysterious half-smile on her lips, and she's wearing a lot more makeup than she needs. But she's Des, and so lovely it makes my chest ache. I find myself touching the glossy image of her face and wondering where she is, and why she never called me. I wonder if she's found a boyfriend.

I blink hard, push it all down, force a polite smile on my face and slide the catalogue back to the mystified girl. "Thanks," I tell her. "Sorry to bother you."

"No—it was not a bother." She smiles at me finally, and then her fingers clench around the bar napkin near her martini glass. "Could you…I mean—"

"Sure thing, sweetheart." I take my Sharpie from my pocket and sign my name on the napkin. "Here ya go."

"Can I help you?" a deep male voice says from behind me. "You bothering my girlfriend?"

I wink at the girl, and then unfold to my full height. The guy is big, but still a third my size. I pat him on the shoulder. "Nope. I just saw someone I know in her catalogue."

He furrows his brow and glances at the table, at the girl, and at the catalogue. "In the fat chick magazine?"

The girl's face falls apart, hurt spreading across her features. She's a girl with curves, sure enough, but she's pretty, with bright blue eyes and wavy brown hair and high cheekbones. The way she buries the hurt so quickly tells me this isn't the first time this asshole has said something like that.

I don't even think, I just react. Before he can finish his next sentence, I've got him across the bar, pinned against the wall with my forearm against his throat. "What…the *fuck*…did you say?"

"I—I—" he gurgles.

"Listen to me, you ugly, sloppy, piece of shit." I get in his face, and I see real terror. "How about you get the fuck out of here, and you leave that girl alone, huh? You don't get to talk to her or *anyone* else that way. Not ever. I should break you in fucking half for talking like that, you pathetic little cocksucker." I drop him, spin, and shove him toward the exit. "Get the fuck out of here, douche-canoe."

He stumbles, lands on his ass, scrambles to his feet and runs out the door. People clap, a few whistle. Oliver is standing guard, keeping the bouncer at bay. I flex my hands into fists, shake and release them, and then sit down across from the girl. She's quivering, fighting back the tears.

I touch her chin, and she looks at me. "Hey. What's your name?"

"Quinn."

"You listen to me, Quinn." I pin her with my eyes, let her see my sincerity. "You don't need a piece of shit like him. If he doesn't appreciate how pretty you are, just the way you are, then he doesn't deserve you."

She searches me. "You think I'm—pretty?"

"Yeah, Quinn, I do. And anyone with eyes can see that, too, as long as they're not shallow, spineless assholes like that guy."

"He's not so bad. He's nice enough most of the time. He just...he wants me to be healthy."

"That's bullshit. He just says that because he thinks it's an easy way to manipulate you. He thinks he can make you believe he's got your best interests in mind, when all he really wants is an easy target." I grab her hands. "But you're not an easy target, are you, Quinn? You're the type of girl who stands up for herself, right? You want a guy to like you for you, who finds you attractive exactly the way you are. Isn't that right? You wouldn't date a pathetic loser just because you think it's all you can get, would you? You aren't that girl, are you, Quinn?"

I can see her processing my words, my challenge. She lifts her chin, and determination hardens her features. "No. I'm not that girl."

I smile at her. "Good."

She tosses back her martini, and stands up. "Thanks, Mr. Trenton."

I stand up too and shake her hand, and then pull her in for a quick hug. "When that loser tries to get you back, you tell him to fuck off. Okay?"

"I will."

I gather my things and stop by the bar, hand a few large bills to the bartender. "Pay her tab and mine, keep what's left."

The bartender's eyes bug out and he nods.

I leave the bar, hand my script to Oliver and tell him to find somewhere to park. I need to walk. Need to clear my head. Seeing Des, even in a magazine, has me flipped out all over again. I'd buried it all, moved on. Or so I'd thought. But obviously, I hadn't.

I walk aimlessly, my thoughts whirling. Every once in awhile I see Oliver pass by me in the Rover, circling me to make sure I'm not getting mugged or anything.

Eventually I realize I'm outside Wayne State University. Students are filing out in singles, twos, and threes. A late class must have just let out. I watch them go, scanning the faces, not sure what I'm looking for, or why I'm here. Des isn't here, I know she isn't. She's in New York, modeling. But I don't walk away; I lean against the pole of a streetlight and watch the students from across the street.

They're gone now. The thirty or thirty-five students have quickly dispersed, and the street is empty again.

I turn away, and then I hear the building door swing open. I glance back, out of instinct, I guess.

And there she is.

Des.

Hands in her jeans pockets, backpack slung across her shoulders, hair in a sleek ponytail.

I'm running across the street without thinking, ignoring the honk and the squeal of brakes. She turns at the noise, sees me, and then I'm in front of her.

She's in my arms, chest to chest, and her warm brown eyes are staring into mine, wondering, amazed, fearful, hesitant. "Adam?"

There are too many things to say, and I don't even know where to start. I feel as if I'm in a dream.

"I'm sorry I never called—" she starts.

A million thoughts skirl in my brain, and I can't even begin sorting them out. All I know is this is Des, here, in my arms, and her lips are wet, like she's just licked them, and I need to kiss her.

So I cut her off with a kiss, my lips slanting across hers, my heart thumping in my chest. She's frozen at first, shocked, and then she's pressing up on her toes and her tongue finds mine, and I know whatever her reasoning was, it's irrelevant now.

She wants this as much as I do.

She moans into the kiss, leans against me as if her legs won't hold up her weight.

I break the kiss enough to whisper to her. "You're coming with me."

She just nods.

CHAPTER TWELVE

IS THIS REAL? IS THIS HAPPENING? HOW DID HE FIND me?

His hand in mine is big and rough and familiar, and his presence beside me is huge and warm. His eyes on mine are the pale pastel green that has my heart flipping and my stomach knotting, because he *sees* me, sees into me.

He wants me.

I still don't entirely know why.

The question is becoming: do I care why, or only that he does?

I'm walking beside him, and then a black Range Rover slides to a graceful stop beside us and Adam slides in, pulls me in after him. He reaches across me, pulls the seatbelt over my chest and clicks it into place. It's a sweet but bizarre gesture, buckling me in. Is he that worried for my safety? Or is he worried I'll bolt? I don't know. But his fingers are twining in mine and the driver seems to know where we're going without being told.

I open my mouth to speak, and Adam shakes his head. "Not yet."

My lips tingle from the force and tenderness of his kiss, and my heart is palpitating furiously and my lungs are expanding and contracting deeply, as if his mere presence beside me requires more blood in my veins, more oxygen in my lungs. I want to crush myself to him, cling to him. I want to mash my lips against his and eat his breath, feel his muscles and tell him to take me, own me, claim me. I also want to run away; being with him will require truth. I'll have to tell him how I grew up, about the foster homes and the things I endured.

The abuse.

NO. I can't go there, not even in my mind. No.

I'll have to tell him he took my virginity. That I gave it to him, and didn't tell him.

I'll have to tell him about New York, and Ludovic.

So much to tell him, so many things I've never told anyone.

I might even have to tell him my real name.

We're pulling into an underground parking garage, sliding into a reserved spot near an elevator.

The driver, a burly man in his mid- to late-thirties with a huge black beard and tattoos curling up his neck and peeking out from the cuffs of his suit coat, pulls open my door and extends his hand to me, helps me down from the SUV. He closes the door behind Adam, follows us to the elevator, and even presses the call button.

Standing in silence waiting for the elevator is excruciating and awkward. I extend my hand to the driver. "Hi, I'm Des."

"Oliver." His voice sounds like stone rasping across stone.

"Nice to meet you, Oliver."

"Same."

And the awkwardness is back. Adam has my hand again, as if he's afraid to let me go, like I'll disappear if he's not physically touching me.

The elevator finally arrives, the doors sliding apart. Oliver extends an arm through the opening and waits for us to board, and then follows us on, reaching out to insert and twist a key, then pushes the top-most floor button.

I find it funny for some reason that a man as intelligent and dominant and powerful as Adam lets someone call elevators for him. "Must be nice," I say, "having someone to push the button for you."

Both Adam and Oliver stare at me as if I've grown a second head.

"My job," Oliver says, one corner of his mouth curling up almost imperceptibly. "He wouldn't let me do it for the first few months I worked for him. He'd get there first, push the button. Get on the elevator first, push the button. Stubborn fucker, makin' me look bad. So I told him he had to let me do my job."

Adam shakes his head and rolls his eyes. "It's ridiculous. I'm a grown-ass man. I don't need anyone to hold doors for me. He all but cuts my fucking meat for me. I swear to Christ, he'd peel the crusts off my sandwich if I asked him to." He snorts. "You're a bodyguard, Oliver, not a goddamned nanny."

"Yeah, well, you need a nanny, you big pussy." Oliver says this with a straight face, but his voice holds humor, and his narrow, deep-set dark eyes hold merriment.

"Twat," Adam says.

I watch the exchange with bemusement. "What is it with men insulting each other? I don't get it."

Oliver and Adam glance at each other, and Adam laughs. "It's just a guy thing."

The elevator stops and the doors swish open. Oliver waits till we're both off, and then somehow manages to move past us without seeming to hurry, leading us down a long, narrow hallway of slate-colored walls and dark hardwood floors. There's a small table with fake flowers up against the wall every dozen feet or so, with either an abstract painting or a mirror above it. We reach a door at the end of the hallway. Oliver unlocks it, ushers us in, and then moves past us once again. He prowls through the kitchen, living room, and through another door, finally returning to where Adam and I wait by the entrance.

"All clear," he rasps. "Need anything?"

"Privacy until further notice," Adam says.

"Cool." He pauses halfway out the door. "Need some carryout, just let me know. I'll grab it."

Finally, Adam and I are alone. "So, Oliver the bodyguard. What's up with that?"

Adam shrugs. "My agent insisted. Said I've reached the level where fans are liable to do crazy shit, so best to be prepared."

"You don't seem like you'd need a bodyguard."

Adam laughs. "Oliver is ex-special forces. Like, black ops. He's trained in all sorts of hand-to-hand combat, defensive and offensive driving, threat assessment techniques, and all sorts of nifty and slightly scary shit. Plus, he's just plain cool." He tugs me by the hand out of the small foyer area and into the kitchen. It's an open-plan apartment, the same dark hardwood floors as in the hallway, large windows facing the street, offering an amazing view of the river and the Ontario skyline. The kitchen is all dark speckled marble and stainless steel appliances, with a round table between the kitchen and living room.

The living room itself has a huge brown leather couch and matching loveseat and chair, with an exposed brick wall and a mounted flat-screen TV.

"Nice place," I say, feeling awkward again.

"It's a short-term rental. Just while I'm here filming."

I decide to bite the bullet. I take a seat in the corner of the couch, curling my legs under me. Adam sits on the opposite corner, facing me. "Adam? Why are you here? Why am I here? How did you find me?"

He takes a moment to think before answering, which is a quality I admire in him. "I'm filming a movie here. I'll be in Detroit for two months."

"So how did you find me?"

"Were you hiding?" he asks. I start to answer, and he holds up a hand to forestall me. "It was totally accidental. I thought you were in New York. Ruth told me you moved there to be a model. Anyway, we were cutting a scene, and I needed to get out for a walk. I just ended up at Wayne State. I don't know how. I was just watching the students leave after a class and…thinking about you, honestly, and there you were."

"Adam, I—"

"Why didn't you call?"

I don't know how to answer. "I just…couldn't. What would I say? Would you have come to New

York? Yeah, you probably would have. But for what? For how long?"

He stares at me for a moment, his eyes narrow in thought, and then he looks away. He puts a palm to his ribs and massages gently, wincing. Finally, he looks back at me. "Why do you seem so dead-set on insisting this couldn't work?"

"*What* couldn't work, Adam?"

He waves between him and me. "There's something here, Des. Between us. There is, and I know you know there is. You're just scared. Of what, I'm not sure."

"Of what? Of *everything*."

"Why?"

I let out a breath. "Because that's what life has taught me." I close my eyes briefly. "I don't trust anyone. I don't know how. My capacity for trust got broken a long fucking time ago."

Adam's face softens, and he just looks at me in silence for several moments. And then he gets up, goes into the kitchen, and pulls two bottles of beer out of the fridge and a bag of pretzels from a cabinet. He twists the caps off the beers and returns to the couch, setting the pretzels on the coffee table between us. He takes a long drink of his beer, chews some pretzels, and drinks again. I do the same, and then Adam is somehow closer to me, his thigh brushing the foot I've got tucked under my butt.

He looks at me, and I can see him sorting out his thoughts, his words. "Des, I almost don't even know where to go with that." Another swig. "I know I promised you last time that I wouldn't ask any questions. Well, I'm breaking that promise. Here's what it is, Des: I like you. I've missed you. God, we spent less than forty-eight hours together, and I just can't forget you. I've tried. I mean, fuck, it's been what, six months? And I can't get you out of my head. I can't get that night out of my head. Two days out of a hundred and eighty, and I can't stop thinking about it. About you. And just so you know now, there's been no one else since then.

"I'm going to give you a choice. If you have any sort of feelings for me at all, then you'll take a chance. On me. On us. On whatever this is, whatever it can be. That means telling me shit about yourself. Answering questions. Volunteering information. I mean, it's not like I'm expecting your whole life story in one sitting, or all your deepest, darkest secrets right here right now. But *some*thing. Take a chance, Des." He pauses, drinks, sets the bottle down. "Or if you can't do that, or won't, then tell me. I'll have Oliver take you home, and you'll never see me again."

Everything inside me clenches. My flight reflex is burning at me. *Don't trust him,* part of me screams. *You can't. He'll hurt you. He'll betray you. Everyone else has and everyone else will, and you know it.*

But the other part of me argues back. *No, not everyone. Ruth hasn't. Adam may not.*

Adam takes my silence as hesitation. He takes my beer from me and sets it down. Grabs my hands and sits angled toward me, as close as he can get. "You can't go your whole life alone, Des. You have to trust someone, sometime. Start with me." He leans even closer, whispering. "You can trust me."

Fight-or-flight wars with my loneliness, my desire for Adam. I blink hard. "Why do you want this?"

"Because I've never met anyone like you. And to be totally honest, I'm not sure I can even quantify exactly what it is about you. I mean, I don't know anything about you. But I'm drawn to you, intensely attracted to you, and I want to know more. Find out more." He pauses again, and then squeezes my hand. "How about this: ask me anything. I'll answer any question you ask me."

"What happened between you and Emma Hayes?" I ask.

He winces. "Wow. Straight for the jugular. In that case, I'm going to need another beer." He gets up, grabs two more, and I use the opportunity to straighten my legs out and prop them on the coffee table. He sits beside me, grabs my ankles, and pivots me so my legs lay across his thighs. "So, me and Emma. We met filming *Blood Alchemy.* We had a kiss scene in that movie, one of only two or three I'd ever done. Typically not my thing. But it was in that movie, and we just…clicked. The kiss was good, I guess. I mean, when you do a scene like that, there's usually like at least six or eight takes, sometimes more. The director wants a variety of angles and different elements, whatever. So it wasn't just one kiss, bam, done. We were on set, kissing in front of dozens of people, cameras rolling, Mike Helms yelling instructions at us and telling us to 'feel it more'. And like I said, we just…clicked. So after we wrapped, we went out on a few dates. That turned into a month, two, three. We got along. Similar interests, I guess. She grew up with brothers, so she could talk football, and we'd both gotten into acting from an odd direction, you know? She was a makeup artist at first. Then an extra got sick and they didn't have time to do an extras casting call, so they put her in. She could do the makeup on herself, and since the role needed heavy makeup effects, that was helpful. Turns out she could actually act, so the director tapped her for a supporting role in his next project. Grew from there. Whatever."

He takes a moment to gather his thoughts, then continues. "I'd had a few casual relationships here and there, right? Girls in high school, some brief flings in college and when I played ball. Nothing serious. Not till Emma. I was always so focused on football and then acting, and I just…never cared about anyone very seriously. It was all just fun. But Emma was different, to me. I thought I loved her, okay? I really did. She was gorgeous and talented and a lot of fun. We dated for a year and a half. We visited each other on set, went on a couple short vacations together.

"And then one day, I was in an airport somewhere. Paris, maybe? Germany? I can't remember. Somewhere in Europe. Oh, I remember now. It was France, after Cannes. I did this bit part in an indie art film, and I'd gone to the festival to support it. Anyway. I was in line in an airport shop, buying some water and a book, and I saw a magazine, a tabloid. And there were these pictures on the front page, photos of Emma and her co-star from her latest project. It was a serious drama, no romance at all. But there they were, holding hands. Kissing." He shrugs, but it's obviously difficult for him to act unaffected. "I flew back to L.A. early, didn't tell her. Showed up at her house in Malibu, unannounced. Ryan's car was there. She's got this big bay window in front, you can see all the way through the house to the ocean behind. I saw them on the deck together. She was wearing his T-shirt, he was in his underwear. Drinking fucking mimosas. She saw me, and she just…fucking waved at me. Like, oh hey. No big deal."

"What? She didn't even care that you'd seen her?"

He shakes his head. "Nope. I was backing out of her driveway and she comes out the front door, still in *his* goddamned T-shirt and nothing else. She stops me. I open my window, and she leans in for a kiss. I was like, *what?* What the fuck is going on, right?" He snorts in derision. "Turns out, she had different ideas about the…exclusivity of our relationship than I did. You know what she told me? 'We never said we were exclusive, Adam. I'm sorry if you assumed that, but I never said it.' She'd—she'd been dating other guys the whole time we were together. I thought it—I thought we'd meant something, I guess. The whole time, a year and a half, whenever I wasn't around, she was banging other dudes. Thing was, she never hid it, or lied about it, she just never told me, and I never thought to ask."

I frown. "God, Adam, that's fucked up."

"That's what I said. She wasn't even upset. I was like, 'Fuck you, we're done. That's messed up.' She just shrugged and said it was fine, like whatever, no big deal. It was all over the tabloid, though. There was a photographer outside her house. He'd seen me at LAX and followed me to Emma's place. Caught the whole thing on film."

"So when that ended—"

He takes a swallow of beer and nods. "Yeah, after that, I swore off women. I was done." His eyes go to me, sharp and hot. "Until I met you."

"How am I different?"

"I don't know, you've got this sense of...you are who you are and that's it. A little insecure sometimes, maybe, but you're not like everyone else. You're tall, and you've got curves, and you're so fucking sexy but I don't think you even really know it." He rests a hand on my knee, glances at me. "So what happened that you're back in Michigan?"

I groan and lean my head against the back of the couch. "A lot of things." I roll my head to look at him. "You want the long version or the short version?"

"Yes."

I laugh. "Okay. Fine. I *hated* modeling. They stuffed me into clothes I didn't always fit in, and I had to get changed in front of other people. Behind a screen usually, but never totally in private. And then I just stood there posing for hours and hours. Never got lunch breaks. Never had time to eat. There was barely time to breathe. The agency had me scheduled all day every day, on one thing or another. I mean, it was great in that I had a lot of work, which was cool. I was in demand. But I hated it. And I hated New York. So loud, so busy. All the time, morning and night, it never ended. So fast-paced, so chaotic. So big. Everyone's rude and in a hurry. No one matters. No one gives a shit." I look away, out the window. "And then there was this photographer. He was a big deal, a total legend in the modeling world. On one shoot, he had his eyes on me. Even when he was shooting other models, he'd glance at me. Watch me. He kept touching me, my hair, my clothes. Looking at me like…I don't even know. Just *leering*. So creepy. So then I get a break and go outside, and he follows me. He fucking propositioned me, like 'I can make your career, baby, all you gotta do is go home with me.' Tried to make me touch him.

"That was the day I talked to Ruthie and she told me you'd visited her. I just couldn't deal with anything else. So then, as if that wasn't bad enough, this photographer got the director of my agency to book me for an exclusive swimsuit shoot in Florida. I had to do it, or else. So I did it. And I hated it. I hate wearing bathing suits. I just…I hate the way I look, the way I feel, and these were bikinis. It was awful. All the other models doing the shoot were actual swimsuit models. Skinny and petite and big-busted and beautiful. I stood out like a sore thumb.

"And again, this nasty-ass photographer shot me last, so it was just him and me and the crew. He finally got all his shots and then he dismissed the crew—so he could get me alone. He propositioned me again, but this time it wasn't implied, like before. The first time it was 'you help me, I'll help you.' Obvious, but not overt. That day on the beach, though, he straight up told me he would make me famous and successful or whatever if I sucked his cock. Outright *told* me I'd never get anywhere if I didn't. Because of the way I look."

I have to pause and gather myself. Anger bubbles up inside me even now, along with shame and embarrassment. "He told me…he said he had a big apartment and a big cock, and I could have both. That I shouldn't refuse him, because it's not like I'd ever get anyone better than him. He said it like it was obvious, because I'm…big." The last word comes out as a whisper.

"Jesus, what an asshole."

I try to shrug and can't quite muster it. "Yeah, I slapped him, and then shoved him away from me. Flew back to New York. Then the manager from the agency met me at the airport with all my bags and sent me home. Like, don't even bother coming back, you're done. So here I am."

He's kneeling on the floor in front of me, his hands on my face. "You're not big, Des. You're beautiful. You're perfect. You're amazing and you're sexy and—"

"Shut up, Adam. You're sweet, but I know who I am, and I'm fine with it. Even after New York, I'm okay with how I look. Maybe even more so, because of everything that happened. I mean, before the stupid fucking bikini shoot, the agency owner and manager told me I had to lose weight. They said that even though I'm a plus size model, to do a bikini shoot I had to lose weight. I had to look a certain way. So I did it, and I hated it." I can't look at him. "It all made me so angry. Fucking Sidney telling me to lose weight. Ludovic telling me I'd never be able to get anyone better than him. The looks from the other models, like 'what is *she* doing here?' It just made me even more...shut down, I guess. I hated it, but I survived it, and I learned from it. I'm better for it. I won't change who I am. I will *not* be made to feel like I'm less valuable or attractive than anyone else just because I'm taller or weigh more, or because I'm shaped a certain way. I can't look any other way than I do. No matter how I diet or work out, I'll never get any skinnier. And, if I try, if I just stop eating like I did in New York, I'll not only be miserable, but unhealthy, too. And honestly, I don't want to look any other way. I like how I look. I'm learning to be comfortable in my own skin."

To his credit, he doesn't try to convince me of my worth, both to him and to me. Instead, he latches onto something else. "And the way you're built, regardless of what I think about it, does that have anything to do with why you're so reluctant to believe I'm genuinely interested in you?"

It's hard to swallow, suddenly. I don't want to look at him, but he's there, his hands are on my cheeks, his thumbs at my chin and touching the corners of my mouth. I have to look into his eyes, and it's so hard, because he just sees so much. "Yeah. Partly. Not entirely."

"Then what is it?"

"Because you're *you!* You're Adam Trenton. You're *famous,* and you look like a fucking god! You can have anyone you want. You dated one of the most famous actresses in the world. And even if you got hurt by her, it just...it seems like you'd feel—like going from someone as gorgeous as her to—to *me,* is...is downgrading. Like going from a Ferrari to a ten-year-old F-150." I talk over his impending protest. "Not just because of the difference in the way we look, but because she's from your world. She's famous. She's glamorous and rich and 'grew up with brothers' and she's...*somebody.*"

"And you're..." he prompts.

"And I'm not."

He frowns, and his eyes hunt mine. He ignores the obvious and goes for the harder question. "'Grew up with brothers,' you said. Why is that important?"

Shit. I pull away, grab my beer from the coffee table and drain it, take the second one Adam brought a few minutes ago. Drink from that.

"Des? What does that mean?"

I shrug, a tiny lift of one shoulder. "I don't have a family, that's all."

"Des." It's a scold.

I can't avoid the question any more. "I grew up in the foster system. My mom was a crack addict. She OD'd when I was three and I went into the system. Bounced from foster home to foster home my entire life." I let out a breath. "Some of the homes I got placed in were okay, and some…weren't."

"What's that mean?" Adam asks.

I shrug. "It's not important anymore."

He scrutinizes me. "Something tells me it is."

I glance at him, hating how perceptive he is. "The bad ones were just…rough. Alcoholic foster fathers, shit like that. There are so many kids in the system that it's impossible to place them all, especially because there just aren't enough families willing to foster. The ones that are, especially in the area surrounding Detroit…it's just extra income for them, most of the time. So it's just rough. You learn early on to be independent, to not trust anyone. You get moved around a lot, you learn to not get close to anyone." I shrug again, hoping he'll let it go at that.

"And?" he prompts.

Of course he can't.

I close my eyes slowly, open them, and take a drink. "I was molested by one of my foster fathers." I can't look at him when I say it, and I hate the sharp inhalation, the boil of concern and anger and—yes—pity—I see in his eyes when I do finally glance his way. "It went on for a year before I got the courage to tell anyone. He got arrested. Turned out I wasn't the only one. But he was so good at manipulating, threatening, making sure you knew no one would believe you if you did tell. He scared me. But eventually I just…couldn't take it anymore. So I told a teacher at school. I was terrified I was going to get in trouble…for not telling sooner, for letting him, even though I kept telling him no, begging him to leave me alone. But the teacher…Mrs. Erwin. She believed me. And the first thing she did was hug me, and tell me she would make sure he never hurt me again. And he didn't." A look I can't parse crosses Adam's features. "What?" I ask. "Why are you looking at me like that?"

"Jesus, Des." He shakes his head, wipes his face with both palms. "No wonder it's hard for you to trust me."

"Yeah." I blink hard, emotion running rampant through me. "You know, I've never told anyone that. Not even Ruth. I mean, she grew up a foster kid too, which is why we're so close, because we both get it, and I think she guesses at what happened, why I'm closed off. I mean, how do you get past that? How do you…how do you deal?"

"How *did* you deal?"

I laugh, and have to sniffle. Not that I'm crying, no way. Not worth crying over, not anymore. "That's just it, Adam. I mean, don't you get it? I haven't. Not really."

"But you seemed to trust me, on Mackinac Island. For a while, at least. I mean, you let me take you to that dinner, and that night, we…we had an amazing time. I thought we did, at least."

I shake my head softly. "Adam, I did too. That night…it was incredible. I mean, it was scary as shit, the whole dinner party thing. All the celebrities and the paparazzi. That was scary, and I wasn't ready for it. But everything after, being with you…" I look at him, let him see into my eyes. "That was honestly amazing. Best night of my life, in so many ways."

He grabs my hand, tangles our fingers together. "Me too."

I hear something in his voice. "But?"

He doesn't answer right away. "But you shut down, later that morning. I could have stayed, I could have figured out a way to have more time with you—but you just shut it down."

"Because I was scared!"

"Of what?" He seems genuinely puzzled.

"Everything! Look at it from my point of view, Adam. I'm a trash girl, an orphan, and I'm just minding my own business and along comes this hot, sexy, rich, famous actor, and he's all into me. It's too good be to true. It's *got* to be too good to be true. Shit like that doesn't happen to me."

"But you went with it."

"Yeah, of course I did. I liked feeling desired. It really felt like you liked me, like you wanted me. And I—I liked that." I swallow hard, keep my gaze shifting, moving, away from his. "And when you had to go, I just had to…let you go. I couldn't handle it if you acted like you wanted more, and then just ditched me for the next shiny new thing. I don't know. It was a special night for me, and I just wanted to have something special, just for me."

"It was special for me too, Des—" he starts.

"No," I say, feeling the truth lodged in my throat, and knowing it's a bomb, knowing it's going to explode and going to cause pain. "You don't get it."

"I do, Des. I really do. It was surreal, and I can see where you're coming from, how you'd think it's too good to be true. But I'm just a guy, at the end of the day."

I blink away tears. "No, Adam. You really don't get it. You can't."

He goes still, quiet. He suspects something deeper now. "Then what, Des?" His eyes narrow, and rove down my body, assessing. "We didn't—I mean, you're not—"

My eyes widen, realizing what he thinks. "No! God, no. I'm not pregnant. Jesus, I'd have told you *that*."

"Then what?"

I breathe deep, let it out. Make my eyes go to his. "That night, Adam..." God, it's so hard to make the words come out. "You were my first."

His eyes close, blink, and he runs his palm over his face, massaging his temples. He leans forward, elbows on his knees. "Tell me you're joking."

I shake my head, but words won't come out. I have to clear my throat of the ache, the tears I'm suppressing. "No one ever made me feel the way you did. There was one guy before you, we made out and he wanted to cop a feel, and I just couldn't. The panic attack, that first day we met? That's what it was about. If guys got close to me, tried to touch me, I would freak. Couldn't breathe. Froze up. I just couldn't let men get close to me, physically or emotionally. Any male that's ever been in my life has, at best, been indifferent, just treating me as one more foster kid going through the system. At worst, they were Frank Platte, sexually molesting me.

"And then I met you. And you *saw* me. Like I meant something. Like I was worth looking at, worth talking to." It's harder and harder not to cry, because Adam isn't moving, looking at me, or responding. "You had this way of...making me feel comfortable. Of not being afraid. And I was sick of being scared of men. I was sick of being a virgin. And you made me feel good."

"I took your virginity." His voice is pained. "Jesus fucking Christ, Des! Why didn't you fucking tell me?"

"Because you'd treat me differently. You'd have wanted to make it a big deal." It's hard to talk, hard to even whisper. Looking at him is totally out of the question.

"It *is* a big deal, Des! It's like, the *biggest* deal. You were a virgin? And I fucked you like—"

Anger blazes through me and I find my voice. "Don't...you...*dare*." I shoot to my feet and stand over him. He peers up at me with conflicted, hurt, and angry eyes. "Don't you fucking *dare* make it less for me than it was. It was *exactly* what I wanted. It was *more* than that."

"Did I hurt you?"

I shake my head and lift a shoulder. "Not any more than it would have anyway."

"So it did hurt."

"Adam. Jesus. With everything that happened before, how good you made me feel, both before and after, that part was like...not even worth thinking about." I pace away. "This is why I didn't tell you then, and why I didn't want to have this conversation. It was my decision to make, and I did so eyes wide open."

He lurches to his feet, drains his half-full beer in three long swallows, and then sets it down on the table far too gently. "I need a few minutes. I need to think." He's out the door, scrubbing a palm over his head.

The door slams, and I'm alone. The only sound is the ticking of a clock somewhere in the apartment.

CHAPTER THIRTEEN

My head, heart, and body are at war. At the moment, my head is winning.

Des had been a virgin.

It all made sense. Her hesitation. Her panic attack. How incredibly responsive she was, how shy in some ways. And then, how hungry, how voracious for more. Even the way she shut down the next morning made sense.

But she hadn't told me. She knew how I'd react, and she'd intentionally not told me. It hurt. It made me angry. That's not something you keep from a guy. It just isn't. I feel justified in being pissed off, but the logical part of me also understands where she's coming from.

Only, logic doesn't mean shit in the face of pain.

I find myself outside, stalking angrily down the sidewalk. And I realize if I walk too far, I'll get lost. Which, at the very least, will just piss off Oliver. So I make myself stop, turn around, and walk back toward my building more slowly. I turn it over in my head, trying to think it through rather than just reacting.

And then I see Des on the sidewalk ahead of me, walking away from my building.

I catch up to her, grab her by the arms and stand in front of her, stopping her forward progress. "Des, where the hell are you going?"

She jumps and gasps in surprise, then jerks free, shoves me backward. "Get off me, Adam." I'm confused, now. Which one of us is supposed to be pissed off?

I growl in irritation and jog past her again, stopping in front of her. "Des, hold on. Just talk to me. Where are you going?"

"You left." She says this like it explains everything, and then starts walking past me once more.

I don't know how to stop her, how to make her listen, how to make her understand. So I do something desperate. I stop her with my body, grab her hand as she starts to shove me out of the way, and then I capture her other hand and tug both behind her back, grab her wrists in one of my hands and pinion her arms behind her back. And I press my body against hers and force her to walk backward until her spine is up against the wall of the building.

"Let me go, goddammit!" she snarls.

I take her ponytail in my fist and tug her head back, chin up, and I slant my mouth over hers. Her body thrashes, fighting me. I've got her wrists captured in my fist, and I'm holding her gently but firmly. Her knee lifts and pushes against me, and I let her, but don't allow her to move me. I kiss her, deep, hard, and sweet. And for all the fighting she's doing, her mouth responds to mine. Her body fights, but her lips move, part, and her tongue slips out and touches mine, and I'm tasting her, putting all my conflict into the kiss.

When I know she's not going to fight the kiss, I release her hair and cup the side of her face, my palm to her cheek, my thumb against her temple.

"Goddammit, Adam. Let me go." She breaks the kiss, speaks the words with her lips to my ear.

"No."

"You left."

"I said I needed a minute. How does that translate into leaving?"

"I told you the truth and you—"

"Needed thirty fucking seconds to process it, Des. Jesus." I've still got her hands in mine, but she's not fighting it now.

"And?"

"And I get it. If you'd told me, I would've…I don't even know. Gone slower. More gently. Made it special. Made it the best night of your life. Something you'd never forget."

"It already was." She leans her forehead against my cheekbone. "It already *is* that."

"Come back, Des. Let's talk about it upstairs, okay?"

She nods, and I let one hand go, keeping the other gripped in mine. I don't exactly drag her back upstairs, but it's clear she's hesitant, maybe a little afraid. Once we're in my apartment, I stop with my back to the door. Des keeps going a few steps into the no-man's land between kitchen and living room, and then realizes I'm not beside her anymore.

She stops, turns back, looks at me. Sees me staring at her. "What?"

I shrug. "Like I said down there, I get it. Doesn't mean I'm not still a little pissed off about it. I feel guilty. I took your virginity and I didn't even know it. I just don't know what to think, what to feel."

"Does it change things between us?"

"Is there anything else you haven't told me? That I should know, I mean."

She shrugs. "No. I mean, I told you about being molested. That's the only other thing I tend to keep to myself. For obvious reasons. People look at you different if they know. I tried therapy on my own, once. With a counselor at Wayne. And she just...she always had this pitying look on her face whenever we talked and I just couldn't handle that shit. So I never told anyone else. That's the big one, for me. Some of the other foster fathers would beat up on me, but that's only a trigger when someone gets in my face or tries to restrain me."

My gut sinks and my blood goes cold. "Like I did downstairs, just now?"

She bobs her head from side to side in a neither-yes-nor-no motion. "At first. More when you came up behind me and grabbed my arms. I don't like being surprised or grabbed like that. That's the trigger. But when you held my wrists and kissed me...?" She trails off and doesn't finish.

"What?" I prompt.

She's blushing. "It was...kind of hot. I feel like it shouldn't be, considering things in my past, but it was."

I take a slow, prowling step toward her. "Des, do you understand, all the way down to your soul, that I'd never, *ever* do anything to hurt you?"

She ducks her head. "Not on purpose, I guess, yeah."

"You've been through so much, Des, and you deserve to be treated—"

She looks up sharply, her eyes fierce. "That's just it. I deserve to be treated normally. I can't stand being coddled or pitied or like I'm…fragile." She says this last word bitterly, like it's the vilest of curse words. "I'm not fucking *fragile*. I've been through shit most people can't even fathom. I was jumped in the bathroom more than once during high school, six or seven girls beating on me just for being new and white. I've been mugged. I've been sexually molested. I've been through a shitload in my twenty-two years, Adam Trenton, and I'm *fucking fine*. I don't need help. I don't need pity. I don't need to be treated like some delicate fucking little flower."

I close the space between us, palm her waist and pull her lush body flush against mine. "Treat you like you're delicate? No." I drag my lips across hers, slip the tip of my tongue along the crease of her mouth, kiss the corner. "Treat you like you're precious? Absolutely."

Her breath hitches, and she tilts her face to mine. "Nice line, asshole," she breathes.

My hands find the lower edge of her T-shirt and lift it, I work my fingers beneath it to find her warm soft skin, and she finally exhales softly, her palms going flat on my chest. I slide my palms up her back, bringing her shirt up as I go, bend my head to kiss the side of her neck. Her head tips back, offering me her throat, and I kiss her there, then down and down to the point of her V-neck. Unable to wait any longer, I lift the T-shirt over her head and drop it to the floor. Her bra is purple silk with white lace running along the upper edge of the cups, her tan flesh mounded and tantalizing. I leave her bra on for the moment, kissing down between her cleavage, down again to her stomach, lowering myself to my knees.

Her hands catch at me as I work the button of her jeans open and lower the zipper. "Adam…what are you—what are you doing?"

I smile up at her as I hook my fingers into the denim and tug down. The jeans come off inside out, and she steps free of them. I push the garment aside and run my palms up the backs of her legs to caress the soft taut silk of her underwear, matching purple with white lace running around the waist.

"I'm glad I wore a matching set today," Des murmurs. "This is the only thing even close to lingerie I have, and I'm only wearing it because everything else is dirty and I haven't done laundry yet—"

She's rambling out of nervousness, which is cute, and unlike her. "Des."

"Yeah?"

"Shut up." When she frowns down at me, I smile back. "You're sexy. And honestly, I couldn't care less what kind of underwear you're wearing. It's all coming off, whether it cost fifty dollars or a thousand. To me, it's all about what's underneath."

I pull the elastic at her right hip down an inch or two and kiss the flesh as I bare it, slide my finger across and beneath her navel, and do the same to her opposite hip. She's not breathing now, and her hands slide through my hair, her fingers combing my short, gelled black spikes. Another gentle tug, and her left hipbone is bared, my lips graze her skin as my fingers drag over her stomach just above her core now. I lower the silk on her right hip.

I do this again and again, teasingly slowly until the top of her pubic hair is revealed. Her fingers freeze on my head, fingernails digging into my scalp. She gasps as I curl the index fingers of each hand into the elastic at her hips and tug her panties off in one quick motion.

"Adam..."

"This is the penthouse," I tell her, "and the apartment beneath is untenanted."

Her brow furrows as I glance up at her. "So?"

I keep my eyes on hers as I touch my lips her pudendum, then her thigh. "So feel free to scream as loud as you want."

I nudge at her inner thigh with my nose and her stance widens, and then I dive in, my tongue going to her hard little clit and lapping at it slowly.

"Oh...shit."

"Balance for me, babe," I tell her.

"What?" she gasps. I grab her left ankle and lift. She leans so her weight is on her right foot, and her hand goes to the wall on her left. I drape her knee over my shoulder and suction my lips to her pussy. "Oh shit. Oh my god, Adam."

Her hips angle forward and her left heel hooks around my back, opening herself to me even further. I taste her essence on my tongue, musky and sweet. Her hands are in my hair and holding the back of my head, her breath coming in short gasps. I don't draw it out or toy with her. I slide one hand up to her ass and clutch one of the globes, keeping her core against me, and I bring the fingers of my other hand to my chin, find her opening and slide in, one finger first. She's wet and hot and tight around my finger, and I slide it in, then out, setting a synched rhythm of finger and tongue, and she's gasping even louder now, a whine at the back of her throat coming with each exhale. Her hips angle forward and pull back, and I can feel the leg supporting her weight trembling.

"I can't—I can't…ohgodohgod, Adam—" she groans, and her spine bows out, pushing her tits forward and her hips into me, her core harder against my face.

I know she can't possibly come while standing on one leg, so when I sense that she's close, both to the edge of orgasm and the end of her ability to balance, I stand up, keeping her left leg in my hand, around my waist. I bend at the knees and lift her right leg. She stares at me in obvious surprise as I lift her and support her weight with my hands under her ass.

"Adam, you're going to break your back, you idiot," she says, wrapping her arms around my neck as if afraid I'll drop her.

She's not light, but I carry her easily across the apartment to the couch. I set her down and kneel between her thighs. She's shaking all over.

"I was so close," she murmurs.

"Yeah? How close?" I ask, nuzzling at her thighs, kissing my way toward her core.

"Right there. Couple more seconds..."

"You want it, babe? You want me to make you come?"

She palms the back of my neck. "Yes, god yes. Please..."

I pause with my face inches from her core. "Then let me see you take off that bra. Show me those gorgeous tits of yours, Des." She leans forward and reaches behind her back, frees the strap and slides one arm out, then other, and then she's tossing the undergarment onto the coffee table. I make a low sound in my throat, a moan of appreciation. "God, you're perfect. Look at them, Des. Big, round, soft—"

"Just like the rest of me," she jokes.

I reach up and strum a nipple with my thumb, and she gasps. "You're sexy, Des. I don't care what words you want to use to describe yourself. You're beautiful all over. Here—" I flick my tongue against her clit, "...Here—" and I lift up to suck her rigid pink nipple into my mouth and flatten it between my tongue and the roof of my mouth, "and here—" I release her nipple and find her mouth with mine, driving my tongue between her lips.

I slide my hand up her thigh, over the side of her hip, up her ribs, caress her back, and then pull her into the kiss with my hand at the back of her head, and then break the kiss to tap her temple. "And you're beautiful here." I bring my palm down, over her breast to where I can feel her heart beating. "And here."

"God, Adam." She leans back, her eyes full of emotion. Her fingertips touch my cheeks, drag down to my jaw, and then wrap around the back of my neck. "Shut up and make me come." She pushes my head toward her core.

I bury my face between her thighs, and she draws her knees apart, leans back against the couch, moaning in relief as I suck her clit between my lips and slip my middle finger into her channel. Her hips roll as I suckle, and then I flick my tongue and move my head in a circle, faster and faster.

And yet, when I feel her tense, I slow. She groans in frustration, which turns into a whimper when I curl my finger inside her, and then add my ring finger inside her. I start a slow in-and-out motion with my two fingers, curling at the in-thrust to scrape at her high inner wall. I glance up at her, and her eyes are closed, the corner of her lower lip between her teeth, a desperate expression on her face. I return my attention to her pussy, reaching up with my free hand to pinch and roll her nipple between forefinger and thumb until she's moaning and her hips are writhing and I feel her walls clamp down around my fingers. Her body quivers, straightens, and she lets out a small scream. One of her knees and then the other hooks over my shoulder, and she lifts free of the couch cushion completely, writhing against my face as I devour her, my tongue circling her wildly, fingers fucking her steadily. Her hips grind, moving against my fingers and mouth and she's gasping breathless shrieks as wave after wave of orgasmic bliss wash over her.

I'm hard, achingly hard from eating her out, from the sight of her nude perfection and the taste of her essence and the sounds of her climax. I need her. I need her pussy around my cock, her mouth on mine, her hands on my skin. Except I'm fully clothed still, and I realize I don't have any condoms. I used the last I had with Des six months ago and never bought more.

She comes down from her climax and goes limp against the couch. I move to sit beside her, and kiss her shoulder, her chest, her throat, unable to keep my hands or mouth off her. I caress her waist, her hip, kiss between her breasts.

"Adam, wait." She pushes me away. "My turn."

She grabs the lower hem of my shirt and peels it off, tosses it aside.

She sees my bruises and gasps. "Adam…? What happened?"

I shake my head. "Just a stunt. I'm fine, don't worry about it."

She eyes me. "You're sure? I don't want to hurt you."

I reach for her. "Babe, the only thing that hurts is how bad I need you."

"Then let's get you naked," she breathes.

She leans into me, kisses my chest, and her hands caress my shoulders and trace my abs, and then her fingers are at the fly of my jeans, unzipping me. I love that, the feel of her hands unzipping my jeans. And the button is popped, and my dick is pressing up at the opening against my underwear.

Des straddles me, pushes me back against the couch and leans down, kisses my shoulder. Her heavy boobs drape against my chest, drag soft as silk against my skin. I can't not touch her, my hands sliding up and down her spine. But then she's off me and on the floor in front of me, dragging at the legs of my pants until they come off, bringing my underwear with them part of the way. I lift up and she tugs both jeans and boxer-brief off at once, her mouth touching my thigh, the other thigh, and then my hip.

"I don't suppose you're on birth control, are you?" I ask.

"No," she says, wrapping one hand around my dick. "Why?"

"Because I don't have any protection."

She pauses and looks up at me. "You don't?"

I shake my head. "Nope. I had three left in my toiletries bag, and I used them with you on Mackinac. I haven't had a need for them since."

"You haven't?"

I shook my head. "No. I told you, there's been no one since you, that night."

"For me either."

My eyes close involuntarily as her fist slides down my length. "We're going to…need condoms," I say between groans.

She rolls her thumb over my head, and then plunges her fist down to the root, then drags it slowly back up. I glance at her, watch her as she stares at her own hand, at my cock, and she glances at my face. "So what do we do?"

"I could go get some."

She shakes her head, and she's leaning over me. "No. I don't want you to leave me."

"It wouldn't take long."

She twists her fist around me, and yes, she's definitely closer, now. "That'd be too long." She looks up at me. "Have your guy go get them for us. Oliver."

"You wouldn't be embarrassed for him to know what we're—"

"I'm pretty sure he already does, Adam."

There's no doubt, now. She's leaning over me, my cock rock-hard and throbbing in both hands now, her fists sliding over me hand-over-hand, and she's watching from an inch away.

"Des?"

She ignores me, reaches to the floor at her side and rummages in the pocket of my jeans, withdraws my cell and hands it to me. I let out a breath and then take the phone, bring up my text thread with Oliver.

Need a huge favor, dude.

He responds after a couple seconds. *Would I find your favor in the family planning aisle?*

God bless Oliver. Yes.

Ok. But I'm not sure you're paying me enough for this.

I'll give you a raise.

Sounds like you've got the "raise" aspect of things covered, boss.

I will fire your ass so fast...

LOL. Stop texting during foreplay. It's rude.

I toss the phone aside and return my attention to Des, who is utterly absorbed in her ministrations. Her hands move slowly up and down my length.

"I want to taste you, Adam." She leans even closer, her lips inches from me.

"Des..."

"I've never done it before, and I want to."

My breath catches in my lungs as her lips wrap around the head of my cock. Her mouth is warm and wet and I can't help a groaning exhale of bliss leave me as she bobs down ever so slightly. My head falls back on the couch and I force my eyes open to watch her. Her mouth is spread wide around me, her eyes raised to look at me.

She pulls back and I leave her mouth with a *pop*. "Was that okay?"

I laugh. "Anything you do is amazing, Des. Just don't bite, and it'll feel incredible."

She moves back down, taking me into her mouth, her tongue swirling around my tip, tasting. Her hand is around the base, just holding, and then she strokes once and I unconsciously lift my hips. She lets out a sound of surprise, and then backs away, sucks once with her lips around the head, then lowers her mouth around me.

"Jesus, Des. You're gonna have to stop soon."

"Mmm-mmm—" She makes a negative sound, and then lifts her mouth off me, stroking me as she goes. "No way. You *really* like this, don't you?"

"God yes."

"More than fucking me?" she asks, and then her mouth is around me again and I can't help groaning.

"Hell no. *Jesus*—!" The last is an exclamation of surprise as she sucks hard and lowers her mouth around me until I'm sure it has to be uncomfortable.

At that moment, I hear my front door open, and a small square package flies to land on the floor. I glance at it, and see that he's bought extra small condoms. "Oliver, you asshole!" I try to sound normal.

I hear his rasping laughter and then another package flies through the foyer to land beside the first, this time a package of condoms that will actually fit me.

And then the door closes and he's gone.

When she heard the door open, Des paused and glanced toward the opening, to make sure he wasn't going to show up. Once she hears the door close, she gives me a wicked grin and takes me in her mouth again. And this time, she shows no mercy. Her fist flutters up and down at the root of my cock, and her lips slide around my girth, going down and down, and then back up, and up, and now she's set a rhythm, slow and steady.

I'm having trouble holding still, holding back. "Des, stop."

I pull at her, but she takes my hands in hers, tangles our fingers. Her eyes go to mine as she bobs her head, watching me. I try to pull my hands free, but she doesn't release them, holding tight and fighting against my grip. Her eyes show humor briefly, and then she's going down on me harder and faster, and I know I can't hold back.

"Fuck, Des, I'm gonna come. You have to stop or I'm gonna—"

She pauses with her lips wrapped around the head and sucks hard, and I know it's hopeless. She moves our joined hands to her head, places my palms on her hair, and then takes my root in her fist and cups my balls in her hands. I tug her ponytail from the elastic band and feather my hands through her black locks, holding it away from her face. She bobs again, stroking my base and sucking.

I'm gone.

I cry out, unleashing suddenly, unable to warn her again, and she makes a sound of surprise, but doesn't stop or slow down. I feel myself explode in her mouth, and she keeps bobbing, keeps caressing my length, and then I hear her gulp and I'm exploding still, groaning and trying desperately not to thrust too hard.

And then I'm done and she's letting me go, moving to straddle me, taking my face in her hands. "How was that?"

I blink up at her blearily, woozily. "Jesus, Des." I rest my forehead against her mouth. "I wasn't expecting that."

"I know."

"But it was…I can't even move."

She kisses me, and I taste myself on her, but I don't care. She's on top of me and I feel her core against my softening member, but her tits are brushing my chest and her mouth is insistent on mine and I've got her full hips in my hands, and I know it won't be long before I'm ready for her, before I can take her the way I need her.

He stands up with me in his arms and carries me across the apartment, into the bedroom. Lays me down, plants a hand on the bed beside my face and kisses me while caressing my breast with his other hand.

And then he's gone, but only for a moment, returning with the package of condoms.

My heart seizes, and my core goes damp.

But he's not ready for that yet. He rips the box open, pulls one square free and sets it aside, then sprawls out on the bed beside me. His hands trace my ribs beneath my tits, down, and find the edge of one of my tattoos. His eyes go to mine, and I see the question.

I roll into him, resting a hand on his stomach, just above his nascent erection. "'The ache for home lives in all of us, the safe place where we can go as we are and not be questioned,'" I recite. "Maya Angelou."

He nods. "I saw it when you were sleeping. What's it mean to you?"

I rest my head in the crook of his arm. "It's just about…home. About belonging. I've never belonged anywhere. Growing up in the system, none of the placements ever lasted more than a year at most, so there was never home. Everywhere I lived, it was just a house. A place to sleep. So that's what I've always wanted more than anything, is to feel safe, and…to have a home."

He traces the tattoo on my hip. The scar beneath it. "And the scars the tattoos cover?"

I close my eyes and bury my face in his skin. His arms curl around me, shelter me. Protect me. "I was sixteen. I'd just been moved to a new family. The dad was…bad. Real bad. On disability, wasted all the time. Got violent. Usually he only went after his wife, but every once in a while, he'd go after their daughter. Her mom would get between the girl and the dad. But once…he hit his wife too hard, knocked her out. Michaela, the daughter, started screaming. He was just…crazed. I don't even know what the fuck got into him. I think he was a Desert Storm vet or something, maybe it was a flashback? I don't know. There was this extension cord on the table, an orange one. Michaela went after her dad, and he knocked her to the ground. Just laid her out. And he grabbed the cord, started hitting her with it. It was long, and he just had a doubled-over section of it, about three or four feet long. He started hitting 'Chaela with the cord, and I just couldn't let him—I couldn't. So I laid over her, covered her. And he just kept hitting. I'd just gotten out of the shower, and all I had on was a towel. The towel fell off, and he just—kept hitting me. I don't think he even knew what he was doing. Maybe he did. I don't know. Part of me thinks he did know what he was doing, because he kept hitting me in the same place, over and over, and then he'd hit in a different spot. Left those fun scars."

"Fucking hell, Des." Adam's arms tighten, his lips touch my temple. "What stopped him?"

"A neighbor. Heard the screaming, realized it was worse than usual, I guess. It took the neighbor and three cops to get me off Michaela. I wouldn't let go of her."

"Des, god, babe."

I lift up and look at him, let him see into my eyes. "It's fine, Adam. It was a long time ago. And honestly, I'd do it again, if I had to. Michaela is just the sweetest girl you'd ever meet. I stayed there…for her, even after that.."

"*What?*" He gives me an incredulous look.

"He spent six weeks in jail, got probation, a tether, addiction counseling, mandatory AA, all that. My caseworker wanted to move me, but I refused. I was sixteen, so she could've insisted despite my protests. Before that, I didn't care. It didn't matter; one home was as good as another. But Michaela…she needed me. Her mom wasn't much good on her best day. She needed a friend, and I was all she had." I smile, thinking of Michaela. "I still visit her, sometimes. She was only five when that happened. She's eleven now."

"And you got the tattoos to cover the scars?"

"Sort of," I answer. "But more out of a need to turn something that came from ugliness into something beautiful—more than because I was self-conscious about the scars or whatever. And that quote...I came I across it my senior year of high school. I was doing a paper on Maya Angelou, and I read a whole bunch of stuff she'd written. I came across that quote, and it just stuck in my head. It resonated with me on a really deep level. Maya, she *got* it, too. She had a hard life, and she turned all that pain into so much beautiful poetry."

"So have you," Adam says.

I glance at him. "How do you figure?"

He smiles, traces my lips with a thumb. "Just you. Who you are. The fact that you can be such a beautiful person despite all that you've been through, that's poetry too, Des."

"Jesus, Adam. You're gonna make me cry." I sniff.

"That wouldn't bother me," Adam says. "You don't have to be strong all the time, you know. It's okay to show weakness. To show emotion."

I shrug. "It's ingrained."

"Un-ingrain it," he says.

I can't help but laugh. "Yeah, lemme just flip that switch real quick..."

Adam laughs with me, letting it go. He knows it's not that easy. He brushes a lock of my hair out of the way. "Des? I have a question, and you have to answer it truthfully. You're gonna want to dismiss it as stupid, but please don't."

I lean back to look at him. "Okay, I'll try."

He takes a deep breath and lets it out. "Why me?" I frown and open my mouth, but he covers my lips with his finger, and then traces my jawline, my lips, the column of my neck. "You're a gorgeous woman, and as ill-fated as it was and as horrible as the industry can be, modeling has to have shown you that that's not just my opinion. So why me? Why did you trust me? Why did you let me take your virginity?"

I don't answer for a long time, thinking about my answer. "Number one, you didn't *take* it, I *gave* it to you. Big difference to me. As for why you? You *saw* me. I'm not sure how to explain that. It's like... you seemed to see who I was, who I am, and you treated me like I am worth wanting. You see what I hide. It's not that anything I've experienced is a secret; it's just that I don't trust anyone enough to tell them. But you...I just *trusted* you, like instinctively or something. I still can't explain why. I mean, I know *now* that you're a strong and kind and understanding man and that you're trustworthy, but I didn't know that then. I *wanted* to trust you. And, honestly, that scared the fuck out of me. That was as much the reason I didn't stick around the next morning as anything else. I couldn't figure out why I'd trusted you, why I wanted you so badly. Or why you wanted me. None of it made any sense, and that just scared me." I smooth my palm in idle, lazy circles on his torso. "You pursued me, like you just *had* to…have me, and that was like nothing I'd ever experienced before."

"You're so different from anyone I'm used to," he says. "You're honest. Not open necessarily, which I understand. You couldn't be, not with the life you've lived. But you just are who you are. I saw a beautiful woman who knew herself, and was comfortable with herself, but she didn't entirely comprehend her own beauty. It's an intoxicating combination." His fingers dance over my hip, and his eyes burn. "And also, I just plain lusted for you. I wanted you, and I intended to have you. I just didn't realize—"

"What you were asking for?" I cut in.

"How much more there is to you than I even first imagined," he answers. "And I mean, I knew from the first conversation we had that there was a lot you kept hidden. There was a lot of complex, beautiful woman to know, hiding somewhere past all those walls." He pulls me toward his body, and I fall against him, breasts crushed to his side, a leg thrown over his, my eyes fixed on his. "I was determined to get past those walls. I wanted to figure you out. I wanted you to trust me, to tell me all those secrets I saw in your eyes."

"Well…now I have."

"Now you have," he agrees, and his mouth finds mine.

His hands span my waist, lift me astride him, and the kiss breaks. I gaze down at him, into his pale green eyes, and I'm lost. I was lost before, but after revealing the truth and all the things I'd kept hidden, I'm drowning in him. I press a kiss to his chest, and then sigh in pleasure as his big strong hands roam my back and my ass and my thighs, and then up to bury in my hair and bring my face to his for a soul-searing kiss. He's there, at my entrance, hard and hot, and I scrub my palms over his cheeks and slide my body up his, cling to his neck and sink him deep inside me.

"Oh *fuck,* Des…god, you feel like heaven…"

"Not heaven," I gasp, writhing upon his length. "*Home.* You feel like home."

"Is there a difference?" he whispers.

I shake my head, lift up so I can see his eyes, my hair falling around our faces. "No, there's not. Not to me."

"Me either." He thrusts up into me, lips touching my cheek, then teeth nipping at my ear. "I love this, Des, feeling you like this. Bare inside you."

"Me too."

"You're not on birth control."

I shake my head. "No. Never needed to be."

"Then we should stop for a second. I've got to put one on." He rolls us over, slides out of me, rises to his knees between my thighs. Snagging the packet he'd set aside earlier, he rips it open and sheaths his cock with the condom. "Now. Where were we?"

I just stare up at him, waiting, expectant. "I don't know. I've forgotten. You should show me."

A smile spreads across my face as he grips his thick cock in one hand and guides himself to my opening, presses the broad head to my clit and rolls it in slow circles. I gasp, and his eyes darken, heat up. He slides into me, pushing all the way in, and then moves his knees closer to me, spreading my thighs farther apart.

So fucking full. He's in me, his heat diffuses over my skin, his eyes penetrate mine and see my soul and he knows my secrets and he's looking at me like he can't get enough. He's so deeply impaled in me that I can't take any more of him. But then he lifts me by the hips and drives deeper, and holy *fuck* it seems I can take more of him, and still I need him harder faster deeper *more*...

And now he's pulling back slowly, sliding his length nearly out of me in a teasingly slow glide, and then he pistons all the way in so hard my tits bounce and I shriek involuntarily, gasping, reaching for him, leaning forward and gripping his hips and pulling at him, because *Jesus* did that feel good.

"Again…" I breathe, "Adam, do that again."

His grin is pleased and hungry. "You like that, huh?"

"Fuck yes."

"You like it hard? A little rough?" He pulls out in the same slow withdrawal, tightens his grip on my waist, and then slams in as hard as the last time, and my eyes cross from the spear of superheated ecstasy that explodes through me when he's deep and hard like that.

"Yes, Adam, yes…god, I do, I like it when you fuck me hard."

"Then I'll give it to you hard." He pushes deep, leans over me and his cock is buried in me, filling me, and his lips find mine, kissing me with a sweet lingering tenderness that has my eyes pricking and my heart swelling in my chest. It's a kiss that tells me, no matter how hard and rough he may be about to fuck me, he's doing so with a heart full of—

No.

Nope.

Not letting myself go there. Even now, I can't let myself believe it's that, *that* word. For him, or me. That would be too much like every girl's fantasy, and too much like everything I've ever wanted, and if I let myself want it or feel it with Adam, and it's taken away, I'll shatter.

So I accept thoughts like "tenderness" and "sweetness", and keep that other word at bay, buried deep, deep, deep in the shadowy recesses of my consciousness.

Adam straightens, lifts my legs and places the backs of my thighs against his chest so my feet extend past his head. He scoots closer to me so my ass is flush against him, and I can't even breathe from how deep he is, can't see from the dizzy, heady splendor of his cock so big and hard and hot and perfect inside me…

And then he moves.

He pulls back, wrapping his hands around my thighs just below my knees, and drives in. It's gentle, that time. A warning shot, so to speak. And god, I'm already breathless, a taut fiery tension coiled in my belly, making my toes curl and my fingers scrabble desperately at whatever flesh I can find. Another thrust, this one a little harder, and a gasp is driven from me.

"Oh *fuck,* Adam…"

"Is it good?"

"So good."

"You want more?"

"God yes, more." My voice shakes.

His eyes don't waver from mine, nor mine from his, as he sets a slow and steady rhythm, grinding deep, pulling out slowly and then thrusting in, faster and faster. Harder and harder. Between my open thighs, I can see his still-bruised torso rippling and tensing as he thrusts, the granite-hard slabs of muscle shifting beneath his dusky skin, the faint scrim of hair beading with sweat. His massive arms cling to my thighs for leverage as he begins to fuck in earnest now, slamming into me with relentless vigor, his flesh slapping against mine, and the detonation inside me is building, ecstasy piling upon bliss piling upon whatever is beyond that.

Nirvana, perhaps?

Heaven?

Completion, maybe.

I lift my hips to meet his thrusts, and deep-throated, unladylike grunts leave me with each clapping orgasmic meeting of our bodies. He's grunting with me, groaning and cursing and his skin gleams with sweat, veins stand out, muscles ripple and flex, and I feel like I'm being ripped apart in the most incredible way by the exploding need behind each pounding thrust of his body.

"Adam…I'm gonna come."

"Let me hear you, Des. Scream for me, babe. Scream my name when you come all over my cock."

"Only if you scream my name too."

"Deal." He grins at me, white teeth flashing and pale beautiful green eyes hot and intent on mine.

I feel my pussy clench, feel the tension snap like a rubber band and tears start in my eyes, a gasping sob borne of raw intensity ripping from me.

And then, in that exact moment, when the orgasm breaks free, Adam releases my legs and bends over me so we're face to face. His cock pistons into me in wildly fast thrusts, mad and manic, and his mouth claims mine, a breathless kiss.

"ADAM!" I shout his name as I shatter, heat suffusing my body, my thighs locked in a vise-grip around his waist and my hips grinding.

And then, inexplicably, at the peak of my climax, he slows his pace. I claw at his ass with my hands, pull at him and shriek with frustration.

He pulls out slow, hesitates, his eyes on mine, and then he slams his cock into me hard and fast, and I scream. "Fuck, Des, *fuck,* I'm coming, I'm coming." He withdraws, an infinitesimal pause, and then his thick pulsing cock rams home.

He's shaking, his thrusts slow and desperate. His eyes are locked on mine, but I can tell it's an effort to keep them open. I cling to his neck, legs around his waist, lips pressed to his ear. "Come, Adam, come inside me. Yes…" I whisper it, writhing my hips. "Yes, keep going, Adam. Keep fucking me. Keep coming." I've got a penchant for cursing, but talking dirty like this is something I never knew I was capable of. Yet with Adam, it just seems right, it just emerges from me involuntarily.

His thrust falters as he buries himself deep. I roll so I'm on top, slide my knees forward and my ass backward, hands on his chest, and push his cock as deep as it will go, push *hard,* and he lifts up with his hips and grips my thighs in his powerful hands and roars loudly and wordlessly. I pull my pussy forward, and then drive back down as hard as I can, watching as his eyes squeeze closed and the veins on his neck and forearms and biceps pulse and his abs go taut. I feel his heat within me, feel his cock throbbing.

Once more, then, I lift up, angling my hips back slightly to pull his shaft away from his body, and sit down hard.

"FUCK!" he groans. "Des…my fucking god, *Des…*"

He's gasping for breath, we both are, and we're both coated in sweat, shaking all over.

I'm still trembling from my own orgasm, after-shocks quaking my body as I impale myself on him one last shuddering time, and then I can't stay upright on him. I pull him free of my body with a whimper, and then fall to the bed beside him.

"Jesus, Des."

"That was…"

His chest is heaving, abs tensing and relaxing with each deep breath. "That was fucking *intense*."

"It's the most amazing thing I've ever felt."

He rolls to his side, facing me, cups my cheek with his palm, eyes honest and sincere. "Me too. I never knew it could feel that way." He slides his lips over mine, a brief, hot kiss.

"It's not always like this for you?"

He shakes his head. "No. Never." Adam plants a fist in the pillow by my head, lifts up, and this time the kiss is deep, soul-scouring, demanding all the emotion in my soul be offered up for the taking, for the tasting. "There's a...*connection*...with us that I never even knew was possible. I *feel* you, Des. I don't know how else to say it. I don't mean just physically, but I mean fuck, yeah, the way sex with you feels is so much more than I've ever felt before, but that's not what I mean. You, me, *us,* it's something more."

I want to believe that. I want that to be true. Because I feel it, too. "Don't lie to me, Adam. Don't feed me bullshit. Don't tell me what you think I want to hear." I'm too vulnerable, too emotional, and my defense mechanisms are kicking into overdrive.

But Adam is there, somehow *inside* me, inside those mechanisms. "Hey. Don't try and shut me out now, Des. Don't you fucking dare." He takes my hand and places my palm over his heart. It's thumping hard and fast. His eyes bore into mine. "Come back, Des. Come back to me, baby."

Babe is one thing. *Baby*...that's got "attached" written all over it. It's deep, familiar. No one has ever called me anything but my name. No one has ever cared enough about me to use terms of endearment. Except Ruthie, of course, who is really all the family I've ever had.

I blink hard and squeeze my hands into fists and fight my fear of emotional vulnerability. "I'm here."

He sits up, swings his legs off the bed. "Don't move. Don't even blink. I'll be right back." He's in the bathroom for a split second, it seems, and then he's back sans condom.

And then, somehow, I'm wrapped up in him. His arms are circled around me, my head tucked beneath his chin, my body tangled with his. I feel the stickiness of his come on his cock as it lies against my thigh. My skin cools as the sweat dries, and I feel his pulse thrumming in his throat, in his chest.

He doesn't ask anything of me. Doesn't demand I tell him how I feel or try to kiss me. He drags the blankets over us both and holds me. And this, it turns out, is the magical key to unlocking the gates. He holds me and the fear reflex, the instinct to protect myself from getting to close to anyone, fades into nothingness.

CHAPTER FOURTEEN

We're sitting in the waiting room of a doctor's office. Adam is beside me, reading a magazine. I notice he's been probing at his ribs every once in a while.

"Adam?" He glances up at me. "How are your ribs?"

He shrugs. "They're fine," he says. "They'll heal."

"Does it hurt?"

He shakes his head. "Not really. Aches a little."

"What was the stunt?"

He closes his magazine. "Jumping from the roof of a warehouse to the top of a moving train. The director wanted the landing to look a certain way, and I kept messing it up. Well, on the last take, the train was moving too fast, so instead of my jump being timed to land in the middle of the car, I hit the back edge, caught it with my stomach. Some bruising, nothing I can't handle." He's obviously trying to make light of it.

"Wait. You were jumping onto the roof of a *moving* train? Like, for real? Isn't that dangerous?"

He shrugs. "It's what I do."

"That's crazy! You could've been killed!"

"It's all carefully orchestrated and planned out. And, honestly, if you think about it, it's no less crazy than putting on some pads and letting other guys tackle you on the field. Playing football, you risk concussion and broken bones every single day. Every practice, every game, you risk injury. In acting, even the most dangerous stunts are planned down to the most minute detail. And this stunt, yeah, it went wrong, but that's one scene out of hundreds. And that's the most difficult one we'll do on this project. It's not a big deal."

"Did we make it worse, last night?"

He winks at me. "Babe, I didn't even feel it. In college, I played injured several times. I played a full game with a sprained wrist once. Bruises like this were so commonplace you didn't even mention them, honestly. A cracked rib would be a different story, but this is just some bruising."

I'm focusing on him, rather than my nerves. We're at a gynecologist to get me on birth control. Adam insisted on going with me, and on having

Oliver drive us. Which meant avoiding Oliver's knowing smirk. God. How embarrassing. Twenty-two, almost twenty-three, and I'm just now going on birth control for the first time. And I was driven to the appointment by a bodyguard, with my famous movie star boyfriend sitting beside me.

Boyfriend? Is that what he is? Is this an actual *thing* between us? If he's willing to sit in a gynecologist's office with me, I'd guess so.

I have a boyfriend.

Holy shit. That excites me more than I'm comfortable admitting even to myself.

Adam catches my giddy grin. "What?"

I shrug and shake my head. "I just…I don't know. It's silly. I'll tell you later."

"Okay, then." He smiles and shrugs.

The door between the waiting area and the exam rooms opens. A young woman with curly brown hair and dark green scrubs stands in the doorway, propping the door open with a foot, an iPad in her hand.

She glances up. "Destiny Ross?"

Adam frowns and looks at me. I blush and refuse to meet his confused gaze.

The nurse looks at me. "Destiny Ross?" she repeats.

I stand up. "That's…that's me." I move toward the nurse, saying, "I go by Des."

"Des, then. Come on back, Dr. Guzman will see you now."

I turn back to Adam, who has a puzzled frown on his face. I shrug at him, and then the door is closing behind me, and the nurse is having me step on a scale and measuring my height, noting the results in her iPad. And then I'm in an exam room, and the nurse is in the doorway.

Her eyes are wide as she leans toward me. "Your boyfriend, is that—?"

I nod, and can't stop a wide, giddy grin from crossing my face. "Yeah."

"Damn. You go, girl!"

I wave her over. "But you can't say anything to anyone, okay? Please?"

She tugs on a brown ringlet. "Can I tell my roommate I met him, at least?"

I shrug. "Sure. Just…don't take any pictures or anything. He's here privately, for me. It's important."

She nods. "No problem." She giggles and shakes her head. "I can't believe you're dating Adam Trenton. That's so cool."

"You have no idea." I'm blushing furiously now.

She seems to realize what kind of office she works in and what the implications are, and her eyes widen. "Ohmygod. Is he as big—"

I cut her off. "There's no way in hell I'm answering that question."

She ducks her head. "Of course not. Sorry." She smiles at me, and then offers a polite, formal smile. "Dr. Guzman will be in to see you in just a moment."

"Thanks."

"A moment" turns out to be fifteen minutes. And I thought it'd be a matter of just saying I wanted to get on birth control and get some pills, but it's not that easy. Since I've never had any kind of medical insurance, I've never had a proper exam, so she insists on that, and then there's the whole conversation of what *kind* of birth control I want. I decide on an IUD, because remembering to take a pill every day is never going to happen.

When I leave the exam room, I hear the hub-bub of voices raised in excitement. My heart stops as I push open the door to find Adam in the waiting room, surrounded by a crowd of women, some of them patients, some of them wearing scrubs. He's got a Sharpie in his hand and he's signing receipts and the backs of cell phones, and he's got his public smile on, but it looks strained. I push through the women, grab Adam by the hand, snatch his Sharpie from him and cap it, and then stand in front of him, between him and the women, all of whom seem a little...rabid.

"Excuse me," I say, giving each one a glare. "That's *enough*."

"But hold on," one woman says. "Can I just get one selfie with him?"

Something has me in its claws. Jealousy? Protectiveness? Possessiveness? "No. You can't have a selfie with him. We're leaving."

"Des, it's fine—" Adam starts.

"It's not. This is a doctor's office, not a fucking press junket."

"Are you his girlfriend?" another woman asks, looking at me.

Adam answers for me. "Yes. She is."

I guess that answers that question.

"Lucky bitch," someone mumbles.

"What's so special about her?"

"I'm prettier than *her*—"

"Come home with me and I'll show you what a *real* woman can do, Adam!"

"We're out of here," Adam growls, and pushes me ahead of him, out the door and into the parking lot. The crowd of women follows us, but Oliver is waiting. The driver's side door is open, the engine running. He flings open the rear passenger-side door, and then moves between us and the crowd, two massive arms spread out to form a barrier. Adam puts himself between me and the noise behind us, waiting until I'm in and buckling before sliding in himself.

And then we're off, the Rover's smooth, powerful engine roaring.

"Well, that was fun," Oliver says.

"Yeah," I say, my voice bitter. "A real hoot."

Adam lets out a breath. "God, Des. I'm sorry you had to deal with that."

"Me? You shouldn't have to worry about being mobbed at the goddamned gynecologist's office."

He shrugs easily. "Price of fame, I guess. I'm used to it, for the most part."

"Where did they come from, though? The waiting room was empty when I went in for my appointment."

Adam nods. "Yeah, well, the one girl in the waiting room sent a text, and a few minutes later three or four of her friends show up, and then the receptionist showed up, and then it was just a fucking circus. Whatever. It's over now." He glances at me. "So, we covered?"

I smile weakly. "Yep."

He frowns and glances at Oliver in the rear-view mirror. "We left before I could pay the bill. Can you call and take care of that for me?"

Oliver nods. "Sure thing, boss. Consider it done."

And then Adam's eyes are on me. "So. Destiny?"

I sigh. "I *hate* that name. There's a reason I go by 'Des.'"

"Why? Destiny is a pretty name. I like it."

I shake my head. "Yeah, I just…I'm weird about it, I guess. I mean, there's nothing wrong with the name itself, it's just—I don't know. 'Destiny Ross' just sounds like a stripper's name or something. I figured I've got enough going against me that I don't need to sound like a stripper on top of it. So I go by Des."

"So can I call you Destiny?" Adam asks, a small grin on his lips.

I glare at him. "Not if you want me to respond."

He chuckles. "We'll have to see about that," he says with a mischievous smirk.

I'm not sure I want to know what that smirk means.

We stop for lunch at a Mexican place downtown, hiding in a corner booth in the back, Adam facing the wall so all anyone can see is me. We eat and chat idly, and then as we're finishing, Adam glances at me.

"So. What had you grinning so big back in the waiting room earlier?"

I shrug and toy with the straw in my glass of Diet Coke. "It's dumb."

"So? Tell me anyway."

"You're my boyfriend." I glance at him. "Right?"

His brows furrow. "I'd hope so, yeah. I mean, I said as much to that crowd at the doctor's."

"That's why I was grinning. You're my first."

"You've never even had a boyfriend before?"

I shake my head. "Adam, Ruth is the only person I ever clicked with. I don't trust anyone. I've known Ruth since my freshman year of high school. As soon as we graduated, we got a place together. She's my only friend, my only family. I'm a very…private… person." I poke at an ice cube with the end of the straw, watching it bob and pop back up. "I told you the other day. There was one guy. I had a few classes with him. He was nice, attractive. Seemed interested. We had coffee, he drove me back home and we made out in his car. That was my first kiss. I was okay with it, it felt nice, and I had no problems. But then he got a hand under my shirt and tried to unbutton my pants and I…wigged out. I had a panic attack. Not as bad as the one I had with you, but bad. That was the one and only time I tried dating, or anything close to it. After that, I just couldn't bring myself to go out on dates. Guys would try to talk to me, and I'd just… freeze them out. So, yeah. You're my first boyfriend. And that makes me smile."

He just grins at me, happy, pleased with himself.

Once it was out there, it didn't sound as dumb as I'd worried about. Or maybe it's just Adam and his ability to make me feel comfortable, to feel good about myself.

Dating a celebrity is never boring. I discover this over the next two months. Some days, I don't see him at all. He films from sun-up to sundown, and I've got my classes and work. But then he'll show up outside the school, a hat low over his eyes, or a hood pulled forward, and he'll whisk me away for dinner somewhere, and we'll end up back at his apartment and I'll invariably be naked before he's even got the door locked behind us.

Ruth is giddy for me.

I'm giddy for me.

We get mobbed every once in awhile. Once, it was at the Somerset Mall, outside Nordstrom. Another time, it was at a Subway—turns out Adam has a slight addiction to Subway. He always handles the attention with aplomb and class. He never refuses to sign, rarely refuses a picture, and always keeps the focus of attention on himself, knowing I'm not entirely comfortable with it.

We're photographed together on several occasions. And the tabloids have a field day with it. Rumors abound. According to the tabloids, we've broken up at least once so far, probably based on a Photoshopped picture taken of me as I'm trying to peel hair out of my mouth and looking, accidentally, like I'm angry or shouting. In the picture Adam is on his phone and he's walking away from me. We'd just said goodbye, he was going to set, and I was going to class. Moments before the picture was taken, we'd kissed rather passionately. But they didn't put *that* photo in the magazine.

He invites me to set to watch filming a few times, which is fun. He's amazing to watch in action. I watch the filming of a big fight scene. Adam is empty-handed, fighting against the villain who has some kind of black stick with green dots running down the length of it. Someone nearby explains that the stick is a stand-in for what will later be a fiery sword created using CGI. Adam is all-explosive energy, back-pedalling under the villain's assault, crossed forearms blocking downward strikes, and then darting past and pummelling his opponent's body with his fists. Even knowing it's choreographed, Adam's punches look vicious, and real. His expression is focused and furious. He's bare from the waist up, wearing a pair of ripped blue jeans and combat boots, and pieces of leather wrapped around his forearms, the same green dots covering the leather. Obviously, some kind of special effects will be added to his forearms, presumably something that will explain how he could block a fiery sword.

Each motion is graceful and powerful, and by the time the scene is finished, he's covering in sweat and his chest is heaving, and my panties are wet with desire for him.

The director calls "cut!" and Adam leads me by the hand to his trailer. He locks the door, pushes me up against the wall, jerks my jeans open and shoves them down. I'm fumbling at his jeans at the same time, and then he's bending at the knees and thrusting up into me, and a whimper escapes me. He covers my mouth with his palm, his eyes burning into mine. He rests his forehead on mine and he thrusts into me until I'm coming and his hand is all that muffles my gasps of climax. And then he's coming into me, his heat shooting into me, filling me, wet and thick.

When we're done, he goes into the small bathroom and comes out with a damp washcloth and cleans me. I wring the cloth out, wet it again, and clean him. And then he's kissing me and we're buttoning up, and he's back to filming and I'm back to class.

It's our secret. Only, guessing by the smirks of certain crew members as Oliver escorts me to the Rover, it's not such a secret.

I don't care.

Okay, maybe deep down I'm equal parts embarrassed and thrilled. Knowing we're fucking with hundreds of people just outside the walls of the trailer adds a layer of excitement to the whole thing.

Another time, near the end of the filming, Adam surprises me at work. It's the end of my shift, around one in the morning, and I'm exhausted. We didn't get much sleep the night before…*ahem*…and I was up for class at seven thirty, and then at work by four that afternoon. So when I feel hands on my waist, I shriek in surprise. He pulls my ear buds out of my ear.

"Hey." His mouth is at my throat and his hands are caressing me down to my ass.

I grin, and set my mop aside. "Hey yourself."

He lets me go, reaches for a small bag at his feet. "So I kind of hate that I can't text you while we're apart. So I got you a phone." He hands me the box to a white iPhone 6. "It's got my number, Oliver's, and Ruth's programmed into it already."

"Adam..." I start, but I'm not sure what to say.

No one gives me gifts. Ruth and I have a standing agreement on the subject, since we're both typically too broke to afford much. We usually just get tipsy together for whatever occasion would require a gift.

"This is a selfish thing I'm doing," Adam says. "I need to be able to call you, or text you. I mean, I like just showing up and surprising you, but it'd be so much more effective if I could just text you and be like, 'hey, I'm coming over to get you, so wear that sexy underwear I like.'"

I frown at him. "I don't have any sexy underwear."

He grins. "Exactly. Those."

I blush. "Adam. I'm not *not* wearing underwear. That's weird."

"You should try it sometime. It's fun."

My gaze travels south. "Are you wearing underwear right now?"

"Where's the fun in telling you?"

So I push him into the men's room, into the handicap stall, and discover he's commando when I unzip his jeans and his cock springs out, hardening under my gaze.

It hardens further in my mouth. I've found out he has a thing for taking my hair out of the ponytail when I go down on him. He likes to bury his hands in my hair, hold it away from my face and 'help' me ever so gently, especially when he's close.

"If this is how you're gonna react when I get you things, I might be giving you more gifts," he jokes as I zip him back up.

I rinse my mouth out and glance at him. "You don't have to give me gifts for this, Adam. Just ask."

He tilts his head. "Really? If I asked, you'd just—"

I wink at him. "Try it, sometime."

Now, I don't precisely *like* going down on him, but I *do* enjoy it very much when he goes down on me—which he does regularly, and voraciously, and skillfully—and I also enjoy his reactions, and the way he thanks me.

So, a few days after he gave me the phone—which I love and can't seem to put down—we're in his apartment, watching a movie. Aunt Flo is in town, shutting me down for business. So he asks, and I do, drawing it out as long as possible, making him go crazy until he's nearly begging me to let him come. When he does, it's a *lot,* and hard, and he's gasping and he can't seem to make coherent sentences for at least five minutes, and I feel very pleased with myself.

The thing with Adam is, he always seems to get the last word.

The credits to the movie are running, white text on a black background, electronic music pulsing. I'm lying on his lap, his jeans still unzipped and unbuttoned but pulled up, and his fingers trail through my hair.

"So. We wrapped filming today," he says. "Which means I'm heading back to L.A. at some point."

I tense. "Oh."

Hello, panic attack. How awful to see you again.

But he's not done, so I try to keep the looming panic attack at bay with some deep breathing.

"Your semester is done when?"

"Next week," I manage.

"And how many semesters do you have left before you get your degree?"

"I have another year. Maybe a little less."

He just nods, and is silent for a moment. I'm still close to panicking. "So *Fulcrum 2* premieres in three weeks."

"Okay." I'm not sure where he's going with this, and I'm afraid to ask.

"Are you locked into going to Mackinac this summer?"

I shake my head, the denim of his jeans scratching my cheek. "No. I said I was, but Ruthie has an internship here in the city this year, and I...I don't know what I'm going to do. Mackinac wouldn't be the same without her."

Adam grabs the remote, clicks the TV off, and tugs at my shirt sleeve, a tacit request to sit up. I twist and tuck my feet under my thighs and sitting facing him.

"Come to L.A. with me." He takes my hand as he says this, twining our fingers together.

"Um...what?" I blink several times. "I'm half-done with my master's, Adam. I can't move—"

"Just for the summer," he interrupts.

"Oh."

"At first, I mean." He pauses. "My agent just sent me a script for a cop movie. It's gonna be filmed here in Detroit starting in the fall. September or October, they're thinking. It sounds like a good script. It's not a big-budget action movie either, more of a cop drama. I want to try my hand at more serious acting roles, and this might be a good way to show my skill at things other than fight scenes and crazy stunts. In the meantime, I could just keep this apartment."

"But this summer?" I prompt. It's not that I don't care about where his career goes, because I very much do, but I want to nail down what he's asking me.

"This summer. Come back to L.A. Go to the premiere of *Fulcrum* with me." He traces my cheekbone with a thumb. "Meet my family."

I swallow hard and have to blink the dizziness away. "Where—um. Where would I stay?"

He frowns. "With…me?" This is said in a *duh* tone of voice. He touches my chin and tilts my face up so I'm looking at him. "Des. When I said I was going back to L.A., what did you think I was saying?"

I shrug miserably. "I don't know."

He has the gall to laugh. "Des. Seriously? Did you think filming would wrap and I'd just…what? Take off and leave? Like, see ya, I had fun?"

I get up and walk across the room, feeling angry and hurt that he's laughing at me. "I don't know, Adam!" I snap. "I don't know what I'm doing. I don't know what this…where we're…I don't know. Yeah, maybe I did think that. I mean, what, am I just supposed to assume you'd want me to move to L.A. with you? And how could I do that? I can't transfer this late in my degree, and I wouldn't want to anyway. And then what? After I've got my degree, what then? I don't know! I don't—I don't know."

Adam is behind me, arms wrapped around my waist, nose in my hair. "Breathe, baby. You don't *have* to know any of that. I don't know either. That's how relationships work, Des. You have your life, I have mine. And somehow, we find a way to make your life and mine fit together, because we like the way life feels when we're together. Right? Do you know *that*, at least?"

I lean back into him, let him support me. "Yes, I know that much."

"Then that's all you need. That's all I need. The rest we take as it comes. We figure it out."

"Okay."

"Okay?" He spins me. "So you'll come to L.A. for the summer?"

I shrug. "Sure."

I ignore the fear that comes with the rest of what he suggested: a big-ticket, high-profile premiere event, as his real official girlfriend, and, more scary yet, meeting his family.

"Good." He tilts my face up, slants his mouth towards mine. "Now kiss me."

"I taste like come," I whisper in warning.

He just smirks, kisses me, sweeps his tongue through my mouth. "Sure do. But then, you kiss me when I taste like pussy, so I guess we're even."

I can't help blushing and burying my face in his neck. "Does it make me dirty that I kind of like kissing you when you taste like me?"

He chuckles. "Yes, it does. It makes you a very dirty girl. I'll have to remember that."

I wonder what I just got myself into. Whatever it is, I'm sure I'll enjoy it.

A lot.

I'm going to L.A. with Adam. I'm going to meet his family.

Shit.

CHAPTER FIFTEEN

I THOUGHT MAYBE WE'D GO TO HIS HOUSE AFTER WE landed in L.A., or maybe to a hotel, or something. I thought maybe Oliver would meet us there, or some other driver. I thought we'd do any number of things.

Instead, there was a tall black man in a fitted black suit standing beside a sleek red sports car, holding a sign that read *A. Trenton*. The man takes our four suitcases and piles them—improbably, it seems to me—into the trunk, hands Adam a key fob, and accepts a folded $100 bill. Adam holds the door and closes it behind me, and then climbs into the driver's seat. He touches a button, pulls the shifter into gear, and then the car darts forward silently. There's no roar of the engine, nor even a silky purr. Just... silence.

I glance at Adam. "What the hell kind of car is this? Is it electric?"

He grins. "Yep. It's a Tesla. Pretty sweet, huh?"

"Where's Oliver?"

"Miss him already?" Adam jokes. "Or is his driving that much better than mine?"

He has the car whipping between lanes, darting around one car and then another, doing easily eighty-five if not more. It's certainly not what I expected when I thought of an electric car. It's sleek and sexy looking, effortlessly powerful, and the interior is done in luxurious tan leather, with a huge touch-screen display where the radio and climate control would be.

"Just…maybe slow down a little?"

He only laughs. "Babe, this is L.A. Traffic will slow me down at some point. Besides, I've missed driving my car."

I don't ask where he was taking us. I should have. I really, *really* should have. But I don't. We don't head into downtown L.A., but up into the hills surrounding it. After a good hour's drive spent in conversation interspersed with companionable silence, he pulls off the freeway and into a suburban area.

We go through a few stoplights, past a few shopping centers, palm trees lining the broad boulevards. It's like a scene from every movie ever set in L.A., immediately familiar even though I've never been here. He turns into a quiet neighborhood and the houses aren't the monster mansions I was expecting, but they are still fairly large. I mean, they're still mansions compared to what I'm used to, but still.

A few turns, and then he's pulling up to a tall two-story house, all brick and adobe and dark beams set on an acre or so. There's a Lexus sedan, an older two-door BMW, and a new four-door Wrangler in the driveway.

Adam pulls up behind the Wrangler, shuts the car off, and gives me a happy grin. "Ready?"

I stare at the three cars, at the expensive but still modest home—modest in comparison to what I imagine Adam could probably afford, even though I have no idea what he's worth. I realize how far we are from Hollywood and the studios, and something inside me makes a connection.

"This isn't where you live, is it." This comes out as a statement.

He grins even more widely. "Nope. At least, not anymore." He gets out, and then ducks his head back in when I don't move to exit the Tesla. "Come on, Des."

I shake my head. "You've got to be kidding me."

He sighs in irritation, closes his door, and rounds the hood to my side. Opening my door, he kneels beside me. "Des. This isn't a big deal. They're excited to meet you."

"I've been on a plane all day!" I hiss. "I didn't take a shower this morning. I'm not wearing any makeup, and I'm wearing fucking yoga pants. Not how I wanted to look when I met your family."

He rolls his eyes. "Believe me, they're the last people on earth who would care how you look, babe. And you look stunning."

"You haven't told me a single thing about your family."

This isn't true. I know he has two sisters and I know their names—Lizzy and Lia—and that they're twins. I know his mom and dad are still married, and that their names are Lani and Erik.

"Liar. I have too." He grabs my hands and pulls me up, and I let him pull me out of the car. "Now, come on. You'll like them. I promise."

He takes my hand and leads me between the Lexus and the BMW, down a walkway lined with dark red stones that leads to the front door, which is easily ten feet high and a rich brown, with black iron fittings. Now that I'm closer to the house, I realize it's quite a bit larger than I'd originally estimated. My heart pounds.

Adam pushes the door open, and we're in a cool, airy foyer, the floor a blue-and-white Spanish mosaic tile, a staircase to the right, a formal living room to the left, and a kitchen visible beyond a short hallway. Adam kicks his shoes off, and I do the same.

That, taking my shoes off before entering the home, is a marker that I'm *really* not in Kansas anymore, Toto. Where I come from, no one gave a shit whether you had your shoes on or not. I mean, why would you take your shoes off? It wasn't like it mattered. Adam takes his shoes off in a way that makes me think it's a life-long ritual. Walk in, take your shoes off.

I can hear voices, a male and several females.

Adam leads me into the kitchen, and then stops just inside. No one sees us at first. There's music playing, top forty pop. A tall, slender woman with dark skin and long, straight black hair stands at an island set in the center of the kitchen, slicing cheese. She's most likely Adam's mother. Her head is down to focus on what she's doing, so I'm not sure yet. Sitting on the stools on the opposite side of the island are three more people.

All I can see of them are their backs, since they're faced away from us, but I can guess their basic identities. The man is even taller than Adam and nearly as well-built, but he has fair skin and wavy brown hair. The other two are his sisters, I think, with Adam's dark skin coloring and black hair.

It occurs to me that Adam comes from an interracial family.

The woman looks up first, sees Adam. He shakes his head, and the woman somehow keeps her expression neutral as Adam creeps up behind the other three sitting at the island. They're all munching on crackers and sliced cheese, chatting and laughing with easy familiarity.

A real family.

A normal family.

It's hard to breathe for some reason.

Adam lets my hand go and tiptoes up behind his sisters, moving with surprising silence for such a huge man. His hands clap down on his sisters' shoulders, and he shouts wordlessly. They shriek deafeningly, jumping on the stools, and then turn and they both leap from their seats at once. They both cling to Adam, and he wraps an arm around both of them, spin them in circles, and then he sets them down and hugs each of them in turn.

They're not identical twins, he told me, but they're almost indistinguishable. Or they would be, if they weren't dressed totally differently, with their hair done differently as well. One wears a skirt shorter than anything I'd ever feel comfortable wearing and a tight top, her hair twisted up in an elaborate knot, and the other is more modestly dressed in a pair of jeans and a tank top, her hair in a low, loose ponytail.

After he's hugged them, Adam turns to his father, who's stood up to wait. He and Adam hug. That's just fucking weird. I mean, I've seen bro-hugs before—bump chests, hands clasped between them, smack each other's back three or four times—but never an actual embrace like this between men. And then Adam is on to his mom, and this is hard for me to watch. He clearly adores his mom. He pauses, holds her by the arms, looks at her, and then he pulls her into a long, intimate hug.

Her hands curl up under his arms and hold onto his shoulders, and when he releases her; she sniffs and drags a finger under her eyes. "Tory…hi, baby. I didn't know you were in town."

Tory?

Adam glances back at me, gestures for me to come to him with a jerk of his head. "Mom, Dad, Lia, Lizzy…this is my girlfriend, Des." He points to each family member in turn. "Des, this is my mom, Lani, my dad, Erik, and my baby sisters, Lia and Lizzy." He glances at Lizzy, the sister in the miniskirt. "And Lizzy, would you like to explain to me exactly what the flying fuck you're wearing?"

Lizzy narrows her eyes at him. "Not you too? God, would you guys give it a rest? It's not *that* short."

"That's what I asked her this morning," Adam's dad says. "I was running late so I didn't have time to argue with her about it."

"Liz, that wouldn't fit a Barbie doll," Adam says.

"Don't be an asshole, Tory. It's not that short. Seriously. You should see what the other girls at school wear. This *is* modest."

I tap Adam's shoulder. "Um. Who is Tory?"

His entire family exchanges looks, and then they all burst out laughing. His mother is the first to answer. She does this by moving between his father and sisters to pull me into a hug. Which is awkward, because I'm *not* a hugger. So I tense, and wonder what I'm supposed to do with my hands, and do I put my face against her shoulder, or what? I don't know. But she doesn't seem to care; she just wraps her arms around me and holds on. She smells like cinnamon, and her hug is soft and never seems to end.

"Des, it's so good to meet you." She finally lets me go, and stands at a comfortable distance. "His full name is actually Torrence Adam Trenton. He went by Tory up until high school, when he decided it was too girly for him, and switched to Adam. But he's been Tory to us his whole life, and he always will be, especially since it irritates him so much." She smiles at me, her teeth flashing white against her dark mocha skin. It's very faint, but I notice a lilt to her voice, the trace of an accent of some kind on certain words.

I turn to him and grin. "Tory, huh. You'd think this would have come up before now."

He narrows his eyes at me, and the glare he gives me is a mirror to the one his sister just gave him. "Is that so, *Destiny?*"

I frown, because I don't exactly have much to argue with on that score. I turn away from him and extend my hand to his father, who ignores the hand and moves toward me. *He's* going to hug me, too? What the fuck? Who hugs this much? It's unnatural. My gut flips and my pulse hammers, because his mother is one thing, but Adam's dad is almost as huge as his son, and I'm uncomfortable at best around anyone, men especially. But I don't want to seem standoffish or anything, so I force myself to stay calm and let him get near me. It feels like it happens in slow-motion, and then his burly arms are around my shoulders, but he's angled slightly rather than face-on, and there's space between us, and somehow it's strangely not as scary as I thought it would be. He smells like cologne and lets me go quickly.

"It's nice to meet you, Des. Welcome." He smiles, and I see where Adam got his eyes, the same pale, intelligent, piercing green.

"You too," I say. "And thanks for having me here."

That's what you say in these situations, right? I don't know. Whenever I was placed in a new home, I'd just say my name and everyone else would say theirs and then I'd find somewhere out of the way to hang out. No one hugged, no one told me welcome or that it was nice to meet me. Just "Hey, 'sup. How are ya?" And then back to the TV or the video game or the joint.

And then his sisters are in front of me, side by side, and they each hug me in turn, because clearly a hug is how this family greets new people, or maybe it's just Adam's girlfriends. I don't know. But I make it through the hugs without panicking or freezing.

"Would you like a glass of wine, Des?" Lani asks, uncorking a bottle.

"Um. Sure?"

"Do you like shiraz?"

I shrug, mystified. "I…I'm not much of a wine drinker, so I honestly don't know. Whatever you're having is fine."

I accept a huge goblet of ruby red wine, and when I taste it my mouth explodes. It's thick, rich, and does something bizarre to my taste buds. I blink and force myself to swallow it.

Adam is watching my expression carefully, and laughs. "Yeah, shiraz'll do that to you. I hate that shit, myself."

Lani looks at me in concern. "Oh, I'm sorry. I guess I didn't realize…here, would you care for something else?" She reaches for the glass, her expression so worried that it's almost funny.

I shake my head and take another sip, which assaults my mouth just as violently as the first time, but it's not entirely unpleasant, just…very different. "No, it's fine. I'll try it."

Lani frowns. "Well, don't drink it just to be polite, not if you don't like it."

The girls have glasses of something pink and bubbly, and I'm not sure if it's alcoholic or not. Adam and his dad have beer, and his mom has a glass of the same wine I'm drinking, and then we all move outside to a long rectangular glass table beneath a pergola. Thank god for HGTV, so I at least know what a pergola is. Lani brings a plate of white, pungent cheese and another plate of hexagonal crackers, and the cheese is arranged in an intricate starburst pattern on the plate and the crackers are stacked in rows, and it looks like something out of a TV show, where people do fancy shit like arrange cheese on the plate before eating it.

I settle into a chair and take another sip, and this time it's actually almost pleasant, the way the wine seems to occupy my entire mouth, exploding and changing as I swallow. I have a hand draped down at the side of the chair, and I feel something wet nuzzle my palm.

I glance over, and then jump so hard my wine spills over the edge of the glass and then I shriek. They have a bear. An actual pet bear. Okay, maybe it's just a big dog, but it's the size of a small bear, with floppy ears and shaggy gray fur.

"What the *hell* is that?" I ask, scooting my chair backward and moving behind Adam, who is laughing.

"That's Iggy," Adam says, pulling the enormous beast to his side. "He's an Irish wolfhound. He's big, sweet, and stupid."

"Iggy?" It seems an incongruous name for such a massive dog. I move out from behind Adam's chair and sit down again.

"He is *not* stupid, Tory!" Lizzy protests. "He's just misunderstood. And a little slow."

"Will he try to eat me?" I can't help asking.

I'm not a dog person. Cats, maybe. Fish, lizards, very small birds…fine. Dogs the size of a grizzly bear? Not fine.

Adam laughs. "No. He might try to sit on your lap and crush you, though. Sit, Iggy." He pats the dog's backside, and he sits, huffing, tongue lolling, a mouth full of huge fangs dripping with saliva. "Iggy. Say hi."

The dog barks, a loud *woof* of sound that has me startled all over again. "Hi, Iggy." I reach my hand out tentatively, and the dog barks again and moves toward me.

I hastily withdraw my hand, but now the dog is in front of me. He's so tall that, when I'm sitting, he can basically lick me in the face without having to lift up. Which he does. Vigorously. I stand up and back away, but Iggy just leaps up and puts his paws on my shoulders. His paws reach my shoulders, and his head is higher than mine. And now his breath is in my face and his tongue is lapping at me.

"Get him off!" I'd like to say that came out as a shriek, but it was actually more of a squeal.

"Ignatius, get *down,*" Erik snaps, and the bear-dog or wolfhound or whatever it is lowers his paws to the ground and stares up at me, tongue lolling, eyes happy and innocent, his head even with my navel.

I wipe my face, and then wipe the slobber from my hands on my pant-legs, trying to contain my disgust. When I finally look up, everyone is trying not to laugh.

I glare, but it's good-natured. "Why on earth would you have a pet bear? That's crazy."

"Wolfhound, babe. Not a bear." Adam is grinning.

"Bear, wolfhound, the size of that thing makes it moot point, if you ask me." I watch nervously as Iggy ambles away, turns in a circle three times, and then lies on the ground behind Adam's chair.

"So did you have any pets growing up, Des?" Lani asks.

I shake my head. "No. I…moved around a lot, so pets weren't really a possibility."

"Oh, was your father in the military or something?" Lani's questions are innocent, but so hard to answer.

"Mom." Adam gives his mother a meaningful glance and a slight shake of his head.

And now it's awkward. I take a fortifying sip of the wine. "I didn't have a…traditional childhood," I say. Everyone at the table is rapt. "I grew up in the foster system in Detroit."

"Oh." Lani's gaze goes soft and understanding. "I see."

That's the look I hate. That right there, even though I know she means well, is the reason I don't talk about it.

I shrug. "There was this one family I stayed with for a few months, and they had a parrot." I can't help smiling. "He was kind of an asshole. I think he was actually a cockatoo, now that I think about it. He was really bizarre. He would climb up your arm and sit on your shoulder when he first met you, and he would just stare at you. It was creepy. You couldn't get him off or try to pet him, or even talk to him until he got down on his own, or he would bite you."

"What was his name?" one of the twins asks. Lia? The one wearing jeans.

"Cartmann."

"Like…the *South Park* character?" she clarifies.

I nod. "Yep."

"That's kind of funny," Lia says, grinning.

"Yeah, until he takes a chunk out of your ear," I say, touching the small divot in the outer edge of my ear where Cartmann had bitten me when I first met him.

"Yeesh." Lia makes a face.

"So, Tory, how long are you in town for?" Erik asks.

"Till September or October," Adam answers.

"Oh, for awhile, then."

Adam nods. "Yeah. All I've got is the premier next month, but I'm off for the summer except for that."

Erik peels the label off his beer bottle, glancing at his son. "So what are you going to do with yourselves?"

Adam shrugs. "Dunno. Show Des the city. Hang out and not memorize lines. Not spend twenty or thirty hours a week in the gym." He glances at me, and there's a glint of humor in his eyes, or maybe it's a promise.

Something tells me those twenty to thirty hours a week in the gym will be transferred to the bedroom, and it'll probably involve me on my back. Or my knees. Or standing up, bent over. He's very imaginative. My core tightens and goes damp at my train of thought, and I force my mind out of the gutter and back to the conversation, which has moved on to Lia and Lizzy's coming transition to college in the fall.

I pay attention and keep quiet, watching Adam interact with his family. It's so incredible to watch. They all know each other so well, they're each so invested in the others, and they each have their own unique way of talking to each other. The girls obviously adore and idolize their older brother, and Adam is fiercely protective, interrogating them each in turn on the kinds of guys they've dated, who they hang out with, and spends several minutes lecturing them on keeping out of trouble when they start college. It's adorable, and a lot sexy. He's tender and respectful with his mom, macho and manly with his dad. And with me, he's a little of all of that. He goes out of his way to include me in the conversations, guides the topics away from anything that might make me uncomfortable.

At some point in the afternoon, Lani quietly leaves the table and moves into the kitchen and begins pulling things from the fridge. I get up and join her in the kitchen.

"Can I help?" I ask.

She smiles at me. "Sure. Would you like to mince a few cloves of garlic for me?"

I smash the cloves with the flat of the knife blade, peel them, and then start slicing. "Adam is really incredible," I say. "You and Erik should be proud."

She beams. "Oh, we are. Very proud. He's accomplished a lot in a very short time." Lani opens two packages of ground beef and dumps them into a huge pan and stirs. When the meat is sizzling, she turns back to me and glances past me, at Adam. "I was worried about him when he signed with the Chargers. I was proud of him then, too, of course, because making it to the NFL is an enormous accomplishment for a football player. But even in the four years he played for Stanford, he got injured several times. Very badly, once, and actually missed half a season. His Achilles tendon, that was. The NFL is so competitive, and I worried for him."

"How do you feel about him acting? Some of the stunts he does are pretty dangerous."

She shrugs. "Well, he's a very tough and athletic man. He always has been. He wouldn't be content doing something that wasn't physically demanding. So yes, I suppose the stunts are dangerous, but the overall risk is less, I think, than the NFL." She glances at me. "Did you know he got a full ride to Stanford?"

I shake my head. "I didn't. I knew he went there and played ball, but…"

Lani's pride is evident. "Well, yes, he played football, too, but his full ride was an academic scholarship, not athletic. He wouldn't mention this, because it's not his nature to brag, but he was Valedictorian when he graduated. He has a degree in psychology. That's on top of starting all four years he played football as well."

My head spins. "Wow, I didn't know. I mean, I know he's smart, but…" I shrug. "When it comes to Adam, though, not much surprises me."

"What about you?" Lani asks, putting water on to boil for pasta. "What do you do?"

"I'm working towards a master's degree in social work."

"What will you do with it?"

"Work with foster kids like me. They need an advocate. Someone who cares, because there's just… there's not enough people in the world who care for the kids who get lost in the system." I slide the cutting board with the minced garlic to Lani, who dumps it into the pan with the now-browned ground beef and tomato sauce. "I want to be someone that I wish I'd had myself, growing up."

"I understand this," Lani says, her voice quiet, her eyes far away. "Growing up in Fiji, I was just one of many children whose parents simply couldn't afford to care for them. But for us, there was no system."

My heart hitches. Something in her carriage, her bearing, her voice, tells me she understands me on a personal level. "But you made it out?"

She nods. "Eventually, yes. I had an aunt; my father's much, much older sister. She had no children of her own. She'd moved here to Los Angeles many years before I was born. I'm not even sure how she made it here, honestly. She visited us in Fiji when I was eleven. And she…brought me back with her. Why me, I'll never know. But she did. Put me in school, gave me an opportunity I would never have gotten otherwise."

"That's awesome," I say.

"Yes, I was very fortunate."

"So, what do you do?" I ask.

"I am a surgeon," she answers. "And Erik is an entrepreneur. He owns several apartment complexes, a shopping center, a chain of gyms, and he also runs a medical supply company, primarily for outpatient home care."

"You must be busy, then."

She shrugs. "Who isn't? He's thinking of selling off some of his holdings now, though, since the girls are both heading off to college in the fall." Her gaze goes to me, and while her expression isn't exactly hard, it's piercing, unwavering. "Tory is kind and loyal to a fault, you know. And he may be a big macho tough guy, but his emotions run deep. He was hurt by a woman recently, very badly. That was…difficult for me to watch."

I let out a long breath and meet her eyes. "Emma. He told me about that."

Lani seems surprised. "He did? He's usually very reticent to speak of that time in his life. That was just so…public, which made it that much more painful for everyone involved. Except her, of course."

I nod. "He made it seem like the whole thing was no big deal to her. Which is just…insane to me. The way he explained it, at least."

"Well, we never met her, but every time I saw him during the time they were dating, he seemed…

stressed. As if keeping up with her, keeping her happy was more a full-time job than even his acting career was." She glances at me. "If you ask me, a person is only as beautiful as the contents of their soul."

"You never met her?" I find this odd. "They dated for what…a year and a half?"

"Perhaps closer to two years, yes. And no, he never brought her here." Lani's expression is thoughtful. "How long have you and Tory been dating?"

I shrug. "Not long."

Adam is behind me, his arms sliding around my middle. "I never brought Emma over because I just…I guess I knew you and Dad wouldn't approve. And I didn't want that conflict. Des is a different story." He moves beside me, leans a hip against the island. "And Des, you're the only girl I've brought home to meet my parents since…what, Mom, high school?"

Lani nods. "Your first girlfriend. Sarah Wexford. That was your sophomore year."

My heart lodges in my throat. "So I'm in pretty exclusive company, huh?"

Adam laughs. "Babe, you *are* the company. I brought Sarah here once after we'd dated for a month, but then she dumped me two days later for the quarterback, who happened to be my best friend at the time. So that doesn't even count."

"Wow." I'm not sure what else to say, so I don't say anything.

The rest of the evening passes easily. I like this family. I like sitting around the dinner table, passing a basket of bread, laughing, talking, feeling as if I belong. Perhaps it's just how kind and open his family is, but I *do* feel as if I could belong. Which is heady, and addictive, and frightening. I pinch my leg under the table several times throughout the evening, but it all remains real. Lia and Lizzy and I discuss fashion for a long time, especially once they discover that I was a model. I tell them modeling isn't all it's cracked up to be, and Lizzy especially seems a little let down by that. I find out Erik used to play football, too, for the USC Trojans, and then second string for the Forty-Niners for four seasons, which explains Adam's build and natural athleticism.

As scared as I was when we first got here, by the time night has fallen and Adam seems ready to go, I feel like I've known this family forever, which makes it hard to leave.

But we do leave, sometime close to ten p.m., and Adam is quiet on the drive into downtown L.A. He takes me to a high-rise condo building in the bustling heart of the city, where a valet parks his car and a porter unloads our luggage and whisks it away. We board an elevator, Adam inserts a small key and presses 'PH', and then we're shooting up, up, up, forty-three floors above the ground.

The elevator doors open directly into a huge foyer where the luggage is somehow waiting for us. It's an open-plan penthouse suite, the kitchen, dining room, living room and a library all sprawled across the entire upper floor, more square footage on one level than I've ever seen before. The walls are white, decorated with black-and-white photographs of old Hollywood, a few framed high-gloss color action photos of Adam playing for the Chargers, and some antique-style maps. The floors are black wood and so shiny they reflect the track lighting. There are floor-to-ceiling windows running along one entire wall, a white couch in the living room area facing a TV that has to be at least ninety inches. It's a beautiful condo, masculine and lived in.

I'm still taking everything in when Adam tosses his keys on the kitchen counter, kicks off his shoes, and then peels his shirt off. His dark skin and rippling muscles catch my eye, and then the gleam in his gaze, the hungry, predatory expression has my breath lodged in my lungs and my core going hot and damp.

"Seeing you with my family was incredible," he says, reaching for me.

"Your family is amazing. They're all wonderful."

"They loved you." He rolls the waistband of my yoga pants down. "I told you they would."

"I felt very welcomed. It was…nice."

"Nice? That's all it was?"

I set my purse on the floor and leave my hands at my sides, look into his fierce, ravenous green gaze. "They made me feel like they could be…like I could—" I can't finish the thought, though. It's too much to hope for.

"Like you belong?" His mouth slants across my jaw.

"Yeah," I breathe, tilting my head to the side, offering him my throat.

"That's because you do."

"I do?"

"Yeah." He takes my offer, nipping across my throat and then down, his hands rolling my yoga pants down a bit further, revealing the indent where my hipbones lead to my core.

"I want to belong." My hands flutter and find his skin. "I've never belonged anywhere before."

He tugs my pants down so I'm nearly bared to him, but not quite, and then his hands cup either side of my jaw. His eyes find mine. "Well, you belong now, Destiny."

My heart stutters at the way my full name sounds on his lips. Words stick in my throat.

"Where do you belong, you ask? Well, let me tell you." He speaks into the silence of my inability to reply. "To me. With my family. In my life. In my home."

"I like all those places," I whisper.

"In my bed."

"I'm wearing too many clothes to belong in your bed," I say, looking up at him.

He peels my pants off, then my shirt. "Let me fix that," he rumbles, his eyes raking and roving over my body as he bares it, bra then underwear.

"And so are you."

"Then you should fix that, too."

So I divest him of his jeans and underwear, and then he's walking me backward, kicking open a door. I pause to look around. The bed is set in a nook to the left of the doorway, on a raised platform. It's a massive bed, custom-made by the look of it, piled with pillows and throw blankets. There's a set of French doors to the right, leading out onto a balcony, and straight ahead is a door leading through to a mammoth walk-in closet that, in turn, leads to a bathroom.

"I like your condo," I tell him.

"Me too." He grins at me, his hands roaming over my ass. "I've only owned it for a year. You're the only person other than my parents, my sisters, and my agent who has been here." I know what he's saying, that Emma has never been here. That the memories we make here are solely ours. He kisses my shoulder, cups my breast. "So, my sexy Destiny…you have two choices. Number one, I lay you on the bed over there and eat you out until you can't breathe, and then I fuck you six ways to Sunday. Or number two, I bend you over the bathtub, and then fuck you *in* the tub. And then maybe the shower."

I reach behind me and grab his erection. "How about option number two, followed by option number one?"

His finger slips between my thighs, finds me wet and ready. "I like the way you think, baby. Guess I'd better get started."

"Guess so."

He moves past me, through the closet—which extends at least two or three hundred square feet to either side—and into the bathroom. The floors are marble, and warm under my feet. There's a palatial glass-walled shower with more heads and nozzles than I can understand, a double sink, several shelves of thick, white, folded towels, and a separate room for the toilet. But the centerpiece is the tub. Claw-foot, circular, and gobsmackingly enormous. Big enough for even a man as big as Adam to lie in, with room for me as well. The faucet and knobs are brass, matching those at the sink and shower.

And, coincidentally, the tub's walls are the perfect height for me to hold on to. I discover this the fun way as Adam guides me to the tub, places my hands on the rim, gently but firmly presses on my shoulder blades until I'm doubled over, and then nudges my feet apart. My hair is still in the ponytail, so he slowly pulls the elastic band free, feathers his fingers through my hair, and then drapes it over my shoulder. I crane my neck to watch him, trembling in anticipation.

He palms my ass cheeks, lifts them and lets them fall with a heavy bounce, slides his hand between my thighs and finds my entrance. Guides himself to the opening and slides in, no warning, no easing in, no foreplay. I gasp and then moan at the sudden fullness of him inside me, lean forward and relax into his movement for one...two...three...four thrusts, and then he's out.

"Don't move," he tells me, giving me a light pat on my ass.

He circles the tub and twists the faucet on, adjusts the temperature, then sets the plug. While it begins to fill, he rummages in a cabinet beneath the sink, finds a bottle of some kind, and squirts it into the stream of water. Bubbles immediately form.

I glance at him in curiosity. "Bubble bath?"

He grins somewhat sheepishly. "I had the place done by a company. They staged all the furniture, picked out everything from towels to silverware. And, for some reason, they provided a bottle of bubble bath. I'm not sure why they stocked a bachelor's condo with bubble bath, but now I'm glad they did."

I reach down and swirl my hand in the water, find it steaming hot. Adam points at me. "I told you not to move, Des."

I put my hands back on the tub. "Well hurry up. I need you."

He grips his cock in his hand and strokes it. "This?"

I nod. "That. Bring it over here."

He shakes his head. "How about you touch yourself for me. Let me watch you make yourself come." So I slide two fingers against my clit and gasp as I circle myself, slowly at first, and then faster. "Stop," he commands, when I'm moments from climaxing.

I halt, quivering, aching, and then Adam is behind me, pressing the broad, soft head of his massive cock to my clit. He cups my tit with his other hand, thumbs the nipple until I moan, and then massages my hypersensitive nub with his head until I'm rocking against him, gasping and moaning.

"Adam, I'm—shit…*shit,* I'm coming!" I feel it hit me all at once, rockets shooting outward from my core, making my knees tremble.

He shoves his cock into me at the moment of my orgasm, and I squeal in shocked pleasure as he fills me. I fall forward, gripping the tub rim for dear life, and then push back into him, bowing my spine inward to get him deeper. He grips my hips and pulls me into his thrust, pushes me away as he pulls out, and then slams back in, and my climax is still ripping through me, stealing my breath and making me dizzy.

And then, abruptly, he pulls out, leaving me fighting for balance and for breath. "Fuck…Adam, why'd you stop?"

"Because I'm not ready to come yet." He growls this, and I can tell whatever game he's playing is costing him in terms of control. He wants to come, and I know he was getting close, but he stopped anyway.

He steps into the tub, helps me in, and then he's lowering himself down and settling me between his thighs, and I'm relaxing against his chest. The hot water swirls around us, bubbles popping and tickling. The sudden heat is relaxing, an abrupt about-face from the frenetic urgency of my climax, which still shudders through me.

But Adam isn't done with me, it seems. We sit in stillness and silence for a few minutes, just long enough for the aftershocks of my orgasm to fade and his erection to subside a bit, and then his hand cradles my stomach just above my pussy, his other hand smearing soapy water across my torso, cupping my boobs and caressing them and fondling them, pinching and rolling my nipples until I'm biting my lip and squirming. And then his hand slips between my thighs, covers my pussy, and his long middle finger slides in.

He massages my clit slowly, so slowly, god, so slowly. Maddeningly slowly. It takes him several minutes to bring me to quivering completion, writhing against his middle finger, just that one inside me, circling my clit and then fucking my entrance, alternating in an arrhythmic pattern.

I come with a sigh, and then he's lifting me by the ass and I'm impaled on him, sitting on him. His knees are spread apart to bear my weight, the water sloshing around us, spilling out. His hands find mine, guide my fingers to my clit, and urge me to touch myself. So I do, and aftershocks become the precursors to something else, something bigger, and his hands are at my tits, holding on and kneading and caressing, and all I can do is ride his thrusts and let him fuck me however he wants.

"Come again, Destiny. Right now." His command works like a trigger.

I come again, *hard*. And this time, I scream.

As soon as the initial wave of climax leaves me, he's lifting me and sliding out of me, groaning and moving shakily, as if the effort to withhold his own orgasm is nearly too much.

"Adam, what game are you playing? Just come, baby," I tell him, watching from my place in tub as he turns on the shower.

He shakes his head. "Not yet."

He hands me up and out of the tub, leads me to the shower, and washes me. He wets my hair, lathers shampoo from scalp to tip, rinses, works conditioner in, and then his hands are scrubbing a bar of soap across my skin. I can't not touch him, so my hands roam his shoulders, slip over the hard muscles sheathed in smooth dark skin, down to his erection, which I caress until he forces my hand away. He washes every inch of me, and then lets me do the same to him.

I run the bar of soap over his stomach, down his hips, then fall to my knees and wash his legs, and take his cock in my mouth. He lets me fondle him with my lips and tongue for a few moments, and then he's pulling me away and pressing me against the shower wall, kissing me until I'm breathless. He kisses me beneath the spray of hot water as if I'm oxygen and he's drowning.

"Jesus, Adam. I'm here, baby. I'm here." I hold his cheek, water splattering off his scalp and onto my face.

He just smiles at me and shuts off the water. "Are you ready for phase two?"

I grip his cock. "So ready."

He grin turns lust-hot. "That's not phase two. You remember what phase two is?"

I pretend to think. "Something about eating me out, right?"

He pulls me out of the shower and wraps a towel around me, scrubs me dry as if I'm helpless to do so myself. "Until you can't breathe, yeah."

I return the favor, drying him off. And then I wrap my hand around the back of his neck and kiss him the way he kissed me, as if I can't exist without his mouth on mine. "I already can't breathe, Adam. Being with you is so…intense…so much…that it's hard to breathe with wanting it to never end."

His expression turns serious, thoughtful, as he leads me to the bedroom, lifts me in his arms as if I'm nothing, and lays me on the bed. "It doesn't have to, Destiny."

I never thought I'd say this, but I love the way my name sounds when he says it.

Shit. I just thought the "L" word.

And, somehow, it's not as scary as it used to be.

CHAPTER SIXTEEN

I SEE SOMETHING IN HER EYES, SOME THOUGHT SHE doesn't share. It's not a look of fear, or nerves, or anything I recognize. It seems more like a realization.

I don't ask, I just slide my face across her stomach, rub my cheek against her inner thigh, bury my face in her core, inhale the scent of her arousal, flick my tongue out and taste her essence. She groans, lets her knees fall open, and writhes her hips. I take my time, wiggling my tongue in slow circles around her clit until she's gasping, her stomach tensing and relaxing with each scrape of my tongue tip against her hardened nub. And when I think she's starting to get close, I suction my lips around her clit and work my tongue back and forth until she's moaning and breathless.

"Yes, yes..." she groans, lifting her hips to grind against my mouth. "I'm there, I'm so close, Adam..."

And that's my cue. I slide up her body, kissing her skin as I go, stomach, ribs, tits, neck, then lips. I align myself with her, nestle my cock against her soft folds, and slide in. She inhales as I slide home, and her heels go around my ass. I give her a slow stroke, two, a third, and then I pause, buried deep, and take a moment to lave her nipples with my tongue until she urges me to move by digging her heels into my ass.

I thrust and thrust and thrust, and she's whimpering and gasping and shrieking in the back of her throat.

"Tell me when you're coming, Des. Say my name when you come." I whisper this in her ear, and she nods.

I'm close myself, but I clamp down and force it away, force my thrusts to go slow and even.

And then she's arching her back. "Adam, god... Jesus, oh fuck I'm coming, Adam!"

I wrench myself out of her and go to my knees between her thighs and suck her clit into my mouth and work it with my tongue until she's thrashing and I have to wrap my arms around her thighs hold her still. She grabs my head in both hands and crushes me against her pussy as I suck and lick her, her hips moving wildly to fuck my face.

And then she's slowing and her breathless screams turn to relieved sighs.

Which is my next cue.

I slide back up and enter her, and now she forces her eyes open and watches me. "Holy shit, Adam. Are you trying to kill me? I'm not sure I can take another orgasm."

"I think you can," I tell her.

She shakes her head. "No. I can't."

I thrust slowly, levered over her. "You can." I touch my lips to hers, briefly. "Touch your tits. Grab 'em, baby. Let me see you play with those big titties of yours."

She cups her tits in both hands and pinches her nipples between finger and thumb. Her mouth falls open and her eyes go wide. "Like this?"

I groan. "Yeah, baby. Lick one for me."

She lifts one of her tits to her mouth and extends her tongue, flicks it across an erect pink nipple, a sigh escaping as she does so. "That turn you on, Tory? Watching me touch myself and lick myself?"

"Yeah it does," I murmur.

She starts to move with me, now, meeting me thrust for thrust. "I like watching you, too. Will you let me watch you jerk off?"

I grin at her. "Maybe."

"What if I let you jerk off onto my tits?"

I feel my balls clench as I imagine that. "Fuck yeah." I dip down to kiss her, slipping my tongue between her lips.

She sweeps her tongue across my lips. "You taste like my pussy."

"So does my cock," I tell her.

She pushes me off her, hooks a leg around mine and twists so I'm on my back. I let her, and then I'm breathless as she bends over me and runs her tongue up the length of my cock from balls to tip. "Mmmmm. Yeah, you do." She licks me again, and then twists her head sideways to slide her lips up my length, and then gets to my head and licks that too, swiping her tongue over it and swirling and licking until her essence is gone and only her saliva remains.

And then she's off me, lying back down on her back with her heels drawn up against the backs of her thighs to spread her pussy apart for me. "Eat me, baby. Lick me until I scream." She drags her finger through her slit and it comes away coated.

Jesus. I'm not sure I can wait any longer. I've been on the verge of coming for so long now it hurts, my balls ache from the come boiling inside me.

She holds her finger out to me, and I close my lips around it, tasting her essence, and then I lower myself between her sweet plump soft muscular thighs once more, taste her juices on my tongue and lap at her relentlessly until she's gripping my hair in her fists and fucking my face with desperate thrusts of her hips, coming, coming.

And I'm in her.

And this time, there'll be no stopping. God no. The games are over.

She hooks her heels together around my back, snakes her arms around my neck, and grinds her hips against me, her lips at my ear. "Don't stop this time, baby. Come for me. Come in me. Let me feel you shoot your load inside me." Her voice is a constant whisper of exhortation in my ear as I feel her pussy clench around me. "Yes, god yes...you feel so good, Adam. Keep fucking me."

I'm grunting and groaning and thrusting with slow, hard movements, trying to make it last. I don't want this to end, this feeling of perfection, this feeling of completion. She's wrapped around me, tangled up in me, and nothing has ever felt so right as her body clamping down on mine, her words in my ear, her hands clawed into my shoulders.

This woman, she is my Destiny.

Fuck, that's cheesy, but it's so true.

"You're my Destiny." I can't help saying it out loud.

She buries her head against my neck and laughs. "Jesus. That was so bad it was good." She lets herself fall back to the bed and my thrusts slow to almost nothing as I fight the urge to unleash. "But I loved it. Because…I am."

My eyes lock on hers, and I know I'm done for, then and there.

This is love.

I won't say it yet, though. I'll save that for a better moment. If I say it now, she'll think it's just the intimacy of sex making me say it. And that's not it at all. Or at least, not entirely.

My movements go shuddery and stuttering. I'm gasping, sweating, and I don't dare look away from her molten brown gaze.

"Now, Adam. *Now.*" She grinds against me hard, and I feel her squeeze with her inner muscles as she writhes against me, fucking me.

And somehow, despite being beneath me, she's in control now. She grips my ass and hooks her heels around the back of my knees and her pussy clamps down, and I have no choice but to bury my face in the generous silken heaven of her tits and let myself go. It's not letting go, though, because I have no control over this. She's demanding my orgasm, taking it from me. Drawing it out of me.

I'm wild, suddenly, manic and feral and rough. And she just shouts "YES, YES, YES!" and fucks me back and growls with me.

"Destiny…I'm coming, Des." My forehead rests on her cheekbone, her breath in my ear, her hands gentling on my ass now but still pulling me and pulling me, urging me. "Oh…fuck…*fuck*…"

"Yes, Tory, give it to me, give it to me, Adam." It should be weird hearing her call me 'Tory' since only my immediate family uses that name, but it's not. Nor is it weird hearing her use both names in one sentence.

It just reinforces how completely we're intertwined.

And then my cock explodes inside her, heat shooting out of me, wrenching my entire being so I can only drive into her hard and fast and explode again, and she's smoothing both hands from ass to shoulders, her hips grinding against mine, and she's moaning in my ear, clamping down around me and everything is gone, nothing exists but this moment, this breathless unity.

"Holy shit, Adam." She kisses my cheek, my jaw, her hands still roaming all over my back.

I collapse on her, and she takes my weight and holds me until I slide off her, but she won't let me go far, cradles my head against her breast and strokes my hair. "It gets more intense every time, Des," I murmur.

"No kidding," she agrees. "I didn't know it was possible to come that many times."

I just laugh against her skin. "I lost count."

"Five," she answers.

"So that last time, when I came?"

She laughs, her tits shaking. "I'm not sure, honestly. I don't know what that was. I felt you coming inside me, and even though I'd just come and I don't think I could have again even if I tried, I was...coming with you. Feeling you come that hard just...did something to me. Not sure what it was." I roll to my back and take her with me, so now she's nooked into my arm. She nuzzles against me, sighing. After a moment she rests a palm on my stomach, flips my still-recovering cock back and forth. "Gonna need this again soon."

"I love how horny you are, baby." I didn't mean to use that word, but she doesn't freak out.

I feel her smile against my chest. "What can I say? I love the way you fuck me, and I can't get enough of it."

"It's not just fucking, Destiny."

She tilts her head to look at me, her eyes deep and knowing. "I know. It's a lot more than that." She touches my lips with her finger. "But let's save that for later. For now, focus on getting ready for me again."

Holy shit am I in deep with this girl.

CHAPTER SEVENTEEN

"QUIT FIDGETING, DES," ADAM SAYS TO ME. "YOU LOOK breathtaking."

But I can't stop fidgeting. It's the premiere, which means it's my first public event with Adam as his girlfriend. My heart is in my throat and refusing to beat properly. And I can't breathe.

He's effortlessly sexy in a custom Brooks Brothers suit, black slacks, white button-down with a bowtie the same shade as his eyes, and a black jacket with the sleeves pushed up past his elbows, the cuffs of the button-down tugged out and wrapped around the edge of the jacket cuffs. His hair is a little longer than usual, per my request, swept back and loosely gelled. He's got two days worth of beard scruff going, which gets me all hot and bothered every time I look at him—roughly every six seconds, since my nerves are on high-alert.

I'm wearing a Betsey Johnson dress in the same pastel green as his bowtie and his eyes. It's strapless, showing off the tattoo between my shoulder blades. It's chiffon, flowing to floor length with a slit up my right thigh, sweetheart waistline. It's been sized and tailored to fit me, donated to me by the designer for the premiere.

Hair and makeup? Rose lent me her stylist, which was…surreal. Having my hair and makeup done for professional reasons was fun the first few times, but it became routine. Sitting in Rose's elegant loft apartment, having my hair fussed over, sipping something sweet and fruity and stiffly alcoholic to soothe my nerves? That was incredible.

But now we're in a rented Bentley, sliding to a stop outside the theater, and I can't breathe. The two drinks I had are roiling in my stomach.

The vehicle halts, and a body appears on the other side of the window—it's a guy in a tuxedo who is preparing to open the car door. Adam is curbside, so he'll get out first. Flashes pop and pop and pop, blinding. Even through the acoustically soundproofed interior, the noise beyond the car is loud.

Adam grabs my hand, squeezes. "Destiny. Look at me."

God. He's got a thing for using my full name when he wants my attention. It's effective, though.

I glance up at him and crush his hand with mine. "What?" My voice is shaky.

"You can do this. *We* can do this. You've done this before, okay?"

"Not…not like this. This is different." My voice falls to a whisper. "What if I embarrass you somehow?"

He shakes his head. "You won't. I'll be right beside you. Now just breathe, smile, and stay calm."

And then he's tapping on the window with a knuckle, the door is opening, the chatter of voices and click of camera shutters washes over me. Adam unfolds from the Bentley with easy, enviable grace, pivots away and extends a hand to me. I slide across the seat, place one wedge heel on the red carpet, and pull on Adam's hand to stand up. A brief glance down to make sure everything is in the right place, the black Prada clutch purse Adam gave me as part of my twenty-third birthday gift in my hand, and I move into Adam's waiting arm. He wraps his hand around my waist, tucks me to his side, and then we're facing the crowd of photographers.

My smile is automatic. I relax, and move with Adam naturally as we pivot slightly to give the photographers a different angle. And then he's twining my fingers in his and we're moving down the carpet toward the backdrop where Rose and Dylan are posing. They move off toward the theater, and it's Adam's and my turn. He has my hand in his, and we stand side by side, hands down and clasped, smiling, turning this way and that, more smiling. I ignore the fact that the flashes have blinded me so I'm seeing spots in front of my eyes.

And then Adam is stepping away from me, gesturing to me with a wave of his hand, smiling at me reassuringly. Oh god. Oh god. I'm standing alone, now, facing what feels like a firing squad of photographers. This is nothing like modeling. That was arranged, composed, one guy and a camera, directing me. I have to do this on my own. I stand with one hand on my hip, a knee popped, lift a shoulder, turn my head this way and smile. Look into one lens, change the tilt of my lips and look into a different camera, adjust my pose, turn and give them a look at the back of the gown, and my tattoo, which is scary. *The ache for home lives in all of us…*

It's a statement, and I chose it to make one, but having it be public, photographed and talked about? Oh god. Panic is bubbling up. The tattoo was always 'shopped out in the shots that went to the clients. That's out of the question now, obviously. It's out there and the conjecture will begin, the questions, the requests for interviews. They've already come, starting when Adam announced me as his date for the premiere.

"What's your tattoo mean, Des?" The question comes from my right.

I face the man who asked it. "Adam is the only one who knows the answer to that," I say, and offer a coy smile.

"He's a lucky man, then," the reporter says with a grin. "In a lot of ways."

Adam steps close to me. "You have *no* idea, pal," he says, a playful smirk on his lips.

And then we're moving, Lawrence and his wife coming up the carpet toward us. Adam guides us into the foyer of the theater, where dozens of couples mill about, talking, laughing, smiling for yet more photographers, posing, doing impromptu interviews. We mingle, and I find myself dazzled by the easy manner with which Adam moves from conversation to conversation, greeting everyone by name, the men with a handshake, the women with a friendly hug. They all look at me, introduce themselves, and include me in their conversations.

This goes on for what feels like an hour, and at one point we're cornered by a photographer and a young woman juggling a notepad, a cell phone and pen. She touches the screen of her cell phone and rests it on the top of the notepad and prepares to scribble. She asks Adam a series of questions about the film, which he answers confidently, and then she glances at me.

"So tell me about yourself, Des. How did you meet Adam? What made you quit modeling?"

I have absolutely zero clue how to answer that without losing my shit. I glance at Adam, swallow hard, and think fast. "I. Um. I met Adam on Mackinac Island when he was there for a charity dinner. And as for modeling…um." I have *got* to stop saying um. Fuck. Get it together. "It just wasn't right for me. New York was too hectic, and the hours just killed me."

"Is there any truth to the allegations that you assaulted Ludovic Perretti?"

I blink. "I—that's not something I feel comfortable talking about."

Adam steps into me, forcing me to move away from the interviewer, putting himself in front of her. "That's enough, Amy. Thank you."

He even knows the names of the reporters. It's crazy. I can't remember anyone's name unless I've met them more than once.

We're moving through the crowd, and then I feel Adam go stiff beside me. "What the holy *fuck* is *she* doing here?" he hisses.

I scan the crowd, and I see her. Medium height with an hourglass figure, monster tits and sleek hips. Pouty bright red lips. Vivid blue eyes, long chestnut hair brushed to a glossy shine and floating in loose spirals around her slim shoulders. She's wearing a scrap of slinky dove-gray silk that exposes as much as it covers without being exactly slutty. Four-inch cream heels, diamonds dripping from her ears and draped around her throat, dangling on her wrists.

God, she's drop-dead gorgeous. It makes me feel immediately inferior, because I can't deny how intensely, sensually lovely she is.

And she knows it. She's the center of attention, the unexpected guest.

Emma fucking Hayes.

She sees me at the same moment that I see her, and she struts straight through the crowd of photographers and journalists and sycophants and panting men. "You must be Des," she says in a voice that dripping with sultry sexuality.

"What the fuck are you doing here, Em?" Adam asks, not bothering to hide his animosity.

Cameras flash, cell phones are held up to record video.

"Well, Adam…I was invited by Drew." She holds her hand out, and a man I remember meeting at the dinner on Mackinac moves to her side.

He's tall and handsome with thick blond hair swept artfully to one side, and his hazel gaze rakes over me briefly. "Hey, Adam."

I think Drew is one of the writers, or maybe a producer? I don't remember. All I know is he seemed like an asshole then, and nothing has changed. He slides his arm around Emma's waist, a snarky, shit-eating grin on his face. He's taunting Adam, I realize, who is tense, taut.

"I see you've finally moved on," Emma says, glancing at me, looking me over, assessing me, dismissing me.

Adam seems at a loss, for once. He wants to lash out, I think, but he doesn't want to make a scene, especially with all the press looking on. I want to say something cutting, something intelligent and witty and hurtful.

"Nice implants," is what I end up saying.

Adam snorts in an attempt to hold back laughter, and Emma goes red in the face, trembling all over. I worry for a moment that she's actually going to attack me. Drew obviously thinks the same thing, because I see his arm tighten around her waist.

She's silent for a moment, and I can see her jaw grinding. Eventually she sneers at me and says, "Just remember I had him first, bitch."

What a comeback. I roll my eyes. "Which only makes me seem that much better."

Adam pulls me away. "And that's enough." He glances back. "Goodbye, Emma. And Drew? Good luck, buddy. You'll need it."

And then we're out of the foyer and moving toward the doors leading into the auditorium.

The reality of what I just did hits me. I just insulted Emma Hayes in a *very* public setting. I got catty. Jesus. What the *fuck* is wrong with me?

I hear people talking behind me, discussing me; the scene that just unfolded, and I twist to see people typing furiously on their cell phones. Tweeting, or Facebooking. Putting the whole ugly exchange out to the world on social media.

I stumble, and Adam catches me. "I can't... breathe," I rasp. "Get me out of here."

He ushers me into a coatroom. A young girl in a theater uniform is leaning against a wall, cell phone in hand, a bored expression on her face. But then she sees Adam and she goes star-struck, stammers a hello, and starts toward him.

"Out," Adam says, and the girl scurries out, ducking her head. He turns to me. "Des, babe, what's wrong?"

I bend over, hands on my knees, and force myself to breathe in slowly. "I just...with Emma... 'Nice implants?' What the fuck was I thinking?"

Adam laughs. "That was probably the worst thing you could say to her, because, and this may be TMI, but they're actually real. It makes her absolutely furious when people say that."

"I insulted her at your premiere. Everyone was watching. There's probably video on YouTube already. I can just see the tweets now: Hashtag catfight, Hashtag Des is a cunt." Adam laughs even harder, and I finally straighten to glare at him. "Why the *fuck* are you laughing at me? Remember what I said about embarrassing you? Well, hello embarrassment. Yeah, that just happened."

He takes a deep breath and pulls me close to him, holds me to his chest. "It was fucking funny, Des. I'm not embarrassed at all. I'm actually a little turned on that you got in her face over me."

"One, you're always turned on. And two, you probably just wanted to see us actually fight."

He snorts. "You'd crush her like a fucking bug, babe."

I press my forehead to his chest. "She's so beautiful it's not even fair." I let out a frustrated sigh. "I mean, her tits are almost bigger than mine, and I'm twice her size. And they're *real?* Come *on*. Not fucking fair."

Adam groans. "Fuck me. You're not going to obsess, are you? She's beautiful, sure. But she's not you, Des."

"Which goes in her favor, I think."

"Are you forgetting what she did to me?"

I shrug miserably. "So she's a skank. I bet she gave better head than me."

Adam pushes me to arm's length. "For fucking real? Destiny. Jesus. She's my ex. She broke my god-damned heart and did so publicly, without a scrap of remorse. And you're comparing which of you gives better head? Come on, babe. Let it go."

I just stare at him. "I notice you're not denying it, though."

"I'm not going to compare, Des. I *won't.* You know why? Because there's no comparison. You're everything I've ever wanted in life. You're tough. You're sexy. You're intelligent and hardworking and you know what you want. You have an absolutely voracious sexual appetite—"

"A voracious appetite, period, you mean."

He nods. "Yeah, and that's sexy to me too. You enjoy food. You enjoy life. You don't play games." Adam takes my face in his hands. "To me, you are better in every way. You kiss me better, you fuck me better, and yes, you go down better. More importantly, you *see* me, as you once said. You know me. You don't just appreciate me for the way I look, or for the fact that I'm famous. You appreciate me for *me.*"

"Smooth talker."

"It's not smooth, Des, it's the raw truth."

"Well, whatever it is, it's working." I can't help a smile from curving my lips.

"Good." He touches my chin with an index finger, tipping my face up. His lips graze mine, his tongue drifts delicately across the seam of my mouth, probing, tasting. "Now let's go watch the premiere, huh?"

And the premiere is fantastic. Adam is incredible. Not just the brutal fight scenes or the heart-stopping stunts, but the way he portrays his character, making him self-deprecating and darkly humorous, yet still badass and utterly, primally alpha.

God, this man is amazing, not just on film but in every possible way.

CHAPTER EIGHTEEN

I NEVER GET NERVOUS ANYMORE. I JUST DON'T. I WAS nervous the first time I started in front of a packed home-crowd stadium at Stanford, I was nervous the first time I jogged out onto the Chargers field, and I was petrified when my first starring role in a big-budget, high-profile film hit the theaters.

But none of those experiences can hold a candle to the nerves blazing through me at this moment.

Which is beyond stupid. I shouldn't be nervous. The chances of her saying no are slim to none. I know my girl, and I know she wants this. But I'm still nervous.

I've waited a long time for this. Months of traveling between Detroit, L.A., and two different shoots in different parts of the globe. I shot the cop drama in Detroit, and then I did a small-budget, character-driven piece shot largely in a studio in L.A. I had two months free which I spent in Detroit with Des. And then that time was followed by a massive historical project filmed in a studio in London and on-location in Germany and Spain.

And the whole time, I knew what I wanted. I wanted her, in my home. In my bed. No more brutal long-distance flights, no more splitting time between cities, no more nights alone. But I had to wait. She worked too damn hard for her degree for me to get in the way. So I waited.

And now she's done. She graduated last week. I arranged the shoot schedule in Spain around her graduation and flew in the day before and surprised her with a custom-designed sapphire pendant. She doesn't let me buy her a lot of extravagant gifts, so when there's a reason to get her something that she can't argue with, I go big.

The pendant was only the first part of her graduation gift. The second part is a secret trip. We're on a private jet right now, flying south out of Detroit. I refused to tell her where we're going, and I only let her pack a handful of dresses, some shorts and tank tops, and a few bathing suits. So she knows we're going somewhere warm, but that's it.

My buddy Dawson and his wife Grey recently bought property in the Caribbean. Now, when I say 'property', I mean half an island. And the only reason it's not the whole thing is because I bought the other half. The salary for the historical war movie I just did was my biggest payout yet, and I haven't spent much of what I've made in the last four years, except for taxes and the penthouse.

So when Dawson came to me with a plan to team up and split the cost of a small island, I jumped at it. Monster, fifty thousand square-foot palaces in Beverly Hills don't appeal to me, and I suspect they don't to Des either. The condo is fine, and still more than two people need. But a sprawling tropical estate on a private island, indoor-outdoor living spaces and no neighbors for literally a hundred miles in any direction—except Dawson and Grey on the other side? Hell yeah.

So we bought it at the end of last year and we've spent the last six months building the houses. Dawson's done most of the work overseeing the construction, since he's taking a two-year hiatus from filming. Everything was finished two weeks ago, and we're meeting on the island for the inaugural visit.

Des hasn't met Dawson and Grey, yet. We've been so busy and those two have been traveling the world. I think they've been in a dozen countries in the last year, and they make a point of staying at least a week in each place. I'm excited for this, honestly.

Dawson is great guy, and Grey is sweet as sugar, but she's tough, too, reminding me of Des in that way.

I glance at Des, who is sleeping beside me, her head on my shoulder. God, I love her.

I pull out the ring and look at it. I spent four months designing it, working with one of the world's premier custom jewelers. It's a flawless, one-in-a-million pink diamond, teardrop shaped, two and half carats. The band is comprised of over three hundred individual strands of filigreed platinum woven together, the strands merging and reaching up to capture the stone in an ornate, intricate web.

I hear Des murmur in her sleep and hurry to nestle the ring back in the black velvet box, and tuck the box back in my backpack. She stirs, stretches, blinks up at me. "We almost there?"

I smile down at her, wipe my thumb across the corner of her mouth. "You've got a little something here," I say. "Yeah. We'll land in about twenty minutes, and then there's another short plane ride to our destination."

"And you still won't tell me where we're going?"

"Nope. It's a surprise."

"I don't like surprises," she grumbles.

"Well, I think you'll like this one."

We land on St. John, transfer our one suitcase to a Jeep, and sit in easy silence as the driver takes us from the airport to the marina, where a twin-engine float plane waits. The pilot is a grizzled, weathered old man with a long graying red beard. He's been hand-picked by Dawson and he's got more flight time logged than any of us have even been alive, Dawson says, and that's good enough for us.

I take our suitcase and shoulder my backpack as well as Des's and we cross the dock. I put one foot on the float, the other on the dock, and toss the suitcase in, and then extend my hand to Des. She takes it, steps to the float and then into the plane.

Ron, the pilot, takes off smoothly, and then we're buzzing a thousand feet over the blue waters of Caribbean.

We're alone in the airplane. I could ask her now.

No. No. I've got a plan; stick to the plan. Dinner on the beach, a moonlight proposal.

I lose track of time scripting out what I'm going to say, and then Des is gripping my hand so tightly it hurts as we sink toward the water.

"Holy shit holyshitholyshit!" Des is shaking, petrified, eyes scrunched shut.

"Relax, missy. Done this a hundred thousand times. Ain't nothin' to it." Ron's voice is smoke-roughened, an unlit cigarette tucked behind his ear.

"It's terrifying!"

Ron chuckles. "First time is a bit scary, I guess. Just keep your eyes shut and hold your man's hand. Be down 'fore you can blink twice."

Sure enough, barely a minute later, there's a light splash, a brief sensation of weightlessness, and then we're skidding across the water. I lean in my seat, trying to get a glimpse of the island through the windscreen. It's all green trees, with a stripe of white sandy beach at the edge. I can see sunlight gleaming off glass, a dock extending several hundred feet out into the water. Ron brings the seaplane to a gentle halt at the edge of the dock, shuts off the engine, and then shoves open his door and jumps to the dock with an easiness that belies his age. He ties the plane to the dock, and then takes the suitcase I hand to him. I jump down, and then hand Des down after me.

She takes two steps past Ron and me and then stops, hand to her mouth, staring in awe at the island. "Adam, this is...incredible."

I just laugh. "You haven't seen anything yet, babe."

Ron gestures toward the island. "Y'all go on. I'll bring your bag up for you."

"What *is* this place, Adam?"

I lead her off the dock and onto the sand, up a stone-lined path leading into the jungle. Unlit tiki torches mark the path on either side. It leads up a steep hill and curves around, following the shoreline and then cutting inland, emerging in a clearing. We're around the curve of the island, so the dock is out of sight. The clearing is easily two full acres, the jungle rising high on three sides, tall trees casting shade on the back of the house that sits in the middle of the clearing. The house faces west, into the setting sun, with another, shorter, rock- and tiki torch-lined path leading down to the beach, smooth wooden steps and handrails in places to assist the way down the hill.

The house itself isn't massive, just over five thousand square feet. But it's all richly appointed, the footprint extending north and south so every room faces the beach. There's a covered porch that wraps around the perimeter of the house, which sits on the cusp of a hill, so there are actually two floors to the home, one at ground level, and the lower one set into the curving hillside, each level connected outside by an elaborate series of walkways, bridges, and gazebos. The porch, walkways, and gazebos are lit by strings of white lights and gas-fed, electronically controlled tiki torches.

Dawson took me on a complete virtual tour last week, showing me every feature, every control panel, every little nook and cranny, so I'd know the layout and how to operate everything. The floor plan of the house is stunning. It's all open plan, but the square footage is spread into cozy nooks and comfortable spaces, every wall a floor-to-ceiling window that can be slid open to let in the constant Caribbean breeze.

I take Des on a tour, pointing out the wine cellar, the gym, the incredible kitchen, and, last but most importantly, the bedroom, which is its own entire wing set at an angle to the rest of the house, connected by a covered walkway. It's glass on all four walls, which like the rest of the house can be opened all the way. There's an en-suite bathroom with an outdoor shower and an outdoor soaking tub set directly into the hillside, shielded from view from the rest of the house behind clever landscaping and design.

She's speechless. "Adam. Seriously. What is this place? Is it a resort of some kind?"

I laugh as we sit on the porch of the master bedroom, watching the waves lap on the beach. "No, babe. This is ours. Welcome home."

She turns to me, eyes wide. "What do you mean, welcome home?"

I grin even more widely. "This is the real graduation present, Des. Not just the trip here, but the island, the house."

"The island. Explain that one, hon. The *island?*"

I love her inability to comprehend this. "We own half of this island."

"You mean you do."

I shake my head. "Nope. We." I lead her back toward the kitchen. "Come on, there's something I need to show you."

On the counter in the kitchen is the paperwork, laid out in piles, with a yellow-highlighted 'X' wherever a signature is needed. I take the pen Dawson left, and sign each page, and then extend the pen to Des.

"Sign, and it's really, truly *ours.* Yours and mine. Both our names." With a provision enabling us to update the paperwork if Des was ever to take my name. But I don't mention that proviso just yet.

She stares at the papers, then out at the water and the sun lowering itself toward the horizon. "I don't understand. How can we own half an island? Who owns the other half?"

"My friend Dawson Kellor, and his wife Grey." I wave toward the other side of the island. "They have a house over there, a lot like ours, with the dock in between. On the opposite side of the island from the dock there's a boathouse, with a sailboat and a powerboat."

"So you and your friend bought a whole island?"

I grin cockily. "Sure did. It's a small one, though, not even a full square mile. It was owned by some rich guy who wanted to build a house here. He actually did most of the hard work, creating a workable, self-contained power and plumbing infrastructure." I tap the papers. "And not just Dawson and me, but you and Grey, too."

She sets the pen down and walks back outside, and leans on the railing. I follow her and lean my butt against the rail, and wait for her. "This is big, Tory. Really big. And really permanent."

God, she's serious. She only calls me Tory when she's feeling emotional.

"Are you scared?" I ask.

She shrugs, and then nods. "You bought a fucking island, Adam. Jesus. I mean, what am I supposed to do on an island?"

"Des, baby. This is a vacation home. A getaway. I'm still going to act, and now that you have your degree, you can do whatever you want. You want to stay in Detroit? I'll buy the apartment. We've got my place in L.A. Where else would you want to live? I'll have to fly back to L.A. for filming, and I'll have shoots in other places—that's not going to change. This doesn't change us, Des. It's just somewhere we can go and get away from the studio and the interviews and the paparazzi, and everything. Just be us, no interruptions."

"Oh." She glances up at me. "Do I want to know how much you and Dawson spent on all this?"

I grin. "Nope. You might pass out." Big numbers make her dizzy.

When I bought her that Prada clutch, she asked how much I spent, so I told her. She got weird. Tried to convince me she wanted me to take it back, even though she had it in a death grip. Another time, I was on the phone with my agent, discussing an offer. It was for sixteen million, and my agent thought that was lowball, so I told her to counter with twenty-five, not realizing Des was standing behind me, listening. So I tried to explain to her how a big-budget payout worked, and she just shook her head, waving me off. She doesn't like to think about money, I've realized. She's lived so frugally her entire life, never having enough of anything, and I think the shock of the change in lifestyle was just too much for her to comprehend. So she doesn't. She's perfectly content to let me take care of money and not tell her about it.

"So," I ask, "are you going to sign or what?"

"It's too much to process," she answers. "Can I think about it?"

I pull her to me and kiss her. "Take all the time in the world, babe."

He's wearing a tux, barefoot, the cuffs rolled up past his ankles, jacket sleeves pushed up. Black bow-tie, hair slicked back and to one side. Fucking gorgeous. Such a beautiful man, so powerful, his arms stretching the sleeves of the coat. His eyes blaze, hot and intense in that unique, incredible shade of green. I never get tired of staring into his eyes. It's cheesy and sappy, but I just can't get enough.

And he's looking at me with those eyes, and an emotion I never thought a man would ever feel for me shines from him, pours off of him:

Love.

I'm fighting tears, overwhelmed by the reality of this island, the stunning, breathtaking beauty of the property and the home. I'm even more overwhelmed by what he's got planned for this evening.

He had a catering company set up a small table, covered in a white tablecloth, right on the beach, near the surf, so the waves lapped against our toes. Torches, planted deep into the sand, flickered in a row behind us, circling us. The torches extend in a double line out into the water, forming a corridor of orange flame on the black, moonlit water. The moon is rising just now, sliding up from out of the waves, up from the horizon, huge and full and white, her light shining in a gleaming silver pathway down the corridor formed by the torches.

Fifty yards up the beach, a violinist and cellist play, surrounded by more lit torches.

Dinner is four courses of light but filling fare, a citrusy soup, a garden salad, some kind of flavorful, flaky fish with jasmine rice and steamed vegetables, and then dessert.

We share a bottle of chilled, expensive white wine that tastes great. I don't tell Adam but it tastes just like any other wine, to me.

Once the food is finished and the last drops of wine have been swallowed, Adam stands up, one hand in his pants pocket, and leads me away from the table, into the water, toward the pathway lit by moon and by fire.

The hem of my dress floats in the water.

He stops, turns to face me, his gaze serious.

I gaze up at him, expectant. As soon as I saw the setup, I knew what this was, what he was doing, and I've loved every minute of it. It's perfect. Incredible, romantic.

But he could've proposed to me in an airport bathroom and I would've said yes.

"You are my Destiny." He leads with this, and with a smile. "I love you."

My throat closes, and my eyes prick. "I love you, Adam. So much."

"Hey, I've got this all scripted out. I'm gonna forget something if you start talking."

"Oh. Sorry." I lean into him, slide my arms around his back. "Continue."

He shakes his head. "No, now I've lost it all. I'm gonna have to improvise."

"You don't need a speech," I tell him.

"I don't?"

I gesture at the table, the quartet. "This is your speech. Just get to the good part."

"See? This is why I love you. I never know how you'll react." He takes a deep breath and lets it out. "You changed everything for me, Des. From the day I met you on Mackinac Island, you changed everything. All I knew was that I had to have you, that I had to know you. I'm so glad I jumped off that carriage. Because it's led me here, with you."

He takes a small black box from his pocket, opens it, withdraws a ring, and slides the box back into his jacket. He holds out the ring so I can see it, and my breath, lodged in my throat, leaves me stunned.

"I designed it myself. You are unique, and you deserve a ring as incredibly one-of-a-kind as you." He takes my left hand, his eyes fixed on mine. "Destiny, will you marry me?"

I'm already smiling, tears sliding down my cheeks, but my smile gets bigger and the tears flow faster, and I can only nod, wait until he's fitted the ring on my finger, and then I lunge into him, wrap my arms around his neck and kiss him everywhere I can.

Finally, I find his mouth, and we kiss until neither of us can breathe and my legs are shaky and weak from desire.

He whispers against my mouth. "Des, I need to hear you say it. Tell me yes."

I bite his lower lip and then whisper back to him, "Yes, Torrence Adam Trenton, I will marry you." I pull back and look into his eyes, hunger in my gaze. "On one condition, though."

His gaze darkens, and a puzzled frown touches his mouth. "What's that, babe?"

"Take me to that amazing bedroom up there, open all the windows, and fuck me till sunrise."

He gathers the hem of my dress in his hand until it's bunched around my waist, revealing the fact that

I'm not wearing any underwear. His hands slide across my skin. "How about right here?"

"The band..." I breathe, pawing at his hands, even though Adam is between me and them.

Adam turns, waves at the quartet, and they scurry away. His mouth finds mine, and he devours my breath. I'm lost in his kiss, so I barely register the sound of a seaplane taking off.

"They're gone," Adam murmurs.

"Then take me."

Clutching the bunched material of my dress in one hand, he reaches up with the other and unzips it. Lifts it over my head and off, drops it into the waves.

"You won't be needing this," he says.

I undo his belt, free the clasp of his pants, lower his zipper, and reach in and find his erection, slide my fist down his length. He gasps a breath in my ear when I cup his balls and give them a gentle squeeze. I smile against his cheek and palm his cock until he's growling in my ear, and then I push his pants down.

"And you won't need these," I tell him.

He kicks them off, his shoes and socks, shrugs out of his jacket. I untie the bowtie, unbutton his shirt, and then we're both naked and our clothes are floating away in the silver path of moonlight, my dress caught on his pants, a sock and a sinking shoe wrapped up in my strapless bra.

His fingers are busy between my thighs, stroking and circling until I'm whimpering and dipping at the knees to ride his fingers to a low, shuddering climax. And then he's bending and sliding into me, gripping me at the knee and holding my leg up near his hip, grunting and thrusting.

I hold onto his neck and laugh as I lose my balance, falling into him, and we go toppling into the water. We splash and disconnect, and then he's gathering our clothes and leading me up to the beach and up the stairs to the balcony, where he deposits our sopping pile of clothes. Further upward, then, to our room.

He pushes open one door, and then turns to me. "Go get in bed, babe."

I grab a towel from the bathroom and dry off while Adam opens all the doorwalls until the sea breeze fills the room. By the time he's done, I'm on the bed, on my back, fingers at my clit, swiping through the wetness of my desire.

Adam stands at the foot of the bed and watches as I touch myself, and then he's between my knees and his tongue replaces my fingers, and I'm breathless, coming again, and he's lapping at the juices as they leak out of me, squeezed from within me by the clenching of my inner walls.

"Adam, I need you…" I gasp, pulling at him. "I need you inside me. Right now, baby, please."

He crawls up my body, nestles his core against mine, leaning over me. He's at my entrance, hard and hard and spreading me apart. I flex my hips, and he slips in, and I'm gasping. He remains still, eyes pale and piercing on mine, hands beside my face. One of his palms scrapes over my nipple and I whimper, wrap my ankles around his spine and lift up, driving him deep into me.

"Like this, babe?" His lips move against mine, somewhere between a kiss and a whisper.

"Almost," I say.

I grind my pussy against him, around him, feel him slide in deep, rough circles inside my body, arching my spine and rolling my hips to fuck him harder and get him deeper.

"I can't get enough," I groan, "I need more. I need you deeper."

I lever him sideways and he lets me roll us so I'm on top. He just grins as I settle onto him, sink him deep, and start a rhythm. I rest my palms on his chest and let my hair drape around us, my tits swaying and bouncing as I ride him until we're both grunting with the impending force of climax.

But it's still not good enough.

"I know what you need," Adam whispers to me.

I slow and stare down at him. "Oh yeah?"

"Yeah." He sits up, slides out from beneath me, and then stands up beside the bed. "Come here, Des.

On your belly. Lean over the bed for me. Show me that fine ass of yours, love."

I do as he instructs, moving to bend over the bed, but when my feet touch the floor, he takes my left leg in his hands and lifts it so my knee is bent up and forward, resting on the bed. I'm bared to him, spread open and bent over, unbalanced.

He slips a finger between my thighs and finds my wet and waiting entrance, touches me and guides himself in, flexing his hips in a slow glide. His foot is beside mine on the floor, his hand on the bed at the crook of my knee, keeping it from slipping off the bed, and his other hand goes to the crease of my hip, pulling me back into him. I gasp at the depth of his cock inside me, and push back, pushing further off the bed. My knee bends so my thigh is pressed to my body, and I'm not so much standing as merely resting on the bed, held up by Adam's impaled cock.

"How's this?" he growls, smoothing a hand over my back.

"Perfect," I gasp, "as long as you start fucking."

He drives in and pulls out, his hand skimming my skin in a circuit from thigh to spine to ass and back to my bent thigh. He pushes on my ass-cheek as he penetrates me, spreading me apart, and I can't help groaning low in my throat as he grinds in ball-deep, so deep I can feel his sac slapping against me.

"Fuck, Adam…yes…" I murmur, breathless.

"You like this?"

"God, yes, baby. I love it."

"Is it enough?"

I shake my head and push back against him. "No. I still need more."

He fucks harder, and this time as he drives in, he smacks my ass with a resounding *clap,* hard enough to sting and startle, and I shriek with surprise but it turns to a groan of need as the slap somehow lets him deeper yet, and now he's fucking and slapping and fucking and slapping, and all I can do is moan his name.

"Adam…Adam…*Adam*…"

"You want me to come inside you like this, babe?" he asks.

I shake my head. "No. I want to see your eyes when you come."

So then he's pulling out and I'm turning over, sitting on the edge of the bed. He doesn't have to tell me what I want, and I don't guess. I just know. He's there, between my thighs, and I'm locking my ankles around his waist and kissing his sweaty, heaving chest as he slips back into me, drives deep home where he belongs. His hands find my cheeks, brush my hair away from my face and his mouth is seeking mine, kissing forehead and cheekbone and chin and jawline and the corner of my mouth and then his tongue is between my lips, and we're kissing in that deep and desperate way, the drowning and lost and mad crazed breathless and needy kiss of soul to soul.

We're moving in sync, grinding and rolling together, and I feel my climax rising inside me even as I feel his rhythm falter. We fall backward to the bed, and I'm scooting back and welcoming his weight on me, clinging to him with arms and legs and my lips are on his neck and my teeth nip and I'm screaming as I come, feeling and hearing his roar of release and our sweat is merged and smeared together and we're gasping in unison, hips crushed together and moving, rolling, grinding, desperate for each fractional moment of mutual climax.

"Destiny, Jesus, Destiny, I love you so fucking much…" He's limp on top of me, and I cling to him, feeling him tense and shudder and flutter his hips in the quaking aftershocks.

"I love you, I love you, I love you." I whisper it into his ear, gasping it, fingers scraping and scratching down his back as my body tremors beneath his. "I love you forever and forever and forever."

We drift and drowse together in the moonlight, sea salt on our lips and moonlight on our skin, sticky and love-slick.

And then he's cradling me from behind, both of us on our sides, and he's surging into me, slowly and lazily. His thrusts are like the slide of glaciers, unhurried and inevitable, and when I feel him start to shake, I slip my fingers between my thighs and bring myself there with him. And we never speak a word, never need to even look at each other.

We sleep, and then I feel his lips on my shoulder and his cock between the globes of my ass, and his fingers slide over my hip bone and to my core, and he's got me writhing with need before my eyes open. And then he rolls to his back so I'm on top of him, my back to his chest, my weight on him. I plant my feet in the mattress and spread my knees as far apart as they'll go and feel him slide in, sigh as he fills me, his huge rough hands cupping my breasts gently, his breath in my ear, his heart beating at my spine, his stomach tensing under me as he thrusts, thrusts, groans my name on a whisper and thrusts, harder and harder until my tits shake and my thighs are tensing as I move with him, my ass grinding down to push him deeper, my hands on his thighs gripped tight and pushing, pulling…

"I love you…"

"I love you…"

I'm not even sure who says it first, who comes first, only that it's all a surging exploding fiery blazing blur of love and breath and his come shooting wet and thick and deep and his hands all over me and his lips at my ear.

The sky is pink with sunrise when he finally cradles my cheek against his chest, both of us sweaty and naked and sated. I watch the sunlight glint off my pink diamond, refracting into rainbows on the ceiling, marveling at the intricate metalwork of the band.

He's nearly asleep, and I'm not far behind him when he speaks. "By the way, I reserved the Little Stone Church for next summer."

"You...what?"

"The Little Stone Church, on Mackinac? Where we kissed that first time? We're getting married there next June. Soonest opening they had, or it'd be earlier."

I can only smile sleepily against his skin. He knows me, god, so well. "I love you, Adam."

"Love you more, Destiny Ross."

EPILOGUE

THE TINY CHAPEL IS JUST THE RIGHT SIZE FOR THE wedding we've planned. Most of the people in attendance are actually *in* the wedding party. My mom, of course, who walked with me down the aisle. And Dad, who gave away Des. She was already crying just from that, and gave my dad a long, emotional hug. My sisters, my grandparents, Rose, Gareth, and my agent Rachel and her husband.

The wedding has been planned in total secrecy, so the paparazzi won't know about this until we announce it. I'm giddy with the fact that we actually pulled off a secret wedding.

Dawson is standing to my left, my best man. He's grinning like a fool.

Ruth, Grey, Lia and Lizzy, and—surprisingly—Rose Garret are lined up at the front of the church, Des's bridal party. I've only got Dawson but he's all I need.

After a short speech about and love and the sanctity of marriage, the minister asks us to exchange vows.

I go first. I'm speaking from the heart. "Des…I honestly never thought I'd get here, you know. In a church, getting married. And then I met you, and I just knew, even then, that I needed you, and that I needed to make you mine. So here we are, babe. I'm making you mine, forever mine. You belong, now. To me. With me. My home is yours, my family is yours, my life, my love, my future…it's all yours."

Des is barely containing her emotions. It takes her a few moments of deep breathing to collect herself, letting out a sigh through pursed lips, blinking her thick black lashes.

"I have a quote tattooed on my body. A Maya Angelou poem." She blinks and breathes, and then continues. "'The ache for home lives in all of us, the safe place where we can go as we are and not be questioned.' That was the one constant in my life, the aching need for somewhere to call home, for someone to call home. Until you, Adam, I…I honestly didn't think it was possible. I was starting to think it didn't exist. Love, I mean. And home. And then you jumped off that carriage and showed me how wrong I was."

She has to stop again, lets go of one of my hands and wipes a finger under her eye, head tipped back.

"I don't ache for home anymore, Adam. You're my safe place. You're where I be exactly who I'm meant to be, and I know you love all of me, the broken and the whole."

I hear sniffles and sighs, and I don't need to look out at the small crowd to know everyone is moved by her words, me most of all. My throat burns, and I have to swallow hard past the hot knot of emotion in my throat. I can't look away from Des, from the tear-shimmer in her wide brown eyes, from the love pouring off her.

I almost miss the minister's next prompt: "Do you, Torrence Adam Trenton, take this woman to be your lawfully wedded wife, in sickness and in health, for richer or for poorer, as long as you both shall live?"

"I do." I haven't taken my eyes off hers during the entire service. I'm not the least bit nervous, just incredibly happy.

"And do you, Destiny Lynn Ross, take this man to be your lawfully wedded husband, in sickness and in health, for richer or for poorer, as long as you both shall live?"

She takes a deep breath, smiles. "I do. With all my heart, I do."

The minister smiles at her addition. "Then by the power vested in me by the state of Michigan, I now pronounce you man and wife." He takes our hands, joins them, and lifts them. "May I present to you, Mr. and Mrs. Adam Trenton!" I was sure to prep the preacher on how to introduce us, and I'm amused by my mother's glare of irritation. She was the one who chose my name, and it's always bugged her that I go by Adam, as much as it bugs me that she continues to refer to me as Tory. It's a game, and this is my latest gambit.

We're out the door, the sun shining bright in the blue sky. A beautiful white carriage is waiting, with two huge, glossy black Percherons stomping their hooves and snorting. The Grand Hotel looms up on the hill, colonnades marching into the distance, flags flying.

I can't take my eyes off Des, her shoulders bare in the strapless white gown, the train flowing around her feet, the bodice cupping her magnificent breasts and lifting them proudly. I stand behind her and assist her up into the carriage, with Ruth at my side arranging her train so it doesn't get tangled.

Ruth smiles at me as she finishes fussing with Des's dress. "I'm glad she found you, Adam."

I just shake my head. "I'm the one who found her, actually," I say with a grin.

Ruth rolls her eyes, but she's grinning. "Arrogant ass."

"You know it."

Ruth is on the step of the carriage, hugging Des, and they're both whispering, crying. I turn and Dawson is there, his dark hair pulled back in a ponytail. He's contractually obliged to keep it long for the role on the HBO original series he's doing. It looks good on him. He grabs my hand and pulls me into an embrace, slapping my back.

"Congratulations, brother." He pulls away and grins at me. "Married looks good on you."

I laugh. "It's been about four minutes, Dawson."

He shrugs. "Best four minutes of your life, though, right?" He leans in and elbows me. "Or is that a different four minutes I'm thinking of?"

I shove him off. "Douche. You must be thinking of yourself."

Grey is at Dawson's side, listening to the exchange with an amused gleam in her eyes. "Hey, now. Don't be knocking my man's stamina like that. He can go for hours."

Dawson stares at his wife. "Um. Okay then.... thanks for that, hon."

She shrugs and endeavors to look innocent. "Wasn't four minutes last night, I can tell you that much. I'm still sore."

"Grey. Jesus." Dawson actually looks a little embarrassed, which is funny as fuck.

Des leans down from the carriage and grabs my arm and pulls me. "Come on, sexy. We've got a carriage ride to go on. You can measure dicks with Dawson later, after I've had enough of yours."

And that's my cue.

"All right then." I walk over to hug my parents and kiss my sisters, and then I'm sitting beside my wife, my Destiny, my sweet and sexy Des, and we're waving to our friends and family. We'll see them a bit later for the reception at the Grand Hotel. For now, though, it's just us.

After the crowd is behind us, the driver turns. "So. A tour or the hotel?" He asks with a knowing grin, having overheard the foregoing conversation.

"Actually, I was here three years ago and I was supposed to do a tour of the island, but I never went."

"Oh no? What stopped you?" he asks.

"I met her," I say, putting my arm around my wife.

He glances us. "Good reason, then. Well, you've got the right man for the job. My name is Dan, and I live here on the island year-round. I can probably tell you more about this place than anyone else, including some pretty freaky ghost stories, if you're into that kind of thing."

"Sounds good," I say.

Des nuzzles into me as the horses lean into their harness and haul us up a hill. "Well, baby. We're married."

I kiss her neck. "You know, I'd never say this to Dawson, but he was right. The minutes since saying 'I do' have been the best of my life."

She turns her head, and our lips meet. "Mine too."

THE END

COMING SOON
from
JASINDA WILDER:

FALLING AWAY

I PUSH THE WEIGHT UP WITH MY LEGS, STRAINING, aching, and fighting the agony in my right knee. I manage to straighten my legs, and I desperately want to lower them and release the strain. I start to do just that…

"Hold it there for me, Ben," Cheyenne says. "For ten seconds. That's all. Ten seconds. You can do it, I know you can."

But I can't. I'm a fucking pussy, and it hurts. But I try. I shake all over, sweat sluicing down my face. I strain, and a growl escapes me as I fight the urge to let the weight go.

"…nine…eight…seven…six! Keep it up, Ben! Five more seconds, come on!" She's kneeling beside me, her voice patient and encouraging as it always is.

My leg trembles, and the pain in my ruined knee is so bad I could almost cry. "I can't—fuck, I can't. I gotta let it go."

I start to lower the leg press, but my knee gives out. And Cheyenne is there, catching the weight and lowering it. I slide to a sitting position, grab my right leg near the knee and lift it over the bench, and then collapse forward, elbows on my thighs, gasping.

The most pathetic thing about this? The press only has a hundred pounds on it. And I only managed two reps of ten. I used to be able to press over twice my bodyweight, six or eight reps of twenty each. Now, a hundred measly fucking pounds pushed twenty times and I'm out of breath, sweating, and my knee hurts so bad I don't dare speak in case the tremor in my voice would show.

I feel her hand on my shoulder, and a white towel appears in front of my face. I take the towel, dab my face, neck, and chest, and then accept the bottle of water she hands to me.

"That was great, Ben. You're making excellent progress." She sips from her own bottle of water, another towel slung over her slim shoulder. She toys with her hair, a sleek blond braid hanging down her back. "Next time we'll try for three reps, huh?"

"I barely managed two today, Cheyenne. Gonna take awhile to get to three." I hate how defeated I sound.

She crouches in front of me, and my eyes go involuntarily to her gray-and-pink sports bra, visible beneath the white tank top, and then to her muscular thighs, encased in black knee-length stretch pants. I force my eyes back to her hazel-green gaze. If she noticed me checking her out, she doesn't give anything away.

"Ben, you're too hard on yourself. It's only been a month. It's going to take some time, okay? You have to be patient with yourself."

"I know," I sigh, and roll my head around my shoulders to loosen the tension. "It's just frustrating to be so limited."

She smiles, warm and understanding. Only the slight crow's feet in the corners of her eyes give away the fact that she's older than me by quite a bit. I don't know how much, but enough. She has a daughter in college, so she's got to be at least forty. But Jesus, what a gorgeous forty.

"I get it, Ben. I do." She pats my knee, the good one. Is it me, or do her fingers linger a few seconds too long? "I went through it too, remember? I know what you're going through, how hard it is. You can do this. You just have to be patient and stay the course." She stands up, turns away and grabs two ten-pound hand weights from a rack.

She's facing away, so I let myself eye her ass. Taut, all toned muscle.

Fuck, what's wrong with me? She's got a daughter in college, for fuck's sake. She's my physical therapist. I should *not* be checking her out. But yet, every time I've been here since being injured in the game that ended my chances at a football career, I check her out. I struggle to keep my eyes off her, especially when she's looking my way.

Like she is now. Shit. She totally caught me staring. But yet, she doesn't turn cold, doesn't scold me, or glare at me. She just offers me the same kind, warm, patient smile she always has for me.

"Come on. Time to walk that knee out, mister. Come on. Up, up, up." She grabs me by the hand and pulls me up to my feet.

Her hands linger in mine, just for a moment, but it's enough to make me wonder. And then she's putting the weight in my hands and gesturing to the track that leads around the perimeter of the gym. She walks beside me, twenty-pound weights in her hands, and sets the pace. She ignores the fact that I'm fighting to keep up, that I'm hobbling so bad it can barely be called walking.

And then a ripple in the carpet catches the toe of my cross trainer, and I trip. I lurch forward, hobble, and my bad knee twists and goes out from under me. I fall, the weights dropping from my hands. My knee crashes into the floor, and pure agony lances through my leg, shooting from toe to hip, throbbing so hard my gut tightens. I roll off my knee, clutching it, gasping, fighting the urge to curse a blue streak.

"Ben! Shit! Are you okay?" She's kneeling beside me, helping me sit up.

Her hand goes to my knee, and she rips open the snaps of my track pants up past my knee, baring my hairy thigh. Her hands are warm and strong, flexing my knee, straightening my leg until I yelp.

"Fuck!" I pull free of her hold on my leg and lay back. "Fuck, that hurt."

"I think we'd better call it a day," Cheyenne says, a concerned expression on her face. "I'm worried that's going to swell."

"Yeah, no shit." My voice is hoarse with the effort needed to breathe through the pain like a man.

"Can you stand up?" She's taking my hand, pulling.

"Yeah, I can fucking stand, okay?" I snap, jerking my hand away.

"Fine then, stand up." She backs away, not quite hiding the hurt before I see it.

I scrub my hand through my hair. "God, Cheyenne, I'm sorry. I'm being an asshole and you don't deserve it."

And just like that, the smile is back. She holds her hand out to me, and this time I take it and let her help me pull me to my feet.

"Okay, see if you can put any weight on it," she tells me, not letting go of me.

I hobble, get my balance, and gingerly put weight on my knee. "Nope, nope, nope. Not happening," I grunt, hopping as my knee gives, wincing.

"Okay. Lean on me." She slides her slim shoulder under my arm and supports me.

She's a lithe little thing, barely five-five to my six-two, and I outweigh her by at least seventy pounds, but she still manages to support my weight and help me limp out of the gym and to the locker room. I lower myself to the bench and straighten my leg, closing my eyes as the motion sends pain shooting through me.

"That set us back, didn't it?" Cheyenne asks.

I nod. "Yeah, I think it did."

She sits down next to me and buttons the snaps of my pants leg. When she's done, she's sitting just a little too close to me. "You need ice on that."

"Yeah, I'll ice it when I get home."

"You have a ride?"

I shrug. "No, I'll just take the bus, then walk, same as always."

She frowns. "Ben, you can't. You'll hurt yourself worse."

"Well I can't drive with my knee fucked up, and I'm still working on teleportation."

She snorts and smacks my shoulder. "Smart ass."

"Better than being a dumbass," I retort.

"Well, you'd be a dumbass not to just ask me if I can drive you home, then, wouldn't you?"

I swallow my pride. "Cheyenne, would you mind driving me home?"

She smiles brightly. "Why sure, Ben, I'd be happy to."

So I wait, leaning against the frame of the door as she wipes down the machines, shuts off the lights, and then locks the door behind us. She hikes her gym bag higher on her shoulder, and I, out of the instinct drilled into by my mom and dad, take it from her.

"Ben, I can—" she starts to protest.

"And so can I. I have a shit knee, but I'm not useless." I hang the bag from my right shoulder and lean on the cane.

She lets me carry her bag, shooting me a smile that's somehow different from the ones she usually gives me. This one is…more personal, somehow. Less politely professional, containing a note of…I don't know what. I can't read Cheyenne, most of the time.

She opens the back door of her F-150, takes the bag from me, and tosses it in. I watch her climb up and in, and then around the truck to open the passenger door. It's not a big truck, not jacked up as high as my Silverado is, but the step up and in is still going to be hellishly difficult. I set my cane—my stupid fucking cane—inside, grab the handle and the seat and lift myself into the seat using only my upper body.

"Nothing wrong with your core muscles, clearly," Cheyenne says, a strange note in her voice.

I glance at her, surprised by the comment, but she focuses on putting the truck in gear and backing out. I have to be crazy, because it almost looked like she was blushing there for a moment. But that's stupid. There's no way a forty-year-old fox of a woman with a grown daughter would be blushing over a twenty-two-year-old kid.

I give her directions to my apartment, and the ride is surprisingly comfortable, no awkwardness. She tunes the radio to an XM country station, and "Cowboy Side of You" by Clare Dunn comes on. I surprise myself by knowing the lyrics. But then, you don't grow up in Nashville, and now live in Texas, without hearing some country music, even if it's not really your thing.

We pull up to my apartment, and she hops out, circles around and hovers near me as I slide out. God, I hate being a damned invalid, having her hover over me in case I fall. But a part of me, *way* deep down, kind of likes having her close, having her hover. Because it means she cares.

And shit, this last year has been fucking lonely.

I have to lean on the cane more than I'd like on the way up to the front door of my apartment, which, fortunately for me, is a ground floor. Cheyenne is beside me, not really hovering now, more just…there. In case. I unlock the door, shove it open and let bang against the inner wall. Hobble through, and glance back at Cheyenne, who hasn't crossed the threshold.

"Hey, so…you want to come in for a second?" I ask.

She hesitates. "I…" Her eyes go to mine, and then she smiles. And it's that *other* smile. Still bright and warm and genuine, but…intimate. I don't know how else to think of it. "Sure, for a few minutes."

I flick a switch to turn on the lights in the kitchen, and then the lamp in the living room. And that's the apartment. Kitchen, living room, a bedroom. Tiny, but mine. Well, Dad's. He's been subsidizing me while I got started in FXFL, the experimental minor league football league. Except now…I'm not sure what's going to happen. I didn't tell him about the hit I took, or what it means. I've been avoiding it.

And fuck, my place is messy. Dishes in the sink, clothes on the floor in the doorway to my room, unmade bed, a pizza box on the counter.

I grimace and glance sheepishly at Cheyenne. "This place is kind of a mess. Sorry."

She just grins. "You're a bachelor. I'd be worried if it wasn't." She lifts the lid of the pizza box with a thumb and forefinger, glances in and closes it again quickly; it's been there a while. "And you should see my place. It's not much better."

See her place. Huh. I'm not sure I'm entirely comfortable with the thoughts that inspires. I think of a cute little two bedroom house in the 'burbs somewhere, and then I think of a king-size bed, maybe a blue quilt, and a bra hanging on the bathroom doorknob. I feel my cheeks heat and turn away from her before she sees.

"I do have some pizza that's only from yesterday," I tell her, grabbing the box from the fridge. "And some Killians."

Her eyes light up. "Now that's the best idea I've heard all day."

So that's how I end up sitting on my couch, finishing off a large pepperoni pizza and a six-pack with my physical therapist, watching *Die Hard 2*.

More confusing, though, is our arrangement on the couch. I'm in the corner, feet propped up on the coffee table, and she's sitting right up against my side, body twisted to face the end of the couch, legs curled up under her, watching the movie. And my arm…it's along the back of the couch. Not around her, per se, but close. Very nearly. And my pulse thunders in my veins, my hand itches to go lower, to curl around her shoulders. I mean, that's crazy talk, right there. But the desire is there.

And I can't help but wondering what she'd do if I did let my arm slide down onto her shoulders. Maybe nothing, maybe she'd welcome it, maybe she'd get upset. But no, she's not that kind of person. She'd find a way to let me down gently, and that'd be that.

Halfway through the movie, she gets up to visit the bathroom, and with my nerves jangling, I let my arm slide just a bit lower on the couch back. She comes back, her eyes flicking to me, to my arm. But she sits down anyway, and she settles in close once more. And now…my arm is around her. She sinks lower in the couch, and actually leans in closer to me.

My mouth is dry.

The exhaustion of the day catches up to me, and I find myself blinking to stay awake. Beside me, Cheyenne is fighting sleep as well, drifting closer and closer to me so that, by the time the movie is over, she's fully propped up against me. For a woman who's fit and taut and muscular, she's also soft. My hand slides down as the credits roll, and it comes to rest against her waist, my fingertips brushing the upper swell of her hip.

I'm nearly asleep, but her proximity, the feel of her against me is heady.

But eventually I can't fight it, and I drift off.

I start, blink, and realize I've fallen asleep. The TV has turned off on its own to conserve energy. I crane my neck and glance at the red numbers of the microwave: 2:23 am.

Shit. We slept for a long time. My therapy appointment was at seven, lasted for an hour and a half, and then the movie…

Cheyenne stirs against me, stretches, making a sound in the back of her throat that has my heart clenching for some odd reason, something to do with how cute it is, how intimate a sound it is.

"Time's it?" she asks.

"Two-thirty."

She jerks upright. "Shit. I've got a client at nine, I've gotta go."

I lever myself to my feet, leaning on my cane. But I forget how weak my knee is and put too much weight on it and stumble. And she's there, catching me. Close. So close. She's looking up at me, hazel-green eyes full of things I don't know how to interpret.

"Okay?" she asks, her voice barely above a whisper.

And she hasn't moved away, and somehow, for some reason, her arms are around my waist…or one is, the other resting on my chest. My breath comes slowly, deeply, because my arms are around her too, resting on her back and sliding lower, and she's not doing a damned thing to stop me.

She blinks, and her tongue slides across her lips, and my eyes follow that movement.

I refuse to think, just let whatever is going to happen happen.

She smells like shampoo and faintly of sweat, and she's small and soft in my arms, and her chest is pressed up against mine, breasts that even a sports bra can't hide despite her svelte, athletic build.

Fuck me, I want to kiss her so bad. I've been so lonely, dealing with such wrenching heartbreak for so long, holding myself back from making a move too soon with Kylie, wanting the time to be right. I waited, and I waited too long. I don't want to make that mistake again. I'm not going to let fear hold me back any longer.

So I lean in and I feel her breath on my lips, feel her fingers curling in my Under Armor shirt…and I feel her lips, soft, damp, warm, against mine…

But then she's backing away slowly and carefully, but decisively. "Ben…god, I can't. We can't." She waits until she's sure of my balance, thinking of me even now.

Embarrassment, hurt, and disappointment all war within me. "No, I'm sorry, I don't know what I was thinking."

She reaches toward me, but doesn't touch me. "Don't apologize, Ben. It was as much me as you. But I just… I can't." She lets out a long, shaky sigh. "I have a daughter your age, Ben. And I'm your therapist. You're my client. I just can't let this...I just can't."

I nod. "I get it." I shutter my emotions, shove them down, force a casualness into my voice that I don't feel. "You're a great therapist, Cheyenne. For real. You've helped me a lot over the last month. I just hope...I hope this doesn't affect our working relationship."

She smiles, but it's strained and slightly closed, now. "It'll be fine." She lets out another breath, and then rubs her eyes. "I have to go. It's late and I live on the other side of town."

And now that I'm paying attention to anything other than how I feel, I see how tired she is. There are dark circles under her eyes. She seems to sag for a moment, and then gathers her strength and straightens.

"Cheyenne, maybe you should..." I hesitate to offer, considering what just happened. "Are you sure you're okay to drive?"

She smiles and shrugs. "Oh, sure. I was an ER nurse for a long time. I'm used to it."

I gesture at the couch. "You can stay here, you know."

She shakes her head and moves toward the door. "No, I should go. But thank you."

I follow her to the front door, leaning on my cane. She pauses with the door open, and I wasn't expecting it, intending to follow her through and watch her go from the front step. So when she stops and turns back, I'm right there, and she bumps into me. And now my arms are around her again, and I don't know what the fuck I'm thinking, but I'm milliseconds away from trying to kiss her again.

She stumbles away from me, less carefully this time. Her eyes seem pained, haunted, as if pulling away is difficult for her. "Ben, stop. Please don't."

I back away. "Jesus, I'm sorry, Cheyenne. I'm sorry."

She stays in place, hands over her face. She suddenly seems so tired, so small. "You don't know how I wish I could…it's been so long, and—" She shakes her head. "But I can't. Not with you, not now. I just can't. I'm sorry, I really am."

She walks away then, and her feet drag. Her shoulders are bowed, as if feeling the pressure of refusing the kiss, twice, of walking away.

"Cheyenne?" I call. She stops with one foot in the cab, holding on to the roof. "Are you sure you're okay to drive? You seem really tired."

She smiles faintly. "I'm fine, Ben. I didn't sleep well last night is all. But thank you."

She climbs into the truck, closes the door, and starts the engine. Backs out. I stand in the doorway, the warm San Antonio night wrapped around me like a blanket. I watch her as she turns onto the main road, and I watch as she waits to make a left turn.

There is no traffic and the streets are quiet. I'm about to go back inside when the light turns green and she steps on the gas.

And then I see it. I see the oncoming older model red Mustang run the light.

She doesn't see him. She's too tired to check the opposite direction, probably, focused on the light ahead of her.

Her white truck is halfway through the intersection when the Mustang slams into her driver's side door, going forty or fifty miles per hour.

"CHEYENNE!" I shout and hobble forward.

Her truck rocks with the impact and jolts to the side, topples, and then momentum and weight take over and the vehicle rolls over to the roof. I watch the cab crumple. Smoke rises from the hood.

I can see her driver's door is smashed in, crumpled.

"CHEYENNE!" I'm trying to run, but I can't. I can barely walk, but I somehow make it out into the street, knee throbbing and protesting.

The Mustang is a few feet away, the hood accordioned, smoking.

I get to her overturned truck, just now remembering my cell phone is in my pocket. I dial 911, heart hammering, fear ramming my pulse into overdrive.

"Nine-one-one, what's your emergency?"

"A car…it ran the light and slammed into her." I don't know how to make sense. "The truck…I think she's hurt…"

"Sir, can you tell me your location?" Her voice is calm, smooth, emotionless.

I glance at the street names and relay them, and then I'm awkwardly, painfully lowering myself to one knee at the driver's side window, which is smashed out.

There's blood on the road.

She's not moving. Her head hangs; her braid is dangling over her shoulder.

"Cheyenne. Talk to me. Hey. Come on. You're okay. Talk to me." I reach in and tap her shoulder hesitantly. She doesn't respond. "No. No. Cheyenne? Come on. Fuck. Fuck."

"Sir?" I'd forgotten the 911 operator. "Sir, are you there?"

"She's not moving, she's not—she's not—"

"Help is on the way, sir. We have your location and paramedics are en route. Just stay calm and don't try to move her..."

But it's no good. I can tell.

They won't be able to help.

And when they show up and check her pulse and vital signs I know from the minute shake of a head...

She's gone.

My gaze falls upon the lock screen of my phone: 2:36 a.m.

Falling Away, coming January 6, 2015

PLAYLIST

So, *Trashed* is another book that does not feature music directly. But, I know you know I love my music, especially when I'm writing, so I've listed for you a few of the artists that I listened to a lot during the creation of Des and Adam's story. Enjoy!

Safetysuit
Green River Ordinance
Matt Nathanson
Chris Thomas King
Niyaz
Mandolin Orange
Beats Antique
Rodrigo y Gabriela
Philip Wesley
Elenowen
The Black Keys
Stevie Ray Vaughn
The White Stripes

ABOUT THE AUTHOR

New York Times and *USA Today* bestselling author Jasinda Wilder is a Michigan native with a penchant for titillating tales about sexy men and strong women. When she's not writing, she's probably shopping, baking, or reading. She loves to travel, and some of her favorite vacations spots are Las Vegas, New York City, and Toledo, Ohio. You can often find Jasinda drinking sweet red wine with frozen berries.

To find out more about Jasinda and her other titles, visit her website: www.JasindaWilder.com.

CPSIA information can be obtained at www.ICGtesting.com
Printed in the USA
LVOW10s1054190616

493237LV00007B/581/P